EVE OF DESTRUCTION
BARRY BROAD

SEVEN LOCKS PRESS
Santa Ana, California

Seven Locks Press
P.O. Box 25689
Santa Ana, CA 92799
(800) 354-5348

Individual sales: This book is available through most bookstores or can be ordered
directly from Seven Locks Press at the address above.

Quantity Sales: Special discounts are available on quantity purchases by corporations,
associations and others. For details, contact the "Special Sales Department" at the
publisher's address above.

Cover Photo by Asaf Fulks
Design by Kira Fulks • www.kirafulks.com

Printed in the United States of America

Library of Congress Cataloging-in-Publication Data is available from the publisher

ISBN: 978-0-9801270-5-8
       0-9801270-5-x

PART I: THE PAST

Chapter 1

SREBRENICA, BOSNIA, JULY 1995

Captain Ivana Svilanovic took a deep breath to try to control her fear. She lay on the ground watching a dozen heavily armed members of the feared Drina Brigade of the "VRS" — the Bosnian Serb Army. The firelight allowed her to see them without being seen. The soldiers were drunk, shouting and singing, indifferent to being overheard.

Svilanovic wiped the sweat from her eyes, smearing dirt on her face with the back of her hand. Her mouth was dry and tasted of dust mixed with bile. She looked back anxiously at the white United Nations Humvee parked on the side of the road. Holding up her left hand, she motioned the other two members of her team to stay where they were. She signaled that there were twelve armed enemies and that they were holding hostages.

All that day, the Dutch UN peacekeepers inside the Bosnian Muslim enclave in Srebrenica were reporting that the VRS was closing in on the city. Escaping refugees recounted horrific stories of men being separated from their families and taken away or simply executed by the side of the road.

Svilanovic was part of the small contingent of US military personnel attached to UNPROFOR, the United Nations Protective Force. At dusk, Svilanovic, who spoke fluent Serbian, and two other American peacekeepers, Sergeant Jimmy Ellison and Private Roberto Perez, were ordered by their commander, a laconic French Colonel named Ullmann, to head east toward Srebrenica and scout the rear area of VRS control. If they came across refugees, they were to radio in their position and UNPROFOR command would try and figure out a way to evacuate them.

Huddled on a log near the bonfire were five women, hands tied behind their backs. They were crying and moaning softly. Ivana assumed the women were Muslim. They ranged in age from a young teenager to a white-haired old woman. One girl lay on the ground with her dress over her body, her legs bloody. She was still and appeared unconscious.

Ivana didn't know what to do. The three American blue helmets were lightly armed and had standing orders strictly prohibiting the use of deadly force unless under direct attack. Under no circumstances were they to initiate offensive operations. But one woman was critically wounded, perhaps dead. If Ivana crawled back to the Humvee, they could drive back for help, but it would be at least three hours before they could return with reinforcements—if reinforcements were even available. By that time, Ivana believed that the women would all be raped or tortured or dead.

A big bearded man carrying a vodka bottle in one hand and a pistol in the other staggered in front of the women. "Shut up, you Muslim whores." Their wailing increased. "Have it your way," he yelled, slurring his words. He walked over to the girl on the ground and calmly shot her in the head. The women went silent. "That's better," the big man said laughing. Ivana took in a breath and bit her lip to avoid making any noise. She unholstered her sidearm and clicked off the safety. She wanted to kill the man.

It was obvious to Ivana that they had to do something to save these women or there would be a massacre. If they ran, which would be the sensible thing to do, she could never forgive herself.

She crawled back to the Humvee. Ellison and Perez were kneeling by the vehicle listening, their M-16s locked and loaded. Ellison handed their shotgun to Ivana. "Captain, I thought you might need this," he whispered in his southern drawl. Ivana holstered her sidearm and took the shotgun. "It's ready to go," said Sergeant Ellison.

The Captain explained the situation to the two men. Ellison responded, "Our orders are that we leave in this kind of situation."

"Is that what you are recommending we do, Sergeant?" asked Captain Svilanovic, the fear and tension making her words sound angry.

"I don't know. I guess I could go for being a hero if you want, Ma'am, but I don't see how we're gonna take them without getting shot up pretty bad and those women whacked in the cross-fire."

"I'm asking you, Sergeant, do you want to let those women die?"

Ellison shook his head. "No, Ma'am, I don't," whispered Ellison stiffly.

"How about you, Private? Do you want to run?"

Perez bit his lip, embarrassed. "No, Ma'am. Not if you put it that way."

Ivana took a deep breath. "OK then, I've got an idea. What if we bluff?"

"Bluff, Ma'am, how?" said Perez.

"I'm thinking that we pull the Humvee a little bit closer. You two spread left and right. When you're set, I'll turn on the lights and then get on the PA system and tell them they're surrounded by the US Army and to—you know—drop their weapons and leave."

"That's the plan? That's it, Captain?" asked Private Perez.

"What if they start shooting at us?" inquired the Sergeant.

"We shoot back," Svilanovic responded. "If you've got a better plan that doesn't include cutting and running, now is the time to speak."

"Can't argue with you there, Irv . . . I mean, Captain," said Ellison. Ivana gave Ellison a cold hard stare, the one the rest of the men called her "hairy eyeball." "Irv" was a nickname she had acquired in basic training. Since most of her fellow recruits couldn't pronounce her last name, they just called her Irv. The name stuck and followed her through her career. Although she would never admit it to anyone, she liked it.

"OK then, let's do it. The bastard who shot the girl is the really big guy with a beard. If we have to start shooting, make sure you kill him first."

"Ma'am?" asked Perez.

"What?"

"Can't we get court-martialed for this?"

"Only if we fuck it up, Roberto," said Ellison, "and then we'll be dead anyway."

Ivana gave Ellison and Perez five minutes to get into place, then got in and started the Humvee. With the headlights off, Ivana drove the Humvee off the road toward the campfire. She stopped the vehicle at the edge of the trees, maybe ninety meters from the fire. Ivana didn't think the Serbs could see much beyond the circle of light cast by the fire. She was betting that when the Humvee's four bright lights suddenly came on the Serbs would think a larger group was confronting them. Hopefully they would be disoriented enough to panic and run or surrender.

Ivana turned the loudspeaker system to the highest volume. It made a high-pitched electronic squeak and she had to turn it down a notch. She spoke loudly and slowly into the microphone in Serbian: "Attention, VNS soldiers. You are surrounded by the United States Army. Do not move or you will be killed. Drop your weapons. Put your hands over your heads. I repeat, put your hands over your heads." Ivana turned on the headlights, sending shafts of light through trees. "Put your hands up. We *will* shoot you," she said, emphasizing the word "will." "You are completely surrounded by the United States Army," said Ivana, making her voice as booming and authoritative as she could. "Drop your weapons now! Do not resist or we *will* shoot you." She repeated the warning in the same measured tones.

From his vantage point on the southern perimeter of the clearing, Ellison could see the men freeze and then look toward their weapons, which were stacked a few meters away. The huge bearded soldier who had shot the girl ignored Ivana's order and started to walk slowly out of the knot of VNS soldiers in the direction of the Humvee. Ellison saw that he had a large automatic in his hand. He put him in his sights and when the Serb raised the gun and shouted something in his own language, the Sergeant fired at him twice. Private Perez must have also fired because Ellison heard another report a split second later. The Serb spun around and collapsed on the ground. He was screaming in pain. No one moved to help him.

Slowly, the men put up their hands. From the Humvee, Ivana could see and hear everything: the Serbian soldiers standing in shocked silence, the young girl's murderer on the ground writhing in agony, the women huddled together wailing. She spoke again in Serbian. "You women, stand up and walk toward the lights. You are under the protection of the United States Army. Get up, please, and walk toward the vehicle. You are safe."

Tentatively at first, looking around to see how the VNS soldiers would react, the women got up. The oldest one was struggling to stand. One of the younger women helped her.

"VNS soldiers, keep your hands up. Turn away from the lights and put your hands on your heads. If you move, you will be shot. I repeat, if you move, you *will* be shot."

The women began to walk faster and made it out of the clearing and into the forest. Both Ellison and Perez moved quickly back toward the Humvee to provide cover. In the few seconds it took them to get there, the women also made it to the front of the Humvee. Ellison and Perez opened the doors and pushed the women inside. Ivana continued to warn the Serbs not to move. One of the women asked Ivana about the girl. But another woman shushed her and said, "Mother, she is dead."

Perez got in the passenger seat and Ellison climbed up into the cupola where a machine gun could be mounted. Unfortunately, this Humvee wasn't equipped with a machine gun. At least he had his M-16 and a clear view of the Serbs, who were still standing quietly, their backs facing the Americans, their hands on their heads.

Ellison said, "Hey, captain, what do you say we get the hell out of here?"

Ivana slammed the Humvee into reverse and backed it up onto the road. Then with a grind of the gears, she put it in drive and headed west toward their base.

The women in the back were crying and laughing with relief. They had returned from the dead. Ellison came down from his perch and began giving them water. Ivana heard one of the women thank him and say, "May Allah be with you all of your days."

"Son of a bitch," said Perez, slapping the dashboard, "that was fucking awesome."

Chapter 2

Tommy Harter liked Goth music. He became deeply immersed in the scene, going to clubs on the weekends and spending hours on the Internet. His parents objected to the black clothes and the makeup, but allowed Tommy his freedom. In their youth, Mr. and Mrs. Harter had explored alternative religions and understood that Tommy might go his own way. Spiritual exploration was emphasized as a positive value in the Harter family and the Harters tried out various New Age beliefs, from Ananda to Tony Robbins.

In 1999, toward the end of his senior year of high school, Tom—he had dropped the Tommy by then—seemed to lose interest in the Goth scene and found a job at an auto parts store. To the great relief of his parents, he cut his hair and started wearing conventional clothes. He began to attend community college the following September. In his second semester, he took a class in comparative religion. He sat next to a student named Mohammed, who happened to be Muslim. Mohammed was a nice guy, mild-mannered and friendly, from a hard-working immigrant family. He and Tom Harter started hanging out together. One of the requirements of the class was that each student had to attend the services of a religion different from his own. Tom asked Mohammed if he would take him to his mosque and Mohammed agreed. Mohammed attended a Sunni mosque, whose members were immigrant families from all over the Islamic world. Tom liked what he saw. The rules were clear, the message was one of acceptance and brotherhood, family was respected, and there was a strong sense of community.

Tom began attending the mosque regularly and soon decided to take Arabic lessons so that he could study the Koran. He approached Dr. Wazzam, the Imam of the mosque, who seemed wary of Tom but appreciated his keen interest in Islam. One Friday, six months after Tom began regularly attending the mosque, he informed Dr. Wazzam that he wanted to convert to Islam. The Imam asked him if he was prepared to say the *Shahadah,* the pledge of conviction of faith, in Arabic. Tom responded that he was prepared to convert and said the words in Arabic: "I bear Witness that there is no God but Allah and that Muhammad is His Messenger." Dr. Wazzam welcomed Tom into the faith. "Have you chosen a name?" he asked. "Abdul-Haq," said Tom.

"Yes," said Dr. Wazzam, "Servant of the Truth. I believe the name fits you."

Tom, now Abdul-Haq, began to attend daily prayers at the mosque and Dr. Wazzam gave him a job as a janitor and groundskeeper at the Islamic Center. A free room came with the job and so Abdul-Haq moved away from home. His parents were pleased at his straight-laced lifestyle but were uncomfortable with his new religion. They hoped it was just another phase in his spiritual development. Mohammed's friendship with Abdul-Haq soon began to wane, as he found the intensity of his friend's religious zeal unsettling.

Abdul-Haq did his job and prayed faithfully five times a day. He read about Islam constantly and began to listen to tapes that were circulated by some of the younger members of the mosque. His views grew more conservative and he took issue with the relatively lax dress of some of the wives and daughters of the members of the community. He stopped wearing Western clothing and grew a thick blond beard. In study classes, he expressed loud opinions about the duty of Muslims to engage in Jihad. These outbursts led to arguments with his fellow congregants, who complained to Dr. Wazzam. Dr. Wazzam repeatedly warned Abdul-Haq to moderate his behavior. When Abdul-Haq chastised Dr. Wazzam for his failure to condemn the United States government in his sermons, Dr. Wazzam felt compelled to fire Abdul-Haq and asked him not to return to the mosque.

Three of the young firebrands who attended the Mosque invited Abdul-Haq to move into an apartment they shared. They were visiting students—one was Egyptian and the other two were Saudis. They lived in a messy two-bedroom apartment filled with tobacco smoke and dirty dishes. Adherents to a militant version of Wahhabi Islam, they prayed continuously and stayed completely away from women, whom they considered unclean. They watched Jihadist video tapes from men such as an obscure militant living in Afghanistan named Osama bin-Laden and the blind Sheik, Omar Abdel-Rahman, imprisoned for life in New York for his complicity in the 1993 bombing of the World Trade Center. Abdul-Haq's vision of the world became increasingly dark and violent. He stopped communicating with his parents. Abdul-Haq now felt that he lived in a sea of immorality and degeneration that could be cleansed only by the redeeming power of flame and death. He viewed Dr. Wazzam as being no better than the infidels because he lived among them and admired their culture. Abdul-Haq loved his new brothers and their religious zeal and was sure that he would die for them if called upon to do so.

One day Omar, the Egyptian, said that he wanted Abdul-Haq to meet someone. This man was very important, he explained. He told Abdul-Haq to wear western clothes for the meeting and to keep his head uncovered. They drove over to a Middle Eastern restaurant in El Monte. Omar led Abdul-Haq to a booth where an older well-dressed man waited. His said his name was Sayeed. Abdul-Haq doubted that Sayeed was his real name.

Sayeed asked Abdul-Haq many questions about his family background and his conversion to Islam. His questions were gentle but persistent. He questioned Abdul-Haq about his views of Islam, which the young man was eager to talk about. Sayeed nodded his head and listened intently to every word. He seemed sympathetic and fatherly. Turning the topic to the question of Jihad, Abdul-Haq expressed the opinion that the world would not be a righteous place until Islam had conquered the last infidel state. What did Abdul-Haq think about those who became martyrs? He admired them, but wasn't sure he was brave enough to become a martyr himself.

"Excellent answer," replied Sayeed. He paused, moving closer to the two young men, and then continued, as if taking them into his confidence. "If you were asked to do a job, a very important job, would you be willing to do it?"

"I would be honored," replied Abdul-Haq.

"It would not involve doing anything violent or illegal. Just gathering information and helping us understand how things work. You would have to shave your beard and go back to your American name. Thomas, is it not? And act like all the other American young men. Our people, Arabs, Persians, Pakistanis, they arouse suspicion. American people keep their distance from us. But you have a special gift; you know their culture. You fit in, Abdul-Haq. You are one of them, but in your heart you are one of us."

"Sir, if that is what is necessary, then that is what I will do."

"Well then, young man, here is what we want you to do. There is a job open at the Wal-Mart warehouse in Ontario. Here is an advertisement."

Sayeed pulled a newspaper clipping out of his jacket pocket and handed it to Abdul-Haq. It advertised a job at the Wal-Mart distribution center starting at $6.75 per hour plus discounts on store items, eligibility to purchase health care, and a 401(k) plan.

"If you get the job, we want you to learn everything there is to know about their shipping system. You must be a superior employee, you must work hard, go to church–not the mosque–and pretend to be the 'All-American Boy.' Do you understand? You must pray in private and seek out no friendships with Muslims. None, that is very important."

"Yes, I understand."

"Good, now as part of their selection process you will be required to take a personality test. You must answer the questions correctly.

We have obtained a copy. Study the answers, although it should be quite obvious to a smart young man like you what to say.

"If you fail to get the job, you will not hear from us again. If you get the job, please call this telephone number." Sayeed handed Abdul-Haq a little slip of paper with a number on it. "Do you have a cell phone?"

"Yes," replied Abdul-Haq.

"Now, Thomas, assuming you are hired, you will need to get a small apartment near where you work. We will provide you extra money for that purpose. But you are to live a quiet life. Do not bring attention on yourself. You may date Christian girls but are prohibited from having sexual intercourse with them. Begin to see your family again. Tell them you have given up Islam. Think of yourself as a spy who must act his part at all times. You will be separated from your brothers, but you will be doing our cause a great service."

A cheerful young woman from Wal-Mart's Human Resources Department interviewed Tom Harter. He dressed neatly for the interview and she found him quite presentable. He evidenced a strong willingness to recognize and follow authority, showed no sympathy toward labor unions, and had a conservative personal philosophy. He clearly wanted the job and admired Wal-Mart for its strong emphasis on hard work and loyalty. Tom passed the psychological profile and had a clean drug screen.

Harter started working for Wal-Mart two weeks later. The distribution center was a vast warehouse complex. Shipping containers from the Far East would arrive there and would then be re-routed to other regions of the country or unloaded and their contents dispatched to Wal-Mart's retail stores throughout Southern California.

Harter impressed management. He was a great employee; hard-working, enthusiastic, friendly to his fellow employees, respectful of authority, and always on time. Harter was just the sort of person the company's founder, Sam Walton, envisioned as the ideal member of the Wal-Mart team.

Chapter 3

Mr. Alfeet Shandu was an attorney with the law firm of Shandu & Shandu. As he entered the spacious glass-and-stone lobby of the Ali Jinnah Business Center, he was struck by the intensity of the air-conditioned atmosphere; the building was an oasis of coolness and calm in contrast to the intense heat and bustle of downtown Karachi. Mr. Shandu wore an elegant business suit, which looked remarkably fresh given the torpid heat of the day. He was a thin and ascetic-looking man, with a high forehead and large eyes framed by thin gold glasses. He took an elevator to the twenty-third floor and entered the offices of Barhani, Barhani & Wafti, where he had an appointment to meet with the youngest Mr. Barhani.

The Barhani firm represented Peshawar General Manufacturing Ltd., manufacturers of corrugated roofing, building trusses, aluminum foil, power tools, and packaging for food products. Among its diversified activities, PGM manufactured cat litter at a factory in Karachi for export and for Pakistan's own burgeoning pet-supply market.

The animal products division of PGM was quite profitable. For the last five years, it had been operating at full capacity as a result of entering into an agreement to supply cat litter to a US company named PetClean Products, Inc., developer of a popular and innovative "all-in-one" disposable cat litter box. Like many American companies, PetClean was taking advantage of vastly cheaper manufacturing costs in Pakistan. The US company was very happy with PGM's work because it enabled PetClean to supply cat litter very cheaply to its largest customer, Wal-Mart.

Mr. Shandu represented a privately owned diversified investment firm named Global Pakistan Ltd., headquartered in Islamabad. For several years, Global Pakistan had been quietly acquiring companies throughout South Asia and the Arab world. It had major holdings in the real estate, manufacturing, transportation, and information technology sectors. It eschewed publicity and allowed its various subsidiaries to operate with a great deal of autonomy. Among its major shareholders were a number of Arab charitable trusts, Pakistani madrassas, and various Middle Eastern holding companies. The CEO of Global Pakistan was a reclusive Lebanese businessman, Abu Hassan Andrenou, who had immigrated to Pakistan in the 1980s and quickly amassed a fortune. Global Pakistan was well regarded in the South Asian business community.

Six months earlier, Mr. Andrenou retained Mr. Barhani to commence negotiations with PGM for the purchase of its pet-supply division. Today's meeting would consummate that deal. Upon agreement, Mr. Andrenou would order the wire transfer of 240 million Rupees to PGM's account at the Lahore Finance Bank. The remainder of the purchase price would be paid in five annual installments and also would include shares in Global Pakistan. Mr. Shandu and Mr. Barhani each stood to make large fees upon execution of the agreement.

Mr. Barhani's office was richly appointed in teak paneling and polished brass. It smelled of leather and tobacco, with just a hint of the sweat, urine, food, and automobile exhaust that permeated up from the streets below. The décor, together with the various photographs and memorabilia around the office, reflected Barhani, Barhani & Wafti's long and distinguished service to the Pakistani elite, dating back to the days of the British Raj.

The two lawyers greeted each other warmly. They had known one another, as had their fathers, since childhood. Both knew that this meeting was largely ceremonial, as the negotiations leading up to Pakistan Global's purchase of PGM were now well behind them. During the first few minutes of the meeting they made small talk, speaking amiably of their families, the weather, and the business climate in Pakistan. The introductory conversation having run its course, Barhani took out two sets of documents and handed one of them to Shandu. Shandu cursorily leafed through the documents.

"Nabil, does this reflect the change we requested in Section 12, paragraph 2?" asked Shandu.

"It does."

"Well then, shall we sign?"

Both men leaned over the desk and signed the document. They exchanged copies and signed again. The men stood up and shook hands.

"Alfeet, I think our clients will be very pleased with this acquisition," Barhani said. Opening his briefcase, he put his copy of the signed agreement inside.

"Absolutely. By the way, where do you plan to spend the holidays?"

"At our home in the mountains."

"We will be there too," replied Shandu, "We really must get the families together."

Chapter 4

TEHRAN, IRAN, JANUARY 2006

The Mullah smiled at the young woman on the bed. Her black chador was weakly illuminated by the fading winter light coming through the high window. He had not made love to her before. He was handsome, with a long brown beard, not yet gray, even though he was fifty-five years old. His wife was now middle-aged and unattractive and this girl was young and beautiful and he hungered for her. One must remain loyal to one's wife, but she lived in their family home in the Holy City of Karbala. Did not the Prophet Muhammed, the merciful, permit "*Mut'ah*"—temporary marriage—when a man lives in a city distant from his wife?

He had met the girl in the class he taught in classical Islamic literature at the Alzahra Women's University of Tehran. She was an able student, quiet, observant, respectful of the traditional values. He felt certain she was not one of those who wore the veil in public but then took it off in private and did sinful things. She was a true Muslim. She read Arabic, the language of the Koran, quite well—as few Iranian girls did.

They had never spoken in private, as that would have been indecent, but he had seen how she stared at him adoringly when she thought he was not looking. Because she wore the veil, he could only see her eyes. The decadent West did not understand that a woman's beauty resided in her eyes and this girl's eyes told of her fervor to serve the Prophet and her admiration of him. He had left her a note asking her to meet him at the apartment he had in the Bagher Abad neighborhood on the outskirts of Tehran. "To discuss further study," the note said. He was taking no risk because he was so revered and she was a mere college student who would never say anything to another soul. If she did not desire to meet him, she would simply fail to come to the rendezvous. But he was right about her as he had been about the others.

Of course, many of his young students looked up to him, not only because he was an influential cleric, a gifted professor, and a leader in the *Ruhaniyat*—the Tehran Militant Clergy Association—but because he had been one of the Grand Ayatollah Khomeini's chief aides at the time of the Islamic Revolution in 1979. When Khomeini came to power, he was put in charge of counterespionage for the new government. He specialized in rooting out Zionist spies. Anyone who helped the Jews and their filthy state of Israel, may Allah wipe it from the face of the earth, had to be caught and destroyed. And he had rooted them out. In those heady days after the Revolution, he had caught them and they were tried, five men who swore their innocence. They were just merchants, so they pleaded, just innocent Jews, family men. But they eventually confessed under his interrogation. They begged for their lives, they cried, they lost all dignity. It was disgusting, these *D'Jinnah*, these sniveling descendents of the Jews who had turned their back on the Prophet and whom he had vanquished outside the holy city of Medina. How right was the Prophet Muhammed about these stiff-necked people who never submitted to Muhammed even after they were crushed. In His mercy, Allah allowed the Jews, who were "people of the book," to live among the Muslims as a subjugated people. History had shown repeatedly that they must be watched and suppressed so that they did not rise again. Now their Zionist entity ruled over Muslims in Palestine; their soldiers controlled the

Dome of the Rock in Jerusalem, from where the Prophet ascended to the heavens on his horse Buraq and received the holy prayers from Allah. Their bastard state must be destroyed if it took two hundred years. The Supreme Islamic Revolutionary Court found the Jewish spies guilty and they were hanged from the gallows on 15th Street in front of the ancient Marariv Synagogue. Their bodies were burned.

He walked toward her and smiled. He stopped two feet from the bed and held out his hand for her to take his and rise. "May Allah bless you, my child," he said in his deeply resonant voice.

She looked up at him, nodded modestly in submission, and without saying a word, undid the veil. She smiled sweetly at him and his heart thumped in anticipation. Then, with the beautiful smile still on her face, from the folds of her black chador, she pulled out a small 9 mm automatic of Eastern European origin—common enough on the streets of the Middle East. The serial numbers were filed off. It could never be traced.

"*Israeli injast*" —Israel is here—she said calmly in Farsi, as she had been instructed to do by the Mossad.

The Mullah tilted his head slightly and looked puzzled. His brain simply could not register the meaning of the combination of the gun pointed at him, the sweet smile of the girl, and the words she spoke. It was understandably confusing for him and, despite his formidable cognitive powers, he really didn't have time to make sense of the situation in the split second it took for her to pull the trigger. Two shots to the chest—it sounded like a flat pop from a car backfiring— and she dropped the gun on the floor, as she had also been taught in Mossad training school. Although the little gun was not silenced, you could hardly hear the report with all the noisy rush hour traffic outside.

He fell to his knees, his hands grabbing the spreading red stain on his chest, with a look of puzzlement in his eyes. "Why?" he said.

She didn't bother to answer him, as she was now rushing to leave the room.

The Mullah was dead by the time he hit the floor.

A debt is paid, she thought, as she left the room, quickly reattaching her veil. Her face covered, her eyes averted, the cold biting her to the bone, she made for the subway station like any other harried commuter. The complicated business of exfiltration was still ahead. As she got on the train at the Red Line station for the long ride back to central Tehran, Hannah Parras could hear the muezzin of the great city calling the faithful to prayer. She always loved that sound. It reminded her of Jerusalem.

Chapter 5

The safe house was in the sprawling working class district of Javadiyeh in the southern reaches of Tehran. Hannah had been cooped up there for nearly three weeks waiting for her handlers to get her out of Iran. She watched a lot of Iranian television; the melodramas, cooking shows, and soccer matches helped pass the time. Like most Israelis, she was addicted to the news, but the heavily censored Iranian news was hard to take. She briefly thought about putting a bullet through the television set when the Supreme Leader, Ayatollah Ali Khamenei, gave a Friday sermon about how the "Protocols of the Elders of Zion" conclusively established the international nature of the Zionist conspiracy and then, without taking a breath, made the assertion that some Jews had not yet given up the ancient practice of murdering children to consume their blood at Passover.

"Do you think that the Iranians actually believe this shit?" she said to Mordechai Nasim, in Farsi. Even in the safe house, they did not dare speak Hebrew for fear that some neighbor might overhear them and call the secret police.

"Yes." Trying to get the taciturn Nasim to engage in a conversation was no easy task. Nasim was many things: her minder, her bodyguard, and her colleague. But he was not her friend. He was thin and he was over 50, old—at least from Hannah's youthful perspective—with a shaved head and gaunt sad eyes. His body didn't have an ounce of fat on it and he never ate much. He had been in the Mossad for years, starting out his career as a member of a Sayeret special forces team working behind enemy lines in the Sinai during the 1973 Yom Kippur War. He was an Iranian Jew, like her, but not, as she was, from an educated middle-class Tehrani family. He was from a poor family from Tabriz in the northwest of Iran and spoke both Farsi and Azeri. She knew he had a wife and two children living in some dusty development town somewhere in the Negev, but, of course, he carried no pictures of them and would not say much about them. If she asked him a question he did not care to answer, he simply ignored her.

She was confident that Mordechai would protect her and, if necessary, give his life for her. He had killed many times and he would not hesitate to kill again. For some reason, she liked him. He slept on the couch in the living area and she slept in the bedroom. If they needed food or to make contact with other operatives in Tehran, it was Mordechai who would go out. He never carried a gun but he had a very slim switchblade knife that he tucked in his sock. Sometimes at night, as they watched the television, he would hone his knife on a small sharpening stone. The safe house was a virtual arsenal. There were two AK-47s and several small automatic pistols, a collection of grenades, of both the fragmentation and stun varieties, and even some Semtex plastic explosive with a collection of detonators.

She came directly to the safe house after she terminated the Mullah; she was supposed to stay there until the situation quieted. Within five minutes of her arrival, she was glued to the television to see how the assassination would be covered in the Iranian media. State television reported that the Mullah had succumbed to a heart attack and the reporter recounted the admirable story of his life. Despite the public cover story, Hannah assumed that the police were engaged in an intensive search for the person or persons who murdered the Mullah. When they got around to interviewing his students and found out that a young woman named Ashraf Bargahzi had simply vanished and it was discovered that she was registered under fake papers, the secret police—the SVAMA—would be brought in. Given the Mullah's curriculum vitae, particularly his early service to the Islamic Revolution, the SVAMA would suspect that the Mossad was responsible. For its part, the Mossad would be busy trying to throw the SVAMA off the scent. There were plenty of options to choose from—Kurds, Arabs, Baluchis, Baktiaris, Turkmen—all of whom had active armed resistance movements. Sadly, with the demise of the Soviet Union, it was no longer credible to try and frame the Russians. Hannah also knew that the Mossad was not above trying to make it look like a CIA hit since, other than the Mossad, the CIA was automatically a suspect in every political killing inside Iran.

Between television shows, Hannah ran in place and did calisthenics in an effort stay in shape. Fortunately, they were on the first floor, so no one could hear her pounding feet.

One cold snowy afternoon, Mordechai game back from one of his mysterious trips and walked straight to the television, which was tuned into a rerun of a popular variety show, and turned it off. "Hannah, it's time to go. Get your things. You leave on the train for Turkey at 19:00 hours."

"Really? You're serious?"

Mordechai nodded yes.

"Thank God," she said, with great relief and excitement. She smiled at Mordechai, who maintained his deadpan expression. "I don't think I could stand this waiting another day."

Mordechai fished in his pocket and brought out a passport. He handed it to her. It was a Turkish passport with her photograph on it. It was issued to someone named "Vashti Palmeni."

Hannah laughed. "Are they serious? Is this a Purim joke? Someone has a good sense of humor in the Mossad's documents section. I'm surprised they didn't go all the way and just call me Esther. When is Purim, anyway?"

"On Thursday. You won't be here," replied Mordechai, matter-of-factly.

"So what's the plan?" Hannah asked, "Are you coming?"

"No. You will be traveling with Shoshana Levi, who is completing another assignment. Maybe you've worked with her. She will pose as your mother and use the name Samineh—Samineh Palmeni. Your father is not traveling with you because he must run the family business. You have no siblings. Your cover story is that you are from the Persian minority in Turkey and you live in the city of Van in the eastern part of the country. You're a student at the 100th Year University in Van. That's "Van Yüzüncü Yıl Üniversitesi" in Turkish, so remember that. Here's your student identification card."

Mordechai handed Hannah a plastic student identification card with her photograph on it. Hannah leafed through the passport. Like all Mossad forgeries, it was excellent.

"You are studying physics. You came to Tehran to shop. It is your first visit here. You are very excited about your visit. You are conservative and religious. Shoshana just spent the last two weeks at a hotel in the Sadeghiyeh district to establish the cover story. So now pack. You have fifteen minutes."

"Moti, I see one really big problem with this plan."

"What's that?" Mordechai asked, pointing at his watch with the obvious implication that she was wasting precious time.

"I don't speak a word of Turkish. My cover story will break down in five minutes under interrogation."

"So don't get caught," Mordechai said irritably. "Hannah, stop wasting time with stupid questions."

"Moti, you're so warm-hearted. Has anyone ever told you that?" asked Hannah.

"No," replied Mordechai.

Thirty minutes later they were on a crowded subway train headed for Tehran's central railway station. Despite the biting cold, the subway car was hot and humid. It smelled like industrial grease mixed with sweat and stale tobacco. Hannah had a dreadful headache and felt queasy. Now that she was leaving, the black chador she was wearing felt like a straightjacket. At least the subway was fast. Trying to take a taxi or a bus at this time of day was an exercise in pure frustration. During her training, they had shown her a BBC documentary about Iran. There were twelve million Tehranis with an addiction to the automobile that rivaled even that of Los Angeles. The traffic was a nightmare, with many of the city's thoroughfares in perpetual gridlock. The smog was so thick that during her time in the city she had rarely seen the surrounding mountains.

It was a relief when they got out of the subway station, Hannah with her little suitcase, Mordechai walking slightly ahead of her. It was 4:30 in the afternoon and it was already almost dark. They went directly to a news kiosk to wait for Shoshana. Mordechai got a newspaper and Hannah sat on her suitcase, looking like another overburdened Iranian woman. Occasionally, she looked up to survey the station for secret police types. There were a few likely suspects, men standing around reading newspapers and smoking cigarettes. Of course, if they were any good at all—and the Iranians had a reputation for having a first-class secret police—they would be hard to spot.

In a flurry of black cloth, up strode an imposing woman lugging an old suitcase and a shopping bag. "Vashti, my girl!" she yelled.

Hannah stood up and embraced the woman. "*Madar*, how are you?"

"Good, good. Ready to go home."

Shoshana kissed Hannah on the cheek. In a barely audible whisper, she said, "*Shalom*."

Mordechai was standing around looking like a bored relative. Shoshana said brusquely to Mordechai, "Don't just stand there, pick up the suitcases and carry them for us."

Mordechai picked up the two suitcases and Shoshana grabbed her shopping bag and they made off toward the platform.

The train was already waiting, steam venting slowly from its undercarriage. It was relatively new. The Iranians had invested heavily in the last decade upgrading the country's transportation infrastructure. The Raja Passenger Train Company, as the government railroad was called, was well managed. The Islamic government prided itself on being responsive to the people's needs. In return, the people were expected not to challenge the strict religious morality of the state. And most did not.

They stopped at the bottom of the stairs. Mordechai fished in his pocket and handed each of them a train ticket.

Hannah laughed heartily. "First class-tickets. Um . . . 'Father' is very generous." The Mossad was cheap and traveling first class was nearly unheard of—unless there was an operational need.

Shoshana hugged Mordechai. Now it was Hannah's turn. Her dark brown eyes met Mordechai's and a little smile crossed his face. He put his arms around her and she kissed him on the cheek. "Thank you, Moti, for everything you have done for me."

In Hebrew, he whispered, "Next year in Jerusalem." He kissed her tenderly on her cheek and, as she let go of him, squeezed her hand. For Mordechai, her gruff and constant companion of the last three weeks, it was a gesture that was as moving as it was surprising. As she and Shoshana boarded the train, Hannah looked back to wave but Mordechai was already gone.

A porter led them to their compartment, put their things away, and informed them that, at 9:00 pm, he would be back to make up their beds. Shoshana happily made reservations for them to eat in the first-class dining car at 7:00 pm. Although Hannah wondered if it wouldn't be better for them to keep out of sight and eat in their compartment, she did not protest.

Hannah asked the porter when the train would cross into Turkey. He replied that they would reach the Razi border crossing at 3:00 the next afternoon. When he left, they locked the door to the compartment, pulled down the shade covering the windows, and took off their heavy black chadors. They would have to put them back on when they went to dinner.

"What a relief to shed those damned things," Shoshana said in Farsi, gesturing toward their chadors bunched up in the corner of the seats.

"That's for sure," Hannah replied. "I just don't know how they put up with it."

"I suppose it's no worse than the . . ." Shoshana cupped her hands and mouthed the next word *"Heredi"*—the Hebrew word for ultra-religious Jews—"with their wigs and long skirts,"

"Same concept, but at least those women are doing it voluntarily."

"Are they? I'm not so sure."

Hannah retrieved a beautifully bound book from her backpack. It was the *Shahnameh*—The Epic of Kings—by the greatest of all classical Persian poets, Abulqasem Ferdowsi. Ironically, the Mullah had assigned her to read it for his literature course. Hannah bought it as a prop to carry with her to class in order to look like an authentic student, but then decided to read it just in case the Mullah asked questions about it. She loved it. Shoshana took out some knitting from her bag and, incongruously, given her matronly demeanor, an iPod and a set of earbuds.

"What are you knitting?" asked Hannah.

"A skullcap, what else?" Shoshana winked, pointing to the top of her head. Hannah understood immediately that Shoshana was knitting a *kippa*.

"And for whom are you knitting that skullcap?

"For my nephew—I mean your cousin—in the Army."

"May Allah be praised," said Hannah and both women laughed.

Although the train was just a few years old, the compartment was paneled in dark wood veneer and was decorated with heavy brocade curtains and a complicated floral pattern on the seats. The lighting was fluorescent but there were also old-fashioned brass sconces for decorative purposes. Iranian, and for that matter, Middle Eastern taste in luxury leans heavily toward the Victorian. Maybe, Hannah thought, it is nostalgia for the lost glory of the Ottoman Empire.

A few minutes after 5:00 pm the train pulled out of the station, heading slowly west toward Turkey. Sometime in the middle of the night, they would leave the Farsi speaking parts of Iran and climb into the mountainous province of Azerbaijan, where the Azeri people predominate. Hannah figured they would be eating breakfast when they passed through Tabriz, a city of several million that is the capital of Iranian Azerbaijan. From there, they would skirt the shores of Lake Orumiyeh, Iran's great salt lake—high in the desolate mountains of northwestern Iran.

At ten minutes to seven, they donned their chadors and made their way to the first-class dining car. If the decorative style of their compartment was heavily Victorian, the dining car looked like Buckingham Palace in 1885. The heavy mauve curtains were trimmed in gold braid and each table had a light fixture that was a replica of a nineteenth-century gas lamp. Each individual table had a traditional Persian tablecloth—a *sofreh*—with the logo of the RAJA Passenger Rail Company woven into the pattern. The waiters looked smart in their short white serving jackets. Hannah thought the whole scene looked like something out of an American movie she once saw—*Murder on the Orient Express*. She could easily imagine Agatha Christie's famous detective Herecule Poirot arriving for dinner in a topcoat and tails.

As they walked down the corridor to the dining car, Shoshana whispered in Hannah's ear, "Whatever happens, follow my lead and maintain your cover story."

Despite the tension of the situation, Hannah enjoyed dining out after all those weeks cooped up in the safe house in Tehran. She and Shoshana both had a surprisingly good kebab and were just beginning to enjoy a pot of mint tea when three military officers sat down at the table directly across the aisle from them. They smiled at Hannah, who smiled back demurely at them. Shoshana affected the stern countenance typical of a mother standing guard over an unwed virgin in the presence of males in uniform.

They were officers of the Pasdaran and one of them, whose thick brown hair was already streaked with gray, looked to be some kind of high-ranking officer. His piercing eyes locked momentarily on Hannah's. They were an intense color of blue—very unusual in Iranians. His look was calculating; he was sizing her up. Not in a sexual way, but professionally, as if he was trying to figure out who she really was. Having a member of the Pasdaran paying attention to her was the last thing that Hannah Parras desired at that moment and it made her feel exposed. She averted her eyes from his intense stare and, as she did so, looked at his epaulettes and tried to determine his rank. In her training sessions in Tel Aviv, they had briefly gone over identification of Iranian military ranks, but she hadn't paid attention because the information wasn't integral to her mission in Tehran. He had a crest plus one star on his epaulettes, so that made him a lieutenant or brigadier general in the Revolutionary Guards. In any case, he was important . . . a "big wig" in the American slang she picked up from her fellow students during the year she spent in New York in the 1990s.

The other two looked much younger, around Hannah's age. Both had the arrogant look of men who knew they were members of an elite. She identified them as captains or majors, probably adjutants to the blue-eyed general. They didn't even notice Shoshana. Both looked at Hannah with expressions that said, "We dominate women; they serve us." Israeli men had a version of that same look. However, the Israeli version did not so much radiate dominance, but something more akin to, "I'm God's gift to women."

Shoshana was reaching her own conclusions, sizing up the three officers with the dispassion and speed of a trained professional. The waiter came up to the officers' table and they turned their attention away from giving Hannah the once-over.

"I think we should order some desert. What do you think, dear?" Shoshana asked. Obviously, Shoshana was sending the signal that she wanted to stay longer. Hannah had no idea what Shoshana's mission was in Tehran. It was not her business to ask, just as it was understood that Shoshana would not ask Hannah what she was doing in Tehran. Compartmentalizing information was the first lesson of tradecraft. But given Shoshana's sudden enthusiasm for extending the meal, Hannah guessed that perhaps her mission had something to do with spying on the Iranian military. The serendipitous arrival of these three officers was a last opportunity for her to ply her trade before they crossed the border. Hannah just wanted to leave and go back to the relative safety of their compartment, but she was nothing if not perceptive. And so, she smiled and said, "Mother, I would love dessert."

They ordered *Shir-Berenj*—rice pudding with coconut and rosewater—and had a pleasant conversation about shopping and the weather.

Shoshana turned to the officers, but was clearly directing her inquiry to the oldest of the men. "Excuse me, sir, for the interruption, but may I ask you a question?"

For the briefest of seconds, the officer looked annoyed. "Of course. What do you wish to know, Madam?"

"Sir, my daughter and I are from Turkey and we have come to Iran for the first time. We arrived in Iran by air, so this is our first time taking the train across the border. When we cross the border, does the customs process take a long time?"

"Not long. At Razi, the last stop in Iran, the passport control officers from our country will enter the train. They will collect each person's passport. Then the train will cross the border and stop again. The Turkish customs people will board the train and stamp the passports of all the passengers entering Turkey."

"Thank you, sir, for the information."

"And if I may be so presumptuous," asked the officer, "what is your destination?" He was taking Shoshana's bait.

"We live in the City of Van."

"You speak beautiful Farsi. Did your family immigrate to Turkey?"

"Yes, but a very long time ago, during the Ottoman period. My great grandfather was a merchant originally from Mashad."

"How fascinating," he replied with a smile. "And is there a large Iranian population in Van?"

"Actually, yes. We are a minority, of course, but the Turks treat us well. We Persians do not rock the boat. The Turks don't bother us; we don't bother them. They hate the Kurds because of the PKK terrorists, but are good to the Azeris, Ossetians, Circassians, and all the others—even the Jews."

"Even the Jews. Yes, so I've heard," said the General. "Their military is so good to the Jews that they even help the Israelis, who should be wiped off the face of the earth, may Allah be willing. If that Hitler had only done a better job, we wouldn't have half the problems we now have in this part of the world. So," he continued, "do you find that there is hostility toward Shiites by the Turks?"

"The state is secular because of the Turkish revolution of Ataturk and so are the army and the schools. So, if anything, they don't like religion generally. They are not any more hostile to Shiites than they are to Sunnis. Religion is encouraged, so long as it is a private thing and doesn't get political. Like in the European countries."

"Ah, yes," said the general, laughing. "The Turks and their overwhelming desire to hide from Islam and to become the bastard stepchild of the West." The general's tone turned intense and angry.

"They have turned their back on history and on the message of the Prophet, blessed be he. Our Islamic Revolution is the future. The revolution of the 'Young Turks' has grown very old and senile and is at a dead end, like the other imports from the West, Arab socialism and Baathism. We Muslims must find our own path, not ape the ideas of infidels and imperialists."

People in the dining car were turning around to see who was saying these things.

Shoshana blushed and looked embarrassed. "Sir, we are not political people. We are good Muslims and mind our own business. We are great admirers of the Iranian Revolution."

The General softened his tone. "My apologies, Madam and Miss," he said, turning his gaze on Hannah and smiling. "Forgive the frustrations of an old fighter. And you, young lady, are you a student?"

"Yes. I am attending the 100th Year University in Van," Hannah replied, a calm smile on her beautiful face.

"It is such an unusual name for a university," said one of the other officers, obviously interested in the conversation now that it was focused on the young woman.

"Yes," Hannah smiled. "As you can imagine, the students have many jokes about that name."

"And what do you study, young lady?"

"I am studying physics," replied Hannah.

"That, Miss, is very impressive."

"Thank you," she said, blushing and looking down. Shoshana beamed, ever the proud mother. Hannah wanted to kill her for getting them into this conversation with these crazy—and clearly dangerous—Iranians. She hoped there was a purpose to all this. If Shoshana was doing this for amusement, she was really *messhuganah*.

"And do you enjoy student life?" the General asked.

Although the conversation was making her very nervous and she wanted to run as fast as she could back to their compartment, she played her part as Mordechai had laid it out for her.

"Yes, sir, I do enjoy student life. I belong to the Muslim Students Association, which promotes the values of traditional Islam in the university."

The General seemed pleased with her answer.

"Miss Palmeni, I will leave you with this question: What will be your contribution to your people? It is something every young person must consider. I wish you the very best in your studies." Turning to Shoshana, he said, "Madam, your daughter is a credit to your family and to the Persian people."

"Thank you, sir" said Shoshana smiling.

The General reached into his uniform pocket and pulled out a small gold case, from which he extracted his business card. He handed it to Shoshana and said, "I am General Yazdi and, if I can ever be of service to you, please do not hesitate to contact me. We Iranians must take care of our own, wherever they live."

"Thank you, General," replied Shoshana. "That is very kind of you. I am Mrs. Palmeni and this is my daughter Vashti."

The three men nodded decorously. "We are pleased to have met you."

"And if I may be so presumptuous, General, are you going all the way to Istanbul?" asked Shoshana.

"No, Mrs. Palmeni, we will be leaving the train in Tabriz. From there," the General said with a laugh, "our movements are a state secret, are they not gentlemen?"

"Yes, sir," they replied.

The General called over the waiter and told him that he would be paying for the women's meal. "You mustn't," said Shoshana, but general Yazdi dismissed her protest with a wave of his hand.

"Madam, it is my pleasure and the least I can do to make up for my earlier . . . shall we say . . . excitability."

The women, who had long since finished their desserts, rose and again thanked the General for his generosity and courtesy.
"Thank you again," said Hannah as her eyes met the intense stare of General Yazdi.

As the women left and headed back toward their compartment, the General and his adjutants returned to their conversation—no doubt focused on important matters of state security and national defense.

When they got inside the compartment and locked the door

behind them, they both threw themselves down on the seat and started laughing in relief.

"What was that all about?" asked Hannah.

"That, my dear, was what we call the completion of an assignment," replied Shoshana, no longer laughing.

"You're serious, aren't you?"

"Quite serious, dear," replied Shoshana. "The trap is laid."

"And my part?

"The innocent bait. I will say one thing: for a peasant, our General knows his *tarof*?"

Hannah laughed. *Tarof* was the Farsi word for the rules of formal etiquette. "For the most part, but there was a point there when he raised his voice that I do not believe is in the *tarof* manual."

"Well, you must forgive him his passionate outbursts, my dear Vashti. As my grandfather used to say, 'you can take the peasant out of the country, but you can't take the country out of the peasant.' That said, I believe we have spoken quite enough about our encounter with the gallant General."

They sat in silence, Hannah dying to ask more questions, but knowing she should not. She resumed reading her book.

She couldn't concentrate and her thoughts kept turning to her role as an accomplice in Shoshana's mission. "Mother," she said, getting Shoshana's attention, "I now understand why Father splurged on first-class tickets."

"As your father always says, 'one must be thrifty with money but never miss an opportunity to make an investment.'"

"Why, Mother, this evening you are just full of the wise sayings of the men of our family."

Shoshana shot her a look of mild disapproval. "Well, as your uncle was fond of saying: 'Silence is golden.'"

A few moments later, the porter knocked on the door of their compartment and informed them that he would be returning in five minutes to make their beds. They donned their chadors and went out into the corridor to wait. The porter was going from cabin to cabin, changing the beds. There were other first-class passengers milling about. Hannah smiled at two children playing with handheld video games. Another man was having an animated conversation on his cell phone. Some things are universal, she thought. Hannah used the sleeve of her chador to wipe the condensation from the inside of the window. The glass was very cold to the touch; it must be freezing outside. She had to get really close to the glass to look outside. All she could see in the blackness was the bare outline of snow-covered mountain peaks. Above the peaks were a sky full of stars and a brightly illuminated moon in the shape of a crescent.

Eventually, the porter worked his way to their compartment. He went inside and lowered the seat backs and made their beds. Hannah had never slept on a train before. The only train in Israel goes from Haifa to Tel Aviv and it takes an hour to make the trip.

The bed was clean, the sheets crisp, and Hannah was asleep within minutes, the rhythmic movement of the train lulling her to sleep. As she was drifting off, the last thing she saw was Shoshana, with half reading glasses, holding her knitting up by the light of the little reading lamp and admiring her handiwork. Shoshana looked up and mouthed the words, "*Lila tov*" — "Good night" — in Hebrew.

In the morning, Hannah woke to a spectacular view. Shoshana was already awake and dressed and had pulled up the shades. They were in the mountains and every few kilometers they traveled over railroad bridges spanning rugged mountain gorges. The Iranians were excellent engineers. Were they excellent nuclear engineers as well, Hannah wondered? For the sake of her people holding on to their tiny swath of land on the Mediterranean Sea, she hoped not.

At 8:15 in the morning, the train pulled into the grimy train station in Tabriz, all black mushy snow and steam vents. On their way to breakfast in the dining car, Hannah and Shoshana caught sight of the three Pasdaran officers walking away from the train in their military greatcoats carrying valises and briefcases. Was it her imagination or did Hannah catch sight of one of the men turning around and staring back at the rail car momentarily and meeting her eyes?

At 1:33 pm the train stopped at the frontier station at Razi and the Iranian customs agents entered their car. When the two officers got to their compartment, Shoshana handed them their passports and answered a few perfunctory questions about their visit to Iran. They stamped their passports with big red exit stamps. When the officers completed their business, the locomotive again began to move slowly forward. Out the window, they could see a white wooden sign with black letters that said in English, Turkish, and Arabic, "Entering the Republic of Turkey." There was another sign that said. "Kapikoy 1 km."

The train stopped again and a new set of customs officials boarded, this time from Turkey. When the Turkish customs officer opened the door and saw the black chadors that Shoshana and Hannah were wearing, he frowned under his thick black moustache, obviously disapproving of their rigid Islamic dress. He stared at Shoshana's passport photograph and then at her face—only to start the whole process over again for Hannah. It made her feel very conspicuous. God, she thought, was it possible for this whole thing to unravel on the Turkish side of the border? It felt like the world had suddenly slowed down and that the Turkish official would never finish with them. Then his expression changed and an incongruously broad smile appeared on his face. He said, "Welcome back home," stamped their passports, turned on his heels smartly and left their compartment.

They proceeded to take their chadors off and stuff them into their bags. "Enough of those," said Shoshana.

"No kidding," replied Hannah as she busied herself with putting her few things back into her suitcase. They went out into the corridor to wait. About twenty minutes later, the train started to move slowly down the tracks. They pulled into the dusty railroad station at Kapikoy. It was a low slung old provincial station, built shortly after World War I.

"This is our stop," Shoshana said brightly.

Most of the passengers stayed on the train at Kapikoy and the few passengers that got off looked tired and poor, farmers from the surrounding area. Shoshana and Hannah made their way through the station to wait to be picked up.

In front of the station, there was a dirt-spattered old Mercedes waiting. Two men got out and came over to the women. One was older, with a slight limp and a middle-aged paunch. The other was younger, thinner, and looked like he'd seen the worst end of a few bar fights.

Hannah knew the older man. Relief washed over her.

"Mazel Tov" said the older one to Hannah. "You did well, Hannah." He hugged her. "Let me help you with that bag."

The other man walked up to Shoshana and grabbed her bags.

"All right, already, Avi," said Shoshana impatiently. "Let's stop wasting time over sentimentalities and get going."

"Shoshana, I've known you thirty years and you're still in a hurry."

Chapter 6

It was Friday evening, the end of another busy week. The Canadian often dined alone on the nights his wife, who was something of a socialite, was at the opera or the theater. Tonight she had gone with a group of her friends on a weekend cultural trip to Paris. He sat in his favorite restaurant, a small bistro that served excellent food.

His name was Hugh Cartwright and he worked in the passport section of the Canadian embassy in downtown Copenhagen. For the past twelve years, Cartwright spent his days issuing substitute passports to distressed Canadians whose passports were lost or stolen. It was a boring job but he was just a few years away from retirement. Cartwright was a competent employee and always received excellent reviews. He was quiet at work and did not socialize with the other embassy personnel.

Cartwright's wife thought he was a bore. They were childless and their marriage had long since become a sterile partnership. They tolerated one another—rarely arguing—but their life together was austere and loveless. Like so many middle-aged men, his life was one of quiet desperation. But his was a restless soul. He read literature voraciously and wrote poetry and dabbled in photography. At their flat in the bourgeois Frederiksberg neighborhood, he tended to his beloved bonsai collection and made polite conversation with his wife. His internal emotional life was as tumultuous as his external appearance was bland. There was something trapped in the soul of this man and, as controlled as he was, he wished it could be set free.

He finished his dinner and walked along the Krystalgade to his favorite bookstore, a small shop called "Chaucer" that specialized in English language books. He was in the poetry section looking at a compilation of nineteenth-century romantic verse. He noticed a young woman next to him. She was Eurasian and appeared to be in her early twenties. She had long black hair tied neatly in a ponytail, high cheekbones, and long legs under her short pleated skirt. Perhaps she was a student at one of the local universities. Cartwright resumed looking at the book he was reading; he did not want to stare. She reached across him for a book. "Excuse me," she said as she removed a volume of poetry by Rosetti that he had been glancing at a few moments before. He moved out of the way to make room for her. She opened the book and began to read. She let out a barely audible sigh of pleasure. Cartwright was acutely aware of her; she was standing slightly too close too him. He could smell her perfume. He did not move away.

She looked up from the thin volume and cast her gaze at him. "I just love the romantic poets, don't you?" she said. Cartwright looked up from his book. Her smile was warm and friendly. Her English was accented, sounding slightly British, typical of the Danes.

He was taken aback by her directness and it took him a second to realize she was talking to him. "Yes, indeed," he said, smiling back. "This bookstore has the best selection of English language poetry in Copenhagen."

"It's true," she responded with her beautiful smile. Her teeth were so white they seemed almost luminescent in the dark, old, wood-paneled bookstore. "I only discovered this shop recently. I am taking a course in nineteenth-century British literature and my professor, who is English, told us about this shop."

"And where are you attending university?" He managed to stammer out the words.

"I am a graduate student at the University of Copenhagen. And you, are you a tourist?"

"Oh, no, no," he said. "Actually I work for the Canadian Embassy here."

"Really," she replied, "That must be such interesting work. Do you speak Danish?"

He switched to Danish. "Of course. It is a requirement of the job. But my Danish is far from perfect."

"Actually," she said, "it's quite good. Danish is a hard language to master. So where is the Canadian Embassy?"

"It is over on Kristen Bernikowsgade, Number 1, on the corner."

The girl switched back to English. "Have you lived in Copenhagen for many years?"

"I have been here for ten years." Even though the questions were a bit forward, he found the girl pleasant to talk to and she was so pretty.

"And before that, were you in exotic places?"

"Well, I was in Ireland for a while and, early in my career, I was in South Africa."

She must have sensed his thoughts, because she blushed and said, "Forgive me for my questions. I am such a curious person. I like to hear people's stories. My mother says I'm way too forward."

"Oh, please," he said, smiling broadly, "you are not at all too forward. We Canadians are a friendly lot."

"And are you a big fan of the Romantic period?" she said, gesturing to the shelves next to them.

"I'm absolutely passionate about the Romantics. I am a particular fan of Coleridge and some of the women Romantic poets, like Joanna Baillie and Felicia Browne. Have you read them?" He couldn't believe he was opening up to this girl like this. He felt an odd nervous energy.

"Yes, their poetry is wonderful. And Mary Wollstonecraft and Charlotte Dacre—I just adore their poetry. My professor has written a book about women Romantic poets. Imagine, all those brilliant and demure British women, so quiet and refined on the outside, so passionate and sensual on the inside." Her dark eyes brightened and she stared straight into his.

The intense way she held his gaze made him uncomfortable, as if she were standing too close to him on the subway or the bus. He glanced away and when he looked back she was no longer looking so intensely into his eyes. "Indeed, they are amazing poets, particularly the women."

"It is nice to talk to someone who shares one's passion. Do you write poetry?"

"Oh, yes, I must confess that I do, but I don't think it's very good." What made him admit this to this total stranger, to a young woman half his age, he could not fathom. There was something about her innocent friendliness that was disarming and it made him want to talk. It felt good, like a confession—a weight off his chest. "And how about you? Do you write poetry?"

"Yes, but I too am very critical of my work," she said, momentarily closing her eyes. When she opened them, she smiled her beautiful smile and suddenly thrust out her hand. "But I am being rude. My name is Alexis Narbayev."

"And mine is Hugh Cartwright."

He shook her hand. Her handshake was firm and confident, like a man's, and her hands were warm. He worried that his palms might be moist. Sometimes when he was nervous he got sweaty palms. He was certainly nervous now—and excited. He hadn't felt this way around a woman in years. It was as though the bundle of feelings that made up his emotional life was suddenly off balance.

"It's a pleasure to meet you, Mr. Cartwright." She held on to his hand just a moment too long.

"Please call me Hugh," he said, letting go of her hand.

"Hugh . . .," she said, biting her lip, and hesitating for a moment. "May I ask you something? You can certainly say 'no' if you wish."

"Please do."

"I don't know why I would ask a perfect stranger this," she continued, "but you have trustworthy eyes. I would like someone to read my poetry to. Someone who doesn't know me. Because, well . .

.," she stammered, "you know how it is because you write poetry too. It's a very personal thing and it would be embarrassing to show it to a friend. Especially if they didn't like it."

"I would be honored to look at your poetry, Alexis. And I completely understand your feelings. After all, I've never shown my poetry to another soul."

"Mr. Cartwright . . . I mean Hugh . . . that would mean so much to me. You can be honest with me. Really you can."

"Of course I will be honest with you." My, God, he thought, this is so amazing. "Would you like to do this now? It just so happens that I am free this evening."

"Hugh, would you really be willing to do this? That would be wonderful."

"Of course."

"I know a quiet little wine bar over by the University that we could go to. I will, how do they say it, 'treat you,'" she said, her beautiful, open smile radiant.

"Well then, Alexis," he said, his heart feeling light as a feather, "let me purchase my book and we can be off."

They walked down the darkening streets lined with linden trees. He felt her presence next to him and they had an animated conversation about their backgrounds. Alexis came from a working-class family. Her father was a commercial fisherman; her mother worked at the airport as a janitor. They had come to Denmark as refugees from Soviet Central Asia when the Communist regime collapsed in the late 1980s. Alexis was the first person from either side of her family to go to college and her family was very proud of her. She had a younger sister and two older brothers. Her sister worked in a hospital cafeteria and her brothers both worked in a warehouse at the port. She told Hugh that she loved her brothers, but worried about them because they drank a lot and ran with a rough crowd. Her brothers were very protective and it had caused her problems in the past. Hugh responded that he understood how that could happen in an immigrant family like hers.

"Now, Hugh, tell me about yourself," she said, as they rounded the corner near the bar.

"Well, Alexis, there really isn't much to tell. I am a career diplomat and, as you know," he said, laughing, "a secret poet. I love literature and bonsai."

"And are you married? Do you have children?"

Hugh paused. Part of him didn't want to answer truthfully, but he was honest, perhaps to a fault. "Married, yes I am, but we have no children."

"Oh," she said.

Hugh wondered whether she was disappointed. He felt a bit crestfallen.

They were quiet for a few awkward moments. The awkwardness was broken by their arrival at the wine bar, which was named Cosimo's. They entered through an ancient wooden door. Inside, the bar was small, with whitewashed walls and a vaguely Middle Eastern ambiance. The Moroccan lamps were dimmed and well-worn Persian rugs covered the dark plank floors. The art on the walls was modern, colorful, and abstract. There were perhaps a dozen tables in the place, with couples and small groups talking quietly. The crowd was young and serious—men and women in their twenties and thirties with earnest expressions. The Danish intelligentsia.

They picked a table in the corner and ordered two glasses of wine.

"Are you sure this is O.K.?" said Alexis, reaching inside her backpack and pulling out a leather-bound journal. She was blushing, embarrassed again.

"Of course. You can feel comfortable with me," Hugh responded. As Alexis leafed through her journal looking for a poem to read to him, Hugh could not but marvel at the breathtaking beauty of this girl.

"Well, here's one." She looked up. "But first," she said, lifting her wine glass, "a good luck tradition from my family. I know it is considered uncouth but we must drink down this first glass of wine." They touched their wine glasses in a toast. "May the sun never set on your heart," she said warmly.

He started to speak, but she reached across the table and put a finger to his lips. "No," she said, "we drink first." And as they looked in each other's eyes, they drank down their glasses of wine.

"Now you may speak," she said with mirth in her dark eyes.

"Alexis, that was a beautiful toast. Really."

"Well then, Hugh, shall we order another glass? Then I will be brave enough to let down my guard and read you one of my poems."

"I believe, Alexis, that that is what we call 'liquid courage,'" Hugh said, laughing.

"I've never heard that—it's funny."

They ordered another glass of wine and Alexis read her poem. It was about the beauty of the mountains of Central Asia—a place that existed only in Alexis' imagination, as she had left her homeland as a young child.

After she was done, she looked up, apprehension in her face.

"It's beautiful. Really it is. Alexis, you have a great talent. Have you ever thought about publishing?"

"I have, or at least it is a fantasy of mine"

They drank some more wine—two more glasses—and Hugh felt warm and happy for the first time in years. They laughed and smiled and they were both pleasantly tipsy. Alexis read Hugh another one of her poems, about a silent child growing up in a strange land.

Then, on a whim, Hugh asked Alexis, "May I read you one of my favorite poems? It's a poem called 'Love's Philosophy' by Shelley. Hugh opened the anthology he'd just purchased and began to recite the poem. But after a few seconds he closed his eyes because he could recite it from memory.

> The fountains mingle with the river
> And the rivers with the ocean,
> The winds of heaven mix forever
> With a sweet emotion;
> Nothing in the world is single,
> All things by a law divine
> In one another's being mingle—
> Why not I with thine?
> See the mountains kiss high heaven
> And the waves clasp one another;
> No sister-flower would be forgiven
> If it disdain'd its brother:

And the sunlight clasps the earth,
And the moonbeams kiss the sea—
What are all these kissings worth,
If thou kiss not me?

His eyes were just opening, when she spontaneously leaned across the table and softly kissed him on the cheek. He was startled.

"You are a beautiful man," she said, "you have a good heart."

"It's true," he said, and they laughed. But he was deeply touched by Alexis. "Thank you for a wonderful evening," he said quietly."

"Yes, it was, Hugh. Thank you so much."

After a moment's silence, Hugh said "It's late and we'd best be going. Where do you live, Alexis? Can I walk you home?"

"Yes you can. It's not far, in the Vesterbro," she said.

They strolled down the street toward the Vesterbro enjoying the evening, each lost in their own thoughts.

"Hugh, may I ask you something?" Alexis asked.

"Yes", he responded quietly.

"Is your marriage a happy one?"

"Honestly? No, it is quite dead, really. My career was never successful enough for her. So we have drifted apart. But we stay married out of habit."

"It makes me so sad to hear such a story. You are such a kind and sensitive man."

When they got to her apartment in the bohemian Vesterbro neighborhood, Hugh took her hand in his. "Alexis, thank you for a magical evening. But it's late . . . ."

She fixed her dark eyes on him and, for the second time that night, she put her finger to his lips. With his hand in hers, she led him up the stairs to the flat. He did not resist.

Hugh and Alexis became lovers that night. For Hugh, there was a sweetness and eroticism in their lovemaking he hadn't felt in years. Or maybe he had never known these feelings. He really didn't know. The girl seemed so innocent, but she made love to him with abandon, their bodies sweaty in the warm night.

The next morning he knew that he was falling in love with her. It was crazy and dangerous, but he could not help himself.

Chapter 7

COPENHAGEN, DENMARK, AUGUST 2006

The short Danish summer was nearly over and there was rain in the streets of Copenhagen. The nights were growing longer and there was a chill in the air.

To Hugh and Alexis it did not matter. In the preceding two months they had fallen for one another totally. They met whenever possible at her little flat and shared their passion for poetry and music. For Hugh, the colors were brighter, the laughter heartier, even food tasted better. He did not question this improbable turn in his life. He just thanked God that he had been given a second chance in life. His heart had been raised from the dead.

Hugh had little difficulty keeping his relationship secret from his wife; Mrs. Cartwright did not pay particular attention to Hugh's comings and goings. Still, Hugh and Alexis were very discreet. A divorce was impossible for Hugh; he was dependent on his wife's wealth to maintain their lifestyle. Besides, if it became public knowledge among the embassy staff the he was involved romantically with a young graduate student, it could lead directly to his dismissal from the diplomatic service. For her part, Alexis had not introduced

Hugh to her family. They would not approve and she did not want to confront them.

This particular evening they had gone out for a quiet dinner and to a film. Alexis was unusually quiet. To Hugh, she seemed nervous and on edge. He asked her several times if something was wrong, but she said it was nothing. It was well past midnight when they returned to Alexis' flat. Alexis and Hugh threw their clothes off and climbed under the thick down duvet. Their lovemaking was slow and passionate. They stared into each other's eyes and kissed deeply. When they were finished, Hugh closed his eyes and was beginning to drift off when he heard Alexis crying softly.

"What's wrong?" Hugh asked.

"It's about me and about my family. Hugh, I've known this for the last week, but I didn't have the courage to tell you."

Just then, as if on cue, there was a pounding on the door of the flat. "Alex, it's Boris, let me in now!" It was a booming Slavic voice speaking bad Danish.

Another man spoke in rapid Russian. He was even angrier.

"Who is that?" Hugh said with alarm.

"It's my brothers," Alexis was screaming. "Oh my God!"

"What are they doing here?"

Just then, one of the men put a shoulder to the front door and burst into the flat. They strode right into the bedroom and turned on the light.

Alexis sat up in the bed and covered herself with the duvet. "Get out!" she screamed in Russian.

"Shut up, you whore," one of the brothers growled.

Hugh jumped out of bed, naked and defenseless. He didn't know what to do.

"What is the meaning of this?" Hugh yelled.

The taller of the two Narbayev brothers strode over to Hugh and, without a word, hit him as hard as he could in the stomach. Hugh doubled over, unable to breathe. He vomited.

Alexis was sobbing quietly. The brothers grabbed Hugh by the arms and hauled him to the chair and sat him down.

"Listen, you British son of a bitch," the smaller one said in Danish.

"You've dishonored our sister and our family. You've gotten the bitch pregnant. You are an old man. You could be her father. You are married, you bastard. I ought to slit your throat and dump you in the Trangraven Canal."

"Pregnant? What are you talking about?" he managed to say.

"If you weren't fucking her she couldn't get pregnant, you piece of shit." He slapped Hugh hard across the face. Hugh could smell alcohol and stale cigarettes on his damp breath.

"Please, Boris, please, Sasha. I love him," pleaded Alexis between sobs.

"Shut up, little sister," said Sasha, the older one, in Russian.

"OK, Englishman, put some clothes on and we will figure out what to do with you." One of the brothers picked up Hugh's clothes and threw them at him. Slowly Hugh got dressed. The brothers lit cigarettes and waited.

When he was dressed, Hugh sat back down in the chair. The room smelled of his vomit, which had simply been ground into the carpet, and sex.

"I will pay for an abortion," Hugh said. "Or if she wants to keep the baby. Whatever. Just don't hurt anyone."

The bigger, dark-skinned brother laughed. "Yes, Englishman, you will pay. And you will not see Alexis again unless you pay what we want. Alex will keep this baby and you will support her and your bastard."

"I can't believe this is happening." Hugh gasped, burying his head in his hands. "Why, Alexis, why?"

She looked down and spoke in a monotone. "I'm so sorry Hugh. So, so sorry. I tried to tell you but I couldn't get up the courage. My brothers found out about us from one of the Russians who saw us together. They followed me to the doctor yesterday and confronted me. I begged them not do this."

"Shut up, Alex. Englishman, you will pay now and this will be over or we will come to your embassy and complain. You have money?"

"Yes, I have a checkbook and some cash."

"Well, Englishman, what are you waiting for?"

"Hugh got out his wallet and handed over the cash he had in his possession. His checkbook was in his sportcoat pocket. He got it out. "How much?" he asked quietly, defeat in his voice.

"600,000 kroners, Englishman . . . to start."

"I don't have access to that kind of money in my bank account."

"Then you will have to find it. What kind of money do you have now?"

"I can write you a check for 200,000 kroners. Who do I write it to?"

"To Boris Narbayev, Englishman."

Hugh wrote out the check and handed it to the Russian.

"Now leave. We will contact you."

Hugh put on the rest of his clothes. As he was leaving the bedroom, he looked back at Alexis, who was looking at him, misery in her eyes.

Chapter 8

For a week, Hugh heard nothing. He called Alexis, but her line was disconnected. He contacted the University and they said there was no student named Alexis Narbayev enrolled there. Sick with worry, Hugh went to Alexis' apartment. No one was home. God only knows, he thought, what those barbarian brothers of hers would do to her.

Hugh was overwhelmed with anxiety. Alexis had vanished. The 200,000-kroner check had not been cashed. If his conduct was discovered, his career would be over. His marriage would end. He was distracted at work and began making mistakes. His coworkers took notice of the mistakes; his wife noticed nothing.

He had been at work for about an hour when he got a phone call. He picked up the line and, on the other end, a man's voice said in bad Danish, "Hello, Englishman, this is your friend. We need to meet."

Hugh felt a wave of nausea. "Please don't contact me here," he whispered into the phone, looking around to see that no one was listening.

The Russian ignored him. "Englishman, you know the Chinese summer house in the Frederiksberg Have?"

"Yes," Hugh answered, "Of course I know it."

"You will meet me there at your lunch time today. There is a park bench by the pond to the right of the Chinese summer house. Sit there and wait."

"And what about Alexis?"

Hugh received no answer. The man had hung up.

At 11:45, Hugh got up from his desk and left the Embassy. He took a cab to the Fredriksberg Have and entered the park. One of Copenhagen's most beautiful places, Fredriksberg Have was verdant urban forest surrounding a former royal palace. In the center of the park was a whimsical Chinese-style house, with dragons and colorful pillars.

Hugh walked along a leaf-covered path to the Chinese summer house. Hugh easily found the park bench and sat down, his breath showing thick in the cold winter air. He was nervous and scared. He watched a group of Japanese tourists descend upon the summer house, snapping photos. They stayed for a while and then left. He waited, glancing at his watch every few minutes.

After about twenty minutes, a man wearing a black overcoat and carrying a briefcase approached the bench. He had dark hair combed straight back and a neatly trimmed goatee. Hugh thought he looked forty or forty-five years old. He smiled at Hugh. "Mr. Cartwright?"

"Yes, I'm Cartwright," responded Hugh.

"May I sit down?" His English had a slight accent, but he couldn't tell from where.

Cartwright said nothing. The man seemed unaffected by Cartwright's lack of response and went right on speaking in his pleasant voice.

"I suppose you were expecting to see our uncouth friend, Boris Narbayev, were you not, Mr. Cartwright?"

"Yes," Hugh responded.

"Well, I'm sure you will be pleased to know that you won't be seeing him any more. From now on, Mr. Cartwright, you will be dealing with me. I am Mr. Able."

"Who are you and what is this about?" asked Hugh, his anger rising.

"These are good questions and you will understand everything in good time."

"What have you done with Alexis?"

"Ah . . . the beautiful Alexis," Mr. Able replied. "You won't be seeing her either, Mr. Cartwright. I can assure you that she is in good spirits and sends her regards. But her work here in Copenhagen is complete."

"What is this?" asked Cartwright, "I'm leaving."

"Go right ahead, Mr. Cartwright, and leave if you wish. But understand this. I am the representative of a country, the name of which is unimportant. Not an enemy of Canada but not a friend either. You, sir, have been photographed with persons known to the Canadian Security Intelligence Service to be agents of a foreign power. Indeed, you have been blackmailed by them and paid them money. It would be no problem to turn over those photographs and your uncashed blackmail check to the CSIS. Wouldn't you agree, Mr. Cartwright, that at a very minimum, you will be fired? Or perhaps the government of Canada will make an example out of you and you will be prosecuted. Your marriage to the lovely Mrs. Cartwright will undoubtedly end. So I suggest you stay right where you are and listen to my proposition."

"I'm listening," responded Cartwright, his chest tightening and his fear rising.

"We just want one thing from you, Mr. Cartwright. We want you to issue legitimate Canadian passports to ten persons. We will supply you their names and photographs and completed passport applications. For your trouble, we are prepared to pay you $250,000 US dollars to be deposited in a bank in Bermuda. Once you have delivered the passports, we will not bother you again. Your life will return to normal and this will all seem like a bad dream with, I might add, some pleasant memories of the lovely Alexis thrown in for good measure."

"Do I have any choice?" asked Hugh.

"Not really, Mr. Cartwright. As a literary man, you will know what I mean when I say that this is the land of Kierkegaard and Hamlet; where the darker emotions predominate. It must stem from the long and dreary winters." Mr. Able laughed in his refined way and continued, "So I suppose, Mr. Cartwright—shall I call you Hugh?—in your despair you could kill yourself, but don't you agree that that seems a bit excessive and so very tawdry? Everyone makes mistakes and yours was not the worst in the world. What is it they say? You need only lay back and think of England."

The leaves were all gone from the trees now and a permanent gray had descended on the city. It was after 8:00 in the evening and getting cold. Hugh Cartwright approached the Turkish restaurant in the Nørrebro district, as he had been instructed by Mr. Able the night before. He went in and asked a waiter in Danish for Mr. Ali.

A young man came from the back of the restaurant. "I am Mr. Ali," the man said.

"I am Mr. Smith, from the solicitor's," said Cartwright, taking out a letter sized manila envelope from inside his overcoat. As he handed it over to the younger man, his hand shook.

Inside the envelope were ten stamped, official, and original Canadian passports.

"Goodbye, Mr. Cartwright. Perhaps we will meet again."

PART II: THE PRESENT

Chapter 9

The Bekaa Valley, Eastern Lebanon, July 5

From the air, the bunker complex looked like a typical Middle Eastern cinderblock apartment building: low, drab, with the usual group of kids kicking a soccer ball around a dried-out field. Two stories beneath the building was the headquarters of the Pasdaran in Lebanon. From this building in the Shiite stronghold of eastern Lebanon, the Pasdaran conducted its clandestine operations against Israel and the West.

The underground bunker smelled of Middle Eastern food, decades of sweat, and damp concrete. It was twenty degrees cooler underground than on the surface, where the houses baked in the harsh summer heat. Except for an old poster of the Ayatollah Khomeini that dated back to the Iranian Revolution, the walls were bare. In one corner, the concrete was exfoliating as a result of a water leak that never went away and nobody bothered to repair. In the other corner, three Kalashnikovs leaned against the wall.

Five men sat around a battered table under greenish fluorescent lights staring at a map of the San Pedro harbor section of Los Angeles. They were drinking mint tea and talking quietly.

Three of the men were senior members of the foreign operations branch of the Al Qods Force, one was a Saudi, and one was a Lebanese member of Hezbollah. The three Iranians and the Arab were in civilian clothes; the Hezbollah operative wore military fatigues.

The oldest man in the group spoke slowly, with obvious authority. "The most important thing is that this must be seen by the Americans and the Zionists as an Al-Qaeda operation."

"Understood," said the Saudi in Arab-accented Farsi.

"That means that there must be no connection whatsoever to us or to Hezbollah."

"Yes, we understand that, General." There was a hint of frustration in the Arab's voice. "We have the proper contacts with Al-Qaeda."

"Excellent," said General Yazdi. "Now, let's talk about funding."

He turned to one of the other Iranians.

The small bearded man put on a pair of reading glasses and spoke quietly. "The acquisition of Pakistan Manufacturing has been successfully consummated. In addition, over the last nine months, $5 million has been transferred to the Bank Punjab Habib in Lahore in the name of Feysal Construction, Ltd., a subsidiary of a Spanish holding company named. . . ." He hesitated for a moment in order to look down at the papers in front of him. "Gaspar Development, S.A." He looked up to see that the others were following him. The General nodded for him to continue.

"Another $1 million has been transferred as an anonymous donation from a Saudi charitable association called Holyland Trust to the Sheik Abdullah Madrassa in Karachi and is being held at the Qatar Development Bank."

With a twinkle in his eye, the little man added, "May Allah bless the charitable." The others laughed.

"Very well," commented the General. "Abdul, is the team in place in Karachi?"

"Yes, sir."

"And the second cadre?" The General turned his fixed gaze upon the Hezbollah operative.

"General, they are prepared, trained, and standing by in a safe house in Beirut."

"Tell me about them," asked the General.

Ahmed Abdullah, the Hezbollah operative, was thirty-five years old, but looked fifty. He had been a fighter since he was twelve. During the first Israeli invasion of Lebanon, he was captured and spent time in the custody of the Shin Bet, Israel's counter-intelligence service. The Shin Bet agents were hard men and they played by Middle Eastern rules. His time with the Jews had been difficult and it had aged him. He had been released during a prisoner exchange when the Israelis withdrew from southern Lebanon. He never confessed to the Jews.

Abdullah handed the general a dossier containing five sheets of paper in typed Arabic script, each with a photograph attached. The General opened the file folder and studied the sheets.

The General looked up and nodded, signaling Abdullah to begin.

"There are four men and one woman. The four men are all Arabs and all Sunnis. Two are Egyptians, one is a Saudi, and one is Yemeni. The woman is a European —a German—and former Baader Meinhof, a convert to Islam in the 1980s. Very dedicated. They all have had advanced weapons training. The woman is good with languages and has done liquidations for us. She speaks English well, also German and Arabic. The leader, Mohammed Dibul, is an engineer by training and fought in Afghanistan. They all speak passable English. The Yemeni was selected because he grew up for a time in Spain where his father was a guest worker. He speaks passable Spanish. This will help in Mexico. The others are good, strong operatives, well-disciplined."

"How about security compartmentalization?"

"We have taken that into account, General. Yacub, one of the Egyptians, has sole knowledge of the primary and secondary targets. The other Egyptian and the Pakistani are the bomb builders. Dibul is in overall command with the German woman providing security. We are dividing them into two teams. Team One is composed of the woman and Dibul, who will travel posing as a married couple. Team Two is composed of the other three men. They will be traveling on the Canadian passports we obtained in Denmark."

"Excellent," said the General, closing the dossier. His blue eyes twinkled with mirth. "Everybody loves the Canadians. They are so inoffensive."

When the laughter died down, he looked around the table and said, "We shall call this mission 'Operation Zaqqum,' Fitting, is it not, my bothers?" The General banged his fist on the table. "Fitting that the infidel Americans should be forced to have a little taste on earth of the *Zaqqum*—the bitter fruit that the damned are forced to consume in hell to increase their torment."

Chapter 10

San Pedro, California, July 22

It was going to be a beautiful day. The spring sun was just coming up over the mountains and the air was cooled by the sea breezes. The trucks coming to pick up intermodal containers were already lined up outside of Terminal L at the Port of Los Angeles. There were at least a hundred of them and it would be like that all day. Between the Port of Los Angeles and the Port of Long Beach right next door, this was the busiest port complex in the United States. It was a hub of constant activity and at the high season in the fall, millions of tons of freight arrived from across the Pacific to fill up the shelves of the big box stores for Christmas. For weeks at a time, ships were lined up at sea miles off the coast waiting for a berth. The portainer gantry cranes were in constant movement, looking like monstrous hands reaching across the dock to offload forty-foot containers onto intermodal chassis. The containers would be dispatched by truck or railroad all across the continent. Locomotive engines belched smoke as they crept slowly along the underground tracks of the Alameda corridor on their way to the big rail interchange yards east of Los Angeles. The 710 freeway was already jammed. It is the only major arterial leading from the port complex and has bumper-to-bumper traffic every day of the year. The line of trucks on their way to the vast warehouses and truck terminals in the desert outnumbered cars twenty to one. You couldn't get a speeding ticket on the 710 if you tried.

"Close this thing down and you close down the country," said Lee Sandahl. He was slight and nattily dressed. His button-down shirt was neatly pressed and his khakis were creased. He looked more like a left-wing intellectual that you might find enjoying a cappuccino in the East Village than a longshoreman standing among the idling trucks, scurrying dock pigs, and general din of a busy marine terminal. He had round, steel-frame glasses and a salt-and-pepper goatee. His smile was loose and genuine and there was a mischievous twinkle in his eye.

"No shit, Lee," said the guy he was talking to. "Maybe next time we should shut the fuckers down rather than let them lock us out." Eugene Lamont was a large African-American man, a third-generation longshoreman, passionate about his politics, quick to laugh, and equally quick to respond to insults—real or perceived.

"Gene, I really wasn't thinking about labor stuff. I was thinking about terrorists. This place is wide open. Osama bin Laden could call his cousin Achmed in Fresno and tell him to drive over here and pick up a container with a bomb in it and, as long as he had a bill of lading, Achmed could just drive right into the place. No questions asked."

"Damn straight. Half these drivers bought their licenses downtown for fifty bucks. You know that, I know that . . . hell, even the cops know that. A lot of them work for trucking companies that are phony operations. They don't own any trucks and they work out of some shithole office with nothing but a phone and computer."

"Yeah. Did you hear about that accident in the Hanjin Terminal?

"Are you talking about the one where the sister got killed by that driver who just split when the accident happened?" asked Gene.

"That's the one," said Lee.

"I heard that when they arrested the guy, he had no license, no insurance, and his trucking company was just an empty storefront. Damned shame. How can they let that happen?"

"That's capitalism." Lee gestured toward the east. "If anyone out there really understood just how wide-open this place was . . .."

"You know," Gene interrupted, "what I don't get is why after 9/11 they stopped having us randomly open up the containers to check for contraband and overweights."

"That was around the time the freight volumes really started to shoot up dramatically and I guess they figured that it was slowing things down. They don't let anything get in the way of moving freight."

"Yeah, well if those terrorists ever got over their love affair with planes crashing into buildings and got focused on this place, we'd be in some serious shit."

"Well, I'm just a marine clerk," Lee continued, "and you're a crane operator and nobody in management or in the government gives a damn what we think."

"And on that sad note, my friend, I think break time is over."

The two men walked off in separate directions, Lee toward the office and Gene toward a gantry crane further down on the dock.

Chapter 11

On the main road that leads south from the center of Jerusalem toward Bethlehem is the office of the Israeli Finance Ministry. As they passed by the ugly concrete structure, the cab driver joked with Bob D'Agostino that Israelis called it the "Third Temple," because that's where all their money went. D'Agostino laughed, although he had heard the joke a number of times before. The cab driver kept right on talking and asking questions of Bob, who said he was an American teaching at the University of California's junior year abroad program and that he was meeting a friend who lived in this neighborhood.

His story was a lie. Bob was the assistant CIA station chief in Jerusalem and he was going to a meeting with his counterpart in the Mossad. The meeting was held, as usual, in a nondescript and slightly run-down three-story office building just down the block from the Finance Ministry. On the first floor was a factory outlet for *tallit*—Jewish prayer shawls—a travel agent, an Internet café, and a corner grocery. Upstairs were offices for lawyers, accountants, and a few small companies.

After he paid the talkative cab driver, Bob took the small elevator to the second floor. At the end of the corridor was an office with a sign on the door that said, in Hebrew, "Kaufman & Kaufman, Import and Export." He knocked on the door and it was opened by an older man with a warm smile and a neatly trimmed salt-and-pepper beard. Like most Israelis, who carefully cultivated an air of studied casualness, he did not wear a business suit.

"Shalom, Bob, come in." Avi Gerstner gestured for D'Agostino to come in.

"Shalom, Avi, said Bob, thrusting out his hand and shaking Gerstner's. "Beautiful day."

"Yes, one of those '*Yerushalayim shel zahav*' days," responded Avi, referring to the famous folk song of the Six-Day War. Gerstner's English had a slight British or South African intonation, observed D'Agostino.

Gerstner led D'Agostino through an outer office with books and papers stuffed into bookshelves and stacked on the receptionist's desk. The office furniture was old and of the utilitarian Swedish modern style popular in the 1960's. The receptionist—a middle-aged woman with bleached blonde hair—was having an animated phone conversation which seemed to switch between rapid Hebrew and rapid Russian. She didn't look up. They walked past the desk down a short hallway lined with small, drab offices to a conference room. Inside were six men and three women milling around waiting for the meeting to begin. At least half of them were talking on their cell phones. D'Agostino wondered whether the Israelis had replaced their legendary addiction to smoking with an equal attachment to the cell phone. Perhaps it was hard to talk on the phone with one hand and smoke with the other.

"OK, everybody," said Gerstner loudly as he entered the conference room. "Bob is here, let's start the meeting." The other Israelis started to move toward the battered conference table. "Schmuel, get off the phone," said Gerstner irritably in Hebrew to one of the men who had gone right on talking. "Enough already," he said, switching back to English. The man named Schmuel held up his hand as if to say, "one second," and took his seat while still talking on the phone. He then hung up and looked up with an expression of wounded innocence. "What can I say?" said Schmuel to no one in particular.

Bob D'Agostino sat down opposite the dusty picture window that looked out over the street. On the balcony of an apartment across the street was a large banner with a caricature of an American Indian on it. The banner said, in English, "Land for Peace? Ask *him* about that."

Gerstner rapped on the table with his knuckles, bringing the meeting to order. The monthly liaison meeting between the Mossad and the CIA always began with reports from each of the regional desks. Although the Israelis were close allies of the United States, they had their secrets. So did the CIA. That was understood. The Israelis did a little spying on the US and the US spied a little on Israel—nothing serious. "OK, so what have we got for Bob today? Natalia?"

A neat woman in her thirties with clear blue eyes, her brown hair in a thick braid, Natalia took a quick sip of her latte and launched into her report.

"Our sources in Lebanon tell us that approximately 20 kilos of the plastique Danubit was stolen from a Greek military arsenal two months ago and is in the hands of the Abu Massaf Group. The plastique was manufactured by Istrochem in their factory in Bratislava. Our informants tell us it is to be transshipped through Syria for use by Al-Qaeda in Iraq. Currently, we believe that it is being stored in Sidon. We could use your help with the Greeks who are, as you know, not friendly to Israel."

Bob nodded and wrote some quick notes down on a legal pad that he had pulled from his briefcase. "I will certainly follow up on this one and alert CENTCOM. The last thing our folks need is another 20 kilos of plastic explosives floating around Anbar Province."

"Your turn, Aaron," said Gerstner flatly.

"We believe," Aaron began, "that there was a meeting between senior staff of Hamas and representatives of Pasdaran counter-intelligence. The meeting was brokered by the Syrians. It took place two weeks ago at a mosque in Gaza City. We think it represents an effort by the Iranians, who have been very cool to Hamas because it is Sunni, to extend their influence over West Bank terrorist activities.

We consider it a serious development. Although we have successfully penetrated Hamas, we did not have anyone in the meeting itself."

Bob spoke, "We have independent confirmation of that meeting from our own sources. Very significant, in our view, as well. The Egyptians and the Jordanians both alerted us to this meeting. Although, I must say, it may currently get the award for best-publicized secret meeting in the Middle East. I'm surprised that it wasn't carried live on Al Jazeera."

"Yes, we had similar thoughts," Gerstner responded dryly, looking up at D'Agostino with his twinkling grey eyes.

"Yossi, what from the Persian desk?" Gerstner turned to a small, wiry man of indeterminate middle age with dark—almost black—eyes and a heavy five o'clock shadow, even though it was morning and he had just shaven a few hours earlier.

Yossi Levi began speaking in a monotone in heavily accented English. "The Mullahs continue their crackdown on what little is left of the independent press. More secret police visits to Kurdish nationalists in the north warning them that they must moderate their speech and have no contact with Iraqi Kurds, who they warn are American and Zionist spies." A slight smile crossed Levi's mask of indifference. He continued, "As I'm sure your people have noticed, we see stepped-up internal propaganda about the destiny of the Iranian people and their right to develop peaceful nuclear technology. The little president continues to talk loudly about the Jews and the Holocaust."

Gerstner interrupted, "And every time the *mumzer* starts one of his rants, the price of crude oil goes up." There was laughter around the table.

Levi continued, "We detect heavily camouflaged building activity in a high desert valley approximately eighty kilometers southwest of the city of Shiraz, near the village of Bala Deh." He removed several aerial photographs from a file in front of him and pushed them across the table to D'Agostino. Levi paused to allow D'Agostino to look at the photographs. D'Agostino picked up the first photograph and began to study it. It showed what looked like a newly paved two-lane road leading to a large area cleared out of a dry ravine that gradually narrowed so that, from the air, the entire area looked like a large letter "v." Because of the shape of the ravine, there was only one entrance to the area and wire fencing had been run up to the top of the two hills that formed the eastern and western sides of the valley. There were what appeared to be concrete guard towers at the entrance to the facility and on the top of the mountains. A wire fence that was at least fifteen feet high stretched across the mouth of the ravine.

"Bob, if you look in the middle of the photograph, there is an open gravel pit and what looks like a concrete pad where a conveyor system is being installed.

"Now look at the second photograph. Our friends are also busy boring into the side of the mountain."

"Yes, I see."

"The next photograph shows the security at the Bala Deh facility. You can see military vehicles and what we believe are barracks facilities. From their size, we estimate that the place is guarded by a full company of troops."

D'Agostino whistled. "Wow. That's a lot of military."

"Yossi, show Bob the photo of the plumbing."

Levi handed Bob a high resolution photograph of what looked like a pump house next to a river from which large water pipes ran to the top of the plateau."

"That's a lot of water for a gravel-mining operation."

"Precisely," replied Gerstner.

"The Iranians would like us to think it's a concrete batch plant going up. There was a story in the *Iran Business Daily* one and a half months ago about the worldwide shortage of concrete and how the government had made a loan of five billion rials to a consortium of construction companies to establish new concrete and cement factories in central and southern Iran for both export and domestic use. The construction activity is consistent with a concrete plant and there's lots of rock at this place. But that isn't consistent with the cave, the pumping station, and the heavy military presence?"

Yossi Levi threw down another photo in front of Bob. It showed a long dark shadow under camouflage netting. "We think that under the netting, this could be a ground-to-air missile battery. Concrete isn't that valuable.

"May I keep these?" Bob asked.

"Please do," said Gerstner.

"Is there anything else, Yossi?" Gerstner inquired.

"Yes. Two other things. From the world of Persian higher education. A Professor of nuclear engineering at Amir Kabir University of Technology by the name of Majid Emami Honari has taken a sudden leave of absence. We believe that he is a central figure in the Iranian nuclear research program. We don't know where he went. His house is empty. He has vanished on—how do you say it in English?—a 'magic carpet,' We don't know what it means. Second thing. Two weeks ago, a Mullah who was a professor at Al Zahra Women's University named Reza Tourani was murdered. The press reported it as an accident, but we have reason to believe it was a crime of passion.

Avi Gerstner interrupted. "Mr. Tourani was known to us because he was a former aide to Khomeini at the time of the Revolution. Not so nice to the Jews. His death is very sad for his family, but not so sad for us."

Bob smiled. "You know, Avi, we are aware of the demise of Tourani. Some of our folks think you guys had him killed. Not that we particularly care."

"It was not us, Bob. If we were going to assassinate a cleric these days—and I speak hypothetically here—I think we would prefer the victim to be our Hezbollah friend and northern neighbor Sheik Nasrallah. As you know, we owe him a great deal. It is safe to say that we wouldn't mind if he was dispatched to a place where he can commune for eternity with the other martyrs of his . . . ilk."

"Anything else on Iran?" asked Bob.

"No" said Levi.

"Of course, I would be remiss," Gerstner commented, "if I did not repeat, as I do at every meeting with you, that Iranian nuclear ambitions are the greatest danger to the security of this region. We believe that the West must act now and act decisively as we did when we destroyed the Iraqi nuclear facility at Osirak in 1981. The world was angry then, but they thank us now."

Bob sighed. "Avi, while we all agree that Iran should not be

allowed to develop nuclear weapons capability, we also all know that
Iran is a much more complicated issue than Iraq was in '81. Air power
alone will not be enough. We cannot act unilaterally or just with you.
The Europeans and our regional allies must agree and they are not
there at this point. There are domestic political issues that complicate
matters. There is our commitment in Iraq. There are the Russians,
the Turks, the Armenians, and the Pakistanis. Hell, half the Iranian
nuclear sites are in Iranian Kurdistan. Besides you guys, the Kurds
are our only real friends in the area."

"OK, now for the Russians. Olga?"

Everyone's eyes turned to an elegant middle-aged woman with
bleached blonde hair pulled back tight in a ponytail. She smiled
serenely as she began her report. Her voice was quiet and her accent
was decidedly Eastern European.

"The Russians continue to kill Chechens. The Chechens kill
Russians. Very nasty business. The Chechens are getting some
Arab money. Not much, but it is increasing modestly. We believe
that there are some Chechens receiving weapons training in the
Waziristan autonomous region in western Pakistan. As you know,
the Russians continue to exchange information with the Iranians
on so-called 'peaceful' nuclear development. Their gambit is to get
some big contract with the Iranians to supply nuclear fuel for energy
production. That way they can find work for all those underemployed
nuclear scientists and technicians and make some money. Maybe
collect some bribes for all those ex-communist bureaucrats and KGB
types that surround President Putin."

"You mean hire some of the ones that are not already on our payroll
or that you haven't gotten to go to work for you at your 'peaceful'
nuclear research facility at Dimona?"

They all laughed, except Olga, who looked slightly irritated.
"Precisely," she said dryly. "There is something more."

"Bob, we believe that this is very serious", said Gerstner, the smile
gone from his face. "Please continue, Olga."

The Russian woman put on a pair of reading glasses. "We have
reason to believe that the Iranians are in negotiations with the Russians
to acquire 25 3M82 Moskit anti-ship missiles. I believe that they are
code-designated by NATO as the SS-N-22 Sunburn missile."

Bob sat up slightly and frowned. This was bad news. Very bad news. "I am well aware of the Sunburn and its capabilities." The Sunburn was the best anti-ship missile in the world. It carried a 750-pound conventional warhead and could also be nuclear-tipped. Twenty-five Sunburns deployed near the Straights of Hormuz in the Persian Gulf could devastate the US Fifth Fleet. The missile was virtually undetectable while cruising just above the water. It was small and could be fitted on almost any vehicle or vessel and was capable of evasive maneuvers that made it almost impossible to kill.

"Where does this information come from?" Bob asked.

Olga looked at Gerstner, not sure whether to answer. "You may tell him," said the Israeli intelligence chief. The room was hushed.

"We have penetrated Mashinostroyeniye, the manufacturer of the missile."

"Is there an actual executed contract for the sale?"

"No, we believe that they are still in negotiations, but it is at a final stage."

"*Zababa*" said Bob, a wry smile breaking across his face. The Israelis laughed at the irony of this middle-aged straight-laced American intelligence officer using Israeli slang for "cool".

The tension broken, Avi Gerstner asked D'Agostino, "So, Bob, what have you got for us? Don't tell us you've discovered that Kim Jong-Il is anti-Semitic?"

Chapter 12

F requently, Jonathan Elliot wondered why he ever said yes to the offer that he take a leave of absence from his university teaching job and go to work for the government. He wasn't the government type. In fact, he wasn't an identifiable type at all. He held a Ph.D. in nuclear engineering but wasn't a great fan of nuclear power, feeling that society was not ready to handle nuclear fission safely. In an area of study dominated by technocrats who disclaimed any interest in politics or culture, or if they had any politics, they tended to be conservative, Jake was decidedly to the left-of-center. He had never voted for a Republican and neither had his parents, both of whom were college teachers. In fact, as far as he knew, neither had his grandparents or aunts and uncles or anybody else that he was aware of on either side of his family. His grandmother revered Franklin Delano Roosevelt. His father, Louis Elliot, venerated Harry Truman and John F. Kennedy. Louis taught political science at California State University Northridge in the suburban San Fernando Valley section of Los Angeles. His mother, Joan Weinstein—she had kept her own name—was a professor in the history department at UCLA. Jake had an older sister named Ellen, who was a deputy public defender in San Francisco. If you could describe the Elliot/Weinstein family, it would be loud, intellectually engaged, warm, opinionated, and very close. Although both of Jake's parents were atheists, he was the product of a mixed marriage. His father was nominally Christian—from a long line of progressive Unitarian ministers—and his mother was a non-practicing but very ethnically identified Jew. They had compromised and Jake's parents had brought up him and his sister with no religion at all. As a kid, Jake was secretly envious of his friends who had Christmas trees or went to Jewish summer camp. The matter was a sore point with Jake's maternal grandparents, who frequently expressed their disapproval at Jake's parents' failure to bring him up Jewish. His paternal grandparents, being open-minded Unitarians, were ecumenical on the point.

Jake's parents still called him by his boyhood nickname "Jakey." During his teenage years, he had insisted that he be called Jonathan, but they had ignored his request. And now he would have it no other way. They would argue about politics and the state of the world, even though they basically agreed with one another. All told, Jake grew up as a pretty good kid. He was a poor athlete as a child and something of a bookworm. He was teased by bullies but prided himself on talking his way out of trouble. Although tending toward the chubby side as a small child, in his teens he grew thin, tall, and athletic. The girls liked his mop of curly brown hair, which fell in ringlets and, once he got his braces off, his beautiful smile. He was a genuinely nice person and his years as an awkward child not only toughened him up but made him empathetic. His form of adolescent revolt was to immerse himself in science and proudly declare that he didn't care about politics, which irritated the rest of his opinionated family. He became a nuclear engineer, which his parents found vaguely embarrassing. The funny thing was that, by his mid-twenties, he found himself more and more drawn to the family's liberal values.

Jake finished his PhD at Yale when he was twenty-seven, graduating at the top of his class. His dissertation was on the potential for development of a closed power-plant design system that could recycle 100% of the spent fuel, thereby eliminating the environmental problem of disposing of highly radioactive waste. It was well received and he was immediately offered a fellowship at MIT and, within a year an assistant professorship. By the time he was thirty, he had published a groundbreaking article in *Science* arguing that through clean and safe nuclear power, intense conservation efforts, and the mandatory adoption of alternative fuels for transportation, the US and its Western allies could wean themselves off of their dependence on fossil fuels. He argued, however, that the current nuclear power plants were poorly designed and should be shut down and replaced. His outspoken opinions angered all sides and pleased no one in particular. But he earned a reputation for intellectual honesty that gained him the grudging respect of all sides in the superheated debate over nuclear power. He was popular with his students and his lectures were well attended—even by students outside of the engineering field. It didn't hurt that he was handsome, witty, and unattached.

Jake's personal life was somewhat less successful than his professional life. Although he had fallen in love and moved in with a fellow graduate student for a few years in his mid-twenties, he and Alicia had ultimately gone their separate ways. Now, at thirty-three, Jake was turning into something of a confirmed bachelor. It wasn't that he wasn't interested in women or settling down and having a family; he just hadn't found the right person. He dated in a desultory sort of way, somewhat dreading the forced conviviality of the dating scene. He wasn't the sort of guy that felt comfortable with one night stands or the bar scene, his mother having managed to drum into him from an early age that sex went with love. In short, Jake was waiting for the perfect woman.

And so, when the letter arrived one spring day from the Secretary of Energy inviting him to interview for a position as a government Research Fellow with the National Nuclear Security Agency, he was intrigued. The letter explained that the Secretary was forming a research group that would be making recommendations on the foreign policy aspects of nuclear energy and nuclear security. He would have to pass a security clearance and the work group's deliberations would be highly classified.

His parents and sister were appalled that he would contemplate working for an administration that they abhorred more than any other since Nixon was in the White House. While he was no fan of the current Administration—in fact, he disliked it intensely—he told his parents that he felt that they needed someone with his intellectually honest perspective to help formulate policy. His father rather acerbically commented that, if intellectual honesty and a high degree of ethics was the benchmark, he'd last about ten minutes working for this Administration. But Jake had felt the urge to serve his country ever since the 9/11 terrorist attacks and this was his chance.

After first having an interview with a panel of department heads from the DOE and then the Administrator of the National Nuclear Security Agency, Jake was offered the fellowship. At his final interview, they informed him that he would co-chair the panel and oversee its deliberations. It was tremendously flattering to Jake and he was excited to be at the center of policy discussions that would directly affect the United States and the entire world community over the next several decades.

Jake rented out his apartment in Cambridge to a visiting professor from Sweden and sublet a condominium in the trendy— for Washington—Dupont Circle area of Washington. The owner worked for the State Department and was headed for a one-year stint overseas.

On a gray February morning, the team first assembled in the conference room of the office of the Secretary of Energy. The Secretary was not present, but Assistant Secretary for Energy Policy Anne Marie Mitchell was there as well as the Administrator of the National Nuclear Security Administration, David Cantwell. The NNSA was the branch of the Department of Energy that was charged with both domestic and foreign nuclear weapons safety. In fact, every nuclear bomb in the arsenal of the United States was technically on loan from the Department of Energy, which had ultimate authority over nuclear weapons production, storage, and nonproliferation. DOE also ran the government's top-secret nuclear weapons laboratories at Lawrence-Livermore in California and Los Alamos in New Mexico.

They were seated at a long table, with name cards placed in front of their respective seats. Jake was seated next to a dark-skinned woman who looked Middle Eastern. Her name card identified her as "Dr. Youghobian, Co-Chair." On the other side of her was a man who was identified as "Eric Johnson, CIA." Johnson came over and introduced himself with a friendly smile as "Eric the Spook." Sitting across the table was an Army officer whose name tag identified him as Lt. Colonel Alfonse Parinello. He turned out to be a former combat officer who now taught at the Army War College and was an acknowledged expert on clandestine military operations. Sitting next to Parinello was a small wiry woman named Cynthia Takemoto, who was a physicist on loan from the Fermi Lab in Illinois and an expert on nuclear weapons design. The final member of the group was an electronic intelligence analyst at the National Security Agency named Antonia Breski.

The Assistant Secretary, Anne Marie Mitchell, welcomed the group on behalf of the Secretary of Energy. She was a beautiful woman in her late thirties or early forties, with a head of carefully coiffed blonde hair and a strong Southern accent that spoke of old money and refinement. She had a smooth, competent, and professional manner. She had barely started speaking in her warm southern drawl when the CIA guy leaned over to Jake and whispered, "Total phony political hack." Jake did not respond, but did acknowledge the wisecrack by raising an eyebrow. The others sat attentively and Jake wondered what they were all thinking.

They had been convened, the Secretary began, as a result of a Presidential intelligence directive mandating that an interdisciplinary group be formed to examine the best available intelligence sources and, based on that information, predict when the Iranian government would be able to achieve nuclear weapons capability. They were to develop and make recommendations to the Secretary of Energy concerning alternative strategies for neutralizing the Iranian nuclear threat short of all out military invasion. She was to be their highest-level contact in DOE management but would not be involved in their day-to-day work. They were to work under the direction of Administrator Cantwell and be housed in an office in the NNSA complex in Arlington. Each of them, she explained, brought a particular perspective or expertise to the group and they were expected to work cooperatively under the joint chairmanship of Professors Elliot and Youghobian.

Lt. Colonel Parinello raised his hand. "May we ask questions at this point, Secretary Mitchell?"

"Please do, Lt. Colonel."

"When you speak of a recommendation for action 'short of all-out military invasion,' do you mean to exclude all use of military assets?"

Anne Marie Mitchell smiled calmly but Jake thought that her eyes betrayed the slightest hint of panic. "Let me defer that question to Administrator Cantwell."

David Cantwell, who had been silent up to that point, cleared his throat in such a way as to convey irritation. "That's an excellent question, Lt. Colonel. The limitation we wish you to place on the use of military assets is that your plan must presuppose that military force must be used only in a clandestine role. Special forces operations, intelligence-gathering missions, and the like certainly should be one of your tactical options."

"Thank you, David," Assistant Secretary Mitchell said graciously. The use of his first name subtlety conveyed that she was the dominant person in the room. Mitchell explained that they were to issue a preliminary report in no later than twelve months so that it could be reviewed by the Secretary and, if necessary, revised before it was sent to the White House.

"That's so they can sanitize it . . . or bury it," whispered the CIA guy. Jake wished he wouldn't keep doing that, but he also wanted to get along with everyone on the team, so he responded with an understanding smile.

Over the ensuing weeks, the team threw itself into its work. The assignment was daunting and they found themselves regularly working twelve-hour days in an effort to meet their deadlines. The first part of their study would assess Iranian nuclear assets, synthesize data on future intentions, and come up with a threat assessment. Much of the work was speculative in nature. But each member of the team had been picked to bring a particular perspective to the project and they made steady, if slow, progress. They had to wade through mountains of intelligence reports and other information on contracts that the Iranians had executed with various governments and private companies. There were many governments that publicly supported U.N. Resolutions on nuclear nonproliferation while privately supplying the Iranian regime with technology in direct violation of those resolutions. They would sell anything they could to the Iranians. Some governments merely turned a blind eye to their large corporations selling sensitive material to Iran. The President of Iran was bragging openly about his country's progress and the team sometimes wondered if it was a bluff. But as the weeks passed into months, it became clear to the members of the interdisciplinary group that the Iranians were making substantial progress in their effort to build a nuclear weapon.

Chapter 13

Diezengoff Square is the heart of commercial Tel Aviv. It's a big concrete circle surrounded by older apartment complexes and businesses with streets radiating out like the spokes of a wheel. By the standards of most of the world's major cities, it's an unassuming place and, like a lot of Israel, appears to have been built in a hurry with minimal planning.

Hannah waited for Avi Gerstner at a coffee house called "Café Sport" on one of the side streets off Diezengoff Square. It was six months since her return from her latest mission and, after an initial frenzy of debriefings, they had given her time off to rest and get herself physically and psychologically ready to go back to work. She visited her parents for a few days over the Jewish holidays and enjoyed the solitude of her flat. She read for pleasure and took in a few movies with her best friend, Sarah. It was a welcome interlude. She briefly thought about quitting and what it would be like to live a normal life, but the truth was that she was dedicated to her job and could not seriously contemplate giving it up. That time would come but it would not be this year.

She looked up to see Avi showing the security guard the contents of his briefcase. Since the massive suicide bombing attacks had begun, every restaurant—and virtually every other public place—had been required to hire a security guard to try to provide some minimal degree of safety. Diezengoff Square itself had been attacked two years before and it was a shock to Israelis that the heart of Israel's most Jewish city was vulnerable. Since then the Government had expedited building the security wall that was intended to separate Israel from the occupied territories, the number of suicide bombings had declined precipitously. As the effectiveness of the attacks decreased, the Palestinians complained bitterly that the wall was an "apartheid" fence.

Hannah waved as Avi came through the door. He was a big bear of a man, probably nearing seventy now, but he still had the looks and vigor of a much younger man. His face seemed perpetually tanned and his laugh was infectious. Avi was more like a grandfather to Hannah than a boss. He had recruited her grandmother into the Mossad soon after their family had left Iran and, as a child, Hannah remembered many a quiet evening in her grandparents' apartment in Jaffa observing Avi in deep and animated conversation with her *Saba* and *Safta*.

Gerstner gave her a big hug. "How are you, Hannala?" Gerstner asked, using the Yiddish diminutive.

"I'm OK, Avi," she responded.

"Are you really?" he asked.

"Yes, but Tehran was hard."

"Yes, Hannah, what you did, what we've all had to do, is never easy. But it has to be done. We take out the garbage for the Jewish state." He waved his big arm around. "All this wouldn't be possible were it not for us garbage men."

Avi got up to order a coffee. Hannah felt both excitement and dread at what she knew was coming next. When Avi sat down, he took a long sip of coffee and when he looked up he stared at her as if making an assessment of some sort. Or maybe a confession.

"Walk with me."

Gerstner drank down his coffee and got up. Hannah followed

him onto the street. They did not speak. They walked two blocks and entered a small apartment complex. At the end of a dimly lit corridor, Gerstner took out a set of keys and opened the door to one of the apartments. Hannah had been there before. It was an apartment which the Mossad used for meetings. They sat down.

"Hannala, we have a new assignment for you. Are you ready?"

"Yes, Avi, I'm ready."

"When you smile like that, you remind me of your grandmother when she was your age."

Hannah knew that what Avi was saying was that she was beautiful like her grandmother had been. It made her slightly embarrassed. "Yes, Avi, you've told me that before. It usually means that you have something difficult you want to tell me."

"Well, Hannah, I guess you can read me like a book. Here it is. Have you ever gone fishing?"

"Once, in the Kineret, with my grandfather," said Hannah.

"OK, this mission is a kind of deep sea fishing. We are calling it 'Operation Job.' You remember, of course, the Iranian general on the train from Tehran with you and Shoshana, that Yazdi character? We want you to make contact with him. We have been trying to penetrate the Pasdaran's foreign operations branch for a long time. We now have our opportunity. We will send you and Shoshana back to Van in Turkey and set you up there in the University under the cover Shoshana developed. These are dangerous people—we're used to that—but they are also very smart; very experienced. You must be constantly on your guard as they will be looking for infiltrators. They know we're after them . . . along with the Americans and the Brits and probably half the espionage agencies in the Western world. For that reason, this mission is voluntary. We don't know what will happen if they want you to go to Iran or an Arab country. If they catch you, they will kill you."

Hannah looked intently at Avi Gerster and said. "Of course I will do it Avi. I'm a dedicated garbage man."

"After this, maybe it is time for you to come home for good."

"As my grandfather used to say, 'from your mouth to God's ears,' Avi."

Chapter 14

General Yazdi stared out the window of his office. The color guard was marching in front of the Monument to the Fallen. They did a slow goose-step in the drizzle. Yazdi's office was spacious, but simply furnished. The walls were lined with his honors and photographs of him with the President of the Islamic Republic and the Grand Ayatollah who headed the Supreme Revolutionary Council. His desk was clean but that was because he didn't spend much time there. He preferred to be in the field or directing operations from his headquarters in Lebanon.

He turned back in his chair and faced Dr. Honari. "Say that again?"

"Well, there are certain common products—bananas, bentonite clay, cement, aluminum foil—that naturally emit radiation. So if I was going to recommend trying to conceal radioactive material in a shipment, I would probably place it with a commodity that naturally emits radiation. That way the authorities would not be surprised if the shipment showed positive emissions."

Dr. Honari seemed very intimidated. The general momentarily

thought about trying to calm the scientist, but he had found over the years that such efforts were usually futile. He liked the man, but unfortunately duty did not permit him to show it.

"Well, General, of course you would want to shield the material with lead or concrete and pack it with aluminum."

"And among these various naturally radioactive materials, is there one in particular which you would recommend that we use?"

"Well, yes. The product we should be looking at is cat litter."

"You mean that stuff that pet owners use for their cats?"

"Precisely. It's made of materials that naturally emit radiation and is often packed in plastic and foil. And it's exported from China, Pakistan, and Bangladesh to the United States."

"I want a report on this on my desk in one week. One copy, for my eyes only. It must be totally secret. Can you do that?

"Allah be willing."

Chapter 15

BANDE ACHE RESTAURANT, GEORGETOWN, WASHINGTON, D.C.
OCTOBER 23

It was Jake's idea that Al Perinello, Fariba Youghobian, and he go out to dinner. But it was Perinello who suggested that they eat at the small Indonesian restaurant in Georgetown. Perinello told Jake that he believed that the hotter the cuisine, the more productive the conversation would be. Al was a voluble man; a great storyteller and a gifted teacher. He seemed to have a lust for life and his big laugh was infectious. He and Jake hit it off from the beginning. Al had a relatively minor role to play in drafting the first part of the report, since his expertise was not in the analysis of technical data regarding the progress of the Iranian nuclear program. But they would soon be turning their attention to tactical and strategic options. Could the Iranian nuclear threat be neutralized without causing a war or the loss of tens of thousands of innocent civilian lives? Jake and Fariba wanted to pick Al's brain.

"Look, Al," said Jake, digging in to one of the restaurant's excellent sambals. "Is what we're doing here just a big waste of time? Are the President and the military simply just gearing everybody up for another war in the Middle East?"

"Well, Jake, let me try and answer it this way. Did you see that latest Seymour Cohen article in the *New Yorker* about the military establishment's resistance to the idea of invading Iran?"

"Yes, I read that. But to tell you the truth, I never know how to assess those articles. I mean, is the military leadership of this country that upset with this Administration?"

"In a word, Jake, yes. Why? Because the military of this country learned its lesson in Vietnam. When they contemplate going to war, they want a defined strategic objective, to meet that objective, and then to get the hell out. And the corollary to that principle is that the American people need to be fully behind the military when it is ordered into combat. So from the perspective of much of the top US military brass in Iraq, we've been sent on an open-ended mission that has no well-defined objective. We've done the best we can with the troop levels that the political branch of government has been willing to commit to the occupation of Iraq and Afghanistan, but the mission has always suffered from—and this is an understatement—a distinct lack of clarity. All I can say is thank God the American people show continued support for the military and, unlike Vietnam, do not blame the military itself for having gotten us into an untenable situation."

"Sadly, Al, I must confess that I have come to agree with you," broke in Fariba Youghobian in her clipped Iranian-accented English. "The regime is moving hard to the right. They're shutting down newspapers, increasing military spending, reinforcing hard-line restrictions on women, and their rhetoric is getting increasingly apocalyptic. It's a very dangerous situation when a nation feels existentially threatened."

"I think the situation is more dangerous than you might think, Fariba," Al said, "You see, the folks that I work for think at this point that we've about run out of good options and that we're rapidly reaching the place where we will be searching for the best choice among bad options. They are worried sick about a nuclear-armed Iran that might be willing to initiate a nuclear exchange with the Israelis or even with us. I mean, let's face it, it was these guys who sent 150,000 of their own children into no-man's land as human mine detectors during the Iran-Iraq war. Can we be sure that mutual assured destruction will work with them?"

"Al, I certainly don't believe for a minute that Israel will permit a radical Islamic regime to obliterate it without retaliating in kind. And besides a blood bath, a nuclear exchange in the Middle East could destroy the region's oil infrastructure, agriculture, and manufacturing base. It's unthinkable."

"Unfortunately, Jake, it is not only thinkable but the Iranians are increasingly starting to talk about it openly. I don't want to be overly dramatic, but that little bastard who is president of Iran and the fascist grand council of mullahs that are the real power in the country are starting to do just what Hitler did. Little by little they speak the unspeakable until the world gets used to it. We've lived with nuclear weapons since 1945 and in all that time he is the first world leader who has talked about using nuclear bombs as an offensive first-strike weapon. And so, yes, a low-cost strategy that might avoid ever allowing the Iranian regime to acquire nuclear weapons or create an internal political dynamic that would cause the Iranian government to abandon its nuclear ambitions is absolutely desirable. In fact, it is critical."

"I've been thinking about something that would fit just that kind of scenario," said Jake, a conspiratorial glint in his eye.

"Do tell . . .," Al said, with one of his belly laughs.

Chapter 16

The Iran Working Group meets weekly in the situation room in the basement of the White House. It is composed of the Secretaries of Defense, Homeland Security, and Energy, the President's National Security Advisor, the Chairman of the Joint Chiefs of Staff, the Assistant Secretary of State for Near Eastern Affairs, the Vice President's Chief of Staff, the Directors of the FBI, CIA, and NSA, and a collection of various assistant directors, deputy secretaries, lawyers, specialists, advisors, and adjutants. There are also representatives of certain organizations that operate in the "gray" world; agencies that don't officially exist and whose funding is hidden within the budgets of obscure boards, commissions, and bureaus. But they do exist, these secret organizations of spooks, spies, and assassins, quietly doing the bidding of one US Administration after another.

As had been the case for some time, the meeting of the Iran Working Group was not a happy affair.

"OK, people," said Secretary of Defense Thomas Banfield, wrapping his knuckles on the table to bring the meeting to order, "Let's get started. Bob?" The Secretary turned to his assistant.

"Yes, sir. Today's agenda should be in front of all of you. The first issue is the nuclear threat. Mr. Director?"

The Director of Central Intelligence, who detested the Secretary of Defense, began his report.

"In the last six months we believe that the Iranian regime has accelerated its nuclear-weapons program. While the regime has sought nuclear capability for the last decade, even during the so-called "reformist" presidency of Mohammed Khatami, it is only in the last few years that the regime has become fully committed to the acquisition of nuclear weapons. It is no longer cooperating in any way with the inspection program of the International Atomic Energy Agency. Facilities are being hardened to withstand attack with conventional weapons. Our sources have determined that the budget for procurement and production in the Iranian nuclear program has doubled since last year.

"The President of Iran, since his reelection three years ago, has become increasingly provocative and now espouses a radicalized vision of war between Islam and the West as a means of restoring the purity of the Islamic Revolution. He has given two speeches in the last month in which he has spoken of the decline of the decadent West and of the emergence of Iran as the first Islamic superpower. While he denies that his country is seeking to develop nuclear weapons and insists that Iran's nuclear program is for peaceful purposes, as you all know, he has spoken in apocalyptic terms of the destruction of Israel. He has increased Iran's funding of terrorist operations abroad, including those of Hezbollah, Hamas, and other terrorist networks in the Middle East. All of this, incidentally, is severely taxing the Iranian economy. On the domestic front, the regime has stepped up attacks against minorities, improper dress by Iranian women, and free expression by university students. It has also continued to attack what remains of the independent press in Iran, closing two additional newspapers in the last thirty days."

"Getting down to details of the Iranian nuclear program, the new section of the Uranium Conversion Facility in Isfahan is on-line with 130 centrifuges. We believe that these new units are 'Zippe' type centrifuges, which use heat to improve the efficiency of the standard gas centrifuge. We believe that Iran has purchased the design from Pakistan . . . our closest ally in the region." This was a dig at the Secretary of Defense, who constantly defended the Pakistanis, despite mounting evidence that they had sold the Iranians and the North Koreans the fast Zippe-type centrifuge along with other nuclear technology.

"As a result," the Director continued, "yellowcake uranium is being converted into highly enriched uranium 235 at an accelerated pace. We believe, and the BND and the Egyptians have similar intelligence, that the Iranians now posses approximately twenty-five kilograms of HEU, which is half of what they need to produce their first nuclear device. With their new centrifuges on line, we think they can produce the remaining fifty percent within one year."

"That's just wonderful news," said the National Security Advisor acerbically. "Our allies on the Hill should have a field day criticizing the President with that. And God knows what the Democrats will do with it." A small round of laughter went around the room.

"Shall I continue, Mr. Secretary?" said the Director of Central Intelligence, impatient with the interruption and, apparently, unimpressed with the gallows humor.

"By all means . . .," replied the Defense Secretary.

"We've alluded to this in previous briefings, but it has become of more concern of late. About forty kilometers west of Shiraz in a remote and rugged area in the Kuh-i-Marreh Mountains near a village named Bala-Deh, they are building what appears to be some kind of hardened military facility. For the last two years, they have been excavating a cave complex and pouring concrete in vast quantities. In fact, the Iranians have a cover story that the location is going to be a concrete batch plant. We believe they are essentially using the aggregate on the site to make concrete to build there. Aerial reconnaissance shows that they have laid heavily armored underground cable to the site and they have tapped into the main north-south electrical grid. They have built a new access road to the location. The project is fenced and guarded by a company-sized force of the Iranian Army. In accordance with the standing directive under CENTCOM CONPLAN 1025, Special Operations Command is inserting a combined unit team there to monitor developments. Incidentally, this would bring to sixteen the number of teams that have been inserted in Iran since the Administration. . . ." He paused now, for effect. "Began to take the Iranian nuclear threat more, shall we say . . . seriously."

The Secretary of Defense interrupted. "Okay, let's get to the point, Mr. Director. So what do we think they are doing with this concrete thing in the middle of nowhere?"

"The site has year round water fed by a small river in the mountains. This makes it useful for various nuclear technologies, from civilian to military. We think that they could be placing more centrifuges there or perhaps—and this is speculative—building a nuclear weapons manufacturing facility. There is no credible explanation for that much secrecy and security if there's nothing there to hide."

"Unless, Mr. Director, it's just a concrete batch plant," replied the Defense Secretary. "You guys have misidentified these things in the past."

"We've all made mistakes and misjudgments," replied the CIA Director, reddening slightly. "But we're doing our best."

"Okay, so we've got a new potential uranium enrichment or even WMD weapons facility. Anything else we need to know?"

"Well," the CIA Director continued, "in a disturbing development, and I'm sure the folks from the Navy will want to comment on this, we have confirmed that the Russians have agreed to sell the Iranians twenty-five 3M82 Moskit—Code name 'Sunburn'—anti-ship missiles. We don't know whether delivery of the first missiles has already been made. This information comes from the Israelis, the British, even the Poles, with our own sources providing confirmation. According to the Israelis, the Iranian and Russian presidents met secretly at Astrakhan on the Caspian Sea last August and finalized the agreement. The Russians will sell the Iranians the missiles and an assortment of other armaments. The Iranians also agreed to buy $1.2 billion in Russian equipment to modernize their refineries." The Director of Central Intelligence looked up to gauge the reaction. There was much murmuring and shuffling of papers in the room. The implications of this development were clear to everyone in the room.

Jake Elliot sat in the corner listening with astonishment to the tense dialogue between these high level members of the Administration. Like every American, he had witnessed the steady decline of the President's popularity, which was now, in his sixth year of office, at rock bottom. Since the President's narrow reelection two years before, the various opinion leaders—the television commentators, the eminent professors, the senior politicians—had been increasingly harsh in their assessment of the Administration. There was a time, in the wake of the 9/11 attacks, when the President's popularity rose to unprecedented heights and the press seemed slavishly devoted to keeping it there. Those days were long gone. But Jake had assumed that at this level, the President's team would at least be cordial to one another. Jake turned to the guy next to him and whispered, "Do they always go at each other like this?"

The man looked over his half glasses and said, coldly, "Please be quiet, I'm trying to listen."

"State?" the Defense Secretary interrupted, the levity gone from his voice.

The Assistant Secretary of State for Near Eastern Affairs, a dapper, handsome man in a neat blue pinstriped suit and regulation tortoise shell glasses, sat up in his chair.

"The Secretary has contacted the Russian Foreign Secretary to protest. The Russians flat out deny that any sale took place."

"That figures," said the Defense Secretary. "All right. Admiral, let's hear what you have to say about this."

The Chief of Naval Operations is the highest-ranking officer in the US Navy. The current Chief was a distinguished and very dignified sixty-year-old Admiral. He was blunt and straightforward and fiercely loyal to the United States Navy. Along with the other members of the Joint Chiefs, he had an increasingly tense relationship with the Secretary of Defense, who sought to "remake" the US military based on the theories of a number of so-called civilian "experts"—professors, journalists, and commentators—whom the military leadership felt were nothing but a pack of ideologues and officious intermeddlers.

"To put it bluntly, the Sunburn cruise missile is a carrier killer. It can be fitted with a conventional 750-pound warhead that can be hardened with depleted uranium or even fitted with a tactical nuclear device. It is small, fast, and highly maneuverable and can be launched from a ship or from land. At speeds approaching Mach 2.5, our Phalanx point defense system would have only 2.5 seconds to calculate a fire solution—insufficient time to stop the missile. Essentially we have no effective countermeasures at this time. As you are aware, the Administration, against our advice, withdrew its funding request for the next generation of sea borne anti-missile technology to replace the Phalanx."

The Admiral paused and looked over his reading glasses around the table. The room was quiet. The Secretary of Defense rolled his eyes and the White House team looked angry.

"Admiral, as you are aware, the Administration had other priorities," interjected the Secretary of Defense. "Please continue."

"Suffice it to say that the Fifth Fleet passing through the Straights of Hormuz or, frankly, operating anywhere in the Persian Gulf region, would be extremely vulnerable to a Sunburn missile attack. Such an attack could be devastating. The Iranians can launch them from their fleet of patrol boats and so-called suicide craft or from fixed or mobile land-based launching sites. And most critically, Mr. Secretary, it substantially increases the risk of an ocean-based invasion of Iran."

"Which essentially rules out an invasion unless we invade over land from Iraq and/or Afghanistan," replied the Defense Secretary. "Is that what you're saying, Admiral?"

"Basically, Sir, that's what I'm saying."

"As long as we're here, let's move on to the update on the contingency plans for Operation Compelling Impact." "Compelling Impact" was the Joint Chiefs' combined-services plan for a preemptive strike to neutralize the Iranian nuclear threat. "You don't mind the interruption, Mr. Director?" asked the Secretary of Defense. The question was rhetorical—the Secretary expected no argument.

"Not at all, Mr. Secretary," replied the CIA Chief politely, "I have some more but it can wait."

The attention turned to the Chairman of the Joint Chiefs of Staff, General John Christian Gundry. Gundry was from the Army and had just assumed the Chairmanship of the Joint Chiefs, replacing a retiring Admiral. He had been a decorated combat officer with the

82nd Airborne Division in the Vietnam War and Desert Storm. He was liked by his men, who referred affectionately to him as "J.C." —out of his presence, of course—in recognition of the near messianic standing he had with his men. Despite his gruff and direct manner, he had an excellent political sense and was popular with members of Congress because he seemed to be willing to tell it like it was. It was speculated that the President chose him as the Chairman of the Joint Chiefs as a way of improving the Administration's faltering credibility after years of inconclusive fighting in Iraq and Afghanistan.

"Here's where we are, Mr. Secretary, with the planning for Operation Compelling Impact," began the Chairman. "As we discussed at our last meeting, there are thirty-four nuclear facilities that we would need to take out. Between radar, air defense, military, communication and other targets, we believe that there are about 1,500 aim points that would have to be neutralized—and the list is growing daily as our intelligence assets increase.

"The following critical sites are hardened and would have to be hit multiple times: the recently opened heavy water production plant at Arak, the light water reactor at Bushehr, the three so-called "research reactors" at Ishfahan, the uranium mine at Saghand, the uranium enrichment facility at Natanz, which is almost entirely underground, the Kalaye Electric Company's centrifuge factory in Tehran, and the Shahid Hammat Industrial Group's ballistic and cruise missile plant, also outside Tehran. These and other hardened sites would have to be hit repeatedly. In addition, we would need to destroy some soft targets, such as the Tehran Nuclear Research Center. While the Air Force believes that GBU-28 bunker-buster bombs may be effective against some of the hardened targets, the only way to be certain that an attack can be one hundred percent effective would be to use tactical nuclear weapons."

The General looked up and spoke steadily. "Mr. Secretary, I know that you have told us not to take the nuclear option off the list, but the fact is the Joint Chiefs feel very strongly that we cannot entertain the use of nuclear weapons in a first strike."

"General," the Secretary of Defense was now visibly angry, "with all due respect, it is not the responsibility of the military to remove options from contingency plans . . . especially the most effective weapon. That is the responsibility of the Commander in Chief."

"I concur with the Secretary," chimed in the National Security Advisor.

"Mr. Secretary, I quite well understand the chain of command," the General said steadily and slowly, "but the American people, let alone the rest of the world, would never be supportive of the use of nuclear weapons in a preemptive strike to stop another country from developing nuclear weapons. Conventional force, albeit overwhelming conventional force, is, in our view, the only viable option. We feel compelled to make this point in the strongest of terms."

The other service chiefs nodded their agreement. It was obvious to everyone that the military was not prepared to be sandbagged by the political branch of government and take the blame for being a bunch of Dr. Strangeloves. "Not on my god-damned watch," General Gundry muttered.

"OK, General, you've made your point quite clear," replied the Secretary, his mouth tight and his eyes angry. "Now please continue."

"Absent the use of nuclear weapons and given the size of Iran, the disbursement of its nuclear facilities, its defense capabilities, the hardness of the targets, the fact that some of the targets are in populated urban areas, the only possibility is a large-scale combined air, sea, and land assault. This would mean a land-based invasion force, coming from Iraq, Afghanistan, Georgia, Azerbaijan, or Turkmenistan as well as airborne operations and amphibious landings. However, as we discussed earlier, we now face a new and potentially deadly threat to naval combat operations in the Gulf."

"And how many men are we talking about?"

"The lowest force commitment that we can envision that would provide significant assurance of success would be about 345,000 combat troops. Our plan calls for the use of five divisions, two of them armored, elements of the 82nd and 101st Airborne Divisions, the 10th Mountain Division, the 11th Armored Calvary Regiment, the 15th, 24th, and 26th Marine Expeditionary Forces, the First Marine Division, and numerous special forces assets, including Navy SEALS, Army

Rangers, and CIA special forces. We would need to make substantial use of Army Reserve and National Guard units. Of course, there would be a massive pre-invasion bombing campaign to degrade the enemy's defenses."

"General," said the Secretary of Defense, "as we all know, we have 494,000 active duty front line combat troops in the US military. With 120,000 troops committed in Iraq and another 20,000 in Afghanistan, we just don't have the force level to make that kind of commitment."

"Mr. Secretary, as you pointed out, we just give you the options. We agree that such an invasion would require stripping our other commitments down to the bare minimum, unless, of course, the Administration is prepared to contemplate restoring the draft. And even if you were willing to make that kind of commitment, by the time we had enough soldiers drafted and trained, the Iranians might already possess one or more nuclear devices; which, in the event of an invasion by us, we believe they would be prepared to use."

"The President has categorically ruled out the draft. That is just not happening, General."

"We do not advocate the draft either, Mr. Secretary, but we see no way under our present force structure that we can commit to an invasion of Iran with fewer troops than is contemplated by Compelling Impact."

"Well, what about our allies?"

"Mr. Secretary, we can expect as much help as we want from the Israelis, but any Israeli involvement would, as you know, be extremely controversial. The British might help, but they are really under the gun because of Iraq. And there are the usual scattering of friendly governments such as the Romanians, Australians, and Poles. Basically, once again, we'd be going it alone. The Europeans and the Japanese have repeatedly expressed concerns that, given their dependence on Iranian oil, if we engage in combat operations, we avoid targets that serve Iran's oil infrastructure. However, even if we tried to avoid the oil refineries, we would need to take out electrical power, natural gas, hydroelectric facilities, roads, bridges, naval facilities, harbors, rail lines, and so forth that the Iranian oil industry depends upon."

"Thank you General, we will take your report back to the

President. In the meantime, try and figure out how to cut the troops significantly. You guys overstated the need when we were planning the Iraq invasion and I hope that's not happening again."

The Generals looked stiff-jawed and offended but they did not respond.

Watching the interchange between General Gundry and the Secretary of Defense, Jake had to admire Gundry's guts and integrity. It was obvious that there was an enormous fissure between the military and the executive branch of government over the ability of the United States to use force in the Middle East. The US military was understandably frustrated with its role in Iraq. It was undermanned, underfunded, and overwhelmed by the nature of its mission. The Administration wanted to wage war on the cheap. Unlike all of America's other wars, the Administration's "War on Terror" did not place any significant demands on the American people, much less ask them to sacrifice their children. There would be no draft, there would be no tax increases, there would be no rationing of consumer goods, and there wasn't even an effort to make the United States less dependent on Middle Eastern oil. The only people to die in the conflict—assuming further catastrophic terrorist attacks on U.S. soil could be avoided—would be the members of the all-volunteer military. This Administration had learned one critical lesson from Vietnam: never permit the corpse of a dead American soldier to be shown to the public. In short, it told the country they could have its cake and eat it too. The problem was that long after the President had declared the war over, American GIs were dying every day. The US had no real allies left except a worn-out Britain and the tiny state of Israel. The Administration's plan—if there ever really was one—had gone seriously awry.

The FBI Director spoke up. "Mr. Secretary, there is no question that, in our view, any attack on Iran would result in a massive increase in domestic terrorism. I need only point out that it was the Iranians that were behind the bombing of the Buenos Aires synagogue and cultural center in 1994 that killed 85 people. They are fully capable and have the resources in place to commit acts of full-scale sabotage within the borders of the United States."

"We concur," said the Secretary of Homeland Security.

"Anybody else on this subject before we move on?"

There was an awkward silence.

It was at this moment that Jake Elliot decided to speak up. He was sitting at the back of the room behind the Assistant Administrator of the National Nuclear Security Agency with the other second- and third-tier bureaucrats. Afterward, he could not figure out what exactly prompted him to speak. It was against all protocol.

"Um . . . Mr. Secretary? I have something to add here, Sir." The whole room turned to stare at him with incredulous expressions, as if to ask, "who does this guy think he is?" He did notice, among the faces, that the CIA Director looked vaguely amused.

The Secretary of Defense turned in his direction. "Son, who are you?"

"I am Dr. Jonathan Elliot, the Project Manager of the Alternative Strategy Group in the Middle Eastern Section of the National Nuclear Security Agency at DOE. I'm on leave from MIT. I'm an associate professor of Nuclear Science and Engineering there. We've been working on non-military scenarios to neutralize the Iranian nuclear threat. I co-chair the group with Dr. Fariba Youghobian, who is a professor of Iranian Government and Politics at the University of California, Berkeley. We have a team of six . . . ."

The Secretary interrupted Jake. "That's all very interesting, Professor . . .," an aide whispered in his ear, ". . . Elliot, but we're all very busy here. Please get to the point."

"Yes, Professor, please get to the point," said Jake's superior, Assistant Secretary of Energy Anne Marie Mitchell. Ms. Mitchell, with her very classic St. John's knits and country-club blonde hair, looked like she wanted to die of embarrassment. A low-level political appointee who had most recently been the Finance Chair of the Republican Party of Jefferson County, Kentucky, Mitchell was in way over her head. By accident, she happened to be the highest-ranking person in the room from DOE, as the Secretary decided not to attend and David Cantwell, the Administrator of the National Nuclear Security Agency, was at home nursing a nasty cold.

Jake was clearly flustered. "OK . . . in a word, Chernobyl," he blurted out.

"Chernobyl?" said the Chairman of the Joint Chiefs, as did at least a dozen other people in the room.

Jake realized he better talk fast because they would probably shut him down very soon and quite possibly his short-lived government career. Oh well, he thought, nothing ventured, nothing gained.

"Yes," he began, taking a deep breath and launching forth, "our group has come to the conclusion that, short of a full scale military operation which, as you've discussed, may not be realistic, the best solution to the Iranian nuclear threat is for a Chernobyl-like scenario to be . . . engineered. Specifically, I am suggesting that a deliberate radiation release at a nuclear facility might cause sufficient political unrest internally within Iran and externally within the international community to force the government of Iran to abandon its nuclear program or limit it to clearly and verifiably civilian purposes. Such action would pose a relatively small risk to civilian populations in comparison to military intervention."

The Secretary of Defense interrupted Jake. "Just how, young man, would you propose to insure that such an 'accident' could be controlled so that it was bad enough to change government policy but not so bad as to cause a worldwide ecological disaster or kill an unacceptably large number of civilians?"

"We have looked at these scenarios and believe that, at one of their gas centrifuge uranium enrichment facilities, an accident could be arranged which would release enough radiation to scare the living daylights out of the whole world while probably killing no more than some of the people working at the site. Such casualties would pale in comparison to the casualties that both sides would endure were there a full-scale military invasion. Moreover, such an option would still be available if the mission was unsuccessful."

"So, Professor Elliot," said General Gundry respectfully, "do you believe that such an option could be fully accomplished by a small team engaged in a fully clandestine type of operation?"

"Yes, Sir, one of our team members is on loan from the CIA and he has significant experience in the area of clandestine operations. It is his belief that, through several different mechanisms, we could successfully cause an accident to occur that would produce the desired result."

Anne Marie Mitchell felt like she was drowning. What was this guy doing to her? She had to speak. In her best refined Southern accent, which she had perfected as she rose up the political hierarchy, she said, "Mr. Secretary, I must interrupt. This is highly irregular. While Professor Elliot's Group has submitted its report to Undersecretary Smyth and Secretary of Energy Kline, it has yet to be approved for distribution beyond DOE."

Jake's face began to redden. "Look, that thing has been sitting on Undersecretary Smyth's desk for nearly six months. I don't think he's even reviewed it."

"Professor, we don't go outside the chain of command in this Administration," commented the Secretary of Defense sternly. "The President believes that loyalty is the highest attribute for anyone serving in his Administration."

Someone from the CIA side of the table said under his breath, "And that's the problem." This caused the Secretary of Defense to look around for the culprit with an angry look on his face.

"I'm sorry, Mr. Secretary," said Jake. "But time is running out. The Iranians are moving quickly. They know how precarious our military situation is in the region. We believe that something needs to be done quickly and we have a viable plan to do it."

"Mr. Secretary, may I comment?" It was the Vice President's Chief of Staff, a young man who was formally the Counsel to the Senate Armed Services Committee when the Vice President was a US Senator. He was a distinctly political animal—of the predatory sort—and had the absolute confidence of the Vice President.

"Please do, Mr. MacRae."

"I think just about enough has been said about this. While I appreciate the Professor's zeal," his emphasis on the word "Professor" communicated the contempt he held for what he viewed as ivory tower intellectuals, "there are proper channels and he should follow them. Directing his attention to Anne Marie Mitchell, he said, "Madame Assistant Secretary, please convey to the Secretary of Energy the Vice President's concern with this unfortunate outburst and urge him to send representatives to this meeting who possess an appropriate degree of self-restraint."

"I apologize for this incident and I will certainly report the matter to the Secretary, Mr. McRae," responded Ms. Mitchell with a deep sense of dread. She would see that little son of a bitch Jake Ellison hung by his nuts when the meeting was over.

"Very well put, Mr. MacRae, I concur," said the Secretary of Defense. "Now let's move on to the economic assessment."

Jake's face flushed with embarrassment, the humiliation complete.

Chapter 17

Jake Elliot was summoned to the office of Undersecretary of Energy Smyth by his Executive Secretary. By the severity of her tone, the meeting would not be a pleasant one.

He arrived at Smyth's office, which was located in the headquarters building of the Department of Energy at 1000 Independence Avenue on the National Mall. Jake's office was located in a suburban office complex in Arlington and he had been to the DOE headquarters building only a few times. The executive offices were on the top floor. As Jake got off the elevator, he was immediately struck by the rich symbolism of the deep blue carpet. It denoted the importance of the floor's occupants in the bureaucratic hierarchy. Andrew Smyth's office was located at the end of the hallway next to the office of the Secretary.

When Jake entered the dark-paneled office, Smyth's secretary looked up from her desk and asked, "May I help you?"

"Yes, I'm Dr. Elliot. I have a 1:30 appointment with Undersecretary Smyth."

"Please take a seat, Dr. Elliot. Undersecretary Smyth is not yet back from lunch."

Jake sat down and waited. He passed the time by reading back issues of the Department's in-house magazine and checking his email on his PDA. At 1:45, he quietly approached the secretary's desk.

"Excuse me, Ma'am, but perhaps I should come back at another time?"

She looked up and smiled patronizingly at Jake. "Dr. Elliot, the Assistant Secretary is on his way. Please be patient; he will be back shortly."

Jake returned to his seat, feeling like he was in junior high school again and waiting to receive a lecture from the vice principal.

About five minutes later, the secretary cleared her throat to get Jake's attention.

"Dr. Elliot, the Undersecretary will see you now."

She rose from her desk and gestured for him to follow. She led him into an office. Standing behind his desk was Andrew Smyth, all pinstripes and straight white teeth, the picture of a person utterly comfortable with the trappings of power. Assistant Secretary Mitchell was there as was a man whom Jake did not recognize.

"Come in, Dr. Elliot," said Smyth with a surprisingly friendly smile. He held out his hand across the desk and shook Jake's. "You know Assistant Secretary Mitchell, of course, and this is Chief of Staff Thomas Wenham."

Wenham shook Jake's hand while Anne Marie Mitchell just glowered at him.

"Please sit down, Dr. Elliot."

Jake did as he was told.

"Well, Dr. Elliot, you've caused quite a stir over at Defense and the White House," said Smyth. "Suffice it to say, the Secretary is not pleased." He paused, putting his hands together as if in prayer and raising them up to bridge of his nose. "I'm not going to sugarcoat this, Professor. You acted totally outside your authority, bringing up a report that has not even been reviewed, much less approved for distribution to other agencies in the government."

"I'm very sorry, Mr. Undersecretary. I just felt compelled under the circumstances to bring up the report."

"Be that as it may, Professor Elliot, you are off the team. During the remainder of your tenure at the Department, you are being transferred to the Los Angeles Regional Office to help work on the implementation of our nuclear detection program at the Ports of Los Angeles and Long Beach. This is important work. Please don't embarrass us there."

Jake considered tendering his resignation but decided it was best to sleep on it.

"I'll do my best, sir," he said. But he was thinking, "Fuck you, you arrogant shithead."

"Thank you, Professor. You can go now."

Chapter 18

When Ivana resigned her commission and began teaching history at a small liberal arts college outside of Buffalo, she assumed that her military days were over. She liked her students, she liked her fellow faculty members, and she loved the little farmhouse she bought in the rolling hills outside of the city. But she was soon bored with academic life. However burnt out she felt at the end of her stint in Bosnia, she now missed the excitement and the sense of mission that had been so much a part of her life. She had a boyfriend—a professor of philosophy—with whom she enjoyed spending time but there was a certain passion missing from their relationship and it eventually ended when he reconciled with his ex-wife. Ivana was hurt but not devastated by the breakup. In truth, she was relieved and ready to move on. She wondered whether she would always feel at odds and out of balance in the world. Her mother thought Ivana's malaise was due to her "mixed blood"—she was half Muslim and half Christian. As a child in Yugoslavia, Ivana was always aware of the disapproval and ethnic prejudice that swirled around her as a result of her parents' relationship. When they moved to America, no one outside of her family cared about her ethnicity, but she never felt truly American. She enlisted in the military at least in part to confirm her sense of American cultural identity. It had worked for a time.

So when, out of the blue, an officer with whom she had served in Bosnia telephoned to say that he would be in Buffalo the following week and to invite her to lunch, Ivana was delighted. They met at his hotel and walked to a nearby restaurant.

Like Ivana, Bill Conti had quit the military after Bosnia. Now he was working for the CIA. He couldn't get into too many specifics with her, but he was serving in the Agency's clandestine paramilitary branch, the Special Activities Division. She asked him if he liked it and he seemed very enthusiastic. Most of the members were veterans of the US military's various special forces units: Army Rangers, Green Berets, Delta Force, Navy SEALS, Air Force Special Operations Squadrons, and the USMC Force Recon. But there were some regular Army types like them. Very smart, very experienced. Was she interested, he asked?

Maybe, she replied.

He said that he would have someone call her.

When the call came, Ivana said yes.

At the end of the spring semester of 2002, Ivana resigned her job at the college and moved to an apartment in Fairfax, Virginia. She decided to keep the farmhouse. Fortunately, she was able to rent it to one of her fellow faculty members.

In early 2003, she was sent on her first assignment to western Afghanistan. She and two other team members crossed the border into the southeast province of Iran to meet with Baluchi separatists. In a remote village they conducted weapons training and taught the Baluchis how to use explosives. Three months after their departure, a powerful car bomb exploded outside the main police station in Zahedan. Three officers were killed and it caused the Iranian government to increase its military presence in the region. Seven months after the bombing there was a demonstration in downtown Zahedan in which the Baluchi Front, the main Baluchi ethnic political party in the region, demanded that more government resources be spent in their impoverished province and that they be granted greater autonomy from Tehran. When the crowd did not disperse, the police fired on them with live ammunition. Six demonstrators died.

The following year, Ivana joined another team to penetrate the northern Kurdish area of Iran, where they assisted a secret cell of PKK separatist guerillas to plant a bomb at the entrance of a uranium mine.

After nearly two years engaged in field operations, Ivana was returned stateside. All that she knew was that she was going home to receive "advanced training."

Ivana boarded an unmarked CIA plane in Mosul and landed some fifteen hours later at Andrews Air Force Base. Suddenly, she was back in America, in a culture that seemed both intimately familiar and strange at the same time. She noticed that, in her absence, Americans had become very overweight. They still moved through life without the collective fear that was endemic to the Middle East. They were open and friendly rather than wary and suspicious. Despite the profound psychological shock of the September 11 attacks on their collective psyche, Americans still felt safe behind their wall of oceans.

Ivana soon fell into the routine of her new life as a commuter spy. Every day she took the Metro from her suburban apartment complex to a nondescript warehouse about two miles from the Company's headquarters in Langley. She and the other half-dozen or so students in her class were being trained to sabotage a nuclear facility in the Islamic Republic of Iran.

Inside the warehouse was a reproduction of a Pakistani model P-2 Zippe nuclear centrifuge. The P-2 was the model centrifuge that Iran had acquired from Pakistan. It was based on a European model whose blueprints had been stolen by the Pakistani nuclear scientist Dr. Abdul Qadeer Khan when he worked at a Dutch uranium-enrichment plant. In addition, there was a large reproduction of a nuclear reactor core of the type that the Iranians were known to possess at their facility in Bushehr. Ivana was spending twelve hours a day learning about nuclear power generation and uranium enrichment.

They were being trained to attack both nuclear reactors and uranium enrichment facilities. Each presented special problems and opportunities for attack. A nuclear reactor contained fuel rods which were composed of enriched uranium. In order to generate nuclear power, those fuel rods were allowed to create controlled nuclear fission. In a conventional nuclear power plant, the heat generated from the controlled-fission reaction was enormous and self-sustaining and could be used to create steam, which would allow electricity to be produced. The key, of course, to avoiding a catastrophe was maintaining control over the nuclear material at the core. If nuclear fission in the core became uncontrolled, then the searing heat that would be generated at thousands of degrees centigrade could superheat all the metal surrounding the core and cause it to liquefy and then explode, releasing a tremendous amount of nuclear material into the atmosphere. This is essentially what occurred at Chernobyl and Three Mile Island.

A uranium enrichment facility is a significantly different enterprise from a nuclear reactor. Enrichment facilities are essentially a group of thousands of cascading nuclear centrifuges. Uranium hexafluoride gas is introduced at the beginning of the process and spun at high speeds as it moves from centrifuge to centrifuge. Before the uranium hexafluoride is fed into the cascade, it is heated to just below its melting point to turn it into a gas. As each centrifuge spins, the heavier U238 molecules move to the outside of the centrifuge and the lighter, enriched U235 molecules move to the center of the centrifuge. At the end of the process, a small amount of highly enriched Uranium 235 is left. This is the stuff that is used to make nuclear bombs.

At first, their training focused on the rather routine job of using conventional explosives to destroy the equipment. There was nothing particularly specialized about the demolitions used; the idea was to pack as much explosive as possible in and around the reactor or centrifuges to reduce them to a mass of molten metal. Such a demolition would be crude, but effective. Naturally, they asked, why not just bomb the facilities from the air using bunker-busting ordnance? Their instructor explained that the Iranians had recently hardened their fuel-enrichment plant at Natanz. Although the 300,000-square-foot facility had been built twenty-five feet underground and was already protected by fourteen feet of reinforced concrete, the Iranians had added additional reinforced concrete and another seventy feet of packed earth. It was no longer clear that such a target could be destroyed by using conventional weapons, however powerful; dropping nuclear weapons, although effective, was not a realistic option for geopolitical and moral reasons.

In addition to practical instruction, Ivana's class conducted practice exercises at a nuclear power plant at the Department of Energy's sprawling complex in Oak Ridge, Tennessee.

About two months into the course, they began a new training "module," as their instructor put it. Now that they had a detailed understanding of centrifuge construction, power-plant operations, and advanced demolitions, they were to receive training in a much more subtle and highly skilled act of sabotage: how to cause a nuclear core meltdown or destroy a centrifuge cascade and make it appear like an accident rather than a deliberate act of sabotage.

They began to study control-room engineering and power-plant construction. The team took a field trip to Three Mile Island so that they could see first hand the devastation of a core meltdown. They took apart a control room console and put it back together. Then they did it again in the dark. They learned to read various equipment and instrument labels in Russian, French, German, Chinese, and Farsi.

A reactor core meltdown could be induced by shutting off the supply of cold water to a nuclear reactor or introducing cold water at the wrong time in the cycle, by removing cooling rods, or by shutting down the system. At the enrichment sites, where literally hundreds— even thousands—of centrifuges were linked, the easiest way to cause an explosion would be to speed up the rotors to a point where they became unstable. Another possibility would be to incapacitate the venting system, which would cause the centrifuges to overheat. The problem with all of these scenarios was that an explosion could not be guaranteed and certain redundant safety mechanisms would have to be overridden.

Ivana was running hard.

Every other day after work, she drove to Rock Creek Park and ran ten miles. On the nights she didn't run, she worked out at the local 24 Hour Fitness Center. She did a lot of reading. Currently, she was on the third book of the Cairo trilogy by Mahfouz. Although she was half-Muslim, she felt no connection to either Islam or Christianity. Her parents raised her in a militantly secular household and her life experience had only increased her hostility to organized religion. She had witnessed religious prejudice destroy the country of her birth. Now the whole world was being engulfed by the flames of religious war.

Having returned from her evening run, Ivana sat on the edge of her bed, the phone cradled to her ear, rubbing skin cream into the muscles of her sore calves. Her mother, whom she talked to every night, asked her what she was running from. "From, Mama? How do you know I'm not running to something?"

"Because, *srce moje*, you've been running away from something since you were a little girl. You need to stop wandering and settle down. You're not a refugee any more."

"Is this a 'why don't you find a husband' conversation? Because, Mama, if it is, I'm going to hang up on you," Ivana said in mock irritation.

"Look, Ivana," her mother said in Serbian, "I'm not going to ask you again why you broke up with that nice professor."

"I hope not . . . because he broke up with me."

"Are you eating well? Should I send you some of my *kiflice*?"

"I'm doing fine. Anyway, it's not fair to bring out the big guns." Her mother's little crescent-shaped cookies were irresistible.

"I don't believe you. The last time we saw you, you looked like a member of the Yugoslav women's volleyball team. Too skinny, big muscles, and not enough makeup."

Ivana groaned. "Mama, I'm in great physical condition. I'm eating very well. I look great. I love my work . . . ."

". . . which you won't talk about," interrupted her mother.

"True, but it would bore you."

Chapter 19

WASHINGTON, D.C., APRIL 8

It was a warm Saturday morning. The winter cold was now a memory and the trees were fully leafed out. Jake was packing up his apartment to get ready to move to Los Angeles. He hadn't brought much with him to Washington—a few books, his laptop, some of his clothes; he could fit it all in a few moving boxes. Most of his worldly possessions were in storage in Boston and his apartment was sublet to a visiting professor from Sweden. Despite his recent exile to the Department of Energy's political doghouse, Jake was in a good mood. He didn't like Washington, with its self-satisfied insularity and ruthless political infighting.

Jake was listening to the "Car Talk" guys on NPR when phone rang. He turned down the radio and answered it. Jake got so few calls on his land line, he really wondered why, other than habit, he didn't just switch exclusively to his cell phone.

"Hello?"

"Dr. Elliot?" The voice was deep; the accent vaguely Texan.

"Yes, this is Jake Elliot.

"This is General Gundry."

Jake paused for a long second, dumbfounded. "Um, yes sir, how can I help you?"

"Well, son, sorry to surprise you," the General chuckled. "I suppose it's not every day that a broken-down old General calls you."

"You can say that again, General."

"Well, let me get to the point, Dr. Elliot. I need to have a few minutes of your time."

"Well, Sir, it will have to be very soon. I've been reassigned by the Secretary to Los Angeles to do an assessment of port security there. I'm leaving in a few days."

"Son, I know all about it. Bum rap. Would you be able to meet today?"

"Today?"

"Yes, Dr. Elliot. Today as in right now. I'm in a green Ford, parked on your street. How about you just come down and we'll go take a spin around Washington for an hour or so?"

"I'm not really dressed for a business meeting."

"That's fine. In Vietnam, I learned to take guys who wore black pajamas very, very seriously. You just throw on some clothes and we'll have our little chat."

"Okay, I'll be right down."

"All right, Son."

The phone clicked

They drove slowly down one of the tree-shaded roads in Rock Creek Park. The driver looked straight ahead and merely nodded when General Gundry gave him orders.

Jake could easily understand how the General had ascended the ladder of power in the Pentagon. When he spoke, he was both charming and authoritative. He was the sort of man who people naturally trusted and were willing to follow. Jake, who had never been in the military, was both intimidated by Gundry and flattered that he had sought him out. He didn't know if he would follow this man into battle but plenty of men had—some to their deaths.

"I've read your report, Dr. Elliot, and had it analyzed by our people. We think you're on to something. It has the twin virtues of simplicity and cost-effectiveness."

"I don't mean to offend you, General, and forgive me if I do, but the saber rattling of this Administration is not going to deter the Iranian regime from obtaining nuclear weapons."

"What makes you think that I and my colleagues are any more comfortable with this Administration's saber rattling than you are?"

Jake felt himself reddening. "I guess I have no reason to believe that, Sir, but I do know one thing, we have got to get the Iranians to abandon their nuclear ambitions."

"Agreed. Chernobyl was more responsible for the downfall of the Soviet Union than most people will ever know. It fundamentally undermined the trust that the Soviet people had in the regime and it was unable to recover. By our estimates, the Iranian people are perhaps uniquely placed to respond in a similar way. And if your plan worked, how many lives would it save, both American and Iranian?"

"I'm gratified that you see it that way."

"You know, son, I understand that they are sending you to Los Angeles as a punishment for speaking up at that meeting. Not much that I can do to help you. But while you're out there fighting the good fight, think about this: we like your plan and there is a strong chance that we will push to make it happen. And if it works, you will know you played a crucial part in it. Not that anyone will ever give you credit."

"And if it doesn't work?"

"It'll be my ass because it's not like the Commander in Chief will ever accept responsibility."

Chapter 20

THE PERSIAN GULF COAST OF IRAN, 0300 HOURS, APRIL 13

It was a moonless night when the Seawolf Class attack submarine, the USS Connecticut—SSN 22—surfaced two kilometers off the Iranian coast and about ten kilometers north of the village of Zir-Rud. From twenty feet away, the ship was nearly invisible. United States Navy submarines are painted jet black and are very quiet when they run on the surface. They are coated with a special anti-magnetic material that minimizes the possibility of radar detection and makes them highly suitable for the clandestine infiltration of special forces units. This was not the first time—nor would it be the last—that the Connecticut's 133 officers and enlisted crew would operate off the coast of Iran.

The crew was quiet, not because they really had to be, but because a hush came over the ship on such occasions. The biggest danger that the ship faced was being accidentally discovered by a fishing boat or Iranian naval patrol vessel that could not see it. And so members of the crew fanned across its 453 foot length and kept a close lookout for surface ships with night vision binoculars. In the radar room, crew members stared fixedly into their screens, looking for any sign of Iranian naval patrol vessels.

If a ship approached, the crew would abort the mission. They were under strict orders not to fire, unless directly under attack. In any event, they would be on the surface for no more than twenty minutes, just long enough for the infiltration team to be loaded onto inflatables, taken to the beach, and the inflatables returned to the ship.

There were four members of the team. Three were Navy SEALS and one was a CIA analyst. They stood under dimmed red lights directly below the forward hatch going over the procedure one last time. Since leaving Diego Garcia five days before, they had repeatedly gone over every detail.

The team members sported beards in the closely cropped style favored by Islamic militants of the Iranian variety. They were dressed in the military uniforms of the "Qods Force" — the special forces branch of Iran's elite Pasdaran, known in the West by the name Revolutionary Guards. "Qods" in Farsi meant "Jerusalem" and the political implication of that name was self-evident. Ultimately, their goal was to liberate Jerusalem from the Jews. The mission of the Qods Force was to train terrorists, engage in counter-insurgency missions, and to smuggle weapons into areas which, in the view of the Iran's radical Muslim government, were in need of liberation. They were highly motivated, well-trained, and dedicated to the goals of the Islamic Revolution. And most importantly to the success of the mission, the Pasdaran were feared by the Iranian people. The Americans hoped that that fear would work to their advantage once inside Iran.

The team members were armed with standard Iranian made Tondar 9mm assault rifles — short, nasty little weapons punched out by the thousands at one of the factories on the outskirts of Tehran run by the government-owned Defense Industries Organization. Of course, if they had to use their weapons it would mean that the mission had gone wrong. In their backpacks, they carried specially made silencers for the weapons.

The mission was led by a forty-year-old SEAL, Lt. Commander Hector Gonzales. Gonzales had been around every hot spot in the last twenty years. He was a veteran of the first Gulf War and had participated in clandestine missions everywhere from the Horn of Africa to the Balkans. Gonzales wore the uniform of a corporal — a

Sarjukhe—in the Revolutionary Guards. He was dressed as an enlisted man in order to minimize the possibility that he would be spoken to. With the exception of a few words that had been drummed into the team during their training, Gonzales spoke no Farsi.

The second SEAL on the team was a twenty-one-year-old Petty Officer Third class named Teodros Amalakai. Known as "Ted" to his friends, Amalakai was from an Ethiopian family that had immigrated to the US from Addis Ababa in the late 1980s. Amalakai wore the uniform of a *Sarbaz Dovom*, the Iranian equivalent of a private first class in the Qods Force. Ted was an expert in demolitions and he carried with him a variety of explosives that would be useful if the team ran into trouble.

The third member of the team was twenty-six-year-old Chief Warrant Officer Anton Murphy. CWO Murphy was a communications expert and would serve as the team's link to the satellites, submarines, and listening stations in the Middle East that would relay the intelligence they gathered back to CENTCOM headquarters in Bahrain. From there, the information would be beamed to America's vast network of intelligence agencies in North America. Murphy was being promoted for this mission and wore the uniform of a *Sotvan Sevom*, a First Lieutenant in the Pasdaran.

The last member of the team was a short, bespectacled, and skinny thirty-one-year-old CIA analyst named Ojay Hamsid. To the rest of the team, he was simply known as "OJ." As they waited quietly in the weak light of the submarine, OJ felt self-conscious among the military men. He was definitely the odd man out. They all had the quiet confidence of military men whereas OJ felt like he smiled too much and that his jokes always seemed to fall flat. To make matters more complicated, OJ was dressed as a *Sargord*, a Major in the Revolutionary Guards. To any Iranian, he would appear to be the commander of the group, but no matter how much training he received, he didn't feel like a commander.

At dinner on the first night the team had met in Diego Garcia, Gonzales had asked OJ if he was named after the ex-football player.

"Actually, in a way, yes," he replied. "Do you really want to know the story?" he asked.

"Sure," responded Ted.

"Well, in Farsi, *ojay* means 'tall' and to my parents, who were thinking about leaving Iran and moving to the United States when I was born in 1975, it seemed like the perfect name for me. In the year before we left, my father had become a giant fan of American football. I guess my Dad thought that it would help me fit in when we got to Los Angeles. He felt that he couldn't go wrong naming his son after the famous and, by Iranian standards, tall O.J. Simpson. In any event, 'OJ' stuck. Unfortunately, I not only grew up to be short but I had to bear endless ribbing after OJ was accused of killing his wife.

"Anyway, in 1978, we won the US State Department lottery and moved to the Echo Park district of Los Angeles. My father, who had been a high school teacher in Tehran, drove a cab and my mother found a job in a grocery store."

Ted asked OJ what his parents thought of the Shah.

"Well, my father is a passionate man and one of his passions is politics. While he hated the Shah and his secret police, the SAVAK, he absolutely detested the Islamic fundamentalism of the Ayatollah Khomeini. I don't know if you guys remember the whole thing with Salmon Rushdie and the *fatwa* the Ayatollahs put out against him."

"I do," responded Gonzales.

"In fact, when my father finally got a job at a private Persian high school, he caused a minor scandal when he read passages from the *Satanic Verses*. My father is a big fan of the Bill of Rights."

OJ's reverie was broken by the sudden flashing of the red light. The midshipman standing by them began to climb the ladder toward the hatch.

"Show time," said Lt. Commander Gonzales.

OJ was returning to the land of his birth for the first time since he left 28 years before.

Chapter 21

THE COAST OF IRAN, APRIL 13

Aqil Khan sat in the cab of his truck smoking a "57" cigarette, the red tip glowing faintly in the night. He had never really thought about it, but it was pretty ironic. Here he was waiting to pick up some American soldiers and he was smoking a cigarette whose brand commemorated the year on the Persian calendar, 1357, that corresponded to the 1979 Islamic revolution. Aqil laughed softly. Well, fuck the Iranian revolution and the Persians and their oppressive Shia state religion. He was a fighter for an independent Baluchistan and the Americans were the enemy of his enemy, so they were his friends.

Aqil looked at his watch for about the tenth time in the last five minutes. His instructions were to turn on the little homing beacon he had been given at 3:30 am precisely. He was to turn it off after sixty seconds, then wait sixty seconds and turn it on for another minute. He was nervous. The army patrolled this sector. Hopefully, he would be able to see them coming from a long way off. Whoever had picked this deserted stretch of coastline knew what they were doing. If the army stopped here, his cover story was good. He had a legitimate load, imported Pakistani pots and pans, headed for Shiraz. Of course, if they searched the load and found the Americans, that would be a different story. There would be shooting and men would die. Aqil had a small automatic wrapped in a rag under his seat. Lots of truck drivers carried them as self-defense against hijackers. He had cleaned and oiled it before he left his home in Zahedan.

He got out of the cab. The coast road was totally deserted and, in the moonless night, he could barely see the phosphorescent sea. Aqil could hear the rhythmic sound of the waves; the surf was low and quiet. A good night for infidels to invade the Islamic Republic of Iran.

At 3:30, Aqil reached into his pocket and, as instructed, pressed the button on the palm-sized device. A small LED light pulsed on and off at half-second intervals.

These Americans and their crazy gadgets. He stared at his watch, as the seconds ticked away. A growing pile of cigarette butts littered the ashtray of the truck.

Somewhere out there at sea, the enemy of his enemies was listening. Or so he hoped.

Although the sea looked calm, the inflatable was bouncing along at a pretty good clip as they made their way to shore. OJ felt a little queasy. He didn't know whether it was nervousness, seasickness, fear, adrenalin, or a combination of everything. Between the moonless night and the all-black outfits of the team, OJ figured that another boat would have to get within ten feet of their craft to spot them. As they left the submarine, OJ kept looking back. Within fifteen seconds of pushing off from the Connecticut, it was no longer visible. As directed, the members of the team maintained silence as the boat made its way toward the place where the beacon told them to land. There was a second inflatable next to them which contained their supplies and equipment.

The trip to the beach took about five minutes, although to OJ it felt like an eternity. As the boats slowed in the shallow surf and OJ stared at the dark land beyond the beach, it felt more like a burglary than a homecoming.

When they hit the sandy bottom, the Navy crew member at the back of the boat cut the engine, while simultaneously the two men in the front of the boat, Gonzales and Amalakai, jumped over the side and pulled the boat onto the sand.

Chief Murphy tapped OJ on the shoulder. "Hey, kid, time to get out." OJ jumped clumsily over the side and walked up onto the beach. The two SEALS were already busy unloading equipment from the other inflatable.

OJ looked up the beach and saw the figure of a man walking across the sand toward them. He was small and wiry and was smoking a cigarette. He had a big toothy smile and said, "Hey, Yankee Doodle, Mr. Yankee Doodle," over and over again as a he got closer to them. They all stopped what they were doing in a kind of frozen amazement. OJ noticed that Lt. Commander Gonzales had a small gun in his hand, which was rested at his side.

OJ smiled brightly at the man and waived. The other Americans were looking at OJ. Oh, yeah, he remembered, there was a countersign. "George Washington," said OJ.

"Hello, American friends," said Aqil, sticking out his hand to shake the Americans' hands. Having exhausted his English, Aqil switched back to Farsi. *"Kosh amadin Irani."* — Welcome to Iran.

OJ felt an unexpected surge of emotion at seeing the friendly face of this stranger. Were there millions of Iranians like Aqil who wanted something more than the straitjacket imposed by their regime?

OJ went up to Aqil and shook his hand. "I am . . . ," and then OJ remembered that they were not supposed to use real names, " . . . Mohammed, my friend, and I am glad you are here to guide us. These are the other American officers."

"You speak Farsi," he said, with a look of puzzlement.

"I was born in Iran."

The other members of the team came up to Aqil and introduced themselves by their code names, "Sinbad" for Lt. Commander Gonzales, "Ali" for Amalakai, and "Baba" for Murphy.

Aqil started to laugh, pointing at the last two Americans. "Ali" and "Baba," he said, "I saw that movie, the one with the forty thieves."

"Sinbad," OJ said, pointing to Gonzales, "he's the commander."

The introductions were interrupted by one of the Navy crew members.

"Hey, boss, we're done here," he said, addressing Gonzales. "Can you help us turn the boats around?"

"OK, no problem," Gonzales replied. "Let's get these coveralls off and into the boats."

The Americans unzipped their black coveralls, revealing Iranian military uniforms, and tossed the coveralls back into the boat.

Then they turned the inflatables around, the crews hopped in, and Gonzales' team pushed them into the surf. In a few seconds, the quiet outboards were started and the boats were gone.

As OJ watched the black inflatables speed off, he felt a sudden rush of fear. What am I doing here?

"OK, gentlemen, let's get the stuff and go," said Gonzales, picking up his backpack.

"Tell him my truck is up on the road about forty meters away," Aqil said to OJ, who obviously got the gist of Gonzales' point.

OJ translated for the other Americans and they began to gather up their things. It would take two trips to move all the supplies.

They grabbed the equipment and followed the Baluchi to a narrow trail that led to the coast road. When they got to the truck, OJ noticed that, in addition to the sound of the rhythmic pounding of the waves on the beach, a new sound could be heard, that of sea gulls squawking. A new morning was approaching; the residents of the Middle East—both human and animal—were starting to wake up.

Aqil opened the back of the truck. He had rearranged the boxes and crates in such a way as to open a small passageway to the front of the trailer, where an empty space had been created for the men to hide. They began to ferry the supplies and equipment into the truck.

The plan was for OJ to ride with Aqil in the cab in case they ran into trouble and an authoritative officer's persona was needed. The other three members of the team would ride in the back until they got to their destination.

As the Americans prepared to get in the back of the truck, they unpacked and loaded the Iranian Tondar assault rifles. They checked their other weapons and communication devices. OJ had a small earpiece that had a microphone in it so he could talk to the other team members during the drive inland. Aqil showed them a trap door in the floor of the trailer that would allow the men to escape in the event of an emergency.

It was 4:45 am when Aqil started up the truck engine and headed north on the coast road. OJ looked at his watch. They had been in Iraq for precisely 45 minutes and OJ already felt completely exhausted. Aqil must have sensed OJ's mood as he handed him a thermos and said, "Drink, my brother, it's going to be a long day."

The tea was hot and strong. It tasted good and warmed OJ. But it did not settle his nerves. This wasn't a game and the fear hung over him like a heavy weight.

Aqil turned on the radio and there was Persian music playing. It wasn't the stuff OJ's father listened to, although he had heard it before a few times. It was called *Bandari* music from the southern tribal area of Iran. In Los Angeles, OJ had once gone to a concert of an Iranian rock band whose music was based on *Bandari* rhythms.

"You're not Persian, are you?" asked OJ, switching to the Baluchi language. "Let me guess," he continued, "you're Baluchi."

Aqil answered in Baluchi. "Yes, I am a Baluchi, from the South. How can you tell?"

"I can hear it in your accent when you speak Farsi," said Aqil. "I study the languages of Iran and I speak some Baluchi. It is a beautiful language."

"The Persians don't think so," said Aqil. "They don't like us to speak Baluchi."

OJ looked to his right, toward the coastal mountains looming before them. He could now see a reddish yellow light coming from behind the hills. The sun would be coming up in a few minutes and the night would no longer conceal them.

They drove for a few moments in silence, the undulating *Bandari* music making OJ drowsy. Then Aqil lit a cigarette. He offered one to OJ, who declined. "I don't smoke," said OJ.

"Is there something wrong with you?" asked Aqil. "Only old ladies don't smoke."

"That may be true in Iran, but it is not true in America."

"OK, Yankee, have it your way," said Aqil, laughing. "Take a look at this," he said, handing OJ a road map of the region they were driving in. "Do you want to know our route?"

Despite the rising dawn, it was still too dark to read in the cab of the truck. OJ took out a penlight and opened up the map.

"You landed north of the village of Ameri. Do you see it?"

"Yes, I see it."

"So we are traveling up the coast road. When we get to Chaghadak, we head east through Ahram into the mountains. We should be in Bala Deh by tonight—if nothing holds us up. From there you walk."

"What could hold us up?" asked OJ.

"Whatever Allah throws at us . . . rockslides, bandits, the army . . . who can say?

By 9:00 am, they had left the coast road and were traveling on east into the mountains. They avoided the main highway to Shiraz. Occasionally, OJ would give a status report to Lt. Commander Gonzales. About an hour later they stopped outside a small mountain village so that they could relieve themselves and stretch. Aqil boiled water for tea on an old primus stove. He also had a big bag of pistachio nuts which he passed around. Murphy reported in their position. Somewhere up above an AWACS plane was circling around their sector of the Persian Gulf listening and relaying their position to CENTCOM in Bahrain.

Within fifteen minutes, they were back in the truck and on their way. There was virtually no traffic on the road except for an occasional pickup truck or old car. Once they had to stop to let a shepherd boy cross the road with a herd of goats. Aqil and OJ talked about their families, although OJ was careful not to use real names or places. The scenery was magnificent: stark, high mountains with a pale blue sky above. In the valleys where there were streams they could see green. They passed through a village. It was tiny and poor, with naked children playing in the dirt with an old dog barking at them. The air felt cooler now. The monotony made OJ drowsy. Although he wasn't supposed to, he closed his eyes and drifted off.

He awoke with a start when the truck slowed to a crawl, its airbrakes hissing. OJ was disoriented. How long had he been asleep?

Ten minutes? An hour? He didn't know. Someone was talking in his ear. "What's happening? Hamsid, what's going on?" the voice was saying. At the same time, Aqil was talking to him in Farsi. "Shit, there's a SSF checkpoint up ahead," said Aqil.

"SSF? The State Security Force?"

"Yes, SSF. I came around the curve and there they were."

They were approaching a police car, which blocked the road. An officer in the front was motioning them to stop. Three other officers in black coveralls stood to the side with assault rifles.

"Oh God," OJ said in English. "'Oh God,' what?" a voice yelled in his ear. At the same moment, OJ realized the voice in his ear was Gonzales. "There's a State Security Force roadblock up ahead. We have to stop for it," OJ whispered urgently. "There's no other option."

"OK, Hamsid, just stay calm and play your part."

The truck slowed and the officer approached the truck. He was wearing sunglasses and had a thick beard. His complexion was dark and his uniform looked old and rumpled. He looked irritated and his hand was resting casually on his holster. Aqil lowered his window and looked down at him.

"Please get down and bring your papers with you," the officer said. His tone was firm, not angry, but with an edge of menacing authority. This was a man who was used to being listened to and obeyed.

OJ leaned over Aqil. "Wait," he whispered quietly to the driver.

"Officer," OJ said with authority, "what is the meaning of this?"

"The meaning of this?" the officer parroted back, a mocking smile breaking across his face. He looked back at the men near the cars and motioned for them to come. "And who are you to ask?"

OJ realized he didn't have his military cap on. He grabbed it and put it on.

"Officer, I'm Sargord Mohammed Bijani of the Al Qods Force. This is military cargo and we need to meet our schedule. Now, please tell me the meaning of this." OJ was trying his best to sound firm, angry, and authoritative.

"I appreciate that, Sir, but I have my orders. You and the driver need to get out of the truck so that we can check your shipping papers and inspect your cargo. There was a truck hijacking not far from here and we have orders to stop every truck."

The other policemen were now surrounding the truck. They looked casual and relaxed, as if the whole thing was routine. OJ had no idea whether this was something that happened all the time or not. But by the way Aqil was looking at him, this was no routine roadblock. He shook his head ever so slightly as a sign of warning. OJ quietly whispered into the microphone, "Gonzales, there is something wrong here. May Day." OJ thought he heard Gonzales say "copy."

Aqil hit OJ on the leg. When he looked over, the police officer had his gun out and he was pointing it through the driver's side window. On the other side, one of the other officers had an assault rifle pointed at the passenger window.

"Please get out of the truck. Now," said the officer firmly.

OJ and Aqil moved slowly to show that they did not intend to resist. When OJ stepped down out of the cab, the officer pointing the gun at him said, "Go over to the other side."

"Now, Sargord, I mean no disrespect, but you are armed. I must ask one of my men to take your gun." He smiled, slightly, the sun reflecting off his sunglasses. "So you will raise your hands please, slowly."

OJ raised his hands. He did his best to look angry. "I can assure you, there will be problems for you over this," OJ said, mustering all the indignation that he could.

"Perhaps . . . perhaps not," responded the officer, equivocally. "But I will still need your gun, Sir."

"What is your name, Officer?" asked OJ.

"The name is Shirazi, Captain Shirazi."

One of the other officers came up behind OJ and took the automatic out of its holster.

"Please now, give me your papers," demanded the officer, holstering his gun.

OJ reached slowly into his uniform coat pocket and removed his forged identification papers. Aqil handed over his identification as well. Captain Shirazi started to examine their papers, looking up at them as he compared the photos to their faces.

"Sir," Aqil said to Shirazi, "the bill of lading is in the truck. May I go get it?"

"Yes, go," responded the officer, distractedly. Aqil walked over to the truck and opened the door of the cab and started rummaging around for the transportation papers. When he was done, he walked back and handed them to the officer.

"Driver, you're name is Khan. You are Baluchi, no?

"That's correct, sir," responded Aqil.

"And your load consists of metalware from Pakistan? That's what you have here?" asked Shirazi.

"Yes, sir," Aqil's tone bordered on the obsequious.

"And since when are pots and pans military cargo?"

"That, Captain," replied OJ, "is not your concern."

"Well, we'll just have to find out, won't we?" Shirazi handed over their papers to one of the other officers. "Go call this in." The younger officer headed back in the direction of the police car. Shirazi looked up. With a wry smile that turned instantly to a grimace, he walked over to OJ and grabbed the microphone unit out of his ear.

"And what's this piece of equipment?" The question was clearly rhetorical. OJ stayed silent but he felt as though a vise was gripping his chest. How could he be so stupid?

"What is this thing?"

"It is a piece of high technology communication equipment we are now using. It is classified."

"Oh really, Sargord Bijani, and who do you talk to on this lonely mountain road?" Shirazi tuned the little black unit over in his hand. Something caught his attention and he looked closely at it.

"Why does this thing have words written in English that say . . . it says something with 'USA' in it? 'Made in USA." Do we now buy our military equipment from the Americans?"

Summoning all his fake dignity and outrage, OJ said, "This is not a matter you are expected to know about, Captain Shirazi." He was hoping his tone came out as controlled anger not the deep fear that he was feeling.

At that instant somebody yelled "Down" in English and simultaneously there were a series of staccato thumping sounds. OJ dropped to his stomach.

The two soldiers nearest Shirazi crumpled to the ground. The one walking toward the car went down next, his head obliterated by a hail of silenced automatic fire. Captain Shirazi instinctively hunched up his shoulders and ducked down, starting to reach for his holster.

"Don't move and put your hands on your head." It was Aqil and he had pulled his automatic from behind his back. He must have grabbed it when he got the shipping papers out of the truck.

Shirazi slowly stood up, his hands on top of his head.

Gonzales, Amalakai, and Murphy came up, their assault rifles in front of them. Gonzales said to Amalakai, "Ted, go check out the one over there and search their vehicle."

Gonzales walked over to Shirazi and grabbed his arms from behind. He put on a plastic handcuff and another larger one around his upper legs, so he could walk but not run. Then he pushed him firmly down by the shoulders so that he was on his knees. He reached around and took off his sunglasses. Shirazi looked stunned.

With a big laugh, Aqil said to Shirazi in Farsi, "*Xoowha'ly zeer-e-wekamet zadeh*". Turning to OJ, who was in the process of getting up off the ground and dusting himself off, Murphy asked, "What does that mean?"

"Well," said OJ, "Roughly speaking, it means 'Happiness is hitting you below the belt!'"

"Are you going to kill me too?" asked Shirazi.

OJ wasn't sure, so he didn't say anything. Gonzales turned to him and said, "Translate."

"His name is Shirazi, Captain Shirazi," OJ informed Gonzales.

"Captain Shirazi, what is the purpose of your roadblock?"

"I will not answer your questions," responded Shirazi.

"He refuses to answer," translated OJ.

Gonzales punched the Iranian in the face. His head snapped back, blood poured from his nose. Shirazi looked stunned.

"Tell me about the purpose of your roadblock."

The Iranian stayed silent. He was a brave man.

Gonzales pulled out his Iranian service revolver and clicked off the safety.

"Tell him to answer our questions or I will kill him."

OJ translated.

"Go fuck yourself," the Iranian officer snarled in Farsi. OJ did not need to translate.

Gonzales put the weapon to the Iranian's chest and fired. The man crumpled, dead.

"OK, clean this mess up and let's get out of here."

Gonzales walked away, shaking his head.

Over the next hour, the Americans went about quickly and methodically cleaning up the scene. The first thing they did was remove any identification from the dead police officers. Then they put the bodies in the car and drove it to the edge of the road. They took some spare gasoline from a jerry can that Aqil kept in his truck and doused the inside of the car. Then they opened one of the windows in the car and proceeded to push it over the side of the road. As the car started to go over the side, Gonzales tossed a TH3 incendiary grenade into the open window. The police car went over the side of the road and began to fall toward the desolate valley floor below. About three seconds after the car went over, the incendiary grenade detonated. There was a flash and an explosion of intense white thermate flames burning at 4,000 degrees Fahrenheit. At the same instant, the car's gasoline tanks also ignited in a secondary explosion. The sound reverberated in the hills like thunder. By the time the car reached the bottom of the gully, it was a twisted wreck of melted metal. A thin greasy cloud of smoke rose from its final resting place. The thermate explosion was so hot that it incinerated the remaining flammable materials in the vehicles. The residual fire burned out very quickly. Hopefully the wreck would not be discovered for some time.

Fortunately, during the cleanup period, no innocent motorists happened to drive down the road. The last thing they needed was another prisoner.

Right before they were ready to leave, Lt. Commander Gonzales took OJ aside and put his arm around him. "Listen, Hamsid," he said in a terse and quiet monotone, "next time we have to deal with Iranians, how about taking the fucking earpiece out of your goddamned ear? We wound up having to kill four Iranians because of that stupid move. Because of you, a bunch of rag heads will grow up without fathers. This isn't a game. Don't make a mistake like that again. Got it?" Gonzales pressed the black earpiece into OJ's hand.

"Yes, sir," OJ replied quietly as Gonzales walked away. OJ walked over to the side of the road and fought back the urge to cry.

It was just after noon when the truck got back on the road.

Chapter 22

The months of training were now over and the mission was finally under way. They arrived at the Port of Limmasol on the ferry from Ladakia, Syria. It was a warm day and the Mediterranean was a deep azure color. As the ship entered the port, the passengers crowded on deck, looking up at the whitewashed houses of the old city. The two teams stayed apart from one another. Mohammed Dibul, the field commander of Operation *Zaqqum*, and the German woman acted out their roles as a cosmopolitan married couple. The men of the other team mingled with the Western passengers, practicing their English and flirting with the European women who were on the boat.

They carried no weapons, no written plans, no codebooks, no tools—nothing that could give them away. They appeared to be ordinary Canadian tourists, down to the small Canadian flags that the three younger members of the group sewed on their regulation student backpacks to politely distinguish themselves from Americans. They had trained almost as hard to act like Westerners as they had in the military aspects of the mission. There was to be no Islam, no mosques, no Allah, and alcohol consumption was not only permitted, but encouraged. They were to live the life of Westerners and they had the financial resources to do it. They each carried a combination ATM-credit card drawn on a Canadian bank account with an unlimited balance.

There was an elaborate system in place to hide the team's financial transactions. Their credit card-bills would be paid each month by a shell Bahamian corporation that had hired an unwitting accountant in Ottawa to manage its Canadian business operations. The accountant, in turn, was to email his bill and the bank statements to an address that supposedly went to the company's headquarters in Athens, Greece. An agent stationed in Athens would receive the email and send to another Canadian bank for payment. This way, should anyone be caught, the trail of evidence would stop cold in Athens and it would be nearly impossible to make a link to the Iranians. The accountant was paid well for his services and even if he thought the whole thing was a bit unusual, he wasn't particularly concerned. As far as he knew, there was nothing illegal happening, so why worry?

Ingrid Meissner had used various names during her long career. As a young left-wing terrorist, she had been known as Red Lise. Later, after her conversion to Islam, Ingrid had taken the name Kahdijah al-Suri—"Kahdijah the Syrian." For this operation, she had been given a new name, Ingrid Christian, the irony of which was not lost on her Pasdaran handlers. Ingrid's assumed her new identity with ease. She simply resumed her life as a German, albeit under a cover story involving her family's immigration to Canada after defecting from the former German Democratic Republic in the 1960s. She cut her long brown hair into a short Cleopatra like bob and dyed it blonde. She studied Western fashion magazines with the same degree of enthusiasm and dedication she brought to the study of bomb-making. She reacquainted herself with the art of using makeup and walking in high-heeled shoes. Her handlers had purchased an appropriately expensive wardrobe for her in Beirut, where there was a burgeoning market for Western women's fashion among the nouveau riche of the Levant. She was tall, thin, and athletic. Ingrid easily took on the persona of an affluent middle-aged woman who was strikingly beautiful and knew it. Her blouses revealed a little too much cleavage and her skirts were a little too short. It had the desired affect on men, who seemed to lose their critical faculties around her. Ingrid did not fit anyone's profile of a terrorist.

Her "husband," Mohammed Dibul, was given the name Mohammed Ibrahim. He also simply assumed the role that he had once occupied, as a wealthy engineer of Egyptian heritage, whose well-educated upper-middle-class family had left Egypt with the exodus of the British after World War Two and found their way to England. Dibul was in fact the son of a well-known physician, had been educated at Cairo University, and had spend a semester on a post-graduate engineering fellowship at the University of Leeds in the early 1980s. He spoke English well, but with a strong accent.

Ironically, Dibul had become radicalized not in Egypt, but in England while attending the university. He had begun to socialize with other Egyptian students, some of whom were secret members of the *Ikwan el Muslimeen*, the Muslim Brotherhood. The Brotherhood was the first modern Islamic fundamentalist organization. Founded as a secret society during the anti-Imperialist period in the 1920s, it had long challenged the Western-leaning military dictatorship of Egypt. Before that it had fought successively against the British, the infamously corrupt monarchy of King Farouk, and Gamal Abdel Nasser's pan-Arab socialist regime. But the Islamic Brotherhood was not only a violent underground secret society, it was also widely respected for developing a huge above-ground network of Islamic schools and charities that delivered social services to millions of Egyptians free from the graft and corruption that was so endemic to Egyptian society. Across the Arab world, the Muslim Brotherhood became the model of a "third way," an anti-imperialist and genuinely Islamic political movement that could deliver on the Prophet's promise of a just society. When the Islamic Revolution overthrew the Shah of Iran, it was to the Muslim Brotherhood that its leader, Ayatollah Khomeini, turned to find inspiration.

The Muslim Brotherhood reached the apex of its revolutionary activities when it assassinated the pro-Western President of Egypt, Anwar Sadat, after he had made peace with Israel. In the bloody aftermath of Sadat's assassination, his successor, Hosni Mubarrak, brutally repressed the Brotherhood and many refugees fled to England, where they began to preach and organize among Britain's large Muslim population. Mohammed Dibul was increasingly drawn to the passionate and heartfelt beliefs of his fellow students in the Brotherhood. They maintained a dignity that promised to restore the greatness of the Islamic Caliphate. But if the Brotherhood was a beacon, it was the Soviet invasion of Afghanistan in 1979 that was the flame that lit the torch in Mohammed's soul.

In the spring of 1982, increasingly under the sway of the Brotherhood, Mohammed dropped out of his graduate program and found his way to a Muhajadeen training camp in the western mountains of Pakistan. For the next five years he battled the Soviet Army and became a skilled and ruthless guerrilla commander. The Red Army put a price on his head and they called him "The Knife" because, as a method of execution, he slit the throats of Russian soldiers that he captured. He was wounded several times and walked with a very slight limp. He had scars on his chest from shell fragments that had been removed and a burn mark across his back. When he left Afghanistan, Mohammed was a man transformed. He was deeply religious and committed to the restoration of the full power of the Islamic Caliphate through *Jihad*. The Crusaders of the West and their debased and evil culture would ultimately give way to the pure truth of Islam.

After the Russians left Afghanistan, Mohammed went to Lebanon and fought the Israelis and the Maronite Christian militias, joining up with a Hezbollah unit. This brought him to the attention of the Syrians and the Pasdaran in Lebanon and he was soon on the Iranian payroll. In 1991, the Iranians sent Mohammed to Sudan to train Al-Qaeda operatives in combat operations. His cadre was then assigned to Mogadishu to work with the Somali warlords who were challenging the American military presence. It was there, through the sights of a high-powered sniper rifle, that Mohammed killed his first American, an Army Ranger Captain leading a patrol through the twisted streets of Mogadishu. He felt nothing. He had killed too many times before.

Mohammed and Ingrid made a handsome couple; sophisticated, stylish, and cosmopolitan. The Americans and the British were looking out for men fitting the 9/11 mold . . . lonely, fanatical, ready to commit suicide for the cause and, as their reward, eternity in Paradise.

The other three members of the team were traveling together, acting the part of friends—recently graduated Canadian college students—on a foreign travel adventure before starting their careers. When they got to the United States, they were under strict instructions not to seek out the Muslim community. As far as General Yazdi was concerned, every mosque in the United States was under FBI surveillance and every Muslim immigrant a potential government informer. They were to play their parts, carry out their mission, then escape from the United States in accordance with the careful plan that had been developed.

Each of the two groups was under orders not to contact one another until they reached Mexico. The three men stayed together at a small pension in central Limmasol favored by student travelers and run by a Lebanese woman and her Greek Cypriot husband. They asked no questions, served a good breakfast, and smiled as the boys set off on their various adventures.

In contrast, Mr. and Mrs. Ibrahim checked into a suite at the Kryos Beach Hotel, a five-star luxury hotel on one of Limmasol's finest beaches. They sat out by the pool, dined on fine food, and had interesting conversations with the other well-heeled guests. One evening, they even had a pleasant conversation with a wealthy Israeli couple.

They waited for the signal that it was time to go.

Chapter 23

There was a tense silence in the room when Dr. Honari arrived at Nuclear Reactor Number 2 to supervise the reactor shut down and the removal of the spent fuel rods. The protocol must be followed precisely to avoid an accidental radiation leak. Only Dr. Honari and a very select group of individuals in the Iranian government and military knew about the process that was to begin today. Fewer still had knowledge about the long and complicated journey that would begin the next day; a journey that, with Allah's help, would end by shaking the arrogant infidels to their very core. The secret must be kept at all costs.

The President of the Islamic Republic had performed his part perfectly. Two weeks earlier, at a widely publicized speech to the Islamic Veterans Association commemorating their sacrifices in the Iran-Iraq War, he had loudly and publicly protested the "double standard" that the world imposed on his country. Everyone knew, he said, that Israel had long had nuclear weapons and wasn't even a signatory to the Nuclear Non-Proliferation Treaty. Iran was fully supportive of the Nuclear Non-Proliferation Treaty and no matter how peaceful its intentions, the West insisted that it be subjected to greater and greater scrutiny. What, he asked, about the principle of justice, much touted by the Americans, that people were presumed innocent until proven guilty? Were the peace-loving Iranian people not entitled to a presumption of innocence? The President banged his fist down on the dais and declared that, until the double standard against the Islamic world was ended, he would no longer allow the UN's nuclear inspectors inside his borders.

In the greenish light of the nuclear reactor, they carefully lifted the spent fuel rods from the reactor core, each containing hundreds of pellets of highly enriched uranium. Carefully, the superheated rods were placed in a sealed lead-lined concrete cooling tank containing water cooled to 2° Celsius and continuously recirculated. Once cooled, all but one of the fuel rods would be transferred to a centrifuge facility where the minute amounts of highly enriched uranium would be extracted and used in Iran's nuclear weapons development program. The last fuel rod was intended to be used for another purpose entirely.

It was well after midnight when, under Dr. Honari's supervision, the remaining fuel rod was taken to a specially equipped laboratory adjacent to the cooling tower. They waited until a dark and overcast night to limit the possibility that a passing spy satellite would photograph their activities. To get to the laboratory, it was necessary to descend three flights of unmarked stairs, pass through a guarded security door, and then go through a second sealed door. The passageway was an airlock, equipped with radiation detectors, protective suits, and emergency showers in the event of an accidental release of radiation. Inside, the room was a brightly lit twenty-foot cube, with stainless steel walls and polished concrete floors. The only sign in the room said "no smoking" in Farsi and French. It was shielded by three feet of reinforced concrete with intermittent layers of lead sheathing to prevent a radiation leak. In the center of the room was a platform on which was placed a sealed transfer system, which looked like a large aquarium with glass walls approximately five inches thick.   The tank had telemanipulator arms sticking into it, which allowed scientists to safely handle radioactive materials that had been lowered into the tank. It was here that the night's real work was about to begin.

Inside the tank three lead containers were stacked. They had sloping sides so that the top of the container formed a larger rectangle than the bottom. Each had a circular hole in the top that could be sealed. Dr. Honari sat at the front of the tank where he could insert his hands into the sleeves of the telemanipulator and control its arms. He was assisted by two other technicians.

On Dr. Honari's orders, the cooled fuel rod was loaded onto a sling and carefully inserted into the transfer tank. The fuel rod was placed in a specially designed vise, which held it firmly in place. Everyone in the room was wearing white radiation suits equipped with internal radiation detectors that would go off if the integrity of the suits became compromised. He carefully used the robot arms to unscrew the top of the fuel rod and expose the radioactive pellets of spent uranium. Slowly, Dr. Honari picked up the fuel rod with the robot pincers and carefully poured out the pellets onto the bottom of the tank. The marble-sized pellets were dull yellow in color and were composed of almost pure Uranium 235 with trace amounts of plutonium and other isotopes of uranium. Because they have a half-life of 704 million years, if they were disbursed by a conventional explosive charge over a large geographical area, the result would be a public health, environmental, and political catastrophe.

Dr. Honari now separated the pellets into three piles. The empty fuel rod was removed from the tank and immediately transferred to a sealed disposal unit. Using the telemanipulator arms, Dr. Honari placed the first of the lead containers on the floor of the tank. He then transferred one of the three piles of pellets into it, one painstaking pellet after another. He repeated the process two more times, until the pellets had all been placed in their respective lead containers. One of the technicians then placed an electric soldering gun into the tank, which Dr. Honari attached to one of the manipulator arms. The three covers were fitted into the holes and using the soldering gun, and were sealed in place. As each container was taken out of the tank it was allowed to cool. They were then placed in a machine which tested its radioactive emissions. All three tested negative. The transfer of the pellets had been a success.

It was 3:00 am when they finished. Dr. Honari and his assistants were pleased with their work but also totally exhausted. Their part of the process had now been successfully completed; others would now take over.

The next evening, a truck with two men inside dressed in civilian clothes pulled up to the entrance of Experimental Reactor Number 2. Outside the compound on the street there were two unmarked cars containing an armed security escort that would accompany the truck after it left the compound. The truck trailer was loaded with fifty-five-gallon drums of olive oil and the driver had a legitimate bill of lading which required the load to be delivered to the Rawalpindi Trading Company warehouse in Peshawar, Pakistan. Rawalpindi Trading Company was a secret asset of the Pasdaran and was used as a front to conduct business operations in Pakistan. Its employees were either Pasdaran officers or Pakistani nationals in the employ of the Pasdaran. Rawalpindi Trading Company engaged in legitimate business activities which provided a perfect front for the Pasdaran to move men and material through one of the world's great centers of international trade and commerce.

The truck pulled into a covered loading dock where three empty fifty-five gallon drums were off loaded and three identical-looking drums were loaded on the truck. The fifty-five-gallon drums that were substituted were far from ordinary. They were specifically designed to be used by hospitals, laboratories, and manufacturers to hold low-level nuclear waste while being transported. The drums had been modified so that the top third held several gallons of olive oil with a sealed panel below it. Should anyone open the top of the drum to inspect it, they would find olive oil. Underneath the false panel was a plastic container suspended in foam, which held the lead box containing the spent uranium fuel. The plastic container was coated with a heavy lead paint which, if the drum was x-rayed, would present itself as identical to any of the other drums that contained only olive oil. The drum with the nuclear material was also nearly the same weight as the other drums.

Once the load was secured, the truck quickly left the grounds of Experimental Reactor Number 2, picked up its escort, and entered the evening traffic of Tehran.

Chapter 24

KŪH-I-BŪZPAR MOUNTAINS, FARS PROVINCE, IRAN, APRIL 13

They continued going east up into the mountains. About ten kilometers south of the town of Farashband, the road turned north. It was nearing dusk and they were behind schedule. In the hours since their confrontation with the security officers, they traveled mostly in silence, each of them lost in their respective thoughts, Aqil's seemingly endless collection of Iranian music droning on.

"So, my American brother," Aqil said, lighting up what to OJ appeared to be his hundredth cigarette of the day, "you seem troubled."

OJ did not know what to say, so he changed the subject. "Hey, Aqil, has anyone ever told you that smoking can kill you?"

"Making friends with Americans can kill you faster."

"You've got a point there."

Another few minutes went by in silence before OJ spoke again. "I've never seen men killed. It . . .," OJ searched for the words, "made me feel sick."

"Your leader did what was necessary. You will get used to it."

"I hope not."

"They would have arrested us and when they were done, you would have wished you were dead."

Another fifteen minutes passed and the mountain road was now totally dark. There were no lights, no road markings, and the moon had not risen yet. Aqil slowed the truck.

"How can you drive for this long, Aqil? We've been on the road for more than twelve hours."

"Yankee, I will confess to you, it isn't easy and I'm getting very tired. And when I drop you off, I still have to drive to Kazerun before I can stop and sleep. Then I have to get up early tomorrow and drive to Shiraz to deliver the freight."

"I don't think I could do what you are doing—I'd fall asleep at the wheel."

"You learn to stay awake, to play music in the head, to think."

They were silent for a few minutes. Then Aqil asked, "So how does it work? Does Commander Sinbad have some secret device that tells us where to stop even in the night?"

"Something like that," OJ replied.

As if on cue, OJ heard Gonzales' voice in his earpiece. "Hamsid, you there?"

"Yes, I'm here."

"Hamsid, tell Aqil that we are within an hour of our drop."

When OJ reported the news to Aqil, the Baluchi slapped OJ on the shoulder and said, "See, Yankee, it is all OK—Allah be willing."

Unaccountably, OJ's spirits began to lighten a little. He was, of course, still in state of shock. But he began to feel a sense of relief. They had survived a deadly confrontation.

As if to confirm their change of fortune, the road straightened out and the truck picked up speed. They entered a wide valley between two mountain ranges. Sensing OJ's change of mood, Aqil said, "Well, brother, that was quite a day, but I think we are on the downward side of the hill, no?"

"I certainly hope so, Aqil. I don't think I could stand any more excitement in one day."

"The SSF will be very upset when they realize that they have lost four officers. They will be looking for the people who are responsible."

"Who do you think they will be looking for?"

Aqil smiled broadly at OJ. "The SSF will be running around like chickens with their heads cut off looking for Communists or Kurdish terrorists or Zionist spies. Since you are none of those things, you are safe."

"That makes me feel greatly relieved," Said OJ sarcastically.

"Unless they start focusing on Baluchi separatists." Aqil laughed. "But I will never give you away, I promise."

Gonzales piped in on the intercom. "Tell Aqil that we need to stop at the bridge over the Dālaki River. It's about seventy-five klicks ahead. That's where we're getting out."

The Dālaki River was unimpressive and so was the bridge spanning it. OJ imagined it to be a wild, raging river and the bridge one of those engineering feats spanning a deep mountain gorge. In reality, it was an old stone bridge over a small, gently flowing river. Aqil stopped the truck just after the bridge in a little pullout that was used for road crews.

It didn't take them long to unload the equipment. They had four backpacks, their weapons, communication equipment, and food. Each backpack weighed about seventy pounds. They had quite a distance to walk before they would get to their observation position. When they were all unloaded, they hurriedly said their farewells to Aqil. Gonzales handed him a fat envelope full of Iranian 10,000-rial banknotes.

"I've already been paid," he said.

"Consider it a bonus for a job well done."

"LC," said Amalakai, "I see headlights."

They all looked up. Coming toward them from up the road were two sets of headlights. Gonzales said, "We're out of here," and they grabbed the packs and ran for the path that led under the bridge.

OJ yelled to Aqil, "Thank you, brother!"

To which the now running Aqil yelled back over his shoulder, "If you are ever in Zahedan, come visit my family."

Chapter 25

For Tom Harter, life was good. He had recently been promoted to a supervisory position at the Wal-Mart Distribution Center. He was dating a young woman named Rebecca that he'd met at the New Life Christian Church, which he attended regularly. The Pastor, impressed by Tom, had introduced them. She was a student at Biola University and was from a good family. His parents were happy that he had given up his dalliance with Islam and was settling down. They liked Becky and hoped that the relationship would continue.

But inside Tom's soul burned the flame of Islam. While he was Tom Harter on the outside, he was Abdul-Haq on the inside. In his heart, he was every bit as radical as ever and committed to the cause. But he had matured and understood the nature and importance of his position. He was at the vanguard of a great movement. As Sayeed pointed out at their regular meetings, some must fight the Jihad in armies and some must struggle alone. His was a crucial mission.

The two men met about once a month to exchange information. The meetings took place at various small family owned restaurants around the area that Sayeed made sure did not employ video surveillance systems. Tom supplied Sayeed with detailed reports on the international and domestic logistics operations of Wal-Mart: how shipping moved in and out of the Distribution Center, the use of transponders to track each container, how the "just in time" inventory system worked. Tom was not sure why this information was useful to the cause and Sayeed did not tell him.

In the wake of the World Trade Center attack, Tom had been asked by management to head up a security committee at the Distribution Center. He was given broad access to review security procedures. At the time, Sayeed seemed particularly pleased with Tom's new assignment. Although some new security procedures were implemented after 9/11, things eventually settled down and returned to normal. In 2003, Tom was promoted again, this time to be supervisor of the Shipping Integrity Department for the distribution center. Sayeed was particularly delighted by Tom's promotion. In the ensuing months, Tom supplied a wealth of new information to Sayeed.

Tom settled into his new life with its enhanced status and increased salary, supplemented by payments from Sayeed. He married Becky in a small ceremony at the church and they purchased a starter home in the Ontario area. Becky finished her studies and became a teacher at the Inland Empire Christian Center. The young couple appeared happy. Becky soon discovered Tom's threadbare copy of the Koran. She was disturbed by having this pagan book in her house and told Tom she wanted him to throw it in the garbage. Tom refused. He said that, before he was born again, he had explored Islam and the Koran reminded him why he came back to the Lord. As they learned to live with one another, Becky discovered that Tom had a quiet, deeply introspective, almost secretive side. He also guarded their privacy zealously. He was not particularly social and the couple did not have many friends. He seemed satisfied to share occasional meals with their parents and to attend church socials.

Tom's marriage to Becky, which Sayeed encouraged, necessitated a change in security procedures. They now communicated through a dead-letter drop. Tom would take the dog on a walk to the local park. Toward the back of the park was a stick wired to the chain-link fence.

If the stick pointed up, there was a letter for Tom. If it was pointed to the side, there was no mail. Similarly, if Tom wished to post a letter, he was to place it under an abandoned sprinkler access cover, and point the stick down.

One day Sayeed told Tom that this would be their last meeting; Sayeed was returning home. Sayeed told Tom that he would soon be receiving instructions from his replacement. The two men had grown fond of one another over the years, but war was war and they both understood displacement and loss were part of the price warriors paid for the privilege of serving their cause. In the parking lot of the Mexican restaurant where they met, the two men embraced, patting each other on the back. "Goodbye, brother," said Sayeed. "Some day, perhaps, we will meet again."

Chapter 26

J ake hadn't lived with his parents for many years but the temptation of saving a lot of money by moving back into his old bedroom was very appealing. His parents seemed pleased to have him around. However, they expected him to fix things around the house, which Jake found tiresome. Although had had visited his parents many times over the years, they viewed his current situation as qualitatively different. As far as they were concerned, he was an adult child who was "moving back in" with them, even if his stay would be temporary. There was an air of failure surrounding the move, as if Jake's return to Los Angeles was a sign that he was having trouble functioning in the real world. His mother's sympathetic and vaguely patronizing tone annoyed him to no end. Of course, to some degree she was right, which annoyed him even more.

On the first day of his job in Los Angeles, he had an appointment with the Director of the Port of Los Angeles and her Chief of Security. They were going to give him a tour of the sprawling port complex and brief him on security matters. Later in the day he would meet with the local federal officials in charge of port security, including representatives from the Coast Guard, the Customs Service, the FBI, and the Transportation Security Administration. It was a typical Monday morning when he joined the millions of other Angelinos in the morning commute along the freeways of LA in his father's old 1979 Volvo. Jake's parents had kept it as a third car so that he would have something to drive when he visited. It had nearly 300,000 miles on it and as far as Jake was concerned, was something of a modern miracle.

Jake got on the San Diego Freeway in Westwood and headed south. The traffic was moving slowly but steadily and Jake passed the time listening to a show called "Which Way LA?" on the local National Public Radio station. They were talking about global warming and international trade. He was down near LAX when his cell phone rang. It was his mother calling to ask him whether he would be home for dinner. He laughed. "Mom, you and Dad just go ahead and eat. I'll fend for myself."

"Are you sure?" she asked, sounding disappointed. How was it that they seemed to be picking up their relationship as if the intervening twenty years had never passed?

"I'm making your favorite dish, Chicken Jerusalem," his mother said excitedly, as if she had just discovered a hoard of gold in the kitchen pantry. Jake hated the dish. He had tried to hint to his mother many times that he didn't like it, but he couldn't come right out and say it because he didn't want to hurt her feelings. Besides, she had the amazing ability to hear only what she wanted to hear. It was actually her favorite dish, but some time in his childhood, she had served it to him. He had politely lied and told her he liked it. From then on, it had become one of his mother's implanted memories, so that by now she would regale dinner guests with stories of how little Jakey had demanded that she make her Chicken Jerusalem from virtually the moment he emerged from the womb.

"Mom, I just don't know how late I'll be tonight and I don't want to hold you up. So you guys just go ahead and eat without me and I'll catch something on the fly." He felt a pang of guilt mixed with irritation, his most common emotional response to his mother.

"Oh, it's terrible, Jakey, that you have to miss your favorite meal.

I'll tell you what, I'll make enough for you and if you get home in time you can eat with us; if not, you can eat later."

"Great, Mom. Thanks."

"All right, Jakey, I've got to go now. See you tonight at dinner."

The woman is a genius, thought Jake. Although she had called him, she managed to convey that she was bearing up well under the burden of taking care of him.   It was going to be a long six months until his assignment was over and he could return to his teaching job.

As soon as Jake hit the westbound ramp to the 710 Freeway headed toward the twin ports of Los Angeles and Long Beach, the traffic slowed to a crawl. Trucks hauling intermodal shipping containers—those with empties heading into the port and those with full loads heading inland—must have outnumbered cars three to one. So this was the infamous "710 bottleneck" they were always talking about. Old diesel trucks were moving slowly in stop-and-go traffic, belching black exhaust every time their drivers pressed down on their accelerators. With every mile the scene got more grimy and industrial. Railroad tracks, lots filled with empty rusting intermodal truck chassis and shipping containers stacked three stories high, and old warehouses dominated the view. These industrial areas were intermixed with poor residential neighborhoods of little boxy 1930s bungalows. He passed kids playing on an elementary school playground right next to the freeway.

About a half-mile from the water, the freeway simply ended. To the left was the city of Long Beach. Jake could just make out the HMS Queen Mary, once the pride of the Cunard line and now a slightly down-in-the-mouth tourist attraction; to the right were the ports with their behemoth gantry cranes already busy at full capacity moving containers from ships and stacking them on the docks.

Jake made his way across the Vincent Thomas Bridge, its soaring lines strangely out of place amid the strictly utilitarian look of the area. As he drove down Beacon Street toward the headquarters building of the Port of Los Angeles, Jake saw something familiar and it was a bit of a shock to him. In the 1960s, the City of Los Angeles decided to redevelop the port area and ordered the old fish-processing plants demolished. They built a retail area of tourist shops and seafood restaurants with the hopeful name "International Ports O' Call." His parents had taken him there when it first opened and Jake remembered it through the excited eyes of a child, all tropical colors and exotic things to buy. Now, more than a quarter of a century later, it looked worn out and it was obvious that the initial investment turned out to be the last. The changing ethnic makeup of Los Angeles was apparent, as several of the restaurants had big banners hung across their entrances advertising "¡Mariscos!"—shrimp in Spanish.

The security guard on the first floor of the port headquarters made a half-hearted search of Jake's belongings before sending him up to the Executive Offices on the fifth floor.

Jake had just sat down when a small whirlwind of a woman came barreling out of her office with her hand extended to shake Jake's. "Professor Elliot, I'm Dr. Caroline Farberow, the Port Director." Jake made a mental note to find out in what subject Caroline Farberow had earned her doctorate.

"It's a pleasure to meet you." Dr. Farberow's handshake was firm and unflinching. She exuded intelligence and confidence. Jake took an instant liking to her.

Jake followed Dr. Farberow into a conference room, where she introduced him to a number of her subordinates. When the introductions were completed, Dr. Farberow turned the meeting over to Jake.

"The Secretary of Energy has sent me here to review port security issues with a special emphasis on the ability of the port to detect and stop the smuggling of radioactive material into the United States. I am on leave from my permanent job as a professor of Nuclear Engineering at the Massachusetts Institute of Technology. I am not a career government employee and I want to hear your frank assessment of the state of port security."

An older gentleman with stark white hair and a buzz cut introduced himself as Al McBride, the Director of Port Security. "With all due respect, Professor, real port security is inadequate to the point of nonexistence. The Coast Guard patrols the harbor with machine guns on their boats and that is a nice show of force, but the fact of the matter is that fewer containers are being opened and screened than before the 9/11 attacks. The armed TSA police look great in their black SWAT team uniforms but they don't actually do much to increase security. Frankly, you can tell the Secretary of Energy that it would not be difficult to smuggle radioactive material into this port. It's a sieve."

"I want to thank you for the candor of your statement, Mr. McBride. I also want to make something perfectly clear. I don't represent the administration in Washington and I'm not here to sugarcoat their efforts. I want to know exactly what is wrong with port security and what needs to be done to fix it. In the end, it will be a bunch of average Americans who are just doing their jobs—not politicians in Washington—that will save us from a terrorist attack. I will compile my report and it will tell the truth. If they don't like it, that's too bad. If they choose to ignore it, then it will be on their heads."

The group seemed pleased by Jake's response. Like the opening of the bureaucratic floodgates, one port employee after another regaled Jake with his view of flawed security situation. No one, it turned out, actually kept track of which trucking companies serviced the port or the drivers that were entering the various maritime terminals. The drivers were all owner-operators and so they didn't actually work for anyone. The gantry cranes were not equipped with scales and so it was impossible to weigh the inbound containers to determine whether they were overloaded. McBride's frustrated assistant, a guy named Mike Baron, explained that there used to be scales installed in the terminals and on the cranes, but that the terminal operators removed them at the request of the shippers because they actually *wanted* overloaded containers to pass through. That way they wouldn't ever have to waste the time and expense of reshifting loads. Besides, he explained, it was some poor slob of a truck driver who would get the overload citation anyway. However, from a port security point of view, it was a nightmare. While the "out of sight, out of mind" policy of the big box retailers who dominated the shipping world may have been good for their bottom line, it also made it impossible to detect one of the primary indicators of nuclear smuggling—overloads due to the super-heavy weight of nuclear material. As Dr. Farberow put it,

"I don't know who first said this, but it is truly a case of us selling the rope to hang ourselves with."

"And any other instrument of self-destruction as well," interjected Al McBride.

Jake laughed. "Dr. Farberow, I may be wrong about this, but if my memory serves me correctly, I believe it was Joseph Stalin who said the thing about capitalism and rope."

"Gosh, Professor, I guess that I'd better find another quote or I am in danger of making the TSA's 'do not fly' list as a suspected terrorist."

"Here's another significant issue," said McBride, "The feds have installed passive radiation detectors that all the trucks have to pass through, but we have a real concern that they cannot detect carefully shielded nuclear material."

"No question about it," responded Jake. "If we're serious about protecting our country from terrorists using the ports to smuggle in weapons or explosives, we're going to have to do a lot more than we are doing now."

"Professor, how about we take you on the tour we promised?" asked Caroline Farberow.

The drive from the headquarters of the Port of Los Angeles to Terminal Island in McBride's old Chrysler took just a few minutes and brought them to the heart of port operations.

They pulled into the gate at Terminal L. Above the gate was a sign that read "United States Stevedoring Company." McBride told Jake that they would be meeting the Customs Inspectors at the Terminal Control Center, a two-story wood-frame building dating from the 1940s that stood between the truck gates and the dock. The terminal was busy with trucks pulling inside the terminal and getting hitched up to chassis loaded with intermodal containers. Then they lined up in a long, snaking line to get checked out and leave the terminal. Jake noticed that most of the drivers looked like immigrants from Mexico or Central America, small, dark men who worked long, hard hours to make a meager living. Forklifts were driving around the terminal.

Jake could see that a big container ship was tied up to the dock and that a pair of gantry cranes was busy moving containers from the deck to the dock.

Jake and McBride entered the building. A bunch of men and women sat facing computer terminals. Some were talking on phones, some were comparing what they saw on the screen to large stacks of shipping manifests, and one was looking out the window toward the terminal gate, having an argument with one of the guys at the gate over whether a truck driver should enter the terminal.

"These are the 'kitchen clerks,'" McBride explained.

"Why are they called kitchen clerks?" asked Jake.

"Hell if I know," responded McBride.

"Because we work downstairs," said the clerk sitting nearest to them, turning around in his chair. "And the kitchen is always downstairs. Hey, do you know what they call the guys who work upstairs?" the man asked with an impish grin.

"I bet you'll tell us," responded Jake, laughing.

"They're called the 'tower clerks' because they actually worked in towers in the old days."

Jake introduced himself to the man. "I'm Jake Elliot and I work for the US Department of Energy. Actually, I'm a college teacher on loan to the federal government and I study nuclear power and nuclear weapons."

"I'm Lee Sandahl," said the marine clerk, shaking hands with Jake, "and I can tell you categorically there aren't any nuclear power plants at this port and I hope to hell there are no nuclear bombs around here either."

Jake heard one of the other clerks say, "Damn straight."

McBride, changing the subject, said, "Mr. Sandahl here is a walking encyclopedia of dockside lore. How long you been working on the waterfront, Lee?"

"Coming on thirty-five years," replied Sandahl. "How about you, Mr. McBride? I seem to remember you over at APL in the early sixties; if memory serves, with a full head of black hair."

"You sonofabitches turned it grey about four strikes ago."

"And the good Lord retaliated for your sinful acts against the working class by turning you old," quipped Sandahl.

Jake was certain another good natured rib was coming, when the door opened and three men came in. Out of the corner of his eye, Jake could see Sandahl rolling his eyes and turning back to his work.

"Jonathan Elliot, let me introduce Customs Agents Smith, Connoughton, and Zeigler. Agent Connoughton is the Chief Customs Agent at the Port of Los Angeles."

They shook hands. Zeigler, the oldest of the three, smiled at Elliot. The other two were much younger, in their late twenties or early thirties. No smiles from those two; they were all business. Zeigler was quite a contrast to Connoughton and Smith. Whereas he was a paunchy overweight guy wearing a windbreaker and a tie, they were both handsome, athletic, and serious-looking men who looked like they came straight from central casting, right down to the Brooks Brothers suits with the regulation small Customs Agent pins on their left lapels.

"Professor Elliot is out here from the Department of Energy in Washington, DC to assess our nuclear security situation."

Jake couldn't quite be sure, but he thought he heard Sandahl say under his breath, "What nuclear security?"

"I don't think it would be appropriate to discuss the matter here," said Smith.

"Oh, I'm sorry," responded McBride, looking embarrassed. "Perhaps we can go to the conference room upstairs."

The second floor of the building looked much like the first, with marine clerks busy working at computer terminals, looking at shipping manifests, and scheduling the arrival of vessels docking at Terminal L.

The conference room was decorated with a large map of the Port of Los Angeles, showing all of the terminals, the Coast Guard station, and the roads leading in and out of the Port. On the other side of the room, there was a picture window with a view of the channel down below. A large ship was pulling into one of the terminals across the channel. It was a beautiful southern California day, with a clear blue sky and a light sea breeze blowing. The conference table was old and made of solid oak or walnut; the chairs, also of wood, were not very comfortable, dating to a time before ergonomic design.

"So, Professor Elliot," said the older agent, Zeigler, "how can we help you?"

"Well," replied Jake, "I'd like you to go over with me your procedures and defenses against any attempt to smuggle illegal nuclear materials into the Port."

"We believe that we have dramatically increased homeland security measures at this port and that, in fact, it is the safest port in the United States," replied Agent Smith, his expression and tone aggressively neutral.

"I'm sure that you have taken all the precautions that have been mandated. But the reason I'm here is to look at our vulnerabilities and make recommendations for additional security measures to the Secretary in Washington. Perhaps we can start with your screening procedures."

Connoughton responded: "At this point five percent of the containers that come through the Ports of Los Angeles and Long Beach are subjected to passive radiation screening by one of the new Westec devices. As you may know, we successfully tested these devices last year at the Port of Oakland. By next year, we are scheduled to have 100% of the containers screened."

"Excuse me, but can I just interrupt for a second?"

"Yes, sir," replied Connoughton.

"What happens if you detect radiation?" asked Jake.

"Well, then we stop the container and inspect it."

"And what if the container contains bananas or smoke detectors or ceramics or some other substance that is naturally radioactive?"

"We don't stop those because that would cause a major problem with commerce and the shippers have objected to unreasonable delays of their consignments. With respect to naturally radioactive commodities, if you had allowed me to finish, I was about to tell you that we have random inspections of those loads."

"I'm sorry, Agent Connoughton, forgive my interruption." However, Jake was thinking he was an officious asshole.

Connoughton continued in his dry monotone. "We have, of course, other precautions. As you know, Congress has mandated increased security at the Port, but the matter is . . . complicated.

Eventually, as I'm sure you are aware, we are supposed to implement the Transportation Worker Identification Card program, but it will be some time before it is operational. At that point, every driver who enters the port and every longshoreman who works here will be identified using biometric screening every time he or she enters or leaves port property. Again, we do not want to have a situation arise where vital imports to this country are delayed because we don't have enough truck drivers to haul the commodities in and out of the port."

"Wait a minute, I'm confused," Jake started to say.

"What Agent Connoughton is attempting to point out," an obviously annoyed McBride interjected, "is that we believe that somewhere between thirty and fifty percent of the drivers that service the two ports down here are either undocumented immigrants, are not properly licensed, or would have disqualifying criminal offenses. So when we finally have a means of identifying drivers, we might lose half the damn truck drivers here. And so we, or perhaps I should say the higher ups, would rather not know who they really are."

"Aren't there enough qualified drivers?" asked Jake.

"Not at the price the big-box stores would like to pay for them, and they import the vast majority of the freight. The Administration in Washington and the big shippers are worried that, if we really secure the ports, the toys imported from China won't be on the store shelves in time for Christmas or would cost a few cents more to import. Sorry to be so frank about this, but it is a big problem." The frustration McBride felt was palpable. "Hell," McBride continued, "God forbid that we pay these guys enough to attract and retain a pool of qualified drivers. If we started doing that, the next thing you know is that we will have to start manufacturing all that crap in America again."

Jake laughed. "What a tragedy that would be." Smith and Connoughton were dead silent. Zeigler pursed his lips like he was trying to stop himself from laughing, but his eyes reflected the obvious enjoyment he was deriving from watching McBride let loose.

"May I continue?" Connoughton asked stiffly.

"By all means," responded Jake.

"In addition to the container screenings, the Coast Guard has armed patrols in the harbor. We are also keeping very close tabs on anyone coming to the port who is not engaged in port-related business activities. That means surveillance of anyone who might disrupt port activities for political purposes. Of course, we receive hourly updates of security threats from around the country. Should nuclear material be intercepted, we have an emergency response team available 24/7 to take possession of nuclear material, shield it, and dispose of it properly. Professor Elliot, that is the basic security system we have in place to protect the port complex. By the way, Agent Smith here will be available to liaison with you during your stay." Connoughton gestured toward Smith, who nodded slightly in recognition of this new—and obviously distasteful—job duty.

"Thank you for that overview, Agent Connoughton," Jake responded, summoning up the most gracious tone he could muster at the moment. "I have a few questions and then I'll let you get back to your business."

"Sure," responded Connoughton looking at his watch, obviously not pleased.

"How do you do security training for the Longshore personnel?"

"Frankly, we consider the risk of a breach of security that might result from integrating them in the security system outweighs the small amount of useful assistance they might provide. Anyway, we don't have the budget to do security training; that is the responsibility of the private employers."

"And are the employers mandated to do any security training."

"Not that I'm aware of."

"Oh, I see. Basically what you're telling me is that the workforce is getting no security training," responded Jake. He was dumbfounded. Weren't the dockworkers the eyes and ears of the port? McBride was similarly unimpressed, as he made a distinct snorting noise that floated over the room for a few embarrassing seconds.

"That's correct," replied Connoughton.

"Well, Professor Elliot, we need to get back to work. If there is anything we can assist you with during your stay, again please contact Agent Smith." Smith reached across the table and handed Jake his card.

"Thank you, gentlemen," Jake responded, taking the card and handing his back. "Until I get settled in with an office and phone, please feel free to contact me on my cell phone, which is on the card." Smith nodded.

"We assumed that your office would be located at the federal building downtown as we don't have any room here," said Connoughton matter-of-factly.

"Well, I was hoping to have a little space down here," Jake responded.

"No problem, we'll find him a spot somewhere," McBride interjected.

"That would be great."

The men got up and shook hands. The two younger agents went downstairs. McBride and Zeigler, who obviously knew each other well, walked down together catching up on family matters. Jake, finding himself ignored, took up the rear. As they passed by the workstations downstairs, Lee Sandahl turned around and shook Jake's hand.

"It was a pleasure to meet you, Mr. Sandahl," Jake said.

"Call me Lee," Sandahl responded. He leaned over and slipped a piece of paper in Jake's hand and whispered, "We need to talk. Call me."

Jake stuck the piece of paper with Sandahl's phone number in his pocket and followed the others out of the Terminal Control Center into the sunshine of another beautiful California morning.

Chapter 27

Jake waited patiently with his cappuccino for Lee Sandahl to arrive. It amazed Jake that, even in this gritty port city, there was a Starbucks, its hip green-and-mustard décor standing in contrast to the drab-looking businesses nearby. The customers were an eclectic mix of people, though few besides the young barista in dreadlocks and a miniskirt would meet anyone's definition of hip. Sitting across from Jake at a corner table was a morbidly obese man who was in a deep sleep. He was holding a well-used newspaper and he had a pair of smeared reading glasses on his nose. Evidently he had fallen asleep while reading the paper. He wore a blue windbreaker that was emblazoned with the word "Security" across its left front. He was so still that Jake wondered whether he was alive and briefly contemplated asking the barista if they should try and wake him up. Jake was staring at the man, trying to discern whether he was breathing, when Lee Sandahl walked up and said, "Penny for your thoughts, Doc?"

Jake looked up at Sandahl a little startled. "Hi, Lee, I'm glad you could come." He glanced at the fat man, who snorted and looked like he was about to wake but then fell right back to sleep, his glasses falling even further askew on his face.

"That guy's not Al-Qaeda, is he?" asked Lee.

"No, I think he's one hundred percent American patriot."

"So," said Lee, sitting down at Jake's table, "Let me get right down to it. Port security stinks and I'm worried that those hard asses from Customs are not giving you the full story."

"Will *you* give me the full story?"

"I'd be delighted to. To start, you're the first person who works for the government since 9/11 who has asked me my opinion about anything having to do with security at the port."

"You're not serious, are you?" asked Jake.

"I'm dead serious."

"Well, what about training?"

"What training? Before 9/11, the Customs Agents used to keep us filled in on what was going on. After that, the government brought in those cop types like you met the other day and they don't even talk to us. I get the impression that the government views us as a security problem, not an opportunity to use our knowledge to enhance security."

"So tell me what you think are the holes in port security?"

"Well, first of all, believe it or not, we used to open up a lot more containers to check on them than we do now. As the freight volumes increased in 2001 and 2002, they told us to stop because it was 'impeding commerce'. Then they took away the authority marine clerks have always had to order suspicious containers opened up. Only Customs can do that now. And get this . . . since everything has been computerized, we no longer actually see the shipping manifest, so we really don't know what's in the container any longer."

"Are you trying to tell me," Jake asked, "that after 9/11, you actually stopped breaking the customs seal and opening up any containers?"

"That's right. They didn't want to slow anything down," responded Lee.

"Who's 'they'?" Jake asked.

"Everybody there: the terminal operators, the steamship lines, the big shippers. I don't know, probably the government."

"What else?"

Lee took a long sip of his latté. "Basically management and the government guys look the other way when overweight containers come in."

"How can you guys tell that they're overweight?"

"The crane operators can tell by way the container feels as it's being lifted. Here's another thing. You can compare the tare weight, that's the empty weight of the container itself, to the gross weight reported on the shipping manifest. That gives you the weight of the commodity. There are some commodities, like cotton, where they know from experience the normal weight of a full container, so if it weighs 20,000 pounds more than the normal weight, you know something funky is going on"

"Aren't there scales on the cranes?"

"No, the only thing close to a scale is a safety device that stops the crane if the load weighs over 67,500 pounds."

"Wait a minute, Lee, doesn't a truck with a load have to weigh less than 80,000 pounds to be legal on the highway?"

"Yes. Well here's the math: the truck and trailer weigh around 26,000 pounds so that a container that weighs more than about 50,000 is going to be overweight. And a lot of them are overweight."

"And who certifies the weight of the container?" asked Jake.

"Well, actually, Professor . . . ."

Jake interrupted. "Call me Jake."

"OK, Jake, here's what happens. The outbound shipper, say the guy in China or India or wherever who loads the container at his factory, is the one who certifies the weight."

"So then what if the shipper understates the weight of the load?"

"That happens all the time. But if we open up a container, then they have to pay for additional Longshore labor and it slows things down. Management doesn't want to do that because it affects profits."

"So they don't ask you to report overweights?"

"On the contrary, they want us to look the other way."

"And the Customs agents and homeland security people?"

"They don't ask us about anything. I kind of think they don't trust us."

"Well how about training on homeland security issues? I assume you guys receive training on what to look for, how to deal with emergencies, and all that."

"Nothing. We have gotten no training whatsoever."

"So, leaving aside the question of who loses money on the deal, let's say that I'm a bad guy and I want to ship a dirty bomb to the United States. Now nuclear material weighs a lot, so if I can get away with understating the weight of the load and nobody systematically weighs the containers when they get here, then the load could pass right into the port. Is that really true?"

"I guess so, Jake. Here's the other thing. The government does two kinds of radiation testing. They have a big machine that they pass over the containers that supposedly works, but because it slows everything down, they only use it when a shipment for a totally new consignee comes in. The consignees that are repeat customers qualify for something called the "Favored Shipper Program" and are exempt from any radiation-detection screening."

"Are you trying to tell me that none of the containers being shipped to one of the big-box retailers are subjected to any serious screening?"

"That's exactly what I'm trying to tell you. So if you're a smart terrorist, what you need to do is to slip your stuff into one of the millions of containers being shipped to 'America's Favorite Store' and it won't get checked. We heard that the decision to create the Favored Shipper Program got made by the politicians in Washington. I mean those big retailers don't make all those political contributions because they care about the safety of our ports."

"What about on the trucking side? Can any trucking company come into the port?"

"Well, generally, all the driver needs to enter the port is a bill of lading showing that they are supposed to pick up the consignment."

"So to the best of your knowledge, nobody determines if the trucking companies are legit?"

"Not that I'm aware of, Jake."

"And what about the drivers? Does anybody check that they are properly licensed or if they are who they say they are?"

"Are you kidding? Who would check up on them? The scam artists that employ them? They certainly aren't going to pay us to do it, I can tell you that. What we've heard is that they're going to implement the TWIC card—you know, Transportation Worker Identity Card or something like that—which is supposed to make sure the drivers are real. But who knows when they will get around to doing it."

"So what you're telling me is that, in the meantime, someone can ship overweights to any port in the United States more or less freely and virtually anyone can drive a truck into the port to pick up the load."

"That's about the size of it," said Lee. "One more thing: they have a low-level screening process they do as the trucks pass through the gates on the way out of the terminal. But they were getting so many false positives from the freight that emits naturally occurring radiation, they turned down the power and now they get no positives whatsoever."

"That's reassuring," Jake responded.

Chapter 28

THE LADIZ BORDER CROSSING, BALUCH PROVINCE, IRAN
APRIL 14

The truck rumbled into the border crossing at Ladiz at almost midnight. Despite the lateness of the hour, there was a long queue of trucks waiting to pass over the border into Pakistan. The drivers, Jalil and Hooshmand, had taken turns driving, but they were dead tired. It had taken a day and a half to drive from Tehran and, as ordered, they hadn't stopped except for fuel and food. They had run out of things to talk about around Yazd, so while one drove the other dozed. Once they crossed the border, they would have to drive another day to get to Karachi, their destination.

Jalil, who was driving, woke up Hooshmand and told him that they were getting close to the border. Hooshmand had been dreaming and he was angry at being awakened.

"Stop muttering to yourself, you fool," said Jalil. "We're on duty."

"All right, all right."

They knew they would be waved through the Iranian border crossing because their superiors would have called ahead to make sure the border guards knew they were coming. They had been given very little information about the mission, except that they were to play the part of civilian truck drivers—which was easy since both had been civilian truck drivers until they had been drafted into the army—and that their cargo was both secret and critical to the defense of their country. They had speculated for hours about what was really in their cargo, since it was obvious that they were carrying more than olive oil.

Jalil and Hooshmand had joined the little convoy at dawn on the outskirts of Tehran, switching places with the original drivers, who were a pair of mean-looking Pasdaran types. The other vehicles in the convoy had stayed with them until just after they passed through the city of Qom and then had peeled off. Both men had driven the Tehran-to-Karachi road many times before during their civilian truck-driving days and they figured that it was that experience that had qualified them to be "handpicked," as their sergeant had told them, for such an important mission.

When they stopped on the Iranian side of the border crossing, they handed their papers and passports to the guard, who looked at them briefly. There was a Pasdaran officer present who nodded to Jalil and tapped the shoulder of the guard, who clearly understood that he was to pass this truck through. He quickly stamped their passports and bill of lading and waved them on.

On the Pakistani side of the border, they were treated like any other truck drivers coming in from Iran. Their load was inspected—although none too thoroughly—by Pakistani soldiers in dark green uniforms. The soldiers didn't look like the local Baluchi population, but came from somewhere else in Pakistan. They were big men with dark skin and thick mustaches. Although Jalil and Hooshmand could not possibly have known the reason why, as it was outside their range of experience, in fact this was a result of a deliberate policy the Pakistani government inherited from the British. The military was disbursed around the country in such a way as to keep soldiers from serving in their native areas. As such, they were more reliable in the event that the violent suppression of the civilian population should become necessary or they were needed to participate in one of Pakistan's frequent *coups d'etat*.

The border crossing process took less than two hours. In Tehran, just before they left, they had been given a cell phone and were told to call a telephone number in Pakistan when they were through Pakistani customs. Hooshmand punched in the number and when a woman answered, he said what they had instructed him to say: "I found your keys."

"Thank you," the woman said and hung up.

About an hour after crossing the border, they pulled into a truck stop for fuel and food. It was Hooshmand's turn to drive and Jalil's to sleep. Hooshmand had a strong coffee and they got back on the road. By dawn, they were just past the Hingol National Park and about 190 kilometers from Karachi. After a quick breakfast they switched drivers again.

By mid-morning they were on the outskirts of Karachi. The city was enormous, with a population of some thirteen million people and possessing one of the busiest ports in the world. As they got closer to the center of the city, the traffic became increasingly dense and chaotic, rivaling their native Tehran. Cars were honking their horns and mopeds moved in and out of traffic. The white-belted traffic officers looked like they came straight out of the British Raj.

They were supposed to pull the load into a warehouse in the Khadda District just across the Lyari River from Fish Harbor. Both Hooshmand and Jalil were familiar with the area because it was where a lot of importers of Iranian goods had their warehouses and break-bulk facilities.

They had little trouble finding the address. The sign above the gate said, in faded letters, "Rawalpindi Trading Co., Ltd." They stopped at a guard shack and a security officer checked their papers, pointed at the loading dock, and told them to pull in and unload. Although they didn't understand what he was saying, they got the basic idea. As they pulled slowly into the yard, the guard picked up a telephone and made a call.

A couple of warehouse workers came out and helped guide them into one of the loading bays. Jalil killed the engine and he and Hooshmand got out of the truck. More dockworkers appeared. They opened the roll-up doors of the loading bay and swarmed over the back of the truck, skillfully rolling the drums of olive oil onto a big forklift that drove them into the warehouse.

The two drivers were standing by the truck, smoking cigarettes, and watching the action when a small, balding man came up to them. "Brothers," he said in Farsi, "I am Mr. Habib, the manager here. Please accept my thanks for what you have done. You are a credit to the army. Here is something for you."

He handed them each an envelope. It contained money and railway tickets back to Iran. "Please," he continued, "follow me and I will take you to the office, where you will have a nice meal. Then one of my men will drive you to the train station."

Chapter 29

KŪH-I-BŪZPAR MOUNTAINS, FARS PROVINCE, IRAN, APRIL 14

They walked silently in single file on a goatherd's path that ran next to the river. Even though the moon was just a sliver, it lit up the terrain. OJ had never hiked anywhere at night and he was surprised at how bright it was once he got used to the dark. Their guns were locked and loaded. Amazingly, OJ was not tired. He puzzled at how this could be; they had left the submarine almost twenty hours before.

OJ had never felt so intensely aware of his physical surroundings. The crunch of the gravel under their boots sounded loud, as did the water in the river running over the rocks. He could hear lizards and rodents scurrying away as they approached. Once he looked up at the cliff above the river and saw an animal that looked like a dog stare at them and then quickly move away. Perhaps, OJ thought, it was a wolf or a jackal. But more than anything, he was aware of the emptiness of his surroundings, the intensity of the stars, and the silver-and-white sheen of the rocks in the reflected moonlight.

After an hour they stopped to get their bearings and report in. Gonzalez had a topo map of the area and a GPS unit, so he knew their exact location. He told them that they would reach their objective in about three hours.

They continued on. As the tension eased and the monotony increased, the physical strain of the day began to take its toll on OJ. In a matter of moments, he went from wide awake to exhausted, his body finally giving way under the combination of accumulated stress, lack of sleep, and physical exertion. OJ began to fantasize about falling asleep. He remembered watching a war movie on TV—he couldn't remember which one—where the dog-faced GIs fell almost instantly asleep whenever they got a moment's respite from the fighting. The muscles in OJ's back ached and his knees hurt; in fact, if he thought about it—and he was trying very hard not to—most every one of his muscles ached. He kept telling himself to take it one step at a time.

As the night wore on, they started to climb. The sound of the river became louder and its flow faster. The vegetation increased and they began to see trees—birches, scrub oaks, junipers—and grasses between the rocks. As if to add more insult to OJ's menu of injuries, they began to encounter boulders that they needed to scramble over. They had to help each other hoist their heavy backpacks over the rocks. OJ was now thoroughly exhausted. He kept himself going, motivated by that primordial male instinct not to appear weak in the presence of other men.

Around 4:00 am, the terrain flattened again and Gonzalez took another bearing of their location. He ordered them to climb out of the riverbed. When they got to the top, they were in a broad plateau with a meadow through which a small stream flowed, empting out into the river below. They found a dry area under a stand of trees and made camp. Amalakai was ordered to stand guard for the first two hours, while the rest of them slept. OJ laid out his ground cover and, not even bothering to remove his boots, collapsed. He was sound asleep within seconds.

"Hey, get up, sleepyhead." Somebody gently kicked OJ's shoulder with a boot and he opened his eyes. It was morning and OJ looked up into the hardened face of Chief Warrant Officer Murphy.

"What time is it?" asked OJ.

"0700, dude."

Great, thought OJ, three hours of sleep. OJ got up slowly. Murphy gave him a hand up.

"God, Chief, I feel like shit." OJ was stiff and sore in places where he never knew a person could feel pain.

"You look like shit, boy," Murphy said, with a lopsided toothy grin. He handed OJ a cup of coffee. It wasn't his usual morning cappuccino, but it was hot and felt great going down. He went to his pack and grabbed four ibuprofens, washing them down with the coffee.

"Where are the other two guys?" asked OJ.

"The Skipper and Ted went out about an hour ago to scout around and get our bearings."

"Did Amalakai get any sleep?"

"Maybe an hour."

"God, how do you guys do this?"

"Shit, OJ, it ain't easy. We just make it look that way."

"Well, that makes me feel slightly better."

"Hey, man, you're doing OK. I've seen worse, believe me."

Murphy handed OJ a MRE, which OJ picked through in a desultory way. He wasn't very hungry. He needed more sleep; more time for his body to recover. He wandered back toward the spot where he slept and this time unrolled his sleeping bag and lay back down. He stared up through the trees at the patches of blue sky and wispy clouds overhead. The trees were some kind of Aspen, whose leaves flashed in the morning breeze. The grass was green and cool. OJ's eyelids felt heavy and he told himself that he just needed to rest his eyes for a few minutes. He closed them and drifted away.

When OJ awoke, it was getting dark. He had slept all day. He saw the other three men sitting a few feet away, with their small tents erected. OJ brushed himself off and walked over to the little group. Gonzales looked up and flashed OJ a smile.

"Welcome back to the world, Hamsid."

"I'm sorry that I slept like that. I hope it didn't cause any problems."

"None whatsoever," replied Gonzales amiably.

"Commander," said OJ earnestly, "I want to pull my own weight."

"Well, OJ, that won't be a problem. We've big plans for you . . . don't we, boys?"

"Yessir," they replied in unison. They looked amused.

"Since you slept today and we didn't, tonight you can stand watch for the first six hours."

"And what does that involve?" asked OJ.

"You will walk the perimeter of our camp and get us if you have the slightest suspicion of any problem. You will carry a silenced weapon, which you may only fire in self-defense and under circumstances in which you have no time to provide warning. Now here's the hard part. Standing watch is really boring and many a GI has fallen asleep while on watch. Some have done so and gotten their throats slit. So don't fall asleep."

"OK, I've got the point."

Gonzales continued. "All right, let's talk about how we're going to proceed here. Back on the ship, we were given general information about this mission. We know that our guys suspect that the facility is a nuclear plant of some sort and that it has a military use. Now that we've had a chance to reconnoiter the area, we know that we're in a good spot for observation. After we've rested tonight, we are going to set up round-the-clock surveillance of the facility. HQ wants as much detail on this joint as we can put together. This will involve a two-on, two-off rotation. One keeps guard, the other observes. Hamsid will be with me. Ted, you will team with Murph. We're going to keep a detailed log of all observations. No detail is too insignificant. They want us to figure out the fuckers' routine and take photographs of everyone who enters and exits the facility. CENTCOM essentially wants us to do the kind of human intel that satellites can't do."

"How long are we going to be here?" asked Murphy.

"Good question, Murph. They haven't given us an extraction date, so I really can't answer that question. However, we've got two weeks of supplies. So if they want us to stay longer than that they will have to resupply us."

"Skipper, are we taking prisoners?" asked Amalakai.

"You mean intentionally?" Gonzales asked, looking at OJ. "Not that I know of. Who knows, that may change."

OJ walked the perimeter of their camp and across the meadow to where the trees ended and the rocky, dryer terrain began. The night was quiet, although from over the edge of the cliff that ran along the plateau he could hear an occasional noise drifting up from the facility below. Gonzales had supplied him with night-vision binoculars. While he was asleep, they had discovered a protected spot in the rocks from which they could observe the Iranians without exposing themselves. He told him to spend five minutes each hour there and to record his observations.

His watch began at 7:00 pm as the men finished eating and the last rays of the sun disappeared over the western edge of the world. OJ walked toward the blind. When he looked back, he could hardly see the camp, which had been expertly camouflaged by the SEALS. Within fifteen minutes, the darkness was complete and the stars once again began to shine. OJ knelt in the blind and looked down below. It was very dark inside the compound, but the perimeter fence was brightly lit and so he could see the outline of the Iranian facility. When he turned on the night-vision binoculars and brought them to his eyes, the entire area lit up like it was noon. Through the intense greenish light, he could clearly see buildings, equipment, and vehicles in the compound as well as some people moving around. Near the front of the facility, just as in the aerial photographs they had studied, there were barracks for the garrison. OJ put his observations down in the notebook. Nothing seemed unusual, although he really had no idea what "usual" would look like when observing a clandestine Iranian nuclear facility.

OJ moved quietly out of the blind and back onto the meadow. He made his rounds and the next time he looked at his watch, only seven minutes had gone by. He now understood what Gonzales was talking about. Keeping alert and concentrating when there was no mental stimulus was difficult. For a restless mind like OJ's, it was especially hard. He kept focused by silently reciting the suras of the Koran he had learned as a child. OJ found the moment surprisingly moving:

the beautiful songs flowing in his mind as he walked on the ground of a homeland he had never known. Here he was, a stranger in a strange land; yet it was the land where countless generations of his ancestors had walked.

Somehow OJ got through the night and stayed awake and alert. He sipped coffee from a thermos, which helped keep him from getting drowsy. A few times he heard noises that startled him, but decided they were animal, not human, sounds. His hourly trips to the blind were uneventful. As it got later in the night, there was less and less activity in the compound. At around 2:00 am, he observed a vehicle enter the facility and park in front of what looked like the administration building. There was a rotation of guards. OJ wrote it all down.

At 5:00 am, as the first light began to show in the east, the other members of the team woke up. OJ was totally spent and needed sleep badly. Gonzales, looking none the worse for wear, said that he and OJ would have the first twelve-hour shift on watch. He ordered Murphy and Amalakai to clean and oil the weapons, get water for their camp, dig a small garbage pit, and further camouflage the area. Their camp was well hidden behind a shallow dip in the land. From more than a few feet away it looked as though nothing was there.

When it was full daylight, Gonzales and a bone-tired OJ made their way over to the blind. Now OJ could see where the facility was in relationship to the surrounding area.

The scene before them looked very familiar. During their training, they had studied hundreds of photographs of the facility taken by US and Israeli drones and spy satellites. Just as it appeared in the photographs, the Iranian compound lay in a ravine that opened up to a large valley. In the distance, OJ could see a road that ran parallel to the fence in front of the facility. At the entrance, there was a concrete guard tower. Essentially, there was only one way in and out, with the sides of the ravine forming steep walls that came to a point at the rear of the facility. Up on the ridgeline were two more guard towers. On the side of the ravine where they were located, the guard tower was off to the right and at a slightly lower elevation on the plateau. Next to it ran a pipe encased in concrete which, from studying the aerial photography of the site, brought water to the facility from the river behind them. There was a jeep by the tower. Hopefully, they were out of the view of the guards stationed there. On the other side of the ravine, another guard tower was in their line of sight. They would have to be careful going in and out of the blind during daylight hours. Once in the blind they were very well hidden, enclosed by two giant boulders leaning against one another. Except for a few moments every day when the sun was right above them, the floor of the blind lay in the shadows.

Gonzales and OJ set up the observation equipment. They had a digital camera with a large telephoto lens mounted on a tripod. The images were uplinked via a laptop computer and satellite phone to an AWACS plane circling high above the Persian Gulf, allowing the photographs they took to reach various destinations around the world nearly instantaneously. They also had a video camera with similar capabilities running on a constant loop. Their equipment was powered by a solar trickle charger that they had carefully hidden in the rocks.

Once they had finished setting up, OJ and Gonzales got settled in for their shift. Prior to their departure, OJ had received six months of intensive training on nuclear-systems development, equipment design, and nuclear-explosives technology. The purpose of the training was to enable him to make sense of what he was observing in the ravine down below. OJ did not feel particularly confident about how well he had absorbed the information he received during his training.

Their initial observations would involve learning the routine of the facility: how security worked, who was coming and going, and what kind of work was being performed at Bala Deh. Based on this information, military and intelligence analysts would build an assessment of the strengths and vulnerabilities of the suspected Iranian nuclear plant and develop contingency plans for how to exploit those vulnerabilities.

For the first couple of hours, they watched perhaps thirty soldiers in the barracks compound go in and out of a building. It was obviously the mess hall. They took close-up photos of the soldiers as they entered and left the building. After breakfast, a few soldiers stood around a trash can smoking cigarettes and chatting.

"Relaxed bunch," commented OJ.

To which Gonzales, lifting his arms as if aiming an imaginary rifle, replied, "Piece of cake," and winked at OJ.

At 8:15 am, a loud whistle blew and about two dozen workers came out of the central processing building. They waited around on the open field that stretched between the processing building and the administration building. Fifteen minutes later, a bus arrived and discharged, by OJ's count, thirty-five men. The men who were waiting got on the bus, which turned around and drove back out of the camp.

The workers looked like common laborers to OJ and, as it turned out, that's exactly what they turned out to be. They milled around smoking and talking to one other in the area where the bus dropped them off. A few minutes later, a couple of soldiers showed up and organized the men into two lines. They were almost immediately joined by two men in civilian clothes who walked across the dusty compound from the administration building. The soldiers checked the identification of the workers and frisked them in a desultory way. Finally, about twenty of the men were led over toward the gravel pit and climbed down ladders. The others went into the large processing facility located next to the gravel pit. The processing building was substantial, built out of concrete blocks with a corrugated metal roof.

Within fifteen minutes, the men in the pit were operating jackhammers and backhoes to loosen the gravel. They were loading the loose aggregate onto boxes that moved up the side of the pit on a huge conveyor belt and headed to the processing plant above.

By mid-morning, flatbed trucks began to arrive at a loading dock next to the processing plant. Workers began loading pallets of what looked like 100-pound bags of concrete onto the trucks, while the drivers stood around waiting for the signal to leave. Through their high-powered binoculars, OJ could read some of the writing on the bags. It said, "Faisal Concrete." OJ observed that, in addition to being stopped at the front gate to present their papers, each driver was briefly questioned and frisked by security personnel.

"They sure have a hell of a lot of security for a concrete plant," OJ commented.

"Agreed," replied Gonzales tersely.

When the trucks were loaded, they headed down the dusty road out of the camp.

At noon, there was a loud whistle and the workers stopped for a break. The men in the pit climbed out and were joined by the workers from inside the processing plant. They gathered near the loading dock, where some of the men began boiling water for tea on small braziers. Then they sat on their haunches drinking tea and eating their lunches. OJ could hear snippets of laughter and voices drifting up from the valley floor below. At 12:45, the whistle blew again and the men returned to work.

The afternoon routine was nearly identical to the morning. OJ and Gonzales took turns taking photographs of the work going on in the gravel pit, the trucks as they came and went, and the action on the loading dock. Gonzales was particularly interested in the shift changes of soldiers manning the guard towers and their level of readiness. They kept detailed notes of their impressions and observations. According to Gonzales, nothing, however trivial, was too insignificant to report. In any event, thought OJ, at least all this busy work helped make the time pass. They didn't talk to one other much, but quietly and efficiently went about their work. Although OJ had slept the day before, he was tired beyond exhaustion and was counting the minutes before he could go to bed.

Finally, at 5:00 pm, after more trucks picking up concrete had come and gone, the whistle blew, the conveyor belt from the pit to the processing plant was turned off, and work stopped for the day. The men from the pit, now dusty and dirty, were joined by the workers from the processing plant on the "parade ground," as Gonzales had named it. The bus that brought them to the plant in the morning pulled through the gate and picked them up a few minutes later. Another group of workers got off the bus; the evening shift. It was a smaller group. There were only twenty-two of them. After they were searched by the security officers, they all went into the processing plant.

At precisely 6:00 pm, Murphy and Amalakai arrived for their shift at the blind. Gonzales briefed them on the day's activities. OJ did not envy the "Nightcats," as Gonzales dubbed Murphy and Amalakai, who had to spend all night staring through night-vision equipment.

Gonzales and OJ made their way back to their base camp, trying to stay out of view of the guard tower further down the plateau. It had been another extraordinarily long day for OJ and he went to sleep without even bothering to eat or wash.

The Nightcats observed very little of interest. A third bus arrived at midnight and disgorged some fifty workers who looked decidedly white-collar. They were led to the cave entrance where large steel blast doors were opened and they were escorted in for the night. The doors were located under a cleft in the cliff face, which would make them undetectable from the air. The Guard detail seemed to change at midnight. Every once in a while a worker from inside the processing plant would walk across to the administration building.

On the third night, just after 10:00 pm, Gonzales shook OJ out of a deep sleep. "Get up, Hamsid . . . let's go. Something's happening down at the blind." OJ fumbled to get his boots on and ran to catch up with Gonzales.

When they got to the blind, Amalakai said, "Hey, Skipper, you got to see what's going on down there. Something's happening.

He handed Gonzales the night-vision goggles, while he continued snapping pictures. Murphy handed OJ another pair.

"Hey, OJ, what do you make of that?" asked Gonzales, pointing across the ravine to a spot near the place were the two cliff sides met. The blast doors were opened, revealing a pale greenish light emanating from the hole in the mountain.

They waited and watched. Two men came out of the cave. One was a civilian in a white lab coat, obviously some kind of scientist. The other was a military officer. The officer had a cell phone or some other communication device that he was speaking into. A few minutes later an all-terrain forklift arrived carrying a large wooden crate chained onto its steel forks. Workers pried the top off the crate, exposing an inner metal container. At the direction of the scientist, the workers put on respirators and then the metal cover was unbolted. The inner metal box contained what looked to OJ like sand. The color was hard to make out in the greenish phosphorescent light of his night-vision device. The scientist put on a respirator and inspected the sand with a small device of some sort. He nodded and the workers carefully reattached the metal top and secured the wooden cover of the crate.

Gonzales turned to OJ. "Hey, OJ, you snap the pictures. I want to look at something else. Hand me the binoculars."

OJ positioned himself behind the camera. When he looked in the viewfinder, at first all he could see was a small part of one of the blast doors. He pointed the camera at the scientist and the officer, who were smoking cigarettes and talking. OJ snapped several dozen pictures of the two men. With the powerful telephoto lens he was able to get very clear close-ups of each of their faces. The scientist looked familiar to him.

"Hey, Commander, I've seen Doctor Weirdo down there before, but I can't place him." He drew a blank on the other guy. He moved the telephoto lens carefully around the interior of the cave, which was dimly lit.

There it was: a box barely visible on the wall about four feet off the ground. OJ snapped several photos of the box. It was in the shadows and although OJ could make out writing on it, he could not read it clearly in the poor light. The analysts would have to digitally enhance the photo to make sense of it.

The operator carefully maneuvered the forklift into the cave. The officer and the scientist followed and, once they were inside, the big steel blast doors were shut. When the last bit of light faded, the mountainside looked like a wall of solid black.

"So what happened before we got here?" asked Gonzales of the two SEALS. Gonzales sounded tired and tense.

"Well, Sir," Murphy answered, "the workers inside the concrete factory moved that big crate on to the loading dock and the forklift came to get it. Then the guy drove it over to the place where those dudes opened the door of the cave."

"OK, you two write it down and we'll send it to OJ's spook friends so they have something to read with their Cheerios at breakfast."

The next morning Gonzales shifted the assignments. He and OJ would become the Nightcats and Murphy and Amalakai would work the days. Although the day was dead quiet except for the mining activity and some deliveries, at night the place was humming with activity—especially in and around the cave.

At 10:22 pm, a truck tractor was driven in front of the blast doors. Several crates containing sealed tubes were unloaded and transported into the cave under the careful supervision of Dr. Weirdo. On the side of each one of the crates was a skull and crossbones and a warning in Farsi. Gonzales asked OJ to translate.

"It says, 'Extreme Danger, Nitric Acid, Poison, Corrosive'."

After they moved the chemicals into the cave, the men unloaded five approximately six-foot-high square-wooden containers. They also had an inscription in Farsi, which read, "Handle with Extreme Care. Fragile." The unloading process was painfully slow and took most of the night. Gonzales and OJ recorded it and uplinked it to the AWACs.

Chapter 30

The Customs Agents provided Jake a little cubicle in an out–of–the–way corner of their office. They told him that they would provide him any assistance that he needed, but they didn't mean it. After all, he was there to assess their performance. He didn't expect much help and he didn't get any. However, they left him alone, which was fine by Jake. He had clearance to go anywhere on port property and he used it to his full advantage. He spent time carefully observing port activities, from the unloading of cargo on the dockside to the loading of containers on to trucks and railroad cars.

Jake felt it was important to get to know the people who worked at the port: the longshoremen, truck drivers, crane operators, clerks, and mechanics that made the place tick. At first he got nowhere. They treated him with suspicion and would not open up to him.

When Jake asked Lee Sandahl about the cold shoulder he was getting, Sandahl laughed and told him that the longshoremen thought he was a spy for the bosses or the government. In the last labor dispute three years earlier, when the employers had locked out the workers, the federal government dropped any semblance of neutrality and openly took the side of the employers, threatening to run the ports with the military if the union didn't surrender to management's terms. Sandahl told Jake that the only way that he was going to get the workers to trust him would be if someone in the union vouched for him. Sandahl was a third-generation longshoreman and his grandfather had been one of the founders of the Union in the 1930s. He was extremely well-regarded on the waterfront. "For some reason," he told Jake, "I trust you. I'll take you around."

The difference was immediate. Sandahl, who seemed able, through some mysterious means, to leave his job whenever he needed to attend to union business, accompanied Jake everywhere. The older man seemed to know everybody. In Sandahl's presence, it was as if Jake had the key to a lock and it changed everything in terms of how people treated him. Where the secretaries had formerly been cold to Jake, they now even flirted with him. The clerks would drop what they were doing and explain in minute detail how freight operations worked. One of the crane operators took him up into the cab or his gantry crane and allowed him to watch while he unloaded containers from a ship. Everyone started to call him "Doc." He'd be walking somewhere and people he'd never met would wave to him and yell, "Hey, Doc."

One day, Sandahl invited Jake to have lunch with a friend of his, an ex-Catholic Priest who was now an organizer with the Teamsters Union. They met at a local restaurant called "Bubbles," which was named after its proprietress, an ex-stripper who was now at least seventy-five years old. She was still a bleached blonde and had a young woman's figure but her face showed her age. She worked every day running the cash register and kept up a steady stream of commands to the staff and customers alike. She called everybody "honey" or "babe" and flirted in a self-mocking way with the young men. Whatever else one could say about Bubbles, the barbeque was damned good.

When he had been a priest, Patrick Johnston was known as "Father Pat" by the members of his poor, Latino-immigrant parish. The young priest soon discovered it was not his parishioners' lack of faith that was their major problem; it was their lack of a living wage.

He became an outspoken advocate for the working poor. He marched in the "Justice for Janitors" strike in the mid-1990s and it was soon evident to him that his true calling was not religion, but social justice. When the Archbishop of Los Angeles became embroiled in a labor dispute with immigrant gravediggers, Father Pat spoke out from the pulpit in favor of the gravediggers and criticized the Church. He was quietly invited to leave the priesthood. The Teamsters offered him a job organizing truck drivers at the Port. He spoke Spanish fluently and he was well known in the community. Johnston loved his work and the drivers loved him. The problem is that he was trying to organize 18,000 immigrant drivers all by himself.

Johnston was a slight man with a pointy beard and glasses. He looked like an intellectual but his wry sense of humor was anything but effete. Jake felt immediately at home with Pat Johnston. He told Jake that if he was serious about understanding the port, he ought to move into the neighborhood. Jake thought that was a pretty good idea. He was getting sick of the long commute back to his parents' house anyway and he thought that it would allow him to get a better feel of the rhythms of the port and its surrounding community.

Jake asked the two men if they thought that some of their respective union members would be willing to keep track of certain things for him.

"What type of things?" asked Johnston.

"I understand the drivers can tell when a container is overweight. I'd like your drivers to keep a log of overweights and the commodity they are hauling so I can develop a profile of what commodities are typically overloaded."

"Yeah, sure, I see what you're getting at. But the drivers can only feel gross overweights because it makes the brakes more difficult to operate. If you really want to know if containers are overweight on a systematic basis, then you have to weigh them at a truck scale. They ripped out most of them years ago so that no one could really complain about overloaded trucks. There are commercial scales down the road, but they cost money and the drivers can't afford to use them."

"What does it cost?"

"About ten bucks."

"Well, I don't have the time or the budget to pay for it on a systematic basis. Even so, Pat, if I were to give you $1,000, do you think some of your guys would be willing to pass through the scales and keep a record of the weight and what commodity they were hauling whenever they had a hunch that the load was too heavy?" asked Jake.

"They might, Jake, but it would have to be kept really confidential. If the shippers or their brokers find out they are weighing the loads, they will get blackballed."

"It will be completely anonymous. To tell you the truth, I need the confidentiality as much as they do. If Washington found out I was getting drivers to document overloads, I'd probably get the boot."

"I can tell you this, Jake," said Johnston, "those drivers hate overloads. They cause accidents and are just another way of ripping them off. So I think I will have no problem finding drivers who will help."

Jake turned to Sandahl. "What about your gantry crane operators? Would they be willing to keep track of overloads for me?"

"Probably, Doc, so long as we told them the purpose was to fuck with the boss."

"Whatever works," said Jake, gesturing with the rib bone he was gnawing on.

Chapter 31

Hannah and Shoshana settled into their new life. A house had been let in a middle-class neighborhood in Van. The Kurdish section of the Mossad already operated an electronic repair shop in Van's business district, from which they ran agents in and out of neighboring Iran and maintained contact with the local Kurds. The Jewish state and the Kurds had long been regional allies, although Israel did nothing to facilitate or support Kurdish nationalism in Turkey. To do so would have been to imperil the IDF's close working relationship with the Turkish army.

Hannah had been given six months of intensive training in the Turkish language at the Army's foreign language institute in Haifa. She lived and breathed Turkish round the clock. At the institute, they spoke only Turkish; no Hebrew or English was permitted. She learned to read and write passably in Turkish, but certainly not at the university level.

In her university classes, she would play the role of the quiet, pious, and studious Islamic type—as she had done in her last mission in Iran—which would limit her interaction with her fellow students, most of whom were aggressively secular Turks. She would wear a *hijab* and modest clothing, making her harder to identify but ironically, in Westernized Turkey, would make her stand out among her fellow university students. Wearing the attire of a religious Muslim was still something of a statement in Turkey, but was becoming far more common as the Islamic fundamentalist movement sweeping the Arab world took hold among the Turks.

No amount of modest attire, however, could stop men from noticing her. She had large, dark, expressive eyes and a sensual mouth. Her smile lit up a room. Her olive skin was clear and she wore no makeup —which was also the case back home. Her hair, which peeked out from under the *hijab*, was jet black; she was one of those Sephardic women with thick hair in tight, wavy ringlets. She could not help it: men were drawn to her and women envied her. Several times she had been approached by male students but had declined their invitations.

After a month in class and settling in to their routines, the next phase of the plan was implemented. Hannah mailed a letter to General Yazdi in Tehran that had been carefully composed by the team's controllers in Tel Aviv.

My Esteemed General Yazdi,

I don't know if you remember me, but my name is Vashti Palmeni and I met you on the train from Tehran to Van in Turkey last year. I am a college student here and a devout Muslim. I have grown increasingly disenchanted with the treatment of Shiites and all religiously observant Muslims here.

Most importantly, when we met on the train, you challenged me to think about what I can do for my people. I have thought deeply about what you said and prayed to Allah, blessed be he, for the answer.

I would like to help our people but I am uncertain as to the best course of action for a person like me.

I know that you are a very busy man, but perhaps you can offer me further advice.

With greatest respect,
Vashti Palmeni

The weeks went by and there was no response. Shoshana and the other members of the team, Zvi and Benni, waited patiently. Zvi and Matti took the roles of her father and uncle and worked in the electronics store. Avi Gerstner had warned them in Tel Aviv that this type of mission sometimes moved very slowly. They assumed that, if Yazdi was interested in her, he would probably have his people observe her. They might wait six months or a year to make contact, if ever.

Hannah continued to establish and deepen her cover. She regularly attended the Shiite Mosque and went to meetings of the Muslim Students Association. She was very reserved, like most of the young religious women, and spoke to men only when spoken to. At the meetings, they discussed politics and culture and sometimes had guest speakers. One evening a new woman came to the meeting. Hannah noticed her. She wore a gray *hijab* and dress that matched her pale eyes and alabaster skin. She sat near Hannah in the back of the meeting room and listened politely to the speaker, who was discussing the oppression of Muslims by the Indians in Kashmir.

As they were having refreshments at the end of the evening, the young woman came up to Hannah and introduced herself as Niaz. She was new at the University and this was her first meeting of the Muslim Students Association. She seemed quite friendly and asked Hannah if she would like to go out with her for coffee. Hannah readily agreed to go with Niaz.

The women walked to a small coffee house a few blocks from the university campus. On the way, Hannah and Niaz exchanged small talk. Niaz came from a large Persian family that had just moved to Van from Yukesova in eastern Van province near the Iranian border. Hannah, in turn, recounted her cover story for Niaz.

The two women found a small table and ordered coffee and some baklava. Hannah had always loved baklava, although she never ate it without feeling a little guilty for consuming the rich, sweet, filo pastry. After the waiter brought their food, Niaz leaned in close to Hannah.

"Vashti," Niaz said in a quiet voice, "I have a message for you from General Yazdi. He wants to know if you are prepared to do your part for your people."

"Oh, Niaz," responded Hannah earnestly, trying her best to sound surprised and swept away by the emotion of the moment. "I had thought that my letter never got to the General or that he had forgotten me. I felt so ridiculous."

"The General was impressed by you and happy that you contacted him. It is a great privilege that he has chosen you as a possible candidate for service to our cause."

"What happens now?" asked Hannah.

"Vashti, we will be contacting you soon. First, our superiors will interview you and if you pass the interview, we will bring you to one of our bases for training. In the meantime, think about your commitment to the cause. Pray at the mosque and ask Allah for His guidance. The rewards for serving our Islamic movement are limitless, the dangers are great, the sacrifices many. Think about these things between now and the time we contact you again." Niaz picked up her purse and looked for something in it.

"When will you contact me?" asked Hannah.

"The group I work with is very secret and very careful and I cannot tell you when we will contact you again. It will not be long. But when the time comes, you must be prepared psychologically, physically, and spiritually." Niaz leaned across the table and took Hannah's hand in hers, her smile the picture of serenity and compassion. "I must go now," she said and with her other hand placed a small envelope in Hannah's hand and closed her fingers around it. "Please consider this a small token of appreciation from the General."

"But I couldn't accept a gift," said Hannah.

"But you must. It implies no obligation on your part. And now," Niaz said, rising from her chair, "I really must be going. May Allah be with you, Vashti." The girl smiled her sweet smile again at Hannah, turned around, and left the coffee house.

"So, Hannala, when your *Saba* took you to fish at the Kineret, did he talk to you about setting the hook?"

"If he did, Avi, I don't remember."

"OK then, I think you will remember this from your fishing days.

You put the bait on the hook, you cast the line into the water and you wait. No? Then when you get a nibble, you set the hook. I know this is what your *Saba* told you, even if you don't remember now. You see, Hannah, when you feel the fish bite, you suddenly pull back on the fishing pole. But you can't pull too hard or the fish gets scared and swims away. And unless it is a particularly stupid fish, they don't bite twice. We are at that point with our fish, our friend General Yazdi. He's taken his nibble at our bait—that's you, Hannala—and now we need to set the hook and land the *mumzer*."

Hannah looked across the kitchen table at Avi Gerstner sipping his coffee. Shoshana was bustling around their kitchen like she really was Hannah's mother. She put a bowl of cut-up fruit on the table and some pieces of bread. Then she brought them some yogurt—thick Turkish yogurt—flavored with herbs.

"It's been a week, Avi, and nothing has happened."

"We have the girl's photograph, but we did not follow her because we did not want to tip off the Iranians."

"Is she anyone we know?"

"No, but the story she told you was completely false."

"So we wait."

Shoshana sat down at the table with them. "Avi, it's so nice of you to come all the way to Turkey to sit down and have a meal with us."

Chapter 32

Jake sat in his windowless cubicle at the Customs office and thought about the container-weight problem. He had hoped to find a pattern, but none was emerging. Jake had no idea how many containers were overloaded, but it was obviously a lot. In Jake's opinion, there was no question that proper security procedures would require that every container be weighed and all overloads be inspected. More critically, each container should be profiled for its expected weight, given the type of commodity. Something light weight and relatively bulky, like stuffed animals for children, which was expected to weigh 20,000 pounds, should not weigh 30,000 pounds.

Jake reasoned that if he was a terrorist and wanted to smuggle in nuclear material, he would choose a commodity that had a natural radioactive signature and that didn't weigh much. That way, the extra weight could be added to the load and it would still not make the container weigh more than the maximum permissible weight. Jake drew up a list of naturally occurring radiation materials—called "NORM" by scientists—and compared it to the list of commodities entering the terminal. What he came up with was a nuclear smuggling profile that could be used to target enforcement activities. It took him three feverish weeks of solid work to do it, but Jake drafted a comprehensive memorandum to the Secretary of Energy laying out his proposal and sent it off to Washington. He received a polite response from the Secretary thanking him and informing him that his recommendations were being taken under advisement. If further information was needed from him, the Department would let him know.

He also gave the memorandum to Connoughton and Smith, who thanked him and told him politely that they appreciated his efforts and would pass his paper up the chain of command at TSA.

It was obvious that Jake's proposal was headed straight for the dead-letter office.

Feeling desperate, he did something that could certainly get him fired and maybe sent to jail. He showed the memorandum to Lee Sandahl. He explained to Lee that it could get them both in very hot water if anyone found out. Sandahl told him he was already on a million government lists because of a lifetime of labor activism and left-wing politics. "They probably have a couple of hundred pages on me from Chicago in 1968 alone," Sandahl said. As they sat in the corner of Starbucks, Sandahl read the paper straight through.

"Jake, this makes total sense. It's what ought to be done. But nothing will happen, I guarantee you. You know what my old man told me on my first day at the job?" Sandahl asked rhetorically. "He said that in this industry, the employers will always do the right thing as long as there's no other alternative. So I don't think anything will happen until a catastrophe is staring them squarely in the face."

Jake took a sip of his latte and stared up at the ceiling. "Absolutely amazing. This isn't rocket science."

"But it takes time and money, Jake, and they want to make as much of it as possible around here and nothing, not even a real terrorist threat, is allowed to get in the way."

"OK, then, how about this?" asked Jake, "If I was to draw up a list of commodities and their expected weights, would your guys be willing to call you when a load felt heavier than expected?"

"Yeah, I think they would."

Chapter 33

RAWALPINDI TRADING CO., KARACHI, PAKISTAN, APRIL 18

Anwar Habib, the cover name by which he was known to his subordinates at the Rawalpindi Trading Company, was certain that the transfer of the spent nuclear fuel from the barrels in which they had arrived to their overseas shipping containers would be a delicate operation. Although it was risky, his superiors in Tehran felt it was necessary to bring in a team of specialists for the operation. They did not wish to take any unnecessary risk of an accidental leak of radiation occurring while the material was still in Karachi. Pakistani-Iranian relations were a very sensitive matter. The Pakistanis were very deft at playing both sides; overtly they were supportive of the Americans, covertly they had been instrumental in supplying Iran nuclear technology. Although there was much cooperation between the Pasdaran and the ISI, this operation was totally black—the Pakistanis knew nothing about it. They would certainly not approve of the ultimate aims of this mission.

The three nuclear technicians were flown into Karachi on an Air Pakistan tourist flight. Naturally, they could not bring with them the tools necessary to transfer the spent fuel safely. Such equipment would have to be obtained—legally or otherwise—from sources in Pakistan. Fortunately, Habib, in his many years as the Pasdaran's station chief in Karachi, had developed many contacts. Among those were members of Karachi's organized crime gangs. Habib liked working with them. They were absolutely trustworthy, totally efficient, and used violence only when necessary. However, they would not hesitate to kill if circumstances demanded it.

Habib arranged to meet with his contact, a man he knew only as "Abu," at a small restaurant in a slum on the outskirts of Karachi. It was a place of dirty streets, half-naked, skinny children, and shanties covered with corrugated iron roofs and cardboard. Farm carts mingled with motorbikes and cars. The whole area smelled of spices, sewage, and discarded food. The police presence was minimal, as these neighborhoods had long been ceded to the control of local crime bosses.

Although it was not strictly necessary, Habib brought with him one of the employees of the Rawalpindi Trading Company, a quiet older ex-soldier named Hassan, who was his bodyguard. When dealing with Abu, Mr. Habib always felt that it was necessary to project the right image—one of strength and confidence.

It was nearly 9:00 pm when Habib and Hassan entered the restaurant. The walls were painted a dirty green color and it was lit by a couple of naked fluorescent lights strung from the ceiling. The floor was bare concrete. There were a few advertising posters on the walls and a well-used hookah on a table in the corner. On one side of the restaurant was an old wooden counter covered with hammered tin. The weak lights cast everything in shadow.

Behind the counter was a little man with a thin moustache and dark, almost black eyes. Otherwise the place was empty. Habib went up to the man and asked if he might speak with Abu. He added that he was expected. Hassan stood behind him, his arms crossed. The man said nothing, wiped his hands on a greasy towel and went to the back of the restaurant through a doorway from which strings of glass beads hung. Above the doorway was a blue enamel sign with white letters that said "WC." The beads made a slight tinkling sound as the man left. Mr. Habib turned around and said quietly to Hassan, "Be alert." Hassan nodded almost imperceptibly. After a few minutes, the little man returned and told them to take a seat at one of the tables. "Abu," he said, "will be here in a few minutes."

The two men sat down. The little man brought a tray with a large brass teapot and two clear glass cups that each held a sugar cube. He placed the glasses on the table and proceeded to pour the tea into the glasses from high above, filling them without spilling a drop. Every man, thought Habib, is proud of his skills, however humble they may be. The tea smelled strongly of mint. As they waited in silence, Habib and Hassan drank the scalding, sweetened tea in small sips. Habib noticed that Hassan would occasionally adjust his body, apparently unconsciously checking that his gun was still in its shoulder holster.

A few minutes later an old and dirty Mercedes sedan pulled up in front of the restaurant. Three men got out. Two were young toughs, who looked up and down the street. They walked into the restaurant and sat down at a table near the front door, telling the man behind the counter to bring them some Arak. A third man then got out of the car. He was perhaps sixty, short, with a graying beard and a big belly. He wore an old brown suit with a white shirt opened at the collar.

Habib and Hassan stood up at their table. The man strode toward them.

"Abu, my brother," Habib said.

"*Salaam Alekim*, my friend," replied Abu, hugging Habib.

"Let's sit and talk business," said Habib, gesturing to the table. The men sat. Abu took out a pack of cigarettes and offered them to the men. They declined. Abu lit one for himself with a gold lighter.

"Abu, I have a list of things that I need." Habib took out a piece of paper from the inside of his suit jacket and handed it to Abu.

Abu unfolded the paper and looked at the list. "What is all this?"

"Look, you will have to find these things in a special place. There is a business near the University called 'M.V. Khan Company.' They process the radioactive waste from X-ray machines and cancer treatments at hospitals. If you go there, you will find the things on the list. Who knows? After you're done, maybe the building will accidentally burn down. Mr. Khan will get the insurance money. Everybody's OK. You follow?"

"Why do you need me to steal it? Why not just buy it?" Abu asked.

"Because some of this equipment is tracked by the government. If the police bother to investigate and think it's a theft, they will look for it to be sold on the black market. But we won't sell it. When we finish with it, we will bury it out in the desert somewhere." Habib gestured with his hands as if he were a magician making something disappear. "Poof, Gone."

Abu smiled. "How will we know what these particular machines look like? I mean, it's not like you're asking me to find you one of those fancy British cars. What do you call it? Oh, yes, a Jaguar."

"We will give you photos of what we're looking for. You will have no problem."

"OK, this is very complicated, my friend. It will cost you a lot of money."

"How much?" asked Habib. He liked bargaining with Abu. "Go easy on me, I'm a regular customer."

"OK, because it's you, I'll give you a big discount. My price is $250,000 US. That's for everything, all expenses paid. If you like to pay in Swiss Francs or Euros, that's OK, too." Abu gestured to the man at the counter. "Bring me coffee and some sweets."

"You kill me, Abu. That's too much. How about $150,000 US?"

"Hey, for that, you should steal it yourself," replied Abu, who laughed, revealing a gold incisor. "I tell you what, because I like you, $200,000 US, small bills. OK?"

"Done," said Habib, "you drive a hard bargain, you old thief." He handed Habib a briefcase containing five hundred $100 US banknotes. "A down payment, my friend, 50,000 US dollars, the balance to be paid upon delivery."

A fortnight later, just after dusk, a small Chinese-made Hino delivery truck pulled into the freight yard of the Rawalpindi Trading Company. Abu's old Mercedes drove in after it. Habib came out of his office to meet them along with several of his men from the warehouse. They quickly guided the truck to the loading dock and began to unload its contents. Abu had obtained everything Habib had requested: radiation suits, Geiger counters, something called a "sealed-drum transfer unit," lead-lined gloves, plastic storage containers large enough to hold 115 gallons of potentially radioactive fluids, and a remotely operated scissors lift. Abu told Habib that, in order to provide cover, they had blown a safe and stolen a large amount of cash, company credit cards, and some government bonds. Habib handed Abu a suitcase containing the remaining $150,000 of the agreed-upon fee. The men embraced warmly. Habib's confidence in Abu and his organization was once again vindicated. He was certain that Abu would maintain total secrecy; men like Abu lived according to a strict code of silence and it was inconceivable that he would break that code.

Over the previous weeks, in a corner of the warehouse, Habib had overseen the construction of a new "storage room" to the design specifications of the three Iranian nuclear technicians. It looked unobtrusive enough from the outside, but it was lined with lead sheathing and was equipped with an airtight door from an industrial freezer. Unlike the rest of the warehouse, it was temperature and humidity controlled, so that work could be conducted in a completely stable environment.

With the arrival of Abu's stolen equipment, Habib moved quickly to complete construction of the storage room. The technicians installed the radiation detection equipment and the drum transfer apparatus. They made several dry runs to test the equipment.

The next day, the drums that had been smuggled in from Iran were moved to the storage room. With Habib observing through a window in the door, the three technicians donned radiation suits. To their collective relief, there was no sign that the drums were emitting radiation in excess of generally expected background levels. Then they began the tedious operation of removing the lead shielded containers of spent nuclear fuel from the barrels. The scissors lift was specifically designed to work in conjunction with the drum-transfer apparatus to permit the unsealing of a 55 gallon drum of radioactive waste without resulting in a radiation leak. The machine, which looked like a large kettle placed on top of the drum, transferred the waste from the drums into specially designed, vacuum-sealed plastic storage bags in an airtight environment.

Habib thought that all the precautions—the space suits and the high tech equipment—were a bit elaborate, but Tehran had insisted that Habib and his men take every conceivable precaution to ensure that the operation was not blown by an accidental release of radiation on Pakistani soil. When the process was completed, Habib was supposed to dismantle the storage room and bury everything out in the desert.

To Habib's relief, the whole process was completed without complications. The technicians successfully emptied and bagged the fluid in each drum, removed the false bottoms, and recovered the lead containers. They took measurements and found only weak alpha particle radiation coming from the spent uranium fuel inside the containers. They could be safely handled using ordinary lead-lined gloves.

When the technicians came out of the room, they looked tired and relieved. Habib offered his congratulations; they could return home to Iran knowing that they had done their job well.

Now Habib needed to get the stuff on board a truck and over to the factory. With any luck, the material would soon be out of the country and his part of the mission completed.

Chapter 34

Avi Gerstner was not summoned to come to the US Embassy on Rehov Hayarkon very often and when he was, it usually meant that the Americans either had bad news or wanted something from him.

He showed his identification to the US Marine Guard and informed him that he was there to visit Bob D'Agostino. Gerstner noticed that the Marine took a barely perceptible double take, apparently recognizing Gerstner, and went back in his guard house to call D'Agostino.

"Sir, someone will be down in a minute to escort you to Mr. D'Agostino's office."

Gerstner was buzzed into a waiting area. D'Agostino's secretary, a pleasant young woman whom he had met several times, was waiting there to escort him to the meeting. She greeted Gerstner warmly. Gerstner had her name on the tip of his tongue, but could not remember it and was embarrassed. A "senior moment," as his cousin Rivka, who lived in Florida, called it. Charm and a good memory for details were great assets when one's avocation was the manipulation of others. Gerstner was still confident of his ability to be charming; he was not so sure about his memory. As they were walking down the hall, her name—Mary—suddenly popped into his head.

"So, Mary, how are those two little boys of yours," Avi asked?"

"Oh, they're great, Mr. Gerstner. The older one, Sean, just started over at the Friends School."

"That's wonderful."

Mary led Gerstner to D'Agostino's spartan office on the fourth floor. Unlike Avi's office, there were no pictures of children or old comrades, no Army citations on the wall, no files in plain view sprawled all over his desk. Nothing to give away his personality. It was if he was borrowing the office for the day.

D'Agostino got up from his desk and came around to shake Gerstner's hand. The men had known each other for many years and were both a little battered and bruised from decades of service in one of the roughest neighborhoods on the planet. They had come to share a sense of camaraderie; they were old allies and genuinely liked one another. They also understood that their nations did not always see eye to eye.

Gerstner and D'Agostino were too familiar with each other to waste time on small talk or subtlety. D'Agostino simply told Gerstner what he wanted.

"Avi, I asked you here today because we need your help. Some months ago, when we met over at your office, you informed me that a certain Dr. Majid Emami Honari had vanished from his university teaching job in Tehran."

"Yes, Bob, I remember. The applied physics professor."

"Well, he's resurfaced, probably under an assumed name, at a location west of Shiraz that we have now identified as a probable nuclear centrifuge cascade. In fact, it was you who first alerted us to existence of the facility. We have reason to believe that he is a high-level scientist in their nuclear weapons program. We are contemplating an operation to neutralize the facility."

"OK, if you're asking my permission, you've got it," said Gerstner, laughing. "Just make sure you know what you're getting into this time. You don't need another Mogadishu on your hands."

"Touché." D'Agostino paused to let the moment of dark humor pass. "You know, Avi, Felix Dzerzhinsky, the founder of the CHEKA, once said that every man has his weakness; if you can uncover it, you can bend him to your will. Do you believe that's true, Avi?"

"I'll tell you this: I believe that the Bolsheviks, starting with Dzerzhinsky, had the finest espionage system in the world until the end of the Cold War. And I believe the old Chekist knew everything there was to know about breaking men. Unlike you and I, Bob, the Russians had the luxury of operating without restraint. So yes, I agree. But what do ancient Communists have to do with nuclear centrifuge cascades in Shiraz?"

"Well, we think that the only practical way we can gain entrance into the cave complex at Shiraz is to turn someone and get them to get us inside. We need a mole."

"And what does that have to do with Israel?"

"Avi, no one ever accused you of being subtle."

"Bob, no one has ever accused any Israeli of being subtle."

"As you know, Avi, we've inserted some small special forces recon teams into Iran, but we have much weaker assets than you do—or so we've been led to believe—in the area of human intelligence. We would like to know, first, do you have assets on the ground in Shiraz and, second, would you be willing to use those assets to place Honari under surveillance, find his weaknesses, and exploit them? We will finance the operation—whatever you need."

"We're so-so in Shiraz," said Avi, shaking his head, although this was meant to convey false modesty. "But for you, we'll—what do they say in America?—'pull out all of the stops.' How soon do you need us to get going?"

"Immediately," answered D'Agostino.

"You know something, Bob?" said Gerstner, launching into what Bob D'Agostino immediately recognized as one of his lectures. "The really nice thing about blackmail in repressed societies is that there are just so many damned shameful things that can get a person into trouble. Everything is a sin. In Israel or Europe or America, if you become a drug addict or a drunk, you get rehab, if you gamble, you get more rehab, and if you're gay . . . well, that's not even an issue anymore. You can even get married. In these Muslim countries, particularly the fundamentalist ones, it's a blackmailer's dream come true. Everything is a sin. They put you to death for some of these things. So in a place like Iran, you can have a field day. It's like the Soviet Union during the end of the Stalinist period. Listen to this, Bob. The old timers that ran the Mossad in those days had such a good time blackmailing those Russians. When I first started, those old guys used to talk about how they had penetrated the Politburo so deeply, that in 1953, I think they knew that Khrushchev was going to shoot the KGB boss Beria before Khrushchev did. They said your guys were amazed with our Russian operations. And we did it on a shoestring budget. Of course, in those days—forgive me if I'm frank with you—the CIA was still running around like a bunch of fools hiring every unemployed ex-Nazi and paying Ukrainian nationalists to dynamite Russian railroad tracks. No wonder you didn't know anything."

"Is that your way of saying, 'Yes, Bob, we'll help you?'" interrupted D'Agostino, impatiently.

"Forgive an old man his stories. Of course we'll help you." Gerstner knocked himself playfully on the side of the head. "Maybe before I promise these things, I need to talk to my Prime Minister. He'll really like the part about you guys paying for it."

Chapter 35

Ivana Svilanovic sat in the briefing room with the Commander of her unit, a former Marine Major named Bill Victorine, waiting for the final person to arrive for the meeting. There was a large illuminated map of Iran on the wall with a highlighted area around a rugged mountainous region just west of Shiraz.

"So, Irv, how's the training going?"

"I think it puts the 'I' in intensive, Bill."

"Well, I think we're about to put your training into use."

"Already?"

"Events are moving faster than we had anticipated," responded Victorine, who looked at his watch. "I hate meetings which start late."

Just then, there was a knock at the door, and a US Naval officer rushed into the room, slightly out of breath. He apologized profusely for being late and introduced himself as Commander Raymond Einhorn from Naval Special Warfare Command. He had just flown in from the Gulf and looked very travel-weary.

Victorine offered Einhorn a cup of coffee, which he gladly accepted.

Ivana thought he seemed like a nice guy. But then she was a sucker for the ones with the intelligent eyes and warm smiles.

Einhorn unlocked his briefcase and took out some photographs.

"As I'm sure you know, we have a number of special forces teams from various branches of the military in Iran gathering intelligence at nuclear facilities, such as enrichment plants, uranium mines, heavy-water-production facilities, laboratories, et cetera. One of those teams, composed of three Navy SEALS and one of your guys, a CIA Analyst from the Iranian Desk . . . ."

Victorine interrupted. "Excuse me for interrupting, Commander, but I believe Ms. Svilanovic knows him. Ojay Hamsid." Ivana must have looked puzzled because Victorine went on, "You know, the short Iranian guy who did that orientation for our people on Iranian culture and politics?"

Then it clicked. "Witty little guy. Yeah, I remember him now. He's in Iran? Wow."

"He may not be the warrior type, Irv, but he's very smart, speaks the lingo, and knows everything there is to know about the people."

Commander Einhorn turned to Ivana. "So you're the famous Captain Svilanovic. I've heard a lot of good things about you going all the way back to Bosnia."

"I guess your reputation precedes you, Ms. Svilanovic," said Victorine, laughing. "OK, I'm sorry, Commander, for getting you off track. Please continue."

"So in the mountains west of Shiraz," said Einhorn, pointing to the map on the wall, "we have discovered a secret facility that we strongly suspect is engaged in nuclear-production activities. It has not been disclosed to the International Atomic Energy Agency and, therefore, exists entirely outside of the inspection regime of the Nuclear Non-Proliferation Treaty."

"No big surprise there, Commander," said Victorine.

"True. Anyway, between the NSA and our SEAL team on the ground, we now have both satellite and close-up photographs and video of the activities going on there." Einhorn laid out several of the photographs. They were stamped "Top Secret." One was an enhanced satellite image of the valley where the facility was located.

The other two were daytime photos of the valley floor and the cave entrance. "Here's what we know. The front of the place is disguised to look like a rock quarry or concrete production plant. At the rear of the small canyon where it narrows, they have excavated a cave in the mountainside. As you can see, it has blast doors and sits under a rock ledge, so it is basically invisible from the air and would be difficult if not impossible to destroy with conventional weapons."

Ivana picked up the photographs one by one and studied them as Einhorn continued to speak.

"Now as you can see from these photographs . . . ." Einhorn put two more photographs on the table; both photos were taken with a night vision lens. They were in color, but had the green monochromatic cast of pictures taken with night vision equipment. ". . . They are delivering ore to the facility. Computer enhancements and color analysis leads us to believe that it is yellowcake uranium. On another day, they were delivering what appears to be a shipment of nitric acid, which is a crucial component in the process of turning yellowcake uranium into uranium hexafluoride gas for use in a gas-separation centrifuge. We even saw them unload what could very well have been centrifuge units themselves. When the blast doors were opened, our guys were able to take photographs of the first few feet inside of the facility. The resolution is not great because of the lack of lighting. To the left of the entrance is a box which, when enhanced, turns out to be part of a gamma spectroscopy radiation-detection system. In addition, some of the personnel who emerged from the cave were wearing plastic dosimeter badges."

Einhorn took out another photograph showing a scientist in a white lab coat. "See the badge?"

"Yes," replied Ivana.

"And here's the kicker. It turns out we know this guy. He went missing from his job as a physics professor at Amir Kabir University a while back. His name is Dr. Majid Emami Honari. Suddenly, he's working at some cave in the middle of nowhere equipped with doors designed to withstand an air attack. He's wearing a lab coat and a Geiger counter and supervising the delivery of what our analysts say looks an awful lot like yellowcake uranium. So now we're quite certain that what we're dealing with here is a newly built centrifuge cascade designed for the purpose of enriching uranium to weapons grade purity. There is no other explanation that fits the facts and it is consistent with the operational and security setup we've observed at the Bala Deh facility."

Einhorn tossed down another picture on top of the growing pile. "All under the watchful eye of a company-sized garrison of Iranian Revolutionary Guards."

"Well," said Victorine, "look on the bright side. They could be taking delivery of nuclear triggers."

"We better hope they haven't gotten that far or our plan will be too little and way, way too late."

"Now, Ivana, here's where you come in," said Victorine. "Between the politicians on Pennsylvania Avenue, the planners at the Pentagon, and the prognosticators here at the Company, they've kicked this thing around eight ways from Sunday. They rejected the obvious solutions, like leaking it to the press or complaining to the United Nations. 'So what,' the Iranians will say. No matter how much we sail the Sixth Fleet around the Persian Gulf and do flyovers, they know we're not going to invade the place. They also know that conventional airpower is not sufficient to destroy their program and we're sure as hell not going drop tactical nuclear weapons on them. That would work, but it's just nuts. So, at the recommendation of the Joint Chiefs, we've come up with a mission we've dubbed 'Operation Whirlwind.' It's a high-risk black job.

"The overall plan contemplates a small team covertly entering the facility and engaging in sabotage operations that will result in a leak of radioactive material into the atmosphere. The objective of the mission is two-fold. First, to destroy the facility; second, to cause a leak of radiation sufficient to alarm and anger the people of Iran and shock the world, but not in sufficient quantities to kill very many people. We hope to trigger an internal political response which turns Iranian public opinion against the government's nuclear ambitions and, if we're lucky, destabilizes the regime itself."

Ivana realized that she must have had a very shocked look on her face, because Einhorn stopped talking and both he and Victorine were staring at her.

"Irv, are you fully tracking this?" asked Victorine.

"Yes, in other words," said Ivana, speaking quietly, "we're going to turn the place into a huge dirty bomb. That's quite . . . an undertaking."

"That's correct, Ms. Svilanovic," replied Einhorn. "But necessary. The President has authorized this mission because he views it as a measured and proportional response to the Iranian refusal to accept international standards regarding peaceful nuclear development. I think we can all agree that Iran must not be permitted to develop offensive nuclear capabilities."

"Essentially what we're talking about, Irv," broke in Victorine, "is engineering a Chernobyl-like incident that will result in the same political repercussions as occurred in the Soviet Union. That accident contributed significantly to the fall of the Soviet regime."

"What is to guarantee that thousands of people won't be killed as a result of our actions?" Ivana asked.

"Ms. Svilanovic, we're not talking about a core meltdown in a hot atomic pile and so it won't be an explosion and disbursal at the magnitude of Chernobyl. Moreover, unlike Chernobyl, this facility is in a location isolated from major population centers and so the casualties will be limited primarily to military personnel at or near the site. But it will form a cloud of radioactive material that will be exceedingly alarming to populations throughout the region, though hopefully minimally harmful."

Ivana got up and looked at the map. "What about the town of Bala Deh? It's just a few kilometers from the target. How many people live there and what casualties do you project?"

"Good Question, Ms. Svilanovic," said Einhorn. "Bala Deh is a medium-sized market town with a population of approximately 15,000 people. We estimate that if the radioactive cloud passes right over the town, and our analysts view that as a 32% likelihood, we would estimate that the rate of lymphomas, thyroid, and pituitary cancers would be expected to triple, and some immune-suppressed individuals, newborns, and the elderly would die."

Victorine must have seen the pained expression on Ivana's face. "Look, Irv, let's face it, if this doesn't work, we're more than likely going to face two possibilities, neither very attractive. One, a US and possibly Israeli military confrontation with Iran in which tens of thousands of Americans and Iranians could be killed; or two, a nuclear armed and aggressive Iran."

Ivana sat down and stared at her hands for a moment, pursing her lips. She looked up, straight into Victorine's eyes. "Bill, the math is hard to argue with, but the ruthlessness of it all is breathtaking."

"Yes, I suppose it is."

Einhorn cleared his throat. "Now operationally, Ms. Svilanovic."

"If we're going to work together, please call me Ivana."

" . . . Ivana, the really difficult part of this mission is that we need to make this look like an accident, not an act of sabotage. No matter what we do, the Iranians are going to blame us or Israel for this incident, but we've got to make sure that our fingerprints are untraceable."

"How are we going to do that?" asked Ivana, skeptically.

"Very carefully, Irv," said Victorine. "We are going to put you on the ground in Iran with the team that is already there. You will be in command of the mission. Although you will come in with a basic plan for carrying out the mission, you will have considerable flexibility on the ground. You are going to have to assess the vulnerabilities of the facility, enter the cave, plant whatever explosives or perform whatever sabotage is necessary, then get out. We will coordinate a diversionary attack at a police barracks just outside of Shiraz using Sunni Arab separatist forces."

"And who are they?"

"Let's just say they are friends of friends."

"How are we supposed to gain surreptitious entrance to that cave?"

"The best case is that Dr. Honari is going to take your team right through the front door into the facility. The Israelis and their local assets will soon begin a blackmail operation against him and we are cautiously optimistic that it will be successful."

"What if he gets a guilty conscience and sounds the alarm once we get inside the facility?"

"Then you shoot him, they capture or kill you, and we deny everything."

"And if we succeed, what do we do with Honari?"

"The plan is for you to evacuate him voluntarily or, if he is uncooperative, involuntarily. We will offer him money and see if we can buy him off. If we can't secure his cooperation, we have a contingency plan to hand him over to the Kurdish separatists and then have them publish his videotaped confession concerning Iran's nuclear intentions. Hopefully, he will be cooperative and we can turn him. He may be Iran's equivalent of Dr. Abdul Qadeer Khan and so his loss will be a major blow to the Iranian nuclear program."

"A. Q. Khan. Isn't that the guy who is the father of the Pakistani nuclear program and sold centrifuges and uranium hexafluoride gas to Iran and North Korea?"

"That's the guy, Irv."

Ivana looked at Victorine and then Einhorn. "Well, obviously this is conceptual. To make it work, we've got some serious operational planning to do. What is my time frame and what kind of help will I get?"

"You will get whatever resources you need," said Victorine. "That's the good news. The bad news is that we want to make this thing happen within ninety days."

"And the team that's there? I assume they can't stay in the field much longer. In any event, we need time to train together."

"We plan to withdraw them to a safe house in Baluchistan in southeastern Iran within a week. In the meantime, they will gather further intel on the operations of the facility and expand our understanding of the strengths and vulnerabilities of its security system. When we're ready, you'll be going back in with them."

Chapter 36

It was past 3:00 am and the night-shift workers had gone home several hours earlier. A truck rumbled up to the factory gate and the driver showed the night guard some shipping papers. It was not unusual for freight to be delivered late at night. On the dimly lit loading dock, half a dozen men gathered, waiting to unload the truck.

The workers were small, wiry men in dirty overalls, wearing sweat-stained turbans. Some wore boots and some wore sandals. They were, however, not ordinary Pakistani workers but members of a small terrorist cell called *Lashkar-e-Tayyaba*—Army of the Pure. *Lashkar* was a shadowy terrorist group that operated in South Asia. Originally funded by the Inter-Services Intelligence Agency, Pakistan's intelligence service, to carry out operations in Kashmir against the Indians, the group was training in an Al-Qaeda camp in Afghanistan when the September 11th attacks took place in New York. Cut adrift from their Al-Qaeda connection when the Taliban regime was subsequently overthrown, the group fled back to Pakistan. Upon their return they found that their patrons in the ISI no longer wished to be associated with Al-Qaeda and cut them loose. They became freelancers and eventually the Iranians hired them. The Iranians had them carry out a few assassinations of Iranian dissidents and, at one point, they were hired out as muscle to break up a dockworkers' strike. They did what they were told and their Pasdaran paymasters insured that they were well compensated.

The men were informed that the unloading and repackaging operation would take several hours and that they needed to handle the material with care. They were not told what it was they were unloading, but only that it was an important shipment and that the operation was of utmost sensitivity. Husseini, a tall man with a thin moustache, looked at the dark faces of the men in front of him, some with complexions so dark they could have been Africans, and wondered if they had guessed the purpose of their mission. He was certain that the members of the *Lashkar-e-Tayyaba* cell would not betray any secrets. These men were fanatics and they also knew that, were they to betray their Iranian patrons, they would spend eternity in hell, very likely dispatched there by a bullet to the head or a knife across the throat.

Husseini, who held the rank of Captain in the Pasdaran, had been sent to Karachi the year before, shortly after the acquisition of Peshawar General Manufacturing. He operated under a cover story that he was "management consultant" for the Pet Supplies Division, assigned to conduct a thorough review of the business operations of the newly acquired company. It was made clear to the factory manager and his staff that Captain Husseini, or as he was known by his pseudonym, Mr. Hassan al-Feisal, was to be given their full cooperation. Although Captain Husseini went about his activities with great determination, he was a congenial man by nature and soon put the Pakistanis at ease. He joked with them and gave out compliments freely, which eased the anxiety of the staff about the takeover of their company. They, in turn, began to trust him and he rapidly earned their complete confidence. The factory manager, Mr. Sindh, was greatly relieved to find that Husseini was such a kind and decent man. Quite naturally, he had feared that he might be sacked as a result of the change of ownership. Mr. Feisal even spoke passable Urdu, although he had a strong accent.

Mr. Sindh's sense of relief filtered down to the assembly line workers who felt lucky to have a job in the relatively high-paid cat-litter factory and who were also worried they might lose their jobs.

For his part, Captain Husseini methodically went about learning everything he could about the cat-litter manufacturing process. There were two shifts, one that began at 5:00 am and ended at 3:00 pm and the second shift that ran from 3:00 pm and ended at 1:00 am. Any maintenance activities that required shutting down the production line took place between the hours of 1:00 am and 5:00 am. The factory operated every day of the year, except on national holidays. Deliveries of the primary ingredients of pet litter—silica, bentonite clay, binders, and perfumes—were made several times a week. Each day, plastic containers and labels for the product would arrive from a packaging supplier.

As Husseini discovered, the manufacturing process was relatively simple. Hoppers of the ingredients were filled and computers would then control the mixing of the product. The product would then be moved along conveyor belts where the plastic containers were filled and heat sealed with aluminum foil. Finally, the product labels were affixed. The packages were then loaded by workers into boxes for shipping. Each box had a unique bar code which contained the lot number and shipping destination. Under the "just-in-time" manufacturing process that was the pride of the factory's customers across the Pacific, production could be timed to insure delivery to the exact location and at the precise time it would be needed. There would be no unnecessary costs associated with warehousing surplus product and the potential for inventory shortages would be minimized.

Within a few weeks of assuming the role of management consultant, Captain Husseini was able to report back to his superiors in Tehran that all was going according to plan. It would not be difficult to gain access to the plant at night to insert the material into the packaging of the cat litter and then track its movement all the way through to the point of final delivery.

He then turned to the next phase of the plan: infiltrating members of the team into the workforce. This turned out to be easy. Husseini informed Mr. Sindh that he would now focus on reviewing the personnel practices of the company. He had members of his team submit carefully falsified job applications and then inserted himself into the hiring process. The obsequious Mr. Sindh and "Mr. Feisal" seemed to have an amazing meeting of the minds when it came to the decision as to which job applicants to hire. After two months, Captain Husseini had members of *Lashkar-e-Tayyaba* working on the night shift, at the front gate, as janitors, and as security guards. He even had a female member of the group working as a clerical employee in the shipping-and-receiving department. Things were going so well that Captain Husseini felt that he might even get a promotion when he returned to Iran.

Husseini stood behind the men as the rear doors of the truck were opened. Inside was an armed guard, a bearded Pashtun, his Kalashnikov hung casually over his shoulder. Tied down to the wooden slats on the floor of the trailer were the three small, sealed lead boxes containing spent nuclear fuel. Husseini ordered his men to bring them into the factory. They were deceptively heavy, each weighing approximately fifty pounds. It was an odd sight to see two men carrying a small gray box, each wearing heavy, lead-lined gloves to protect them from radiation exposure.

The containers were brought to the shipping department, where they were shrink-wrapped in aluminum foil. As Husseini understood it, the aluminum foil would further deflect the radioactive signature of any gamma rays that managed to pass through the lead shielding.

Husseini then directed the men to remove four cases of the product from one of the intermodal shipping containers sitting outside in the company's freight yard. The men opened one of the cat litter boxes from each case and emptied its contents. They then substituted the foil-wrapped lead containers into the three empty plastic, cat-litter packages, resealed, and repacked them. The repacked cases were put back in the container. According to the bar code on the shipping boxes, these particular cases were bound for a Wal-Mart distribution center in California.

Captain Husseini gathered the men, told them their job was completed, and that over the next month they were to quit their jobs and disappear from Karachi. They would be contacted later for further assignments. Husseini thanked them for their service.

The last thing that Captain Husseini did that night was drive to a secret drop where he left the computer printout of the shipping details for the three cases of cat litter. The intermodal container they were in would sit in a warehouse near the docks for several months waiting for freight to be consolidated on the South Korean registered container ship OPCL Pusan. Sometime in the early summer it would be loaded bound for the Port of Los Angeles.

The next morning, Captain Husseini informed Mr. Sindh that he had completed his duties. He thanked Mr. Sindh warmly for his cooperation and added that he was extremely impressed by the performance of the Pet Services Division and by Sindh's management style. Mr. Sindh bid Husseini farewell, flattered by the compliments and relieved that his operation was probably now safe from corporate interference.

Chapter 37

Their vacation in Cyprus was interrupted one morning by the delivery of a small package containing instructions, airline tickets, and several thousand dollars each of Mexican pesos and US dollars. They were to board an Olympic Airlines flight to Madrid and from there they were to continue on an Aero México flight to Mexico City. Even though they would not be returning to Madrid, they were round-trip tickets. What was not revealed was that another set of agents, members of a sleeper cell which had been recruited in the United States many years earlier, would impersonate them and, using skillfully forged passports, return to Madrid. By that time, Mohammed's group would be safely in the United States. General Yazdi, meticulous planner that he was, would never make the mistake of allowing them to travel on one-way tickets, which would set off alarms in every security-related computer program from Madrid to Washington, DC

Shortly after the team's arrival in Mexico, they would rendezvous with an operative who would give them their US passports, California drivers' licenses, Social Security cards, and credit cards. They would also receive the keys to two vehicles and two apartments in suburban Los Angeles. The sleeper cell was never intended to engage in active missions. Rather, its function was twofold: to provide a plausible identity for arriving agents to assume and to help make preparations for future missions. The members of the sleeper cell had driven to Mexico in two cars lawfully registered in California. When Mohammed's team reached the Mexican border in the two vehicles, they would appear to be returning Californians who had driven to Mexico. Once they had entered the US, they were to slip into the identities of the departed members of the sleeper cell. At some point near the end of their mission, they would fly to Canada using their American identities, rent cars in Vancouver, and reenter the United States using their Canadian passports. Then when their mission was completed, they would use their Canadian passports to leave the United States, making it appear that they were Canadians who had entered and departed the United States as tourists.

The flight was uneventful. Like the other passengers, they slept, watched movies, and read books. They kept to themselves, but tried to appear friendly and unthreatening. The boys in the back of the plane smiled and said "Merci" to the flight attendants. In the first-class section, "Monsieur and Madame Ibrahim" took full advantage of the luxuries of first-class travel. They toasted their successful "marriage" with a complementary glass of excellent champagne. For all of them, this was a continuation of their brief interlude of relaxation, when the mind could easily separate itself from the stress and danger that would come rushing back into their lives when they landed in Mexico. From the moment they landed, they would be in hostile territory, the discovery and apprehension of individuals such as themselves being the main object of the massive counter-terrorist infrastructure of the United States. General Yazdi and their handlers had warned them repeatedly not to underestimate the will of the United States, a country whose commitment and ability to wage war had been repeatedly underestimated by its adversaries. Contrary to popular beliefs, Yazdi had explained at their final briefing in Beirut, Americans were not soft, corrupt, or inept. They were sometimes arrogant and almost always naïve; their complacency was a result of their long history living on the continent of North America surrounded by two oceans and friendly neighbors. It was that complacency that would give the team their opportunity to strike, but if they let their guard down and became complacent or arrogant themselves, they would be killed or captured and the mission would fail. On the other hand, if they succeeded, Allah be praised, they would strike a permanent blow against the American imperial colossus by destroying forever its fundamental sense of security. The Islamic Republic of Iran's effort to become the first Muslim superpower would be immeasurably advanced.

They arrived at Mexico City's sprawling airport tired and nervous after their all-night flight. This would be their first test. But the immigration officials at the airport passed them right through customs and, after retrieving their luggage, they found themselves at the taxi stand. Their "itinerary" had them checking into two small, upscale hotels in the trendy Zona Rosa neighborhood of the federal capital, conveniently located near the Embassy of Iran on the Paseo de la Reforma and Chapultepec Park.

On their third evening in Mexico City, after dinner and a lovely stroll along the Reforma, the front-desk clerk informed Señor and Señora Ibrahim they had a message and handed them a note. In English it simply said, "Please meet me in the lobby of the Hotel María Isabel across from El Angel at 7:30 pm tomorrow evening and we can go have a drink." The note was signed, "Julio". Since they did not know a Julio or, for that matter, anyone else in Mexico City, it was obvious that he was to be their contact to receive further instructions. Mohammed decided that, for overriding operational reasons, it was now necessary to break the silence between the two teams and work directly together. He contacted the other team members and instructed them to meet for breakfast at 7:30 at the café located just to the left of the entrance of Chapultepec Park.

The next morning, as they sipped their Mexican coffees, the chocolate and cinnamon flavors a new taste experience, Mohammed explained the plan for the day. At 2:00 pm, they would meet at the 1910 Revolution Memorial statute in the Colonia Tabacalera, which was a short walk up the Reforma from their hotels. In the meantime, the

Pakistani, Fareed, who spoke Spanish, would have the responsibility of purchasing a set of small high-quality microcommunication devices so that the team could communicate with one another while conducting surveillance of the rendezvous area prior to the meeting. They would also purchase some digital cameras so they could photograph any suspicious individuals whom they might detect during their surveillance activities. They were to get in position two hours before the scheduled rendezvous to detect any suspicious activity. This way, Mohammed explained, if they observed anything indicating that "Julio" was a double agent, they would be able to abort the meeting and flee. Only Mohammed—Señor Ibrahim—would attend the meeting, minimizing the exposure of the team.

As planned, at 2:00 pm they met in the quiet little park surrounding the old monument to the Maderista revolution and Fareed handed out the equipment he had purchased. They studied a street map of the city and practiced using the communications devices. They would speak English and they developed simple code names for one another. If they needed to abort the mission, one of them would say, "I'm tired, let's go home."

At 5:30 pm, the team was in place at various spots along the Reforma surrounding the famous El Ángel de la Independencia. The monument was suffused in gold light, with the bare-breasted, winged angel atop her column pointing her crown of laurels toward downtown. It was a spectacular sight, but none of the team particularly noticed or cared for the aesthetics of Mexico City. They were in their assigned places looking intently around the area for suspicious activity. Fareed was at a café sipping a cappuccino and reading *USA Today*. Ingrid was window shopping the fashionable stores up and down the Reforma. Asim was posing as a tourist taking lots of photographs of the sights. Nasir was at an outdoor restaurant on the other side of the street and down the block from Fareed, enjoying an early dinner. At around 6:30 Nasir and Fareed switched places.

There was a significant presence of uniformed police in the area. However, the team was unconcerned; they were there to protect the tourists and the wealthy from the city's sizable criminal population and were not interested in looking for terrorists. Mohammed's group had been well trained by the Pasdaran to be patient and attentive when conducting surveillance operations. They had spent countless hours in the streets, restaurants, and souks of Beirut and Damascus perfecting their tradecraft. And so they systematically scoured the faces of those passing through the Plaza de la Independencia looking for the sort of persons who might be looking for them.

Mohammed entered the modern lobby of the Hotel María Isabel five minutes early. Ingrid was already there and was seated on one of the couches. If something went wrong she could take immediate action. Mohammed behaved as if he was waiting to meet someone, figuring that this was a common enough activity and would arouse no suspicion.

A few minutes after the appointed time for the rendezvous, a man walked up to Mohammed with an extended hand and a big smile. He was of medium build, with a handsome, open face, dressed in a stylish business suit, and holding an attaché case. He looked to be in his early thirties.

"Señor Ibrahim," he said in Spanish-accented English, "I am Julio Sanchez. Welcome to Mexico City." He pronounced the word Mexico "Mejico."

"Ah, Señor Sanchez, it is a pleasure to meet you," replied Mohammed.

"Perhaps we can walk down the Reforma and find a nice place to discuss our business?"

"That would be fine."

Together they walked out of the hotel lobby. Perhaps forty-five seconds later, Ingrid got up and followed. As she went through the doors of the hotel, she quietly said into her earpiece, "Let's go shopping." This was the team's signal that the rendezvous had taken place and Mohammed and the contact were on the move.

As Ingrid followed discretely behind, she could see the Mexican and Mohammed walking up the Reforma. At the corner of Rio Santa Gèvova, the two shook hands and parted, with Julio turning left down the street and Mohammed continuing down the Reforma. However, Ingrid could see that Mohammed was now in possession of the attaché case.

Mohammed must have stuck the earpiece back in his ear as a few seconds later he said, "Let's go home."

When they were up in their room, Ingrid and Mohammed examined the contents of the attaché case. It contained keys for two cars and claim tickets for a garage in Mexico City, five California drivers' licenses, five US passports, the keys to two apartments in Los Angeles, the addresses and telephone numbers of the apartments, maps, and, under protective foam, three Beretta 21 automatics with extra clips. There was also a small slip of paper that said in Arabic, "*Wa Jazakum Allah Khair*" — "May Allah be with you all." Mohammed said "fools" upon reading the note, tore it into shreds, and flushed it down the toilet.

Chapter 38

Central Iran, May 2

Aqil was loudly singing a Baluchi folk song as he drove down the road with the windows open. He was happy because he was going into action again with the Americans. His voice was raspy from smoking too many cigarettes. Smoking, he mused, had become a definite problem in his life. His wife Lalla was a soft-spoken woman of infinite patience and Aqil readily conceded that patience was required of any woman who could be married to him. For five years she had been gently, if relentlessly, asking him to quit smoking. He said he could not. But what if he quit right now, this minute, as he drove down the highway to the rendezvous point? He tossed the cigarette out of the window, feeling virtuous, wishing he could call his wife on the telephone and tell her the good news. Think of all the money he would save and how happy Lalla would be. Within five minutes, he was dying for another cigarette and his resolve was waning, but he resisted and did not smoke.

Aqil was to meet the Americans at 2:00 am at the same bridge over the Dālaki River where he dropped them off nearly two weeks earlier. He arrived at the bridge at midnight and pulled over to the side of the road to wait. He decided to lie down on the front seat to catch an hour or so of sleep. They would have a long night of driving ahead of them.

The bangs on the door of the cab worked their way into the plot of Aqil's dream, then came flooding into his consciousness when he awoke. He sat up with a start. There were flashlights pointing into the windows.

"Open the door and get out," a voice yelled with authority in Farsi. In the reflected light of the windows, Aqil could not see who it was yelling at him. It must be the police. Better them than bandits. He looked at his watch. It was 2:15. The Americans were late.

Aqil unlocked the cab door and one of the men pulled it open. A was gun pointed at him. "Get out, brother," the man said, "and we won't hurt you." The man's head was covered by a turban that was wrapped around his nose and mouth, so that even in the bright light of the full moon all he could see was his dark, alert eyes.

Aqil put his hands up. "What do you want from me?" Aqil asked.

The man did not answer, but another set of hands grabbed his shirt and pulled hard. Aqil lost his balance and started to fall out of the truck, but caught himself on the door handle. "Not so rough, brother," said Aqil, stepping out of the truck and jumping down to the ground.

"We must take your truck. I am sorry."

Fifty yards away, deep in the darkest shadows of the bridge, Gonzales and his men were watching the situation unfold. The SEAL leader used hand signals to instruct Murphy to cross the road and get into firing position. Amalakai pulled down his night vision goggles, and lay down in the dirt, leveling his assault rifle at the men holding Aqil at gunpoint. OJ whispered to Gonzales, "Let me try to talk them down." Gonzales nodded his assent and took his position next to Amalakai, his own weapon ready. It was a vote of confidence and in the second before fear flooded back into his veins, OJ felt proud.

He stepped out in front of the bridge onto the tarmac. He was in the darkest part of the shadows and figured that, if they started firing, he would dive to the ground. His mouth was dry and he wondered whether his voice would come out sounding like an adult male's, let alone someone with authority and confidence. He took a deep breath, lowered his voice as best he could, and yelled in Farsi, "Drop your weapons, this is the military police. Drop them now."

The men whirled around and pointed their guns in OJ's direction. He instinctively dropped to his knees, but yelled, "Drop your weapons."

Aqil fell flat on his face on the tarmac, figuring that shooting was about to start. But the men looked at each other, nodded in resignation, and put their rifles down. "We surrender. Don't shoot us." The two men slowly put up their hands.

OJ got up and unholstered his sidearm. "Now stay still and you will not get hurt." He started to walk slowly toward the men, his gun pointed at them, with Amalakai and Gonzales coming up behind him. "Aqil," OJ yelled, "grab their guns."

Aqil grabbed the two hunting rifles and crossed to the other side of the road where Murphy, his weapon leveled at the men, was advancing slowly toward the bandits.

When OJ reached the two robbers, he told them to sit down with their hands behind their backs. Ted ran behind them, pulled out some plastic handcuffs, and bound the men's wrists. OJ told Aqil to unwrap their turbans. After a few questions, the two men told them that they were a father-and-son team who hijacked trucks and robbed isolated travelers. They spoke in the distinct accent of Shirazi tribesmen. The father was missing most of his teeth. They begged for their lives, offering OJ and his men money. OJ reminded them that the penalty for armed robbery was death. Aqil, who was enjoying their discomfort, demanded that OJ shoot them right there on the spot. OJ said, as fiercely as he could, they were busy and did not have time for petty thieves. Gonzales and Murphy stood them up and walked them over to the bridge and down to the riverbank. They bound their feet together with more plastic ties and then tied the two men together back to back. It would take them all night to figure out how to escape. When Gonzales and Murphy rejoined the group, Aqil had the back of the trailer open and they were loading their packs and equipment into it.

"Hey, Aqil," Gonzales asked, "why is it that we are always saving your life?"

OJ translated the Lieutenant Commander's question into Baluchi.

Aqil laughed. "Tell the General that I am just trying to get him into shape to deal with the Pasdaran." He thanked them profusely and told them it was time to go.

Already late, the incident had put them almost two hours behind schedule.

Murphy held up the two rifles. "Hey, Commander, what do we do with these?"

"Toss 'em in the back. It'll make a nice gift for Aqil."

They resumed their old spots: Aqil driving, OJ riding shotgun, and the rest of the team in the trailer. At 3:10 am they started driving northeast in the direction of Shiraz.

They caught the main north-south highway east of Shiraz and by the time it was light, they had made good progress and were well on their way to the south of the country. Their destination, the southeastern territories of Iran, bordering Afghanistan and Pakistan, had always been the area least under central government control. Most of the people were ethnic Baluchis, who were primarily nomadic. They moved back and forth over the porous international border as if it was meaningless; to a significant degree, it was. They did not share the same language, customs, or sect of Islam as the Persians and resented the central government's ham-fisted attempts to "Iranize" them.

Aqil drove the rest of the night and most of the next day toward their destination. He was dying for a cigarette, but when OJ found out that Aqil was trying to quit, he was so enthusiastic and congratulatory that Aqil sheepishly had to give up on his secret plan to resume smoking. He pulled off on a side road at mid-day so that they could all stretch their legs and relieve themselves. As they stood near the back of the truck eating some dried apricots and almonds that Aqil had brought, Gonzales told OJ that he'd "done good." The others agreed. "Hey, man," Murphy said, "you're almost SEAL material."

"Let's not go overboard," Gonzales replied.

Just a few kilometers west of Zahedan, they turned north onto a narrow road that headed up into the mountains. They drove for another two hours on the narrow, winding road and then Aqil stopped the truck. "This is it, brother," he said to OJ. They climbed out. It was cold and very dark. On the right side of the truck, illuminated by the moonlight, was a field. They had just unloaded the last of their equipment when they heard the sound of an engine off to the right. It was a light-duty-vehicle engine and within a few seconds, a Toyota pickup came bounding through the field into view. The driver and Aqil hugged each other warmly. "My brother's son," he said to OJ, when he walked over. "His name is Nawab. He is a good fighter." The boy, no more than a teenager, smiled and shook OJ's hand.

"Nawab will take you to my Uncle's farm." Gesturing to the east, he said, "It is over there in the mountains."

The boy was dressed in a sheepskin coat and had on a faded orange turban. An old dog was with him in the cab of the truck.

They piled all their belongings in the back and hopped in. Nawab gave the men some thick wool blankets to spread over them. The blankets smelled strongly of sheep and mildew, but they would keep the Americans warm. Aqil shook all their hands effusively and walked back to his truck. He felt a little sad; he liked the Americans and would miss their camaraderie. He hoped they would need him again.

The boy started the truck and headed back up the same dirt trail that he had come down. The men could feel every bounce of the truck as they slowly climbed up out of the valley floor. It got colder and they began to see snow on the sides of the road. They were not dressed for winter conditions and the blankets were a godsend. They huddled together under them against the increasing cold and got lost in their private thoughts. OJ fell asleep.

When the truck came to a stop, the eastern sky was just starting to lighten. They had turned off the dirt road that wound up the mountainside and were entering a high valley. There was an ancient stone house in front of them, with a low door and a heavy timber roof. A thin trail of smoke was coming from the chimney. Several dogs, which had been sleeping in front of the house, came bounding up to the truck, barking and wagging their tails. Sheep with long coats of thick, twisted wool were grazing nearby.

The Americans were stiff and sore but glad to finally arrive at their destination. A bearded man who wore a fur hat came out of the house to greet them. He hugged the boy and welcomed the Americans to his home. Gonzales wanted to unload the packs and equipment, but the old man waved them off, saying his grandson would bring their things inside. OJ could sense this made Gonzales nervous. When Gonzales asked OJ to inquire if they could bring their guns with them, the man laughed and said, of course they could, provided they did not shoot them off there. This seemed to put Gonzales at ease. The old man smiled and waved them in.

The ceiling was low and a smoky fire was burning in the fireplace. The atmosphere was redolent with the odors of animals, kerosene, food, and burning dung. Oil lanterns and candles dimly lit the interior. An old woman was there, who gestured for them to sit at a long, rough, plank table. She gave them cups of strong hot tea that tasted of butter. Then she brought cheese, onions, and baked flat bread to the table. After living off MREs for nearly two weeks, the strong flavors of real food tasted wonderful. Their conversation picked up and they began to relax.

"Good evening, gentlemen," said a female voice. The men looked up to see a tall, thin woman in camouflage fatigues, come through one of the doors leading off the main room. She smiled. "I'm Ivana Svilanovic. We'll be working together."

Ivana walked over to the men and stuck out her hand. When she got to OJ, she said, "Mr. Hamsid, I believe we've met before at Langley. You gave an orientation to a group of us who were assigned to do work in Iran."

OJ didn't remember her, but he smiled and said, "Oh yes, Ms. Svilanovic, I remember that." He shook her hand. "Call me Ivana," she said, impressed by the way he actually pronounced her last name correctly.

When she was done shaking the men's hands, she accepted a cup of tea from the old woman and sat down at the bench.

"I don't know if Lieutenant Commander Gonzales has briefed you yet, but as soon as you've rested, we will start training for an intensive mission that's being called 'Operation Whirlwind.' You will be under our joint command." At this, Gonzales nodded to indicate his affirmation. "I am formerly US Army. I left with the rank of Captain. Several years ago I joined the CIA and have served on several missions in this region. I have recently received training on neutralizing nuclear targets. This, in essence, will be the nature of our mission."

"May I ask a question, Ms. Svilanovic . . . Ivana?" asked OJ.

"Of course."

"Will we be returning to Bala Deh?"

"Yes."

Chapter 39

D r. Adarhormazd Boomla was in his forty-eighth year of dental practice in Shiraz, the city where he had lived all his life. His father had been a dentist before him and when Adarhormazd got out of dental school in 1958, he went into practice with his father.

The Boomlas were members of Iran's small Zoroastrian religious minority. The Zoroastrian faith was the old religion that was replaced by Islam when the Arabs conquered Persia in the seventh century. The Zoroastrians were despised by the Mullahs because they refused to accept Islam.

As a young man in the 1930s, the senior Dr. Boomla was active in reformist circles. His group of friends included other young professionals. Among them were a number of members of Iran's minority religions: Zoroastrians, Jews, Bahais, and Christians. They shared a commitment to fight the persecution of religious and ethnic minorities by Islamic religious fanatics and dreamed of the creation of a Western, secular, and democratic Iran. His closest friend in the reform movement was a Jewish lawyer named Efriam Yamin. They became business partners in the 1950s and 1960s. Boomla and Yamin initially welcomed the overthrow of the Shah in 1979 because they thought that, with the end of the monarchy, Iran would, at last, become a Western-oriented democratic republic. When Ayatollah Khomeini and the forces of fundamentalism took over the revolution and imposed a reactionary regime in Tehran, Yamin sold his property to his old friend Dr. Boomla and moved to Israel.

The elder Dr. Boomla died in 1983, bequeathing to his son Adarhormazd his wealth, his dental practice, and something less tangible: the leadership of the spy network that he and his Mossad-agent friend Efriam Yamin established in Shiraz in the fall of 1961.

It was the end of a long day spent filling cavities and cleaning teeth, when Amin, the bakery delivery boy who did courier work for Dr. Boomla, brought him a long coded message. The message had traveled far that day, starting its journey in Tel Aviv. It was then transmitted to Istanbul, from there to Yerevan in the Republic of Armenia, then to the American airbase outside Ashgabat in Turkmenistan, and finally into Iran. The message was simple. Locate Dr. Majid Emami Honari, now working under an assumed name, an eminent nuclear scientist working for the Government, track him and his family, determine their personal weaknesses, and report back to Tel Aviv.

It didn't take long for the team to locate Dr. Honari and get a sense of his routine. Five days a week, at 6:00 am in the morning, a driver and a guard in an armored Mercedes sedan picked him up and drove him to the nuclear facility at Bala Deh. It took them about an hour to get there. He was dropped off by the same guard in the evening, usually around 7:00 pm. Sometimes he spent the night in the nuclear facility, which they dubbed "Mecca." He generally took Saturdays and most Sundays off. On Saturday, he was not under guard or surveillance and spent his free time with his family. He had no friends. Dr. Honari's home was in an upscale neighborhood in the foothills just east of old Shiraz. The house was behind low walls. He, his wife, and children had moved into the house about six months previously. They kept to themselves and did not socialize much with their neighbors.

After three weeks of intensive surveillance, Dr. Boomla's team came up with nothing significant. Dr. Honari had no mistress, did not visit prostitutes, did not like young girls or boys, did not gamble, and was not a drunk or drug addict. He didn't even smoke. The guy was, as the Americans would say, "clean."

Dr. Boomla sought instructions from Avi Gerstner.

Chapter 40

Yossi Levi, who ran the Boomla Group in Shiraz, stood in front of Gerstner's desk and said, "Avi, we've got *gornisht* on this Honari character. He's clean. Boomla wants instructions."

Gerstner did not reply for a few seconds. "Yossi, we've promised the Americans on this. So tell the dentist to keep on Honari and to start looking for stuff on the wife and children."

"I can tell you this already. The wife is traditional. She stays at home and all she does is shop a little. I don't think we're going to get anything on her. The kids . . . I don't know. The two girls are in high school and the boy is in college in Shiraz. Hard to believe there's much there."

"Well, keep digging. We do have one bit of good news. Boomla just got a woman on his payroll a job working in Honari's house as a domestic servant."

"That's good, Yossi. OK, so go and get to work," said Gerstner, dismissing Yossi. But then he remembered something else. "Yossi, one more thing. Start hacking into this guy's computer. See what you come up with there. You never know, maybe he likes child pornography."

"We've already started that."

"I knew you were a smart *boychick*. That's why I hired you."

Chapter 41

Ingrid knew that she wanted Mohammed from the moment she met him, but she dared not violate the strict prohibition against agents forming personal relationships with one another. Although she had shed her Western sexual immorality upon her conversion to Islam, she had her share of lovers among her comrades. Arab men seemed to find her white skin, hard, supple body, and blue eyes extremely desirous. Even if she was a Muslim and wore the *hijab* and modest attire, her sexuality was no less apparent than if she wore provocative Western clothes. Her lovers were often aggressive with her. She was, in their eyes, a Western conquest—the fulfillment of a deep sexual fantasy driven into their collective consciousness by Western films and television, forbidden pictures on the Internet, and by the boyhood stories of Islamic conquest of the West. Having her was a kind of revenge, a ravishment, something wanton and forbidden. They would follow her and stare at her with their sullen eyes. Ingrid was always the more experienced lover and she particularly enjoyed freeing the repressed and explosive sexual energy of the young men around her. The roughness of their sex was, she felt, a perfect match for the roughness of their lives. Her gift of her body to these brave *muhajadeen* was a reward for the risk they took in the name of Islam. For many, she would be the only lover they would have before they died a martyr's death.

Mohammed was different. He was her age and no stranger to the joys of women. Ingrid felt an intense sexual desire for Mohammed from the moment they met in the training camp. Initially, he did not seem to notice her but that only caused her attraction to him to increase. She felt a desire to submit to him, to serve herself up to Mohammed.

In the false reality of their cover story, she acted more and more like a wife. Surely he must feel the heat of her desire? If he did, he did not show it and kept a puritanical distance between them. He would sleep on the couch or the floor, insisting that she take the bed. He was pleasant and businesslike with her. It was all very correct. He began to appear in her dreams and some mornings she awoke with memories of those imagined erotic encounters.

After they checked into the hotel, they walked down the main street to a restaurant. The other members of the team were at a hotel on the other side of town. Although they kept in contact through their cell phones, the two teams kept their distance from one another to avoid suspicion and to compartmentalize the mission. If something went wrong with one team, the others could go on. The trip from Mexico City to the border would take three days. They were halfway there.

It was a quiet town named Cruz de Piedra, a regional center in the middle of Sonora State. There was not the grinding poverty of the shanty towns surrounding the Federal Capital, but neither was there the wealth. Men walked the sidewalks in cowboy boots. The women and children were short and dark and looked like Indians to Ingrid, who thought that this must be the "real" Mexico of her childhood imagination; the Mexico of hot-blooded men and long-suffering mestizas.

It was a short walk down the main street of the town. There weren't many restaurants and they picked the one called Restaurante Adelanto. The man behind the desk at the hotel had said it was the best place in town, but in making the suggestion, his tone was apologetic. Mohammed and Ingrid sat at a table in the corner. They both ordered *arroz con pollo*—chicken with rice. Just on the other side of the entryway was the bar. Ingrid and Mohammed watched two men play pool. The men were young and had slicked-back black hair. They were drinking heavily and when the waitress came up to give them another beer, the taller of the men stroked his hand casually across her cleavage. She looked angry but didn't say anything. The men laughed. The bartender, an older man, looked up from the bar with displeasure on his face.

About halfway through the meal, Ingrid got up to use the toilet. She walked by the pool table and the two men gave her a lustful stare. Mohammed watched silently from the table. One of the men ambled toward a jukebox and put in coins. Mariachi music began to play. The taller one looked over at Mohammed, as if to take his measure as a man.

When Ingrid came out from the bathroom, the taller man blocked her way. He asked her to dance in heavily accented English. She said, "*No, gracias,*" and attempted to sidestep him. He moved to block her way. "*Por favor,*" Ingrid said, but again he blocked her path. The man spoke in rapid Spanish. He touched Ingrid's arm.

Mohammed moved quickly out of his chair to Ingrid's side. It would not be good for there to be a confrontation or for police to become involved and Mohammed knew that he must try and diffuse the situation.

"Please, *Señor,*" Mohammed said softly, almost apologetically, "this is my wife, my *esposa.*" Mohammed put his hand lightly on the man's chest to back him away. The man laughed. He had beautiful white teeth under a thin black moustache. He turned to his friend and said something in rapid Spanish. When he turned back around, his smile was gone.

"*Basta!*" yelled the man from the bar. They all looked over at him. He had a shotgun leveled at them. Mohammed and Ingrid instinctively took two steps back.

"*Bueno,* Hector," the man said, and put his hands up in supplication, as if to tell the bartender not to overreact.

"*Ya vete!*" the bartender said, gesturing toward the door. The man by the pool table put his cue down and said something in Spanish to his comrade. The taller man turned to Ingrid, grinned, and kissed the air. "*Adiós, chica,*" he said. They left the bar, but not before one of them reached into his pocket and threw a bunch of money on the pool table. Mohammed watched them get into a pickup truck parked outside the bar and drive off in a cloud of dust.

The bartender and the waitress apologized profusely to Ingrid and Mohammed for the behavior of the men. Ingrid and Mohammed feigned graciousness but then quickly paid the bill and left.

As they walked down the street back to the hotel, Ingrid and Mohammed talked about the incident.

"What would you have done if the bartender had not intervened?" she asked.

"I don't know. I guess I would have had to put the man down without hurting him too badly. The last thing we need is to call attention to ourselves."

"I was thinking the same thing," replied Ingrid, "but I thought it would be worse if a woman did it."

"That is probably true. Anyway, Ingrid, it is a lesson in how quickly things can go wrong. Until we are across the border, perhaps we should eat in our room or in the hotel."

"Yes, perhaps."

They heard the screech of brakes from behind them and turned around. A pickup truck came to a halt in front of them. The two men from the restaurant got out. Mohammed instinctively pushed Ingrid behind him. A confrontation was now inevitable. The men were thoroughly drunk and they weaved as they walked up to Mohammed and Ingrid. Mohammed briefly thought about simply running. He and Ingrid were almost certainly in better shape than the Mexicans, but they did not know the town or speak the language. Although the old familiar tension and fear came to him, both he and Ingrid were armed and they could always kill the men, but that would be messy. They would have to flee the town and the police would certainly be looking for the perpetrators; it could potentially result in their entire cover being blown or worse.

"*Ach*," Mohammed said in resignation, as the two Mexicans swaggered up to them. Ingrid quickly dropped back another step into the shadows and pulled the small Beretta 21 automatic from her purse. She flicked off the safety and held the gun close to her side.

The two men stopped in front of Mohammed. Mohammed said in his accented English, "We want no trouble."

The man who confronted Ingrid in the restaurant laughed loudly. "Go away," he said to Mohammed. "Our business, *Señor*, is with the woman." The other man looked nervous and unsure. Mohammed knew he must act quickly to take the initiative. He stepped forward to grab the man, but the Mexican moved with amazing speed. He had a switchblade knife in his hand, which he opened and slashed wildly in front of Mohammed. The knife cut Mohammed's forearm but the wound did not stop him. He put his left hand on the Mexican's arm to immobilize the knife and with his right hit the man in the face with all his strength. As the man groaned and started to crumple, Mohammed kneed him hard in the groin. The man went down in a limp pile and Mohammed kicked the prostrate man in the ribs repeatedly. The man rolled over and vomited. Mohammed picked up the knife and slit the Mexican's nostril and then tossed it into the bushes. Blood spread all over the man's face. The other Mexican stood still, a look of shock on his face. He raised his hands to show that he meant no harm and kept saying over and over, "*Lo siento, Señor*" —I'm sorry.

Mohammed turned around to Ingrid and said in Arabic, "Let's go before something else happens."

Ingrid put on the safety and carefully put the gun back into her purse. As she walked by the bloody and groaning Mexican, she kicked him in the face. "*Schwein*," she said under her breath as she stepped over him.

"Let me see the wound," Ingrid said as Mohammed unbuttoned his shirt. He sat back down on the bed to let Ingrid examine it. Mohammed held up his right arm. There was a slash wound in the flesh of the inside of his forearm.

"It isn't bad, although my shirt is ruined," he said. "It is quite painful."

She looked at it closely in the light of the hotel table lamp. The wound was about two inches long and perhaps an eighth of an inch deep.

"This needs to be sewn up," she said, holding his arm gently in her hands.

"Then do it," Mohammed responded, a grimace of pain on his face.

One of the things they had purchased the day before they left Mexico City was a physician's first-aid kit. It included lidocaine, a syringe, sutures, and a needle. Fortunately, Ingrid had first-aid training. She cleaned his forearm with betadine and injected the lidocaine all around the perimeter of the wound. Once it was anesthetized, she pulled the skin apart and carefully cleaned the wound with antibiotic liquid soap.

"Do you feel anything?" she asked him, as she stuck the threaded needle into his skin.

"No. Nothing," he replied.

Mohammed kept his arm perfectly still as Ingrid stitched. He could see her breasts rising and falling through her thin cotton blouse as she concentrated on her work. He wanted to touch them. He closed his eyes to divert his attention.

A few minutes passed. Ingrid cut the last suture. "There," she said, "I'm all finished." Impulsively, she leaned down and kissed his arm. He gently stroked her hair and she raised her face to look at him. Her lips were thick and puffy, her blue eyes unblinking. Ingrid's eyes showed the strain of the last few hours.

"I cannot ignore it any longer." He leaned down and kissed her on the mouth, a hard kiss that expressed the fullness of his passion. She kissed him back.

"Mohammed," she said, but she did not have time to finish the sentence as he was on her.

Chapter 42

Two weeks after their meeting at the cafe, Hannah received a message on her cell phone from Niaz. She said that she was inviting her to a weekend in the country; she would meet Niaz the following Friday at noon in front of the main entrance of the University. She would be returned home by Sunday evening. If she could come, then she should wear a blue *hijab* to class on Tuesday, Wednesday, and Thursday. Niaz said that she should not tell anyone where she was going.

When the Israelis traced the phone number back, it was from a pay phone at the central railroad station.

So this was it, thought Hannah. She would, once more, be with her enemies beyond the reach of help from her own side. This time, unlike Tehran, she would be with professionals; people, like her, who were trained to be wary and ruthless, and to kill without remorse. She fully understood and accepted that the odds of her making a mistake and being discovered were high. There was a good chance that she would lose her life and never know the joys of motherhood or the pain of growing old. It made her sad to think about it. But it was the choice she had made. She could back out now, but she knew that her sense of duty would not permit her to do so.

On Friday night, she stood in front of the entrance of the University waiting for Niaz to arrive. It was a cold, clear night; the evening before, a late snowstorm had covered the surrounding mountains in a thick blanket of white. The moon was up and the stars were out. She wrapped her wool scarf tightly around her head and neck and waited. Her breath came out thick in the cold air. She felt fear in the pit of her stomach. What if they knew who she was and were simply going to pick her up, torture and execute her?

Somewhere out in the night Hannah's fellow Mossad agents were watching her with their night-vision equipment. Around her neck she wore a cylindrical charm locket—a *taweez*—popular with Muslim women. Imbedded in the locket was a micro-transponder. Even if they searched her, it was unlikely they would discover the transponder unless they used sophisticated, highly sensitive electronic detection equipment.

In their final conversation, Avi Gerstner had informed Hannah that, as long as she had the *taweez*, they would be able to follow her anywhere and track her slightest movement by satellite. "We'll be going to the bathroom with you, Hannah," he said, trying to reassure her. When they stopped laughing, the conversation turned serious. Gerstner explained that, if she stopped moving for a period longer than 24 hours or the transponder ceased transmitting, they would assume she was dead or had been caught—which meant she was as good as dead. Her orders were to find out as much information as she could and get out alive. If she survived the mission, they would have a wealth of information on Iranian covert operations. She would be on her own and would have to make decisions on her own.

A small Japanese car pulled up across the street and Niaz got out of the back seat. Looking around, she crossed the street and approached to Hannah.

"*Salaam Alekeim*, Vashti," said Niaz warmly.

"*Alekeim Salaam*, Niaz," replied Hannah. The young women embraced. Hannah felt Niaz's sincerity in her embrace. She really was glad to see Hannah; Hannah was glad to see her, too. She liked Niaz. She hoped she would not have to kill her.

"It is good to see you. I'm so glad you could come. You will not regret it," Niaz said in Farsi. She picked up Hannah's overnight bag and gestured for Hannah to follow her. They crossed the street to the car. The driver, who was a short, muscular man with a thick neck, got out and opened the door for Hannah. She gave him her bag, which he put in the trunk. In the front passenger seat sat another, younger man, who turned around, nodded and smiled slightly. Niaz got in on the passenger side. The car started up.

"I know this is silly, Vashti, but you understand, we must follow security precautions. I have to put a blindfold on you. Where we are going is a big secret." Niaz pulled out a black scarf and tied it around Hannah's head. "Vashti, I must also take your watch. You understand why?"

Hannah said, "I understand completely, Niaz."

"I'm so glad," replied Niaz, patting Hannah's hand.

Hannah's lack of eyesight made her hyper-alert to sounds, but traffic was light and there wasn't much to hear. The men in the front seat were silent except for occasional grunts and the sound of cigarettes being lit or put out. They spent some time—Hannah figured about thirty minutes—driving in city traffic. They took many turns and even backed up once. They were probably trying to make sure that they were not being followed. Niaz kept asking Hannah questions about her background and family. Not terribly probing or deeply personal questions, but Hannah had to concentrate on answering correctly. Niaz kept hold of Hannah's hand, obviously intending to reassure her. Once, almost in a whisper, she leaned in close and said, "Don't be scared, it will be OK." In fact, Hannah was scared, but not for the reasons Niaz would have assumed.

After a while, they left city traffic and were driving on a winding road. The conversation with Niaz became intermittent and then they drifted into silence. The longer they drove, the more Hannah's fear that they would simply kill her and dump her by the side of the road abated. She tried to stay alert but the sound of the engine and the darkness made her drowsy. Eventually she drifted off to sleep leaning on Niaz's shoulder. Niaz put her arm around Hannah and stroked her head. She dozed on and off for what seemed like hours.

Hannah awoke with a start when the car stopped. "Wake up, Vashti," Niaz said, pulling off the blindfold. It was dark and they were in the country somewhere. The car was parked in front of a house. The driver opened up Hannah's door. He looked at her with disinterest as she got out. Her legs felt cramped, her nostrils were clogged with the smell of cigarettes, and she had a headache. The air was warmer than when they left Van, but still quite cool. They were in the high desert somewhere. They could still be in Turkey or in Iran, Iraq, or even Syria for that matter. Somehow she thought they would not take her across the border for a weekend, unless, of course, they already suspected her and she was to be interrogated and executed. But then, why bother with that kind of drama? They could have just killed her on the streets of Van or at any time since they picked her up.

They led Hannah into the house. It was dark and they had to turn on the lights. The front room had a couch and a couple of arm chairs one end of the room. On the other end, there was a battered old table with some more chairs around it. There was a dirty rug over the tile floor. "Vashti," Niaz said, "there is a girl's dormitory to the left. We will go there and shower. It will be morning soon and things will begin." They walked down a dark hallway with closed doors on each side. Bedrooms, wondered Hannah? At the end, there was a large room with some steel bunk beds. In the dim light, Hannah could make out dark outline of sleeping women. Niaz led Hannah silently through the room to a bathroom and turned on the fluorescent ceiling light. It was a tiled bathroom, with a toilet on one side, a shower in the opposite corner where a bathtub had once been, and a sink. It was clean but the white tile was cracked and yellowed. There was an old green towel on a hook.

"You will feel better after a shower, Vashti. I will wait for you outside the door. Everyone will be getting up shortly."

Hannah stripped off her clothes and ran the shower. The water was lukewarm and there was almost no pressure, but it felt good anyway. Hannah used the remains of an old bar of soap that stood in a cup in the corner. She washed her thick hair as best she could and even washed out her nostrils to try to remove the lingering the smell of tobacco. When she was done, she dried off with the towel, which was still damp from the last user, and put on her clothes. They smelled like cigarettes too, but there was nothing she could do about it; Hannah had no idea what they had done with the rest of her clothes. Above the sink, Hannah found a tube of toothpaste in a cupboard and brushed her teeth as best she could with her finger. The toothpaste was a Turkish brand. So perhaps they were still in Turkey.

When Hannah went back out in the bedroom, the lights were on and the other women were in the process of getting dressed. There were two women and Niaz introduced them to Hannah. One, named Durrah, seemed about Hannah's age. The other one, named Zeheerah, was probably a few years younger than Hannah. They smiled demurely when Niaz made the introductions. But there was little conversation. Niaz was obviously the leader and she told them to hurry up as it was time for breakfast.

Niaz led them back down the hallway and through the front room to a kitchen with a large table in it. She gestured toward some rolled-up prayer rugs piled in the corner and led them in prayer. After their prayers, Niaz dished out some oatmeal from a large pot. She smiled at the women and murmured words of encouragement in her soothing, motherly way. Niaz spoke Farsi, so these women must be from the Persian minority in Turkey. The women were not sure if they were supposed to talk to one another and so they ate in silence. Niaz poured them each a mug of hot, sweet tea.

They were led back into the front room and seated. Sitting at the table was a man in camouflage fatigues. He fit Hannah's image of the swaggering, Middle Eastern terrorist, replete with holster slung low over his hips, checked Palestinian style *keffiyeh,* and sinewy body. He was handsome, clean-shaven, with a strong chin and dark, intelligent eyes. He had a scar across his cheek, like one of those Prussian dueling scars in an old movie. He looked to be in his mid-thirties, maybe a little older.

"I want to welcome you. I am Commander Zaid." He paused and looked at each of them directly in their eyes. The other two girls averted their gaze; Hannah did so as well but looked up slightly more quickly than the other girls. She could tell that he took note of her gesture. "You have been chosen to serve the Islamic revolution and the cause of anti-imperialism." He spoke in heavily accented Farsi. Hannah could not detect by his accent where he was from, but guessed he was from one of the Gulf states.

"For the next two days we will assess you and your capabilities. At the end of that time, we will discuss with you what our expectations are for you. You may be asked to stay with us and accept an immediate assignment or we may ask you to return home and wait for us to contact you." He looked again at the women one at a time, as if taking his measure of them.

"During these next few days, we must be rigorously honest with one another. It is the only way we can both know if you are right for this work. We already know a lot about you. You have been investigated and watched. We know you are committed individuals, but not everyone is right for our work."

He paused for a long time. The silence hung heavily in the room. Zaid took a deep breath and began to speak more softly. "The work we do is dangerous and you may be killed. But we are not suicide bombers. We are soldiers for Allah, but we act in the shadows, in the quiet. We fight the Zionists and their Mossad, the CIA and the British MI-6. When we die, we die anonymously and sometimes alone. But our deaths are not any less glorious because they are not public."

"Vashti," he said suddenly, startling Hannah and the other women. "Could you act the part of a Westerner, give up the mosque, live apart from your community and your family?"

"I could, Commander," replied Hannah earnestly.

"Have any of you traveled to America or Europe?" Zaid asked.

The two women smiled shyly and Durrah replied, "Commander Zaid, this is the farthest we have ever been from home in our lives."

"Vashti, what about you?"

"I've only been away from Turkey one time. Last year, my mother and I went to Iran on vacation. I've never been to America, but I took English in school. Everybody takes it."

"The Turks have forgotten everything important in their slavish love of the West," Zaid said disdainfully.

"Also, Commander, I don't know where we are now. We could be abroad, but I'm certain that we are not in America." Hannah's humor broke the tension.

"That much I will concede, Vashti," Zaid said, "but if you make any more inquiries as to where we are, I will have to conclude you are a Zionist spy." They all laughed.

"And you, Zeheerah, have you ever fired a gun?"

"I have never fired a gun, Commander Zaid, I don't know how."

Zaid smiled, "And if we taught you?"

"Yes," the girl replied shyly, "I could."

"Darrah, could you kill a man if necessary?"

"Yes, if it be the will of Allah," responded the older woman, calmly and with resignation in her voice.

Zaid looked at them again, one by one. "All right, follow me."

He walked across the room and flung open the front door. Bright sunlight entered the room. The women got up and followed Zaid outside. Hannah tried to imprint what she saw in her mind. They were in a high desert valley surrounded by snow-covered peaks. There were a few stone houses maybe half a kilometer away. She could see a road in the distance, bifurcating the valley. The surroundings gave no hint where they were.

Zaid led them around to the back of the house. There was a car there and an old truck. Beside the truck a man with a black hood over his head was tied to a chair. His head was bent down, as if he was asleep. Zaid stood next to the man, reaching over to pull his head up by the hood.

"This man betrayed us to the Americans and he must die."

Zaid unholstered his gun. It was an old military revolver. He pointed it up in the air and pulled the trigger. The sound was deafening in the empty valley. It echoed several times. The women all jumped, startled by the sudden loud report.

"One of you needs to kill this man," Zaid said.

Hannah could hear one of the women suck in her breath.

"Come on, it's easy. Just come here and I will give you the gun. Then you put it at the side of the head of this pig and pull the trigger. It will be over in a second." Zaid put the gun against the man's head. "Boom," he yelled. He looked back at the women and laughed loudly at his joke. His expression changed to a look of disgust.

"You, Zeheerah, you do it. Come on."

Zeheerah shook her head. "No, I can't." The words came out as a froggy-sounding whisper.

"Well, then, Durrah. Are you brave enough to pull the trigger against this traitorous dog? The Koran says we should behead him. You are lucky I'm not asking you to do that." Zaid turned the gun around in his hand and held it out. "He would slaughter you or your parents or your brothers and sisters without mercy if he had the chance."

Durrah fell to her knees, crying. "I cannot do such a thing. No. No. No," she whimpered, shaking her head. She buried her head in her hands, ashamed by her fear.

"So Vashti, what about you? Are you also paralyzed with fear?"

Hannah walked the ten feet toward Zaid in measured steps and as she got close, she held out her hand. He gave her the gun. She held it like it was an unfamiliar object. He took her hand between his and put her index finger around the trigger. He brought her hand up to the man's lolling head. Was he conscious under the hood? His hands cupped hers with great gentleness and strength. As he pulled his hands away, he said in a whisper, "Just squeeze the trigger, Vashti."

She looked at him squarely in the face. His eyes were bright with excitement. Another crazy terrorist, thought Hannah. She was momentarily tempted to shoot Zaid. But she closed her eyes so as to reinforce the impression that she had never done this before and pulled the trigger.

There was a click. The two women moaned. And then silence. Hannah should have known; the gun felt a little light. She opened her eyes.

After a few seconds, Zaid took the gun from Hannah and put it back in his holster. He pulled the black hood off the man's head. It was the driver from the night before. "So you're the one who tried to kill me. I'll have to watch out for you." The man shook his head and laughed. "Untie me, Zaid," he said.

Zaid untied the man, who rubbed his wrists and ankles before he got up, nodding toward Hannah. "I didn't think it would be this one."

"You can never tell. Niaz, take these two inside and we can resume."

When Hannah turned around, Niaz was helping the other two women up, murmuring to them in her motherly way.

Zaid stood next to Hannah. "When the moment came, you did not hesitate. That's excellent."

"And what of the other two women?" asked Hannah.

"Vashti, we are all put here by Allah for a purpose. They may not be able to pull the trigger, but there are many different kinds of soldiers needed to make an army."

They walked back into the house in silence. Above her, Hannah saw a hawk circling lazily in the strong morning sun. So far, this was working, a thought which made her weary.

Niaz and the two other women were waiting for them. There were mugs of hot tea on the table and a plate of little anise-flavored cookies. When they settled down, Zaid began to speak again.

"Zeheerah, Durrah, you are not to feel ashamed about what just happened." His tone was soothing and warm. "Almost everyone reacts as you did, especially women, who are by nature more peaceful than men and slow to violence. We have different work for different people. Now you, Vashti, I want to tell you that since I have been doing this, only one other woman showed no hesitation." He pointed at Niaz, who was busy pouring more tea for the women. "Niaz. Would you believe that underneath her calm smile beats the heart of a ferocious warrior?"

Niaz looked up and smiled shyly. "Thank you, brother," She said, returning to her work.

They spent the rest of the morning listening to Zaid lecture. He described the enemies of the Islamic Revolution: the Americans, the Israelis, the British, and their corrupt lackeys, the Saudi princes, the Egyptians, and the Jordanians. He recounted the history of the overthrow of the Shah and the battle against the Russians in Afghanistan. He talked of the valiant struggle of the Palestinians against the Jews. He became especially emotional when he discussed the Jews: their secret conspiracies going back centuries, their trickery in inventing the so-called Holocaust so that they could gain sympathy from the gullible Christians, their control of the press and the banks. He said these things matter-of-factly as if they were laws of nature, like the tides and the seasons. Hannah was not surprised by his message, as this was the age-old anti-Semitic bigotry and fanaticism, printed and reprinted every day in the Middle Eastern press, but she was astonished by the viciousness of the tone. Zaid really believed these things. They were not the words of a cynic but of a man who knew his subject and knew it well. She had an epiphany. This is what even educated Nazis must have sounded like in the 1930s, as though the most virulent racist myths were simply scientific facts. The sun rose, the sun set; the Jews stabbed Germany in the back, the Jews carried special diseases. Would it ever change?

At noon, they ate a small meal of lentil soup. Zaid ate with them. The conversation turned lighthearted. They talked about their childhoods. It turned out that Zaid was from Syria and had grown up in Aleppo. He told some funny stories about running wild in the Souk with a gang of other boys. Niaz was from Abadan in Iran, near the Iraqi border. Her family was from the ethnic Arab minority of Iran and they were Sunni Muslims. When she was a child during the Iran-Iraq war, they had spent hours playing in bombed-out buildings. One, a destroyed mosque, they called "Buckingham Palace," but she couldn't remember why. Hannah asked her if she attended University and it turned out that she had graduated with a degree in English. For a while, she had even taught English at a language institute in Tehran before she joined the Jihadist movement.

Durrah and Zeheerah had known each other all their lives. They were both ethnic Persians who had grown up in a small village just across the border from Iran in the province of Nakhichevan. Before 1989, it had been part of the Soviet Union. Their families, who were devout Muslims, smuggled them across the border into Turkey so that they could be educated in a religious school. After the breakup of the Soviet Union, there had been fighting between the armies of Armenia and Azerbaijan for control of Nakhichevan. Their village was destroyed and their families became refuges in Turkey and Iran. Although their childhoods had been hard and poor, the women had warm memories of village life.

It was obvious to Hannah that all of the talk was yet another—softer—method of interrogation. When they turned to her, she talked of long afternoons spent at her father's electronics store in Van and of their excursions to Lake Van and Mt. Ararat. She talked about her close-knit family and the neighbors. She had no trouble regurgitating the biography the Mossad had supplied her. It would hold up—for a while—unless they began digging really hard into her background. The Mossad had set up the electronics business years before and people would know the family. Through a little bribery, the Israelis had managed to plant certain information in the records of public offices around Van, from forged tax returns and birth certificates to voting records and deeds.

After lunch, Niaz took Durrah and Zaheerah off toward the bedrooms and Zaid asked Hannah to take a walk with him. They walked around the back of the house and across the valley in the direction of the hills. The sun was warm, although the air was cold and brisk. A perfect early spring day.

Hannah could sense the self-assurance of Zaid and something else, his sexual energy. He was very attractive. She had known men like this, been involved with men like this, and been hurt by men like this. But Zaid was the enemy. He was a terrorist, a killer of the innocent, and he stood for everything that she fought against. She felt a sense of revulsion at feeling sexual attraction for this man. It made her shudder and close her eyes momentarily. He noticed. "The sun is intense here. We are very high up and the air is thin. It can make you lightheaded when you exert yourself."

"I think I'm mostly suffering from a lack of sleep. We drove all last night and although I dozed in the car, it wasn't very restful."

"If you become an agent, you will have many sleepless nights."

"Zaid," she said, "that is what I want. I want to do something important with my life. I am so sick of the mindless materialism of the Turks, especially the students at the university. They want to be European; they care nothing for Islam."

"Tell me," Zaid said, stopping and turning to face her, "what did you feel when I asked you to pull the trigger?"

"Do you really want to know?"

"Yes"

"Nothing. Nothing at all."

"Did that shock you?"

"Yes it did."

"Could you do it again?"

"If I had to."

Zaid did not reply. He looked into her face for a long second and turned and started to walk again.

For several minutes they walked in silence.

"Vashti, if you come with us, there is no turning back and there is no going home. Even if you live, you will still give up your life. Our enemies will try to hunt you down; you will always be looking over your shoulder. Who is that strange man on the bus? Is he Mossad, a contract killer for the CIA, or just an ordinary passenger? You will know fear like you cannot imagine. You will see your comrades die and no one will bury them or mourn them or hold their hand while they suffer. Think hard on this."

"I understand," she replied.

"And what do you think of Niaz?"

"She seems to be a very good person; a righteous woman. She is trustworthy and loyal."

"All those things are true. Would you like to be paired with her on a mission?"

"I would."

"Well, there's a lot that must happen first. But I sense that you two would work well together. Vashti, I think we should go back." Zaid gently touched Hannah on the shoulder to turn her around. His fingers lingered lightly on the material of her coat. The meaning was clear. She did not flinch; nor did she gesture back. He moved his hand away.

They turned and walked back toward the house.

"Tonight a man will be arriving who would like to talk to you about your studies at the university."

"What sort of man?" asked Hannah.

"He is a specialist in advanced technology. We know that you study physics at the University and we want to see how you might be helpful to our plans."

"I would be glad to talk to him."

When Hannah returned to the house, the two other women were gone. Niaz told her that they had been taken home. They were good women, she said, highly suitable for certain work. Niaz did not elaborate on what work that might be. Zaid joined them at the kitchen table. Hannah asked if she could sleep for a few hours. Zaid agreed that that would be a good idea and the two of them went to the back of the house. Niaz asked her how she felt. "Tired, really tired." Niaz led her to one of the metal bunk beds. It was freshly made, with clean sheets. Like her mother had done as a child, Niaz tucked Hannah in. "Sleep well," she said, but Hannah was already drifting away. Unconsciously, she fingered the *taweez* around her neck. Somewhere, out in the world, Israel was watching over her.

"Vashti, wake up. It's time for dinner." Hannah felt Niaz gently shaking her. She wanted to go back to sleep, but after the Army and the Mossad, she knew how to get out of bed quickly. Hannah could tell that Niaz was surprised by the speed at which Hannah moved. A somewhat more perceptive person than Niaz might have wondered about this, but Niaz merely thought it was another of Vashti's positive attributes.

When they got to the kitchen, Zaid was there with another man. There was food on the table—hummus, pita, a chicken stew, pickled vegetables. Zaid introduced the man as Professor Azam, a "great teacher and friend of the Islamic Revolution." He was a small, round man, well past sixty by Hannah's estimation. He wore a cardigan sweater over a white shirt that was slightly frayed at the collar. He had old-fashioned, black-plastic glasses with thick lenses that made him look like an owl. But what was truly extraordinary looking about him were his eyebrows, which were black, very bushy, and touched one another. He had a thick, gray beard that he stroked repeatedly when he talked. His eyes were intelligent but they had an abstracted, vaguely wild look about them.

"Miss Palmeni, we understand that you study physics at the 100th Year University in Van," the Professor began, as they passed around the food. His tone was kindly, trusting, grandfatherly.

Hannah had dreaded this moment but she knew it was coming. She had studied hour after hour, day after day for this moment; the moment when she would have to demonstrate that she was really a graduate student in nuclear physics. Avi Gerstner had even gotten her a tutor from Hebrew University and Hannah had traveled up to Mt. Scopus three days a week to meet with Mordechai Hirschfeld. Professor Hirschfeld sat in his book-lined office and smoked a pipe while teaching her how uranium was enriched, how a centrifuge was built, and how to make a nuclear bomb. When she talked about Hirschfeld to Avi Gerstner, he laughed and said that Hirschfeld "cut his teeth at Dimona." The two academics—Hirschfeld and Azam— seemed to be almost mirror images of one another.

Professor Azam began by asking Hannah about her classes and the names of her professors. She dutifully regurgitated the information, starting with her first year at the university and moving through her last. He asked about her decision to enter the graduate program in nuclear engineering. They discussed fun and amusing topics, like quantum mechanics and black holes. He asked her about whether she thought fusion power was possible, to which Hannah responded, "Some day perhaps." Since Zaid and Niaz could add nothing to the conversation and Hannah was in no position to ask questions of the Professor, as the minutes passed, the conversation became more obviously an interrogation. The questions got harder and were asked more quickly. Azam asked her about the different types of centrifuges and how to calculate relative centrifugal force. "By the way," he inquired, dropping any pretense of subtly, "have you studied nomograms?"

"Yes," she replied, "in my Systems Management class." Oh God, Hannah thought, was that Systems Management or Systems Engineering? He produced a nomogram from his briefcase and showed it to her. "Do you recognize this?" Azam asked.

"Oh, my word, that takes me back. I haven't seen one of these for three years. It's a chi-square nomogram," Hannah was reaching hard now, "I think it's a Bates correction, is it not?" Hannah could see the anxiety in Niaz's face. She didn't want Hannah to make a mistake.

"That's right, you have a good memory, Miss Palmeni."

Professor Azam beamed. He seemed as pleased as if Hannah was his favorite student and had just passed a tough exam. Zaid watched Hannah carefully and when she glanced at him, she could tell he was focused on her reactions.

He asked her about various isotopes of uranium, their radiation signatures, and how one would go about making weapons-grade uranium. Now she was back on more familiar ground. Hannah talked of the isotopes of uranium and plutonium; their weights, degree of radioactivity, and how they were manufactured and enriched. She confessed to not knowing how nuclear bombs were made. It was not the sort of thing they learned in her classes, but the students sometimes talked about it. They were simple things, really. The hard part was obtaining enough enriched uranium—or better yet, plutonium—to make a bomb. If it wasn't enriched enough, the bomb would have to be as big as a house.

After nearly two hours, they moved into the front room, where Niaz served them tea and little sweet cakes filled with sesame paste. Hannah was hoping that the interrogation was over, but Dr. Azam just moved on to new topics.

"Let's talk about quantum mechanics."

"I've taken several classes in that area."

"Tell me what you know about the Ehrenfest theorem."

Here we go again, thought Hannah. Fortunately, this one she knew cold. "It relates the time derivative of the expectation value for a particular quantum mechanical operator to the commutator of that operator. And then compares that with the Hamiltonian of the system."

"Correct!" She could tell that Professor Azam was impressed. "And what is a Hamiltonian?"

"I feel like this is a final examination."

"It may be," said Zaid dryly. "It would not be good if you failed it."

For a split second, Niaz looked at Zaid with a flash of anger in her eyes, then her face returned to its more serene natural state. But the comment left a pall in the room.

Hannah dove right in. They had driven this stuff into her head.

"A Hamiltonian is a comparison of the observable relative to the total energy of a system. When you're talking about observables, it is necessary to look at its spectrum to determine all the potential outcomes."

The questions dragged on for another hour. Hannah's head ached. Finally, after what seemed like the millionth question, this time about "eigenvectors," she said, "I'm really very tired and I don't want to do this any more." She put both her palms to her temples. Turning to Zaid, she said in a voice harsher than she intended, "Enough! Either you trust me or you don't. I am not a Zionist spy; I am just a student at a Turkish University. I want to return home now."

Professor Aziz looked crestfallen. He had clearly been enjoying himself. Zaid said softly, "You are right, Vashti. This has been exhausting, but you must understand, it is necessary."

"Of course, I understand," replied Hannah, her tone gentler now. "But I can't go on any more. My head feels like it will explode."

"Well then, I will talk with Professor Aziz while the two of you go to sleep. Tomorrow morning we will drive you back to Van."

Later, as they lay in opposite bunks, Hannah and Niaz talked quietly.

"Vashti, you know so much. I was amazed at your knowledge."

"I learned a lot in school, but the things we were talking about were the things that any college physics student would know."

"Obviously, Vashti, they are trying to make sure that you are who you say you are."

"And, am I?" responded Hannah with a gentle laugh.

"You've convinced me. I hope, God willing, you have convinced them."

"Me too. I wouldn't want to wind up sitting in a chair with a hood over my head and with you having to pull the trigger."

"No, no, Vashti, as it says in the Holy Koran: 'When you meet the unbelievers in the Jihad strike off their heads.' The sword," Niaz said with a mischievous chuckle, "is the chosen method of execution for traitors and enemies in this Jihad."

"Fortunately, I am a believer," responded Hannah. But the image of herself on her knees with a curved blade descending on her exposed neck made her shudder in the darkness of her bed. Hannah felt a great loneliness descend upon her. She was a stranger among her enemies. Hannah touched the *taweez* once again and it comforted her. In her mind it was transformed into a talisman, a *mezuzah*—but with a radio transmitter inside.

Niaz put her arm across the space between the two beds and lightly touched Hannah's arm. "Sleep well, Vashti."

In the morning, Niaz and Hannah sat down to breakfast. Zaid strode into the kitchen soon after. He instructed Hannah to pack her things. She was to be driven back to Van. Over breakfast Zaid said that he was very pleased with her. He would make a report to his superiors and then, if she was accepted, she would receive her orders. She should resume her normal life and await further instructions. If she was given the honor to serve the Jihad, she would have one more chance to say no. After that, there would be no turning back.

"How long will it be?" she asked.

"Not long," was Zaid's vague response.

Within twenty minutes, they were back in the car, driving down the bumpy dirt road that led to the highway further down the valley. Niaz was sitting next to her in the back and the same two men that drove her were in the front. Niaz put the hood over Hannah's head again, gently patting her, and said, "I'm so sorry, Vashti, but this is necessary. You understand, don't you?"

"Of course," Hannah replied, fighting back the image of a gun held to the side of her shrouded head.

Hannah and Niaz talked for a little while, but the hood over her head made it hard to keep a conversation going and they soon lapsed into silence. The road wound up into the mountains. Hannah tried to stay alert but it was difficult and she fell asleep.

A while later she awoke, but Niaz was asleep, so she just listened. She could tell that they were on a highway, as she could hear other cars and trucks. They must be getting close to Van, thought Hannah. Niaz woke, grabbed Hannah's hand, and the two women began to talk again.

The car came to a halt. One of the men told Niaz to take off the hood. They were in front of the University, just where they had picked up Hannah on Friday. It was afternoon and the bright winter sunlight hurt Hannah's eyes. Hannah hugged Niaz and she got out of the car. The driver was already outside getting Hannah's bag out of the trunk.

As he handed it to her, he said to Hannah with a deadpan expression, "If there was a bullet in that gun, you would have killed me." He broke out into a smile, "You're a tough one. May Allah be with you." His smile vanished and he closed the trunk. Without looking at Hannah, he got back into the car and drove away. Niaz turned and waved from the back seat.

Hannah stood on the curb for a minute and looked around. It was a quiet Sunday afternoon. Traffic was light. A few students were leaving the University and there were some families strolling across the street, window shopping.

Hannah saw a taxi parked across the street. She hailed the cab, relieved that she would not have to call and wait for one. The driver waived to signal that he saw her and drove the car up to the intersection and made a U-turn to pick her up. When the taxi pulled up to the curb, Hannah opened the door and got in.

"*Shalom*, Hannala," said Avi Gerstner. "I knew you were coming and so I borrowed Zvi's taxi to come and pick you up." He pulled into the road and headed toward the house.

Hannah felt a great sense of relief wash over her. She was safe again. When she went to speak, her voice choked up. She felt like crying and that made her feel ashamed. Israelis were supposed to be tough. She could see Avi looking back in the mirror.

"You're still alive. You did well, Hannah. They accepted you. No?"

"Avi," she said, her voice controlled to keep it from breaking. "I am so glad to be home."

"I know, Hannala. I know," Gerstner responded softly.

"I think they accepted me. They will contact me to go for further training. Where was I?"

"The tracking device in the *taweez* worked well. We tracked you to a remote area called the Heshmand Valley in the mountains just north of the Iraqi border. It was about 400 kilometers from here."

"So you were able to follow me the whole time?"

"The Americans even took satellite pictures of you taking a walk with someone behind the house."

"That was Zaid. He was the instructor, an intense guy."

"Who else was there?"

"Besides Zaid, Niaz was there and two Persian women from just north of the border between Turkey and Azerbaijan. They weren't killers and they were sent home Saturday afternoon. There was also the driver and the guy who came with him when they picked me up. There may have been others that I didn't see. And then, of course, there was the Professor they sent to interrogate me. They said his name was Azzam, but who knows if that was true."

"We have photographs of Zaid, Niaz, the driver, and the guy in the passenger seat," said Avi. "As soon as you take a look at the photographs, we will send them back to Tel Aviv to see if we can identify them."

"Did you get a photograph of Professor Azzam."

"Unfortunately, we didn't get a picture of any academic types. The place is pretty well guarded."

"And now what?" asked Hannah.

"We start the waiting game again. I suspect that they will be contacting you in the near future. From what we know of their modus operandi, they will send you for basic training and then on a mission."

Hannah threw her head back on the seat and closed her eyes. "Avi, I can hardly wait."

Chapter 43

THE OTAY MESA BORDER CROSSING, OTAY MESA, CALIFORNIA
MAY 6

On the Mexican side of the border, the line of cars snaked toward the US Customs facility. Ingrid was driving. She was very nervous and felt queasy. She was actually starting to worry that they were going to have to stop the car so she could throw up. Maybe it was the food they had the night before. An American in the bar of their last hotel had talked about something he called "Montezuma's Revenge," which she understood to mean a gastrointestinal attack—although she was not clear what the Aztec King Montezuma had to do with it. She did know that the American was making a joke and that she was supposed to laugh. They had avoided Mexican water and raw fruits and vegetables, but it was impossible to avoid the food. Mohammed, however, showed no signs of illness. He too was tense, his jaw locked in an expression of concentration, as if he was expecting the US Border Patrol or the Mexican Federales to launch an assault at any moment.

The other men were in the line about half a kilometer behind them. They had decided to stay a little apart so that, if one group was stopped, the other group could get through.

At the Mexican checkpoint, the officer asked for their passports and gave Ingrid and Mohammed a quick cold stare. He nodded and waved them on toward the American side of the border.

The American Immigration officer was a woman, who smiled, and asked them how their stay was in Mexico. Ingrid managed to smile back and said that they had had a wonderful time in Mexico, but were tired and ready to go home. She ran their passports through a computer while another officer in blue coveralls examined the outside of the car and looked in the back seat and the trunk.

When the cursory inspection was completed, the woman officer smiled at them, handed them their passports back and said, "Welcome home."

Ingrid felt a sense of tremendous relief. "We made it."

"Praise Allah," said Mohammed, a big grin on his face.

They drove a few miles up the road and parked at a combination gas station and 7-11 convenience store off the highway to wait for the other group to call them. An hour and a half later, they were still waiting, the windows down to keep the car cool.

"Should we call them?" asked Ingrid.

"Yes, go ahead, they should be here by now."

Ingrid punched in the speed dial of the cell phone. It rang three times and then someone answered, "*Sí.*" Ingrid hung up.

"Mohammed, a Mexican voice answered the phone. What do we do?"

The cell phone rang.

Ingrid looked at Mohammed for guidance. "Should I answer it?" She looked at the screen on the phone. "It's them."

"Answer it."

She pressed the green button on the phone and put it to her ear.

"Hello," she said.

"Hello, Yankee," said the voice.

"What do you want?" asked Ingrid in her thick German accent.

"Oh, so you are a girl," said the voice, laughing. "Your amigos say 'hello' to you, Señorita. They are here at the police station and they are in bad trouble. They had an *accidente* with another car and they had no Mexican insurance *carté*. So they got searched. In one of the men's pocket, there was some *drogas*. Heroin. Very bad for them. You need to come here and pay the bail or they will stay in jail."

Ingrid, horrified, pressed the button to end the call.

"Mohammed, it is the Mexican police . . . ."

". . . or people who say they are the Mexican police," interrupted Mohammed.

"Whoever it is has them. What do we do?"

"Hand me the phone." Ingrid gave the cell phone to Mohammed, who opened the car door and stepped outside. He opened the back of the cell phone and took out the battery. He pulled the little SIM card out of the back and put it in his pocket. He then casually tossed the rest of the phone on the ground and stepped on it several times, crushing it into small pieces. Mohammed picked up the pieces and walked over to a garbage can by the gas pumps and tossed in the crushed remains of the phone.

When he walked back to the car, he said to Ingrid, "We need to go. They are on their own and our mission is compromised. Hopefully, they will keep their mouths shut. In the meantime, we can only hope that they don't connect us to them."

Ingrid closed her eyes and put her head back. "*Scheisse*" she said.

"Now drive, Ingrid."

Ingrid felt a renewed wave of nausea come over her. "I don't think I can. I feel really sick."

"I will drive, then. Let's switch places."

Ingrid got out of the car and the sudden movement made her dizzy. She put her hand on the side of the car to steady herself. Mohammed was coming around from the passenger side.

"Are you all right?" His voice was quiet and tender. He put a hand on her shoulder.

"No, I'm going to be sick." She vomited at her feet, so violently that Mohammed had to step back to avoid getting vomit on his shoes. Ingrid felt humiliated and shaky, but the nausea abated. She looked up and her eyes met Mohammed's. She wiped her mouth with her sleeve.

"Ingrid, get in the car. I will go and get you a coke to settle your stomach."

Ingrid got in the passenger side and lay back on the seat with her eyes closed. A few minutes later, Mohammed knocked gently on the glass. Ingrid opened her eyes and Mohammed handed her the 32 oz. plastic cup and the straw. She had never seen a drink that big. No wonder the Americans are so fat, Ingrid thought. Fat and decadent. But the icy cola tasted good and settled her roiling stomach.

Mohammed drove the car out slowly out of the parking lot and got back on Highway 905 headed toward San Diego.

"Are we blown, Mohammed?" asked Ingrid.

"I don't know. There is a contingency procedure for this situation and I think we should use it."

Chapter 44

St. Petersberg, Russia, May 7

The Internet site was maintained by a man named Sergei, who ran a small and modestly successful Internet web page design business in St. Petersberg. The relationship began with a telephone call three months earlier. The female voice spoke Russian with an accent. She wanted Sergei to set up a secure retail site to sell Russian nesting dolls. After their initial conversation, Sergei and the woman—she said her name was Sasha—communicated by email. She was not very selective and seemed only mildly interested in the Web-page design, agreeing immediately to his first suggested design. Sergei received $500 in crisp new US fifty dollar bills in the mail and he wasn't about to ask questions. Sergei had no idea whether the business was successful or even where it was located, but he knew one thing, every month the postal service delivered an envelope with another $50 bill in it. He monitored the hits on the web page. There were under ten each month.

One of the features of the web page, which was common to many retail sites, was an ability to contact the owner of the business through email. What Sergei didn't know was that any emails sent to the web site would be routed and rerouted several times until they wound up at their destination, the central communications branch at Pasdaran Headquarters in Tehran.

Chapter 45

Just after the 10:00 am opening of the Inglewood branch of the Los Angeles County Public Library, Mohammed Dibul sat down at a computer terminal reserved for public Internet access. Mohammed and Ingrid had been in the United States for less than thirty-six hours. On the screen appeared the website for Russdolls. com. He didn't waste any time perusing the various nesting dolls available for purchase, but clicked on the "contact us" section. Up popped an email box. Mohammed was instructed to use the website only in the event of an emergency, but he believed their current situation definitely qualified as an emergency.

Mohammed typed out three simple sentences: "I have a nesting doll that is missing its bottom half. It is a doll of the President of Mexico that I bought in Tijuana. Do you sell parts for dolls?"

The message Mohammed sent was a one-time code, one of the many he and Ingrid had memorized during their training in Lebanon. As their Pasdaran trainer had explained, the one-time code, a series of seemingly innocuous phrases known only to the parties, is one of the most difficult codes to break. There are no ciphers and no key and unless one of the parties is captured or compromised, it is impossible to decipher.

This message meant that the members of the other team—the bottom half—had been apprehended by the authorities. They had been arrested in Tijuana, Mexico. The remaining members were now requesting instructions.

The cipher clerk in Tehran who received the message went running to his superior officer two stories upstairs from the basement communications room. Immediately recognizing the crisis at hand, they, in turn, contacted General Yazdi.

An emergency meeting of the control team for Operation *Zaqqum* was called for midnight.

The men gathered in the subdued light of one of the many conference rooms in the building. As the others arrived, General Yazdi was there, looking grim-faced, waiting for the meeting to begin.

"Let's begin. What do we know, Munir?" asked the General.

The head of the foreign communications branch rubbed his eyes with one hand, pushing his black plastic glasses onto his forehead. "What we know is this, Sir. We received an email on the secure Russian site using the correct one-time code. One member of Team One, either Dibul or the woman, al-Suri, sent the message, which originated in the United States at a computer located in a public library in the city of Inglewood, California. The message indicates that the members of the other team are in the custody of the Mexican police or army at or near the city of Tijuana."

"What are our assets in Mexico?" Yazdi asked, turning to a man in uniform, a Colonel, who was in charge of the North American desk.

"We have a full team operating out of the Embassy in Mexico City. They have good connections with the police and the government, but our people are under constant surveillance by the Americans, who have a huge counter-terror presence in Mexico. On issues related to foreign espionage operations, the Mexicans will not cooperate with us and will run directly to the Americans with any information. They are lap dogs in the so-called 'War on Terror.' The Israelis are quite active in Mexico as well."

"So, in your view, can we go to them with an issue such as this?"

"There is no way. We could try to bribe them to let our people go. They call it the *mordita* in Spanish—'the little bite.' In our case it would be a big bite. But they could take our money and still go to the Americans. A big arrest of suspected terrorists along with Iranian Embassy personnel would be a disaster that we can't risk and that the Mexicans would find irresistible."

"Agreed," said the General, brusquely. "We need to stay a million kilometers away from this situation. We cannot be connected to these men. So where does that leave us?"

The Colonel hesitated and began to speak slowly. "General, the first option is to hire a Mexican lawyer to try to get them out of jail, pay the necessary bribes, and then move them out of the country. The downside risk is that we don't know what kind of interrogation they are being subjected to, whether their cover stories will hold up, and whether their Middle Eastern origin will trigger suspicion and attract the attention of the Mexican intelligence service and the Americans. They are traveling on Canadian passports. If the Canadians examine the passports, the cover story will unravel. A connection could be made to Team One and then the Americans will begin a nationwide manhunt to locate them. It could destroy the whole mission."

"The first option isn't an option, Colonel. What else have you come up with?" asked the General, thumping his fingers down on the table.

"Well, General, if I may be permitted to speak freely."

"Yes, yes, go on," said Yazdi impatiently, waving his arm.

"We have developed good connections with parts of the Mexican underworld; in particular a drug gang who we have allowed to import heroin through Iran without interference. From time to time we have engaged them in black operations. One year ago, we hired them to eliminate a Kurdish nationalist who was living in exile in Mexico City. They made the man disappear. Very neatly done; the body was never found. We could engage them to . . .," he looked around the room at each of the expressionless faces, ". . . eliminate the men in prison."

There was a silence in the room. Yazdi continued to drum his fingers on the table as he looked at each person.

"A very unfortunate predicament. Do we really have any other option, Colonel Sharif?"

"Given the risks, I would say no."

"Then make it happen." General Yazdi's mood suddenly shifted. "Well, brothers," he said smiling, "there are many ways that the righteous can achieve martyrdom. Some ways, unfortunately, are more glorious than others. Any questions?" There was silence.

"One more loose end, Gentlemen. Once this matter is concluded, we need to find a replacement team to go to California. I do not want a repeat of what happened this time. And get them in there without going through Mexico. Is that understood?"

"Yes, sir," they said in unison.

Yazdi rapped once loudly on the table like a judge bringing down his gavel to adjourn his court. "This meeting is concluded."

Chapter 46

La Mesa State Penitentiary, Tijuana, Mexico, May 10

I n the summer of 2002, the current *Commandanté* of La Mesa Prison in Tijuana was just a *Tenente* in charge of a squad of heavily armed members of the Federal Preventative Police. On a hot August morning, he and 1,500 of his fellow officers were ordered to storm the prison. Their aim was to return the prison to a state more fitting a penitentiary.

After gaining control of the prison yard, the city that had grown up within the walls of the prison, known as "*El Pueblito*," was leveled. The vendors, women and children, prostitutes, and other people who were residing there, but were not actually prisoners, were evacuated. Gone forever were the private apartments, taco shops, brothels, and other makeshift buildings that had grown up inside the courtyard of the prison. The Mexican government promised that henceforth the prisoners would be treated humanely but firmly. La Mesa would be transformed into a model prison. Reform was in the air in Tijuana that summer of 2002.

By the time the three Middle Eastern prisoners were transferred from the dingy holding cell in Otay Mesa to La Mesa Prison, the promises made in 2002 had long been forgotten and La Mesa had settled into its natural role as just another dreadful Mexican prison. For enough money, anything could be bought, from sex, to drugs, to men's lives.

The three prisoners were confident that their handlers would come to their rescue. The police had made it plain enough: a substantial bribe would secure their release. They had asked them a few perfunctory questions about their plans, where they had been in Mexico, and where they were planning to go when they were released. It was obvious that the police had no interest in digging into the real story of these men. Why they were singled out was unclear. Perhaps it was their dark complexions or strange faces. The three prisoners prayed daily and assumed that it would only be a matter of time before they would be set free. They waited for some contact, but none came. However, they were men of faith and their confidence did not wane. They believed their rescue was imminent.

The other prisoners kept their distance from the three Arabs. Many spoke English and could have communicated with them, but they sensed that these men—intense, quiet, quick of glance—were not the typical sort of *Norte Americano* drug addicts and hustlers that wound up incarcerated in Mexican prisons. All three of the men were no strangers to prison—Arab prisons—and so they were wary but felt little fear. Nobody tried to shake them down or rape them or sell them heroin. In fact, it became evident to the men within a week of arriving at La Mesa that the other prisoners were avoiding them. This was oddly disturbing; what did it mean?

In the mornings, the prisoners were let out onto the big courtyard that had once been the site of the crowded little alleys that constituted *El Pueblito*. The three members of Team Two sat on a bench in the shade of a building observing the other prisoners. They knew instinctively that they should always keep their backs to the wall. It was going to be a hot day and the skin of the omnipresent weightlifters, who were stripped down to the waist, was already shiny with sweat. A small group of transvestite prisoners, whose sexual favors were much sought after, watched the men lifting weights and tittered appreciatively. The light-skinned Americans were off in another corner nursing their sob stories and waiting for the good news their Mexican lawyers were always on the verge of bringing but which rarely arrived. A mixed group of prisoners was playing soccer. Guards with shotguns patrolled the walls, smoking and paying little attention to the activities going on beneath them in the prison yard.

With a speed that seemed unnatural, two groups of prisoners, perhaps twenty heavily tattooed, hard-looking men in all, converged in the yard just a few feet in front of the Arabs. Fareed, the Yemeni, asked the other two if they should leave. "No, let's just stay here quietly. If we get up they may draw us into it," one the Egyptians responded. This turned out to be an error in judgment.

As the war of words escalated between the two groups, they drifted closer to the bench, until they were just a few feet away. Other prisoners noticed and were running in the direction of the fight to watch. The three Arabs now knew they should move, but they were effectively trapped by the crowd. Any sudden movement on their part might be misinterpreted as a signal that they intended to become involved in the conflict.

Like a crazy dance, two of the men pulled out knives and began to thrust them at one another. As the yelling reached a crescendo, they went for each other, tumbling on the ground in a cloud of dust. Without warning, six of the men closest to the bench pulled out knives of their own and attacked the three Middle Easterners. Although they tried to defend themselves, they had no real chance. While one attacker went for the body, the other went for the head, slashing and stabbing. Just as a warning shot went up from the wall, someone yelled "*vamanos*" and they all walked rapidly away in different directions.

Two of the three Arabs were dead in pools of their own blood and the Yemeni was near death. He bled to death thirty minutes later as he lay in La Mesa's infirmary.

The prison gang members who did the hit were paid in drugs and sex and a few pesos.

Chapter 47

During the day, Hannah resumed going to classes. But for four nights, her fellow Israelis relentlessly debriefed her, reconstructing every moment of her weekend in the house. It was amazing the detail that Hannah could recall under the questioning. Avi mostly just sat there, adding the occasional question. Her most intense interrogator was Noam, who worked the front counter of the Palmeni family store. But they all participated: Zvi, a big bear of a man, who was supposed to be Hannah's Uncle, Adem, a Turkish Jew originally from Izmir, who acted the role of an employee of the store, Benni, who played the role of Hannah's father, and, of course, her "mother," Shoshana.

Within a week, they had positively identified the driver and the other man as low-level muscle—*stharkers*, as Avi called them in Yiddish—for the Iranian foreign intelligence service. But they came up with nothing on Commander Zaid.

"And Niaz?"

"Nothing, Hannah, the trail is dry there. She's not Turkish, Jordanian, or Egyptian. So maybe she's telling the truth and is an Iranian Arab from Abadan."

"She is an odd mix. Devoted to the cause, obviously, but such a sweet woman." Hannah looked up at Avi, "I like her. She's nice."

Shoshana broke in. "Hannah, my dear, never forget that there are a lot of nice people who hate us and would not shed a tear if every Jew on the planet was murdered."

"I know, I know," replied Hannah irritably. "I'm just saying she's a paradox; such a sweet woman mixed up with such evil."

"So we have a mystery." Gerstner held up one finger. "Why do you think they asked you the question about going to America?

"Then there's the other mystery," said Zvi. "What do they want with our Hannah and when are they going to come to take her away?"

"Very amusing, Zvi," Hannah said, reaching across the table and slapping him on the arm.

Six weeks had passed since the weekend in the Heshmand valley and Hannah was beginning to wonder whether the whole mission was at a dead end. She half wanted it to be over because she was tired and yearned desperately to go home for good, find a nice, stable, boring husband and start a family. Maybe she could teach on a kibbutz and forget about guns and spies and killing. The other half of her hated the thought that the mission might be a failure. She liked to win and having a hot lead run cold was disappointing.

Then one Tuesday afternoon as she was walking down a path on the University campus after finishing a graduate seminar she heard her name called quietly from behind. When she turned, it was Niaz. Spontaneously, the two women embraced. Hannah was genuinely glad to see Niaz, but seconds later she felt her stomach knot; this was it, the Iranians had taken the bait. They sat down on one of the park benches that lined the path.

"Vashti, the time has come. They are waiting. You must come with me now."

"Now? But what will my family think if I disappear? What about my clothes?"

"When we are in the car, you will use my cell phone to call your mother and tell her that you have fallen in love with a man who is not Muslim. You must show great emotion and say that you know that your parents will disapprove. You will tell him he is a Jew and that you are going to live with him in Israel; that you can't bear to disappoint them. Tell them you will contact them when you can. As for everything else, we will give you everything you need—clothes, passport, a new identity. You may not be back for a long time."

Hannah did her best to look stunned into silence. Niaz took Hannah's hands in hers and looked into her eyes.

Seconds passed; seconds that felt like hours.

"Vashti, you must decide now. They are waiting."

Hannah nodded slowly up and down, weighing the gravity of her decision.

"Niaz," Hannah said, "I will do it."

"Then let's go."

Hand in hand, Niaz and Hannah made their way out of the west entrance of the University. As they passed under the arched gate, a car pulled up. Inside was the driver from last time, looking as deadpan as ever, and his thin friend. Hannah and Niaz got in the back seat.

"You know the routine, Vashti," said Niaz, as she placed the hood over her head. Niaz asked Hannah to lie down on the seat. She gently stroked Hannah's shoulder. "I'm sorry, but it is better that you not be seen."

Hannah felt the car start to move.

"I will call your mother on the cell phone. What is her number?" asked Niaz. Niaz punched in the numbers and handed Hannah the cell phone, which she had to fit under the hood.

Shoshana answered the phone. Hannah began a tearful and emotional rendition of the story she had been told to tell. When she got to the part about eloping to Israel, Shoshana was totally silent. She said, genuinely, "Are you joking with me?"

"No, *Madar*, I am not."

"Vashti, my daughter, what has happened to you?" Shoshana adapted quickly to the changing plot. She raised her voice, half yelling and half crying. "It is one thing to fall in love with a Sunni, but my God, to fall in love with a non-Muslim. You have always been a good girl, obedient to your parents, observant, and moral. A Jew, my God, girl, what have you done? When your father hears this, it will kill him." Shoshana's voice turned harsh and bitter. "You must come home now."

Niaz whispered into Hannah's ear, "Tell her you can't come."

"I can't, *Madar*. I can't come home." Hannah was sobbing. She hoped it sounded real. Niaz was patting Hannah's shoulder.

"Vashti," said Shoshana, "come home right now. "

"I can't do that; I must go with him."

"If you commit this sin and bring shame upon your family, you will be dead in our eyes."

Hannah was silent for a moment as she contemplated the implication of her "mother's" threat. "Please, Mother, don't say that. Please."

"Vashti, say you will come home now or I will hang up. And if I do that, don't call back." Shoshana spoke slowly and her voice was controlled and hard. "My daughter will be dead."

"I can't do that, *Madar*. I love Yehuda."

"Then it's goodbye, Vashti," and Shoshana hung up.

Hannah put her hands around her head and sobbed heavily. Niaz tried to comfort her, murmuring supportively.

"Vashti, you did a very difficult thing. I know it is hard, but muhajadeen must do hard things. If you told your mother what you were doing, you would put your family's lives in danger. You are making a sacrifice and some day, God willing, they will understand."

Hannah replied in a measured tone, "Niaz, I will mourn silently. I will never speak of this again. I will never cry over this again. I know that what I did was the right thing to do."

They stopped talking and the men in the front turned on the radio. For a long time, they listened to the music. At some point, Niaz told Hannah she could sit up because it was dark. Hannah felt stiff.

The car pulled off the highway and drove in another direction along a straight road.

They stopped. Niaz pulled off the hood. It was dark, very dark. The night was moonless. As Hannah got out of the car, she noticed a small airplane, painted black, sitting on what appeared to be a dirt airstrip. A man standing by the plane ran toward them. With a bang, the twin engines on the plane coughed to life. The pilot revved the engines up and then throttled them down to a steady roar. The man ran up to them and said loudly over the din of the airplane engines in formal Farsi, *Shab bekheyr, sarkar khanoma*—"Good evening, dear ladies." He bowed theatrically. "Now, shall we be off? We're in a bit of a hurry." He ran toward the plane, waving them to follow.

Hannah and Niaz ran behind the man. As they got close to the airplane, they felt the propeller wash. The air was cold and it blew their hair all about. Hannah and Niaz instinctively tried to hold their head scarves, but it was difficult. When the man got to the plane, he opened a door on the side and pulled down a steel ladder. He stood by the side of the steps to assist Hannah and Niaz as they climbed in. When Hannah and Niaz were inside the plane, the man climbed in, bringing the steps up and closing the door. Pointing to two rows of seats, he gestured for them to sit down. He yelled to the pilot, "Go!" and the pilot immediately released the brakes and let out the throttle. The plane taxied quickly down the bumpy runway and took off just seconds later.

It was dark inside, except for the muted lights on the instrument panel in the cockpit. The running lights on the wings and tail were turned off.

The man chuckled and said to them, "Welcome, ladies, to Pasdaran International Airways. Make yourselves comfortable. This is a very quick flight. We will be in the air for about fifteen minutes and then we will land."

"Can I ask where are we going?" asked Hannah.

"You may, Miss. We are flying back to Iran. From there, I don't know where you are going. But I'm going home to my wife."

He gave each of them a bottle of water and wandered up to the cockpit and sat in the copilot's seat.

After a few minutes, the airplane's running lights went on. Hannah guessed that they had crossed the border and were now over Iranian airspace.

Chapter 48

General Yazdi sat smoking a cigarette at a conference table in the office of the military attaché at the Iranian Embassy on Mezzeh Street. Looking out the window, he could see the maple-leaf-emblazoned Canadian flag flying in front of a building. Beyond the Canadian legation were the embassies of Australia and Chile. There were something like fifteen embassies on Mezzeh Street, which made it the unofficial "Embassy Row" of Damascus.

General Yazdi turned his gaze back to the man who was talking. Yazdi was impatient; he had another meeting to get to and Zaid was reporting at length regarding his recent activities as the Commander of the Pasdaran's Clandestine Branch in eastern Turkey. Yazdi's adjutant, Captain Rajaei, looked bored.

"We've succeeded in pairing the female agent named Niaz Najjar with Vashti Palmeni. Both of them fit the description we want: excellent English, strong commitment, loyal, intelligent, and resourceful. Palmeni has turned out to be a very promising recruit. She even looks like a Jew."

"Oh, yes," Yazdi said, and turning to his adjutant, "Remember her, Gheysar? The one with the curly black hair and the pretty eyes?"

"Yes, Sir, I do. She was the girl on the train."

Drumming his fingers on the table, Yazdi said, laughing, "I have not lost my touch scouting potential agents."

Captain Gheysar interrupted. "They will be transported to Lebanon where they will undergo intensive operations training."

"It will be interesting to see how they react when they find out what their mission will be."

Chapter 49

JEBEL ESH SHARGI, SYRIA, MAY 21

The Jebel Esh Shargi is a mountain range that separates the Syrian Arab Republic from Lebanon. The main north-south highway that runs between Damascus and the Turkish border is called the M-1 in Syria. In theory, but for the limitations imposed by modern politics, it is possible to drive from the Holy City of Medina in Saudi Arabia all the way to the city of Adana in southwest Turkey. Along the M-1, about 80 kilometers north of Damascus, lies the ancient market town of al-Nabk. From al-Nabk, there is a small, one-lane road, little more than a jeep track, that winds its way west over the mountains to the city of Baalbek on the Lebanese side of the border. Baalbek is the cultural and economic center of the Shia population in the Bekaa Valley and the headquarters of Hezbollah, the Shiite militia and terrorist organization.

Hannah and Niaz had been sitting all morning on hard benches in a little waiting area near the main entrance of the Syrian Border Police headquarters. Just after they were dropped off, a taxi brought two young men, who sat on the opposite side of the room. They were silent, following strict instructions not to speak with anyone. It was obvious to the four of them that they were all going to the same place, but they obediently observed "cadre discipline," as they had been taught. Niaz, to Hannah's surprise, leaned over and whispered in her ear, "The one on the left is very handsome."

Hannah smiled and whispered back to Niaz, "Allah's lock on your chastity seems to be loosening."

Niaz reached over and pinched Hannah's arm. "You are evil," she said.

The two boys across the way ignored them, but Hannah could tell that they were dying to talk to the two women dressed in Western attire. They were brought these clothes, along with Syrian passports, just before they were taken from their hotel to Mehrabad International Airport in Tehran to board the Air Arabia flight to Damascus. Niaz clearly felt awkward in the fitted jeans, cotton top, and light jacket she was wearing. She acted scandalized and offended, but Hannah could tell that she was pleased. Hannah thought the outfits were a bit matronly by Israeli standards, but they were a far cry from the long dresses that Niaz was used to. They still wore the *hijab* to conform to the public dress standards required by the Islamic Republic, but now had assumed the look of the more secularized Arab women of the Levant. They were instructed to take off the headscarves when they got on the plane and to keep them off. Niaz told Hannah that it was the first time since she was a little girl that she had been without a head covering.

Since leaving Van, Hannah had learned a lot about Niaz. She was recruited two years earlier in Tehran, where she taught English and Arabic at a girl's secondary school. She was trained to be a courier and was assigned to carry messages and money between Iran and eastern Turkey. Her intelligence, sunny confidence, and personal warmth impressed her superiors and they expanded her role to include recruitment. That was how she came into Hannah's life.

Niaz wanted more; she wanted to be an active agent. She asked Commander Zaid repeatedly if it was possible for her to receive advanced training and he repeatedly told her that she was not ready. Finally, Zaid relented and agreed to talk to his superiors about Niaz's request. The gentle persistence of Niaz paid off and General Yazdi ordered that she receive advanced training and be reassigned.

In truth, Zaid did not want to see Niaz transferred because he was deeply taken by her. In keeping with the absolute prohibition in the clandestine service against fraternization between agents, he was careful not to reveal his feelings. The situation was made more complicated by the arrival of the new trainee, Vashti, whom Zaid also found very attractive. But when the decision was made to pair the two and transfer them immediately to Lebanon for training, Zaid was actually relieved. The whole situation had become too complicated for Zaid and he celebrated his release from the chains of emotional complexity by spending his first evening in Damascus at a whorehouse near the Souk.

An old mud-spattered Russian UAZ jeep pulled up in front of the waiting area and stopped in a cloud of dust. The driver wore mirrored sunglasses, a black-checked *kaffiyeh,* and an olive-drab military uniform. "Hey, you four, let's go," he yelled in Arabic, waving impatiently. "Come on, come on."

The two men got up and the good-looking one said, "You first, ladies."

"Shukran," Hannah responded. She noticed that Niaz was blushing.

They climbed in the jeep. One of the men sat in the front and the rest of them crammed in the rear.

The driver looked down over his sunglasses at the two women in the back. "We will be driving for two hours—maybe a little less if we go fast. It's a rough road and this thing has Russki shock absorbers, which means no shock absorbers, so hold on." With that, he turned around and, with great ceremony, took a cigarette out of a pack stuck in the visor, lit it, inhaled deeply, and as he exhaled a dense plume of smoke out of his nostrils, popped the clutch, and off they went in a cloud of stinking bluish exhaust. The noise was incredible and after a few efforts at conversation, Hannah and Niaz stopped trying.

The road west over the mountains was treacherous. The driver seemed to take some crazy pleasure in the discomfort of his passengers because every time they went over a pothole or through the mud, he turned around and gave them a triumphant smile.

At noon they reached the border. It was nothing more than a checkpoint in the mountains manned by three bored-looking Lebanese Army soldiers who simply waved them through. Hannah's spine hurt from the repeated jarring of the jeep and she kept squirming in her seat in a vain attempt to find a comfortable position.

As they came down the western slope of the mountains, they got their first view of the Bekaa Valley. It was very green and dotted with farms and villages. In the far distance, they could see a city. In the mountain ravines they saw the remaining stands of the *Arz Ar-Rab*, the Cedars of Lebanon, that once covered much of Lebanon and northern Israel. In her mind's eye, Hannah thought they would be bigger, an image shaped by the mythic Bible stories of her childhood.

They pulled off the main road about five kilometers east of Baalbek and turned north on a small dirt road that ran along side a stream. A few minutes later, the driver turned into what looked like an old school from the French-colonial period. It was a two-story stucco building with a tile roof. It was painted a pleasant pale ochre color. The second floor was lined with large, white, double-hung windows.

Two muhajadeen carrying Kalashnikovs guarded the entrance of the compound. One of them came up to the car and the driver gave him a piece of paper. The guard examined it and then looked at each of the four passengers. He nodded in the direction of the gate.

"Welcome to the University of Martyrdom!" the driver yelled as they drove through the gate. He laughed heartily at his own joke. Hannah thought: Whoever said that terrorists didn't have a sense of humor?

As they pulled in front of a big, block building, an officer in camouflage fatigues came out of the thick carved wooden door. He stood on the steps and waived at them in, greeting them as the vehicle came to a stop.

Hannah was relieved to have finally arrived. Every bone in her body ached and when she stood up her legs felt like jelly. Her mouth tasted sour, she felt filthy, and she needed to find a toilet immediately. The others looked exhausted as well.

Niaz turned to the driver and thanked him politely for the ride.

"I got you here alive," he said, "and that's what counts."

Chapter 50

Avi Gerstner studied the photographs in front of him while Ari Levin gave his report. They were taken with a long-range telephoto lens at the farmhouse in the Heshmand Valley.

"We finally figured out who this guy is. His *nom de guerre* is Commander Zaid. We ran his photograph and name by everybody— the Europeans, the Americans, even our new friends the Vietnamese. Nobody could identify him until we talked to the Kurds. They identified him as a member of a paramilitary hit squad by the name of Nizar Hussein Al-Jamil, who was posted by Saddam's people to Mosul right after the first Gulf War. His group infiltrated the Kurdish zone and kidnapped and tortured suspected Peshmurga guerillas. The Kurds would love to get their hands on him."

"So, Ari, is that it?" asked Gerstner.

"No, there's more. When we ran the name Nizar Hussein Al-Jamil, he came up on our database. You're not going to believe this, but this guy's a Palestinian. We've got him as part of the Hezbollah team that participated in the Buenos Aires Jewish Community Center attack for the Iranians in 1994."

"So what was he doing with our friend Saddam if he was an Iranian agent?"

"We don't know. Maybe the Iranians ran him into Iraq to keep an eye on things. Hey, they hate the Kurds too."

"What are our options?" asked Gerstner. "He's a small fish. Please do me a favor and come up with a plan to deal with this Zaid or Al-Jamil, or whatever his name is, that doesn't cause a lot of *tsuris* with the Turks. You know how literary I am, Ari. I'd like a little . . . what do the Americans call it? Poetic justice."

"Yes, yes, I understand," Levin responded impatiently. "I've got two ideas. One, we tell the Turks that the house in Heshmand Valley is filled with wanted Kurdish separatists. They'll bring a bunch of special operations types and odds are they'll kill everything that moves. Two, we leak to somebody . . . I don't know, probably the Russians, that this Zaid works for us. Big-time Zionist spy. Then the Russians tell the Iranians and they take our little friend out one night and put a bullet in his head. Very clean, no Jews involved."

"I like the second option. It's good. So go talk to Yaakov and David and make it happen."

Chapter 51

The apartment that Mohammed and Ingrid inherited was in a complex like so many others in southern California: white stucco with a fake Spanish tile roof, a pool and sauna, and an exercise room that nobody used. It was called "Casa de las Palmas" and, to prove the name was justified, there was a line of lanky palm trees out front. They were badly in need of a trim. The complex was about twenty years old and well on its way to seedy. Children's tricycles and toys were scattered about the common areas and the pool needed to be cleaned. But for Mohammed and Ingrid's purposes, the place was perfect; they weren't looking for friends, they were looking for anonymity. They hardly ever saw their neighbors and the manager stayed out of people's business. The tenants were from all over the world, although the majority were Hispanic. There were a few Iranian couples, but Mohammed and Ingrid kept their distance.

They had been directed to get settled and wait to be contacted. Naturally, Ingrid and Mohammed were very anxious to find out what happened to the other team and worried that they might have broken under interrogation. The previous team had hidden two handguns, an M-16, and some ammunition in the attic access panel in the ceiling of the closet. Ingrid and Mohammed decided that, if the police came, they would rather die on their feet than be taken alive.

About a week after they arrived, they received a coded email message. Mohammed sat down at the kitchen table to engage in the laborious task of decoding the message. The code had been devised by the Al Qods Signals Branch. It was simple and virtually unbreakable. Each group of numbers in the code was keyed to a word in the previous day's Los Angeles *Times*. The first number represented the section of the newspaper where the word would be found, the second number indicated the page, the third number the column, and the fourth the word. Thus the grouping "2,3,2,25" would mean that the word would be found in section 2, page 3, in the second column, and would be the 25th word in the column. If the word was a proper name, then the word would be "name" and the first letter of each subsequent word would spell out the name.

The message was short and direct.

"Team 2 down. Cover intact. Replacements arriving. Contact instructions to follow. Proceed per plan."

Mohammed shredded the email message and deleted it from both his computer and the server.

"Mohammed, what now?" asked Ingrid.

"We do what we've been ordered to do as if the mission was not compromised in any way."

"What do you think happened to them?"

"They must have been arrested by the Mexican police on some unrelated matter and are rotting away in a jail somewhere. Or perhaps they were robbed. If they were caught and the police suspected their true mission, then our controllers would certainly have ordered us to get out. They don't want us caught."

"Who will they send to replace them?"

"They told me that they were training a back-up team, but did not inform us who they were. We'll find out soon enough."

Mohammed and Ingrid drove around the Wilmington area with the newspaper classified ads looking for warehouse space to rent. They wanted something that was large enough to store a truck and tractor-trailer with a sizable work area. They eventually found a small warehouse a few blocks from the marine terminals. They paid the owner, a Korean man named James Oh, $4,500 in cash for two months. Mr. Oh seemed delighted and not at all curious about what they wanted to do with the property. Ingrid signed the lease as "Danielle Smith, Controller," for a fictional company called "Smith & Jones." Mr. Oh, who insisted that they call him "Jimmy," told them that they would need to get a business license from the City and they could use that to switch over the electric service.

The process of getting a business license took all afternoon. They drove downtown to LA City Hall. After wandering through the hallways, they finally found the City Clerk's office. They stood in a long line, which snaked its way toward the clerks' windows. When it was finally their turn, the clerk informed them that the $350 business license fee could be paid in cash, but first they had to fill out an application for a Business Tax Registration Certificate. Ingrid and Mohammed stood in the hallway and struggled over the application, which taxed their English skills. They used the names and Social Security numbers that they had been given by the other team. However, they left blank the section of the application that required that they fill in the "NAIC Code" for their type of business. They didn't know what an NAIC Code was and after a short whispered argument decided that it would be best to leave it blank. They got back in line. The clerk was a fiftyish African-American who showed neither interest nor sympathy for the fact that Mohammed and Ingrid were having problems with the form. She informed them that she could not accept it because it was incomplete. Mohammed started to ask questions, but the clerk had difficulty understanding his accented English. She directed them to another office on Spring Street where they could get assistance with starting a new business. After a circuitous walk, they finally found the "Office of Small Business Assistance." The waiting area was crowded with would-be entrepreneurs and they had no choice but to take a number and wait.

To their irritation, a man sitting next to them decided to start a conversation. He explained to Mohammed and Ingrid in heavily accented English that he was from El Salvador and was trying to open a restaurant. He was very talkative and didn't seem to notice that Mohammed and Ingrid were not the least bit interested in chit chat. Nevertheless, he was nothing if not persistent and coaxed all kinds of information out of them, virtually none of which was true. When they complained about the bureaucracy, he laughed, and told them it was nothing compared to El Salvador, where you not only had to wait in endless lines but you had to bribe the government officials for the privilege of doing so.

Finally their number was called and they sat down at a desk in a Formica lined cubicle with a pleasant young Hispanic woman named Ms. Ortiz. She explained that the letters "NAIC" stood for "North American Industrial Code" and that it was a uniform code that was used throughout North America to identify businesses. She directed them to a public computer workstation where they could access the list of codes and pick the one that described their business most accurately.

It was past 4:30 pm when they finished and by the time they got back to the City Clerk's office, it was closed. They would have to come back the next day.

As they crawled along the Harbor Freeway in rush hour traffic back toward their apartment, Mohammed said to Ingrid, "After today, I now understand why God wants to destroy America."

They turned on the radio and listened to the traffic news. There was a sig alert on the 405, so it would probably take them another hour to get home.

"Is this how these people live all the time?" asked Ingrid.

"Allah willing, we will make things infinitely worse for them," replied Mohammed dryly.

Chapter 52

In an odd way, Hannah was enjoying terrorist boot camp. It was a review course in things she knew already. How to break down and reassemble guns. How to throw a hand grenade. How to use knives. How to do everything related to bombs. How to build truck bombs, shoe bombs, letter bombs, and pen bombs. How to load bombs with shrapnel in order to maim people in addition to killing them. Bomb tactics. How to time detonations so that a second bomb exploded after the emergency response personnel arrived. Different types of detonators. Different types of explosives: Semtex, fertilizer bombs, even TNT. Poisoning people, following people, blackmailing people. Self-defense. Hannah had to laugh. Their instructor, a man named Qaboos, taught them straight out of the IDF's *krav maga* training manual, but he insisted that it was a special self-defense technique invented in the 1940s by the Muslim Brotherhood in Egypt. The inventor of *krav maga*, Imi Lichtenfeld, would roll over in his grave if he thought that the Arabs had appropriated his self-defense method originally developed for Jews to defend themselves against fascist thugs in 1930s Budapest.

Niaz was an excellent student, as was Hannah, who had the advantage of years of combat and espionage training, not to mention real experience carrying out combat and espionage missions. At times, it was hard for her to conceal her superior knowledge. On written tests, however, Hannah had difficulty with some of the Arabic and didn't do as well as Niaz. It was just as well. She was constantly worried about raising suspicions among the staff and students of the training school.

Within a few days, Hannah and Niaz settled into the camp's routine. They arose at dawn and trained for fourteen hours a day, seven days a week. After breakfast, there were religion classes, then weapons training until their midday meal, history and ideology after lunch, physical fitness in the afternoon, and more training in the evening. They also prayed five times a day. There were about twenty recruits, about half men and half women. They were each assigned a partner for training. Hannah and Niaz were delighted to find that they were paired with one another.

After two weeks about six of them were selected for special training in Western social skills. For the women, the training included lessons in fashion. Hannah found it odd and secretly amusing to be required by terrorists to study back issues of *Vogue* and *Elle*. They even required the women to practice using cosmetics. The women tittered like schoolgirls playing dress-up. Niaz found the whole thing deliciously wicked and sinful. She enthusiastically embraced these new instructions to look and act Western. Hannah whispered to Niaz that she thought she looked beautiful in Western clothing.

Ever since their weekend in the Heshmand Valley, when Commander Ziad asked about then about going to America, Hannah and Niaz speculated whether America would be their final destination. As the days wore on, they received increasing amounts of training regarding the United States and the women felt certain that they would be sent to North America. They watched American television and movies, learned about the weather and public transportation, telephone manners, and even tipping practices in restaurants.

On their fifth Sunday of training, just as they finished their dinner, Baqir, their instructor in ideology, gently tapped the shoulders of Hannah and Niaz and told them to follow him. The rest of the trainees pretended not to take notice. Silently, he led them to the door of the Commander's Office, which was on the second floor of the building. He was known by his *kunya*—Arabic for *nom de guerre*—as Abu Khalid. Khalid did not mix with his students much, although a few times Hannah had noticed him in his camouflage uniform and black-checked *kaffiyeh*, observing them with one of his officers. Once, they had a military parade by front of the school, with Abu Khalid standing at attention and saluting them as they passed smartly by in ranks of four.

Baqir knocked quietly at the door. From inside, a deep voice responded, "Enter." Baqir opened the door for the women and gestured for them to go inside.

The room was paneled in dark wood, lined with mostly empty bookcases on the back wall. The big wooden desk had nothing on it but a little bust of a man Hannah didn't recognize and a gun belt with a holster. A small black automatic was in the holster. There were some spare clips on one of the bookshelves. Abu Khalid came from behind the desk as they entered and gestured to them to sit down in two wooden chairs facing the desk. His greeting was warm and fatherly. To their left, sitting on the couch under the window that overlooked the front of the school, was a distinguished man in a neatly pressed business suit. He was big, with green eyes and a well-trimmed moustache. He stood as they entered. He bowed slightly and then took his seat.

"May I introduce Abu Bashir," said Abu Khalid.

The women said that it was a pleasure to meet him. Abu Khalid sat on the corner of the desk.

"I have reports that the two of you have excelled in your training. This is excellent."

"Thank you, sir," replied Hannah.

"As you may have surmised, you have been selected for a mission. God willing, you will be going to the United States to rendezvous with a team that is already in place. This is the reason why you have been trained in Western cultural attitudes and attire. In two weeks, after you have received further training, you will be transferred to another location for specialized instruction and final preparation for the mission. This mission is very dangerous and you may be called upon to make the supreme sacrifice for our cause. Is that understood?"

"Yes, sir," they replied in unison.

Abu Bashir began to speak. "For the trip overseas the cover we are asking you to assume is complex and you will need further training in the next several weeks to assume it properly. We want you to pose as Western, assimilated Jews. Not Israelis, as that would require you to speak Hebrew. You will be traveling on Canadian passports and your cover story is that you are sisters from Iranian Jewish immigrant families living in Canada. This way, you can speak Farsi and English and your accents will not give you away. Your story is that your family left Iran when you were very young children at the time of the Islamic revolution with your rich parents, who were supporters of the Shah. A common enough story, is that not so, Abu Khalid?"

"Indeed," replied the man with an nod.

"Since you are assimilated, not religious, Jews, you will not need to practice the religion or keep their kosher food rules or any of that nonsense. But you will have to learn something about the Jews so that you can play the part. For security purposes, you must travel together and must remain with one another at all times. If you are separated at any time, it will be considered a breach of security and will subject you to the maximum punishment. When I say maximum, I mean what I say. Once you have safely arrived in the US, you need no longer maintain the cover story. By the way, we are supplying you with a second set of Canadian passports and a set of US passports. They will be used when you leave the United States at the conclusion of your mission. Do you have any questions?"

"Why Jews?" asked Hannah.

Abu Khalid answered. "It is good cover, that's all. Who would suspect them?"

The women stayed silent. Abu Khalid's question demanded no answer. The two men stood.

"All right, then, you are dismissed," said the Commander.

With an elegant bow, Abu Bashir said, "Good evening and good luck."

Chapter 53

Once they finally got the electricity turned on, Mohammed went about systematically purchasing the tools necessary to complete their mission. There was a Home Depot in Long Beach that carried most of what they needed. They also purchased protective gear from medical supply houses around Los Angeles.

Mohammed and Ingrid established a routine that to an outside observer was not likely to draw attention to them. Monday through Friday, they joined the morning commute with millions of other residents of the Southland, arriving at the warehouse between 8:30 and 9:00 am and returning home around 6:00 pm. They took weekends off.

Although they were making productive use of their time, in reality they were basically in a waiting pattern. The arrest and detention of the other team members in Mexico left them feeling isolated and tense. Mohammed and Ingrid began to quarrel. Their sexual relationship made it no longer possible for them to act like comrades; they were now a couple and there was a heightened emotional dimension to every decision they made.

A second email arrived eleven days after the first. When decoded it said:

Meet Replacement team 2 females

Arrive AF # 64

Date: 3-28

Display sign: Cohen

Ingrid looked at the decoded message and laughed derisively. "Is this a joke? 'Cohen' is a Jew name."

Chapter 54

"So, Avi," began Schmuel, "Hannah is now in the Bekaa at a training camp that the Iranians run with Syrian support. We've done some over flights and have pictures. But they don't show much."

"And what else?" asked Gerstner, looking up over his half-glasses.

"We have Hannah in the pictures. She and the other girl, Niaz, are wearing Western clothes."

"So, Schmuel, what do we make of that?"

"The rest of the students are in fatigues. Only Hannah, the girl Niaz, and a few others are dressed in Western clothes. So we think they are training them to go West, Avi."

"Well if it's Israel that they are sending them, then it will be a short and unsuccessful mission and Hannah will be home shortly. But somehow, I don't think it's Israel they are targeting."

"There is too much competition," replied Schmuel.

Chapter 55

Hannah fingered the *taweez* as she and Niaz listened to a man tell them about how to be Jewish. Hannah was having a difficult time stopping herself from laughing. The lessons were a combination of deeply held anti-Semitic stereotypes and conspiracy theories intermixed with the occasional truth. Their tutor was a Lebanese Imam named Dr. al-Sari who was an expert on Jews. He matter-of-factly explained to them that assimilated Jewish women wore a lot of jewelry and, as everybody knew, gestured a lot with their hands when they spoke. They wore name-brand clothes as status symbols. They prized beauty and were always well-groomed and kept their fingernails long and manicured to show that they did no work. At that, Hannah glanced at her hands with her short fingernails. There was more. The Jews had a keen understanding of money and finances. Since they were young and unmarried, they would be interested in finding wealthy Jewish husbands. The Iranian Jews in particular were highly materialistic. As Sephardic Jews, they had lived under Islamic rule for centuries and, therefore, knew how to act secretly and conspiratorially, and had very tight-knit family structures.

In terms of religious observance, he explained that most assimilated Jews went to the synagogue for their holy days, Rosh Hashanah and Yom Kippur. In America, they also celebrated Hanukah and had lavish Passover Seders. Traditionally, Jews had been guilty of killing children and using their blood in the baking of matzos, but this was rarely done today. The last time it had occurred in the Middle East was in 1840 in Damascus. He made them memorize several prayers: the *Sha'ma*, which he said every Jewish child was taught and the blessing over the lighting of the Sabbath candles, which he said every Jewish woman must know.

They practiced the Hebrew words to the *Sha'ma—Sha'ma Yisrael Adonai elohenu Adonai echad* . . . "Hear, oh Israel, the Lord our God, the Lord is One." Hannah felt very strange. She was not particularly religious, but here they were saying the oldest and most central prayer of her people; said for three millennia in secret, in crisis, in fear and in happiness, in the synagogue, before sleep and battle, said at those moments when a Jew reaffirmed his or her position in the world. Niaz mouthed the words as if they were poison; the Imam with contempt; Hannah with secret reverence.

Two days later, they were brought once again to the office of Abu Khalid. He informed them that they would be leaving within a few hours. Abu Bashir would come to pick them up. They would be taken to Beirut to complete their training and receive further details on their mission.

Abu Khalid put down his cigarette and said to Hannah, "Vashti, please give me your *taweez*. You both must wear these." He picked up two gold necklaces that were sitting on his desk. From one a small Star of David was attached and from the other a little filigreed *hamsa* with the Hebrew word *"chai"* on it. She gave the Star of David to Hannah and the *hamsa* to Niaz.

"Please, sir, that is a family heirloom. May I keep it?" asked Hannah, putting her hand over the *taweez* as if to protect it and trying to look as hurt as possible.

"I am sorry, Vashti, but it identifies you as a Muslim and you cannot take it with you. But I will keep it here in my desk for safekeeping until your return. It will be safe here." Abu Khalid put his hand out waiting for Hannah to hand him the *taweez*. She unclasped it and gave it to the Director, who walked behind his desk, opened a locked drawer, and tossed it in.

"And if I am killed, sir?" Hannah asked.

"It will be returned to your family in Turkey."

Hannah thought: You, Mr. Terrorist Commander, are a walking dead man.

That evening Hannah and Niaz were in a black Mercedes heading west toward Beirut with Abu Bashir and his driver. In the trunk were two suitcases full of their new clothes, everything from miniskirts to makeup. As Bashir happily pointed out the large ruins of the Roman city of Heliopolis, Hannah marveled at the irony of her situation. She was an Iranian Jew pretending to be a Muslim who was pretending to be an Iranian Jew. Now that the *taweez* was sitting in Abu Khalid's locked drawer, she was on her own, unarmed and in hostile territory. Avi Gerstner would conclude that she was most likely dead. Shortly, she and Niaz might very well be on their way to the United States to participate in a major terrorist attack. She couldn't just walk away when they got to the US. She had to find out what the specific target was and then find a way to alert the Israelis and the Americans without getting herself killed.

Chapter 56

PORT OF LOS ANGELES, WILMINGTON, CALIFORNIA, MAY 27

T he crane operator had been working on the docks for more than two decades and knew his business. He picked up the container from the ship and immediately knew it felt wrong. It was heavy, very heavy. The bill of lading said it was a container of after-market auto parts from China, which should weigh approximately 50,000 pounds. The readout on the screen in front of him said that this load weighed almost 28,000 kilograms, around 62,000 pounds, which would make this a seriously overloaded container. He picked up the phone and called Lee Sandahl. This was not standard procedure. Actually standard procedure was to ignore overweights.

Several weeks earlier, they had had a meeting at the union hall where Sandahl introduced a professor who told them he was working on port security, getting no cooperation from the TSA, and asking for their help. If they unloaded a container that was significantly overweight, they were supposed to call Sandahl who, in turn, would get in touch with the Professor. The Professor made his pitch and then he fielded a bunch of questions from the brothers and sisters, who were angry because they thought that port security was way too lax. They liked him. He obviously cared about the issue and he respected their knowledge and expertise. After the Professor left the meeting, they voted to help him. As usual, if the government or the boss wouldn't help them, they'd help themselves.

"That's the one, Jake," said Lee Sandahl, pointing about half way up a stack of containers that had arrived from Hong Kong that morning.

"The third one from the bottom, right?"

"Yeah."

"And you're positive about the severe overweight and the type of freight?" asked Jake.

"Absolutely, it's heavy and it contains auto parts."

Auto parts were at the top of Jake's threat matrix. They contained large amounts of aluminum and filter parts, both of which could emit naturally occurring radiation.

"So let's pull it out and open it."

"I don't have the authority to order that. Do you, Jake?"

"Strictly speaking, Lee, probably not. But if we're right, then nobody will question my authority. If we're wrong, they will get really angry with me. Those Customs guys are already really pissed off at me, so I don't see what I have to lose. Anyway, if I call them to get their permission, they will go ballistic and say no. The absolute worst thing that could happen to me is that I get fired and go back to my teaching job. So here's what I want you to do. Call your supervisor and tell him that I've ordered an overweight container opened for security reasons. I want him over here and I want him here fast."

"OK. You know, Jake, this is going to cause a real shit storm around here. If we start opening overweight containers, it's going to slow things down, cause a bunch of loads to be readjusted, and generally piss off the shippers."

"It'll piss them off a lot more if a nuclear bomb goes off, don't you think?"

"Hey, I agree with you, but I'm just an average working stiff. What do I know?" Sandahl laughed and shook his head.

"Probably more than you think. Anyway, we might as well get this show on the road and see what happens."

Within about two minutes of Lee calling him, the Walking Boss, a guy named Kent Telfer, was standing dockside with Jake and Lee. Even though he was a supervisor, he was a member of the union and sympathetic to Jake's demand that the container be pulled out of the stack and opened.

"So you are making me do this, right?" asked Telfer.

"Yes, I'm ordering you to get that container."

"OK, so here's what we're going to do. We're going to pull that container, cut the seal, and start looking inside. Then I'm going to call management, who are going to go ballistic because we all know that just being overweight is no longer a reason to open a container. Then we'll see what happens."

The unmarked government car drove up to the Customs impound section of the dock where the container was opened and the longshoremen were starting to unload it. Sandahl and Telfer stood back, pretending not to be totally enjoying the incident unfolding in front of them.

Agent Connoughton flew out of the passenger side of the car and strode over to where Jake was standing. Zeigler, who was driving the car, arrived a few seconds later, a look of total amusement on his face.

Connoughton tore off his reflective aviator sunglasses and said, practically yelling, "Dr. Elliot, what in the hell do you think you are doing?"

"Just what it looks like, Agent Connoughton. I've ordered this container, which is seriously overloaded and matches the nuclear-smuggling profile, unloaded and inspected."

"I want to talk to you over there, privately." Connoughton walked off toward the car. Jake looked at the longshoremen, who had stopped working to watch the confrontation, and at Sandahl, Zeigler, and Telfer. He shrugged his shoulders, winked at them, and walked over to where Connoughton was waiting.

Connoughton put a finger against Elliot's chest. "Let me make something perfectly clear to you. This is my Port, Elliot, and nothing security-related happens without my permission."

"Precisely. This is your Port, that's right, and nothing security-related happens here, period. Since I've gotten here, I've gotten nothing but resistance from you people. This is serious. Even if there's nothing in this load and it's just way overweight, it's dangerous to public safety and should never leave the port in that condition."

"Look, Elliot, they sent you here because you fucked up in Washington. All you need to do is relax and let us do our jobs. Our job is not to make sure that overweight containers don't screw up the highways. We're not in the highway safety business. That's the problem of the local police. We're in the commerce business and the security business. We absolutely do not want to interrupt commerce unless we really have to. That's why we have radiation screening equipment and inspectors on the other side of the ocean watching the freight."

"You can delude yourself all you want, Connoughton. But this port is wide open and we're crucifying the security of our people on a cross of gold. So I'm going to do what I think is right until somebody stops me. And that somebody isn't you. You want to call the Secretary of Energy or the head of the TSA or the goddamned President of the United States? Be my guest."

Jake started to walk away. Connoughton grabbed his shoulder. "I'm not done with you, Elliot."

Jake pulled his shoulder away. "Well I'm done with you, asshole." And he walked back to the group of men.

"Let's get this thing inspected and see what we have," said Jake calmly.

The container incident was a fiasco. It turned out that there was no contraband inside; it was merely a simple overweight. Someone at a factory in China just put more in the container than was legal. The motive was profit, not international terror. Nevertheless, now that the overload was discovered, it had to be separated into two containers.

This made the steamship line and auto parts-retailer who were paying for the shipment extremely unhappy. Someone, probably from the Union, called Dave Lifsher, who published a fiercely independent Internet newsletter that reported on the West Coast maritime scene. He reported the incident to all his subscribers, including the AP stringer who covered the waterfront. A story went out on the wires that a "security-related incident" had occurred at the Port of Los Angeles involving a container of auto parts being shipped to a major retailer. The company was identified by name. Wall Street took notice and the company's shares began to drop. At midday, the furious CEO of the company called his old hunting buddy, the Vice President of the United States. Shortly before the close of business on the Eastern seaboard, when Assistant Secretary of Energy Anne Marie Mitchell was directed to call Jake, the United States government was prepared to have him drawn and quartered.

"What do you think you're doing out there?" she asked, her voice shrill and hysterical. "You have no authority whatsoever to break customs seals and order the inspection of containers."

"Look, Anne Marie, I'm trying to wake people up. The security system out here is simply a sham. America is not safe. The threat is out there and we're just going through the motions. Real security means taking the threats seriously. If we don't do something, we could be facing a devastating attack that makes 9/11 look like child's play. I've called you people, I've written reports to the Secretary, I've developed and sent you a threat-assessment profiling system that I think will greatly enhance security. I've tried everything and it has been ignored. Today I did what I thought was necessary."

There was a pause on the line.

"The Secretary has asked that you tender your resignation and leave government service. He does not wish to terminate you but the situation has become intolerable. You know how influential the Vice President is in this administration. They want you out. The CEO of the company happens to have been a 'Ranger' in the President's campaign and is a major, major player."

"Fine, Madame Assistant Secretary, I will resign, effective in two weeks, if you don't mind. I need to get my things in order."

"That would be fine, Professor Elliot. But be sure and fax that resignation letter here today."

It had been a very long day and Jake was exhausted. He sat at the bar at Bubbles, nursing a boilermaker and eating an order of buffalo wings. He didn't normally drink and he certainly didn't eat buffalo wings, but after the day he had, he felt like indulging all manner of sin.

"Hey, bro, what's happening?" Jake felt a gentle hand on his shoulder. When he turned around, it was one of the longshoremen, the big guy named Eugene Lamont. Standing behind him was Pat Johnston, the Teamster business agent, Lee Sandahl, and some of the other guys from the Port.

"We heard what happened to you. That's fucked up, if you ask me," said Lamont.

"What do you expect from our ass hole government? They don't give a shit about us," said one of the longshoremen.

"You can say that again," replied Lee.

"Come on, let's get a table and commiserate." Jake had a tender feeling for these guys. Then again, alcohol always seemed to make him sentimental.

They sat down and ordered a mound of ribs and beer and proceeded to have an impromptu party. Lee and Pat Johnston, who were not big drinkers, got fairly drunk. By midway into the evening, the longshoremen were planning to shut down the whole West Coast in protest of Jake's treatment. Jake got really plastered and by 10:00 pm found himself dancing to some old R&B from the jukebox with a strapping Latina named Carla. Carla was a welder at the port and, in Jake's inebriated state, was the most beautiful woman he ever met. After that, he didn't really remember what happened, but the next morning he woke up in a strange bed with a hangover the likes of which he hadn't experienced since college.

Carla came in the room, dressed for work in Levis and a tank top. "Wake up, hon. Here's some coffee." She put the coffee down on the nightstand and bent over and gave Jake a gentle kiss on the cheek.

He was looking at her breasts—an imposing sight. But then the pain came rushing into his head and he groaned.

"Oh, Jesus, I feel like shit," he said. "You got any aspirin or ibuprophen or something like that?"

She laughed and wiped the hair out of his face. "You were feeling pretty good last night."

"Really? To tell you the truth, I'm a little blurry on that, Carla."

"There's aspirin in the bathroom."

"Thanks, Carla, for everything. Dancing last night was really fun. I haven't done that in years."

"Yeah, I had a good time too." She paused. "I've got to go to work. You can stay here today and rest if you want. It's quiet. Maybe you can go back to sleep."

She bent down again and kissed him. Then she turned around and walked to the door.

"Goodbye, sweetie," she said, grabbing her car keys from the top of the dresser. She turned back and said, "That was nice. Let's do that again."

Chapter 57

Avi Gerstner had a headache which just wouldn't go away. He washed down two more aspirin with a glass of seltzer water. Maybe he was getting sick. His daughter and her children had been visiting over the weekend and his grandson, Eitan, had all sorts of stuff coming out of his nose. Bertha, his wife, told him to stop sharing food with the boy, but Avi kept right on doing it, insisting that they couldn't expect a child to eat food that a grown up wouldn't eat. Bertha called him a foolish old goat. As usual, she was right.

There was a knock at his office door.

"Come in, already," he said, impatiently. It was Natalia and Aaron. He could tell by the looks on their faces that something was wrong.

"So?" said Gerstner.

The two of them looked at one another, waiting for the other to speak.

"Natalia, out with it."

"It's about Hannah. The homing device has gone absolutely still for over seventy-two hours now. It has not moved a centimeter."

"And where is it?"

"Within a ten meter radius from the headquarters building of the camp in the Bekaa."

"So what you're telling me is that Hannah is dead or captured or she took the thing off."

"Hannah would never take it off voluntarily Avi," Aaron said, shaking his head.

"If she's captured, she's probably better off dead." Gerstner paused to keep his voice from breaking. "Do we have any intelligence reports that are current?"

"Yes, Avi," responded Natalia. "The pictures show the training activities still going on."

"Well then, please inform the Prime Minister's office and the joint military command of this development. As far as I'm concerned, the Air Force can flatten the place whenever the timing is right."

The two Israelis stood there, silently. Natalia was starting to tear up.

So was Avi Gerstner. "Come on, you two, get out of here."

When they left, Gerstner put his hand on his forehead. In his life, he had seen so many young people die. Each time it became harder for him to bear. Bertha was right. This was not a job for sentimental old men.

Chapter 58

Abu Bashir, or Dr. Bashir as he preferred to be called, knew a lot about many subjects. He was a delightful teacher. He and his wife had a sprawling apartment in the southern suburbs of Beirut in the area under Hezbollah control. His wife was a small, round, cheerful woman who cooked wonderful food and fussed over Hannah and Niaz. Dr. Bashir teased her and she teased him back; the good feelings in the Bashir home were infectious. They had a son named Khalid who was an engineer living in France. Khalid was married to a French woman and they had two small children, whose pictures were proudly displayed all over the Bashirs' apartment.

Hannah was puzzled by Dr. Bashir. He seemed so good-natured and apolitical. He made no speeches about Islam and, in fact, did not seem particularly observant. He did not say much about the Israelis or the Americans and what he did say sounded more mildly critical than fanatical. Dr. Bashir loved classical literature and art; most of all, he loved science. He taught chemistry at Beirut Arab University. However, with his infectious laugh and erudite manner, he set out to teach Hannah and Niaz all about making bombs, the use of different types of explosives, and the construction of timers and detonators from commercially available materials. As the days stretched into weeks, Bashir taught them how to make bombs that would disburse radioactive waste more efficiently. He made them learn about gasoline tanker trucks and how they burned so hot they could melt the structural steel of a bridge. Finally, he took them to an X-ray laboratory at Najjar Hospital on Maamari Street where they learned how to handle radioactive materials safely.

After nearly a month of instruction, Dr. Bashir told them that it was now time for them to take what they had learned and put it to practical use. The next morning they would be picked up and taken thirty kilometers south of Beirut to a Hezbollah training camp. That evening Mrs. Bashir prepared a wonderful final meal for them. Hannah could hardly believe that these warm people were her enemies.

The next morning they were picked up by an off-duty taxi driver who drove them to the camp. When they arrived, it looked like an old South Lebanon Army military base that had been taken over by Hezbollah. Hannah and Niaz were the only women there. The rest were an unfriendly and suspicious group of young men of various Middle Eastern nationalities who were training to make suicide bombs. They were not, Hannah learned, going to deliver the bombs themselves; other desperate young men would be doing that. They were devout Muslims and they treated Hannah and Niaz as if they were invisible. Hannah and Niaz studied apart, ate apart, and slept apart from the boys.

The training camp was run by a tough little pockmarked man named Gamal, who wore an eye patch and was missing three fingers from his right hand. Their first day, he pulled off his eye patch to reveal his empty eye socket and told them that this was not the worst thing that could happen to them if they were not careful. They got down to business quickly, building bombs of various types and then detonating them in a concrete revetment that had once been used to store artillery shells. Gamal told them that constructing a bomb was an art, as creative as any painting or poem, but an art form whose aesthetic realization was only achieved upon its disappearance. Were it not for his deadly earnestness, Hannah would have viewed Gamal as the embodiment of self-parody.

Two weeks after their arrival, they were driven to a safe house in Beirut to await their departure for America.

Chapter 59

Shiraz, Iran, June 11

The agents working for Dr. Boomla continued to follow Dr. Honari between his house and his job at the centrifuge facility they called Mecca. But they now added Honari's two daughters, his son, and his wife to the list of people under active surveillance. The females of the Honari family were clean. His two daughters went to school at an elite private academy. They were quiet, studious, and did not draw attention to themselves. The wife was also uninteresting. But they hit the jackpot almost immediately with the son, Abid. He was homosexual. It didn't take more than a few days for Boomla's agents to observe Abid frequenting places where the highly secretive Shirazi gay community were known to meet. While ordinary citizens of Shiraz knew little of such matters, Dr. Boomla made it his business to know such things. Although Abid was discrete, he was not discrete enough to hide his sexual orientation from someone carefully watching him. He often went to a coffee house and bookstore near the university that quietly tolerated gay couples. He was seen late at night briefly embracing another man in the darkened entrance of a student dormitory. On another occasion,

Boomla's agents photographed Abid holding hands and kissing another man on a hiking trail in the hills outside the city.

Dr. Boomla duly reported the information to Avi Gerstner in Jerusalem.

As Gerstner stared at the photographs that Yossi Levi had just dropped on his desk of the two Iranian boys kissing one another, he shook his head solemnly. "It's very sad that we have to do this, Yossi. You know, my sister's middle son, Moti, he's gay. Nobody cares anymore about gay people except for the ultra-orthodox and I don't even think they really care. He and his boyfriend are adopting a baby. And now we are planning to blackmail the father because the son is a nice gay boy who never hurt anyone."

"Avi, what's wrong with you? Isn't it better we should sacrifice one *feigala*, then a million Jews should die because these crazy bastards drop a nuclear bomb on us?"

"You think they would really do that?" Gerster looked at his subordinate with his intelligent eyes. "I don't know. They talk like crazies all the time, those Mullahs and the little President, but they know that Iran would cease to exist if they attacked us with nuclear weapons. We're not going to disappear from history without a fight."

"Maybe they would and maybe they wouldn't. But our people and our politicians do not want to see countries that hate us get nuclear weapons. It would be a catastrophe for Israel. Avi, you and I both know we will attack them before they develop nuclear bombs. So forget the morality of the situation."

"Of course, Yossi, you're right. Listen, I've ordered the assassination of many people. You don't have to tell me that the end justifies the means. "

"So what do we do about it?"

"Well, you know what they say, one gets more with honey than with vinegar."

"OK, I get it, so what do you want me to do?" replied Yossi.

"Our friend Dr. Boomla will know."

Chapter 60

SHIRAZ, IRAN, JUNE 13

At night, the ancient *Darvāzeh Ghor'ān*—the Koran Gate—is lit brightly. According to tradition, travelers leaving the city of Shiraz receive protection from an ancient copy of the holy book that is kept on top of the gate. Where once donkeys passed under its arch, now cars and trucks speed along their way.

Not far from the gate is the tomb of the great medieval Persian Poet, Saadi. Surrounding the blue dome of his mausoleum is a park resplendent with roses and towering cypresses. In the spring, when the roses are in bloom, lovers come to walk hand-in-hand in the park. This is not only because the park is a romantic place, but because Saadi was a muse of love and the gentleness of the human spirit. For some, the beauty of Saadi's *ghazals* are in the meter and rhyme of his poetry. For others, his poetry holds a deeper meaning. Although it is a crime to utter such thoughts in contemporary Iran, Saadi's poetry, along with that of the other great Persian mystical poets, Attar, Rumi, and Hafez, is plainly homoerotic. The object of the muse's love is another young man.

At the Tomb of Saadi, as day turns to night, young men come to stroll in the garden. They come alone but sometimes they leave in pairs; for the tomb of Saadi is a place where gay men come to find one another. It is a very dangerous activity. Under the fundamentalist regime of Iran, homosexuality is ruthlessly suppressed and the punishment is death by slow strangulation. But loneliness and the desire for love, companionship, and sexual gratification drive people to take great risks.

The sun had already set. It was an early summer night and the air in the garden was heavy with the fragrance of roses and pine sap. A bearded young man with dark eyes and long lashes walked along one of the paths near the tomb. He carried a leather-bound book under his left arm. The title of the book, *Gulistan*, which means "Rose Garden," was engraved in gold lettering on its dark-leather cover. It is one of Saadi's most famous works. The young man, Abid Honari, loved the poetry of Saadi, but carried the book for another purpose, to signal his availability to a potential lover.

As he walked down the path, he saw another young man approach. He was dark-skinned and clean-shaven. A college student like himself, Abid thought, and very beautiful. As the two approached one other, they smiled. Abid said "hello" to the other young man, who stopped, and asked Abid if they knew each other because he looked so familiar.

"Perhaps," answered Abid, "I am a student at Shiraz University. I just started there at the beginning of the semester. I was at Tehran University, but we moved to Shiraz because my father changed jobs. And you, what is your story?"

"I am a student at the University as well."

They began to talk about their classes and professors and the things they had in common. The other man's name was Sepehr and he was from Bandare on the Gulf Coast. They decided to go have coffee and left the park together.

It was, literally, love at first sight between Abid and Sepehr. Their romance blossomed and deepened with each passing day. It was an illicit love and had to be hidden from the world. But the desperation they felt only deepened the passion of their private moments.

Abid explained to Sepehr that he lived at home with his parents and sisters in a suburb of Shiraz. Unlike Abid who lived at home, Sepehr lived in a dormitory on campus. The opportunities for them to be together in private were limited but somehow they would find a way.

Sepehr asked Abid whether his parents suspected that he was gay. Abid doubted it. While they *should* have suspected his sexual orientation from his utter lack of interest in women and marriage, Abid joked that such a fate was just too tragic for them to contemplate.

Abid brought Sepehr home to meet his family. Doctor and Mrs. Honari liked his new friend, Sepehr, very much and Abid's two teenage sisters developed crushes on Abid's handsome friend.

Sepehr was quickly welcomed as a regular visitor to the Honari's home.

Chapter 61

After the initial intense passion that marked the beginning of their relationship, Abid and Sepehr settled into life as a gay couple in the hostile environment of Iranian society. At first, the very conspiratorial nature of their relationship was a source of excitement itself. But as time passed, the secrecy which surrounded every aspect of their relationship and the sheer energy it took just to spend time with one another became a source of increasing frustration for the two men. The one thing that helped was that Abid and Sepehr were able to find other gay couples, even a lesbian couple, at the University. They socialized in secret and this helped counter their sense of isolation.

As a result of the oppressive nature of living a secret life, Abid and Sepehr began to think about taking a trip somewhere where they could be themselves. The obvious choice was Dubai in the United Arab Emirates, which was a short flight across the Persian Gulf. There were cheap fares and hotel deals and one of the other couples they knew, who had been there together, said there were nightclubs and even hotels that were friendly to gay people.

The cultural freedom of Dubai, sandwiched as it was between the reactionary Sunni Saudis to the west and the equally reactionary Shiite Iranians to the east, was something of a Middle Eastern miracle. With its paucity of oil revenues, the Emirate of Dubai had developed a huge tourism industry. The majority of its population were European expatriates and foreign workers.

Abid and Sepehr became increasingly excited about the idea of going on a vacation together in Dubai. They decided that they would take their trip when the university was closed for the summer holiday in August, and fares were heavily discounted. They found a great deal on a tourist package that would cost them twenty million Rials—the equivalent of $2,200—for a fourteen-day trip to a gay-friendly resort in Dubai City not far from the beach. Sepehr, who came from a wealthy family, offered to pay.

Chapter 62

Dr. Honari sat in his study and opened up his personal email account. He didn't receive as much correspondence as he used to because he was under orders not to communicate with colleagues or friends. Emails sent to him at his old email address received an automatic reply indicating that he was on temporary assignment out of the country and would not be available. Most of the emails he got now were from people who worked in Iran's nuclear program and had security clearances. He wasn't sure if his emails were being read by the security forces or not but he was careful what he wrote.

Although Dr. Honari did not know the person who sent the email— a person named "Dr. Khamenei"—he decided to open it because it was from an address at a science institute in Tehran that performed research on centrifuge development.

The title line simply said, "Personnel Problem."

But when Dr. Honari read the text, he went into an immediate cold sweat and his chest began to pound. The letter was not explicit, but its thinly disguised meaning could not be misunderstood.

My Esteemed Dr. Honari,

　　We are having so much trouble with two of our young researchers, Ms. Abid and Dr. Sepehr. They began as friends but their relationship has turned romantic and I am afraid that their courtship will interfere with the work at the laboratory. I am also concerned that, since they come from prominent families, their families may object. They have attempted to keep their relationship a secret, but others have begun to notice and I fear that if it becomes known that they are romantically involved, it could cause great difficulty for their parents, particularly for the father of Miss Abid.

　　I am having difficulty determining what course of action I should take. Your sage advice on this matter would be most appreciated. Time is of the essence.

Your Colleague,
Dr. Khamenei

Dr. Honari stared at the computer screen, his heart racing. It was a blackmail threat; there was no other way to interpret it. The blackmailer was threatening to expose his son and his son's friend as homosexual lovers. Could this allegation be true? The boys were close friends, true, but filthy sodomites? He had been told over and over that if there was an attempt at blackmail, he should report the matter directly to the SVAMA. If the accusation was false or the infraction small, there was nothing to worry about. But homosexuality was another matter.

If this was true and his beloved son was a deviant, then Abid certainly would be tried and imprisoned. If they wanted to make an example of him, he might be executed. The anger and repulsion that Honari felt at the thought that his son could be homosexual was mixed with overwhelming fear for the boy and for himself and his family. The shame that this would bring down upon his family would destroy them all.

What should he do? After thinking about it for a few minutes, Honari decided that he would ignore the email. Maybe it was some kind of practical joke or hoax and he would never hear from the sender again. He deleted the email and went into his server and deleted it there as well. He congratulated himself on having the foresight to purchase special software to wash his hard drive. He hoped it would work.

That night, Dr. Honari could not sleep. He lay awake for hours thinking about the incident. He finally fell asleep at 4:00 am. The next day, he felt awful, but somehow managed to get through his work. He struggled all day to suppress his growing anxiety. He tried to convince himself that the email was just a strange mistake, a hoax, or a practical joke. But in his heart he feared the worst and his sense of dread would not lift.

Honari arrived home that evening exhausted from lack of sleep and stress. He avoided going into his study. After dinner, he talked for a while with his daughters, who were doing school work in the bedroom they shared. Eventually, Honari could delay no longer and he went to his study. He turned on his computer. It was there waiting for him: another message from Dr. Khamenei. He considered simply deleting the message, but his curiosity and fear compelled him otherwise.

There was no text, merely a JPEG attachment. When he opened the attachment, it was a fragment of a letter. He immediately identified the neat, flowing script of his son, Abid. The letter was dated just two weeks before, and it said:

> My Sweet S,
>
> When we are apart, I yearn for you and think constantly about when we will see each other next. I can hardly concentrate on my studies because of the heat of my passion and the depth of my love. You are both tender and strong. Our stolen moment last week was something so pure and wonderful.
>
> I do worry that my parents will suspect. If they find out about us it will be so shameful. I could not face my father, who I love dearly, but who could never accept us. I do not want to bring shame on him or our family. But I cannot be apart from . . .

The fragment ended. Dr. Honari banged his hand on the table. Oh, my God, why this? What has this boy, Sepehr, done to my Abid?

He began to sob.

In his desperation, Dr. Honari clicked on the "reply" icon.

"Who are you and why are you doing this to me?" He pressed the button which sent the message into cyberspace.

Honari immediately regretted that he had responded. He waited for a reply but there was none. Exhausted and terrified, he fell asleep on the old leather couch in his study.

Chapter 63

Abid and Sepehr couldn't wait to tell Abid's parents about the trip to Dubai. When they got to the Honari house, Abid's two sisters came to the door to greet them, excited as usual to see Sepehr. Abid's mother had made a huge *Adas Polow*, one of her specialties—meat, fruit, and lentils piled high over saffron rice. Mrs. Honari was an excellent cook and after a week of bland and starchy dormitory food, Sepehr eagerly anticipated a home-cooked meal. Mrs. Honari doted on the appreciative Sepehr.

Dr. Honari, however, was not his usual self. He was sullen and looked tired. Abid hugged his father and asked him if he was feeling well. Honari replied that he was fine but his tone said otherwise. He voice sounded brittle and angry. The others noticed and there was a momentary awkward silence before the conversation resumed. Dr. Honari shook Sepehr's hand, but his greeting was not warm.

Not long into dinner, Abid said that he had an announcement to make. He and Sepehr were going to take a trip to Dubai for two weeks. Abid's sisters clapped and the younger one, Yasmin, asked if they were going to visit the artificial island jutting out into the Persian

Gulf from Dubai City that was shaped like a huge palm tree. Sepehr
said that they would try to visit it, but that he wasn't certain they were
actually finished constructing it. Mrs. Honari asked Sepehr if his
parents approved and Sepehr answered that his father had not only
given his consent but offered to pay for the entire trip.

Dr. Honari stood up, wiped his mouth with his napkin, and
threw it down on the table. "I don't suppose you planned to ask my
permission, Abid?"

"Of course, Father," responded a surprised Abid, "but you have
always said young men should travel and so I assumed that you
would encourage us to go on this trip."

"You must excuse me," said Dr. Honari, "but I am feeling unwell."
Honari abruptly left the table, leaving the rest of his family members
shocked and puzzled.

Chapter 64

The entire team that was working on the Honari matter was gathered around the battered old conference table waiting for Avi Gerstner to arrive. They had called Gerstner at home as soon as they learned from the Mossad Communications Center in Tel Aviv that Honari had replied to the email. He told them to get everybody together so that they could reach a consensus on their next move.

It was nearly midnight when Gerstner arrived. The rest of the team was drinking coffee and looking bleary-eyed. Gerstner, who was twice their age and who had been awakened from a deep sleep, was alert and ready to work. He liked the hunt and now the prey was in his sights. In a line of work that often ended in frustration and dead ends, it made him happy to be making progress.

Yossi Levi reported on Honari's email response to them.

"So you woke me and, more ominously, my lovely wife, Bertha, so you could get my permission to ratchet up the pressure on this gentleman?" asked Gerstner.

"We wouldn't think of depriving you of the fun," said Aaron.

"OK, then," said Gerstner, all business, the levity gone from his voice. "I think we dump all of the coded stuff and get directly to the point with Honari.   After all, we're Israelis, and subtlety isn't our strong suit. So how about this for a response? 'We would like to be friends. You have a problem with your gay son and we can make sure that that no unfortunate facts are disclosed.'"

Chava, who assisted Yossi Levi on the Iranian desk, asked, "Chief, what if their counter-intelligence people are looking at his email? Shouldn't we do something more in code? We could blow this guy's cover immediately."

Gerstner cocked his head and nodded in agreement. "All right, how about this idea? Suppose we make it look like . . . what do you call that fake email business?" he asked nobody in particular.

Several voices responded "spam" at once.

"Yes, spam," said Gerstner, rubbing his face to hide a yawn. "Maybe a travel advertisement—'want to get out of Iran for vacation? Fly to . . . I don't know . . . how about a nice friendly country? How about . . . Israel?" They all laughed. Gerstner continued . "With a tag line that says, 'You got a problem, we got a solution.' What do you think of that?"

Levi, who had been cleaning his glasses, put them back on his nose and said, "Well, Avi, all joking aside, given our other news, I think that might be a better idea that you could know."

"What other news?" asked Gerstner.

"We've been hacking the son's email," said a woman named Deborah Metzger, "and he and his good friend Sepehr are planning a little romantic trip to Dubai to enjoy the gay life there."

"Ah," said Gerstner, smiling broadly. "Then it's perfect. Honari will be aware of their trip. He will put two and two together and he will know that we know about the trip these boys are planning."

"And if they actually go to Dubai," broke in Aaron, "we can have people there to meet them and make sure they have a good time."

"Where's Jack?" asked Gerstner.

"He's in Tel Aviv," answered Chava.

"Then get him," Gerstner said tersely.

Chapter 65

While they waited for orders to return to Bala Deh, the SEAL team and the two CIA operatives trained hard in the high mountain air. Physically, it was tough, but it kept them focused and disciplined. OJ and Ivana were amazed at the endurance of Gonzales and the other SEALS and struggled to keep up.

Ten days after their arrival, Gonzales received a detailed message from CENTCOM. He had a grim look on his face when he handed the decoded message to Ivana and OJ, who were sitting on the front steps, enjoying a hot cup of goat milk.

"We've got our orders," Said Gonzales.

Ivana read the message. She looked at Gonzales. "This is suicide," she said.

"Yeah," he responded flatly, "it kind of looks that way, doesn't it."

Ivana handed the orders to OJ. He looked up and smiled, rolling his eyes. "The odds seem to be going down that we will ever see our pensions."

Gonzales went to find the rest of the men so that he could give them the news.

"Have you ever worked with the Israelis?" asked OJ.

"No," replied Ivana.

"We're going to be totally dependent on them and their local organization."

"What I've heard is that their planning is poor and their execution great," Ivana said.

"Well, we have the opposite reputation. Between us, maybe we'll get it right."

Ivana took a sip from her cup. OJ watched the steam from her breath curl up from her mouth in the cool morning air. "From what I hear, though, the Israelis are pretty fast on the trigger. They love a good firefight."

"Irvita, are you trying to say they're crazier than our group of Navy SEALS?" asked OJ.

Ivana smiled at OJ. "Irvita? I thought Irv was bad enough. Now it's going to be Irvita?"

"Hey, I can't help myself, I'm from southern California. It's the heavy Latino influence. 'Irvita,'" he said slowly, "it has a nice ring to it. Kind of like 'Evita.' I could envision you as a glamorous Perónista queen."

"You know, OJ, you're a little nuts . . . but entertaining in a culturally eclectic sort of way." At that moment, Ivana felt anything but glamorous, in her military fatigues and thick wool watch cap, her skin dry and dark from weeks in the sun.

"One culturally eclectic type is as good as another."

"I guess we share the melting pot together."

"Here's to ethnic confusion," OJ said, raising his mug and clinking it against Ivana's.

"I suppose we better get ready to go. Our ride will be here in a few hours."

"Yeah. And then it's 'show time,' as Gonzales would say."

"You're not going to bring up Hollywood now, are you?" asked Ivana, as she rose slowly and brushed the dirt off from her pants.

"No, Irvita, but I can do a mean Eddie Murphy imitation," responded OJ.

Ivana noticed that his thick black mustache showed a little milk line on it. Impulsively, she reached over and gently wiped the milk from OJ's mouth. There was something intimate about the gesture and it embarrassed both of them.

Ivana said, "See you a little later, OJ."

Chapter 66

SHIRAZ, IRAN, JUNE 30

The next email message that Dr. Honari received was from a company called "Magic Carpet Travel" advertising vacation packages for tourist destinations throughout the Middle East. It advertised trips to the Caspian Sea, the Holy Cities of Mecca and Medina, and the seaside resorts in Lebanon, Syria, and Dubai. In small print under the description of the trip to Dubai was a sentence highlighted and bolded that said, "Boys can really enjoy themselves in beautiful Dubai."

Dr. Honari did not miss the point.

Chapter 67

The Orient Pacific Container Line freighter Pusan was being loaded at its berth. It could hold 7,227 TEUs—twenty-foot container units—and the gantry-crane operator was just finishing loading the last of the containers. It was bound for the Port of Los Angeles; the voyage across the Pacific would take two weeks. On its deck, the containers were stacked six high and twenty across.

Somewhere in the middle of the load was a container of cat litter bound for distribution to various retail outlets across the western United States. Inside that container was one box heavier than the rest, because it contained spent Uranium 235 fuel enriched to a high level of purity. The US Transportation Security Administration had prevailed on the government of Pakistan to install radiation detectors and to screen outgoing containers. Although the container of cat litter registered as emitting some radioactivity, its radiation profile was normal given the fact that it contained bentonite clay, a mineral with naturally occurring radiation. The TSA official who reviewed the findings the day the OPCL Pusan left Karachi found nothing unusual.

A man named Habib sat on the park bench along the shoreline esplanade watching the loading process through a pair of binoculars. To a casual observer, he looked like just another middle-aged man who enjoyed bird watching. When the ship cast off at noon and headed out of the port, Habib made a cell-phone call to the Iranian consulate and asked to speak to Mr. Kormani, the Deputy Commercial Attaché. Habib informed Kormani that he was delighted to report that he had seen the rarest of egrets flying out to sea. Kormani seemed pleased with the news and promised he would tell the rest of the members of their bird-watching club. Within minutes, Kormani sent a secure coded cable to General Yazdi in Tehran reporting that the OPCL Pusan had sailed from Karachi.

Chapter 68

The night before they were scheduled to leave on their mission, Hannah and Niaz were driven to a restaurant south of the Green Line. Armed guards were positioned in front of the restaurant and across the street. Two armored black Mercedes were parked at the curb; their drivers stood leaning against the hood smoking cigarettes and talking.

The driver and guard, both Hezbollah operatives, escorted Hannah and Niaz into the restaurant. It was dark inside; the only illumination was a small oil lamp on each table. In another world, the atmosphere might have been described as cozy, even romantic. But to Hannah it was just menacing. Most of the tables were empty, but two were occupied by older men talking to one another. At another table, some younger men, obviously bodyguards, were eating, their assault rifles lying on the ground ready to be grabbed quickly. They stared at Hannah and Niaz when they entered. No one smiled.

Their driver said, "We go to the back," and nodded in the direction of a staircase at the rear of the restaurant. At the top of the stairs there was a private dining room. Three men were sitting at a table sipping tea. They stood up when the women stepped into the room.

Hannah felt a lump in her throat. Even in the dark Western-style business suit he was wearing, she immediately recognized General Yazdi.

The General smiled, his blue eyes mirthful. "So we meet again, young lady."

While the two other, younger men stood at attention, General Yazdi walked around the table and thrust his hand out to Hannah. She shook hands with him.

"I see that you've learned your lessons in Western etiquette."

Yazdi turned to Niaz and bowed slightly. "It is good to see you again, Niaz. You are a faithful servant to our cause."

"I believe, Vashti, you remember my adjutants, Major Mazandarani and Captain Rajaei."

The two younger officers bowed to the women, who looked down and bowed back.

"Please sit down," said General Yazdi graciously.

The food began to arrive, classics of the Levant: shaslik, dolmas, kofta, mutabbel, and even the spicy dried beef delicacy called pastirma.

"I thought that you would want to eat some decent food before you landed in America," said General Yazdi, staring straight at Hannah.

"That is most kind of you, General," replied Hannah.

"I am told that the Americans mostly eat that debased food, what do they call it, Rajaei?"

"Fast food," responded the adjutant in English.

"Yes, 'fast food,' that's it. Such a rich country and they feed their people garbage at their Mickey Mouse and Donald Duck restaurants. It is an offense to Allah."

"I understand they are fat and sickly there because of their unhealthy Western diet," said Major Mazandarani.

The General held up a piece of the pastirma. "Vashti, this is called Pastirma or Bastirma all over the lands where the Turks once ruled. Niaz, do you know what it is called in Romania, which the Ottomans ruled for three hundred years, until their decadence caused it to be lost for Islam?"

"I do not, Sir," replied Niaz quietly.

"Do you Vashti?"

"No, General," she said, but she could guess the answer and her stomach tightened.

"It is called 'pastrama.' The Jews from Romania stole the recipe from the Muslims there and called it "pastrami." I understand it is a great delicacy in America and the Jews have tricked the Christians into thinking they invented it."

"Is there nothing too small for the Jews to steal?" asked Captain Rajaei, shaking his head. It was a rhetorical question.

They talked about the weather and other pleasantries through most of the dinner, but when the dessert was served, the General cleared his throat.

"Vashti, Niaz. I want to talk to you now about your mission. I will be frank with you. You are replacing three operatives who were detained on their way to perform their mission. I cannot give you more details, but suffice it to say, they were arrested by the police and imprisoned. Sadly . . . how shall I say this?" Yazdi paused, searching for the right words, "They were beaten to death by the other prisoners."

Hannah and Niaz must have looked shocked because General Yazdi said, "I'm sorry to have to tell you something like that so bluntly, but such are the risks of our work. You know why we fight and why we die. Those men died a martyr's death so that others, like you, could take their place and bring our Jihad to the doorstep of the Great Satan."

The General suddenly stood up and removed his jacket.

"I want to show you something." He rolled up his right sleeve and held out his arm for the two women to look at. His whole upper arm was nothing but scar tissue.

"When I was sixteen, my father, who was a mullah in our village, was arrested by the SAVAK. They thought he was an enemy of the Shah and a supporter of Ayatollah Khomeini. He was not political; he was a simple and righteous man who followed the Prophet and sought justice. They took him to Evin Prison and tortured him. They beat him so badly that his kidneys ruptured. The SAVAK pigs dropped him at our front door, barely alive. As he lay near death that night, with my mother and sisters weeping, he grabbed my arm with a grip that I did not think he possessed. He said to me, 'My son, avenge my death, seek justice, always follow the path of the Prophet.' And he told me another thing. In the torture chamber at Evin, there was a blond-haired foreigner who never spoke but only whispered into the ear of his interrogator. One of the other prisoners told him he was an American CIA agent. When my father died that night, I swore that I would avenge his death and rid Iran of the poison that was destroying it: the Shah and his American masters, the Jews, who leach and steal from the Muslims, and all the nonbelievers who wage war on Islam."

Yazdi paused and in the silence that followed, Hannah realized she was holding her breath. She had never heard anything like the burning intensity of this man. The General's face was turning dark with the blood that was rushing into it. He began again, his voice rising in pitch.

"I became an underground fighter. Eventually, the SAVAK caught me, but they had no proof and I would not confess. My body is covered by the burns the SAVAK torturers gave me to try to make me talk. And I knew then with absolute certainty that the day would come when I would look my torturers in the eye and watch them die. And that day came in 1980 at Evin Prison when I personally put the noose around the neck of the SAVAK dog who did this to me."

Yazdi thrust out his arm again to show them his wounds. Spittle was gathered at the corner of his mouth and his blue eyes looked unfocused. Then abruptly his became calm once more. He dabbed his mouth with his napkin.

"So you must be single-minded in your determination to carry out your mission, no matter what. Your life is but a tiny thing measured against the opportunity to strike at the heart of the beast." Yazdi held up his right index finger and waved it in front of the women. "In one split second, you will avenge five hundred years of humiliation of the Muslims. From the moment you strike, everything will be different and whether you live or die, every Muslim child for a thousand years will know your name. I know you have been briefed and you know your mission. Obey your commander. Do not waiver; conquer your fear and I know you will be successful."

The General stood up and bowed to the women. "May Allah be with you and may he guide you to victory."

Hannah said, "We hope, General, that we are worthy of the great responsibility you have given us. And we thank you for this chance to serve our cause, which we know is just."

Turning to the Captain, General Yazdi said, "Captain Rajaei, please accompany our guests to their car and escort them back to their quarters."

"Yes, Sir," he responded and, gesturing to Hannah and Niaz to accompany him, they left the room.

When they had gone down the stairs, the General turned to Major Mazandarani and said, "There is something about that Turkish woman that bothers me."

"General, I didn't notice anything out of the ordinary," replied Mazandarani.

"The handshake, Mazandarani, it was a bit too firm and her expression changed slightly when I mentioned the Jews. No matter how much training you give Muslim women—even Turks—they cannot easily master the firm handshake. You will communicate with Dibul in Los Angeles. He is to observe Vashti closely and report any suspicious activities. He and Niaz need to be together all the time, involved solely in their primary bomb construction activities or other general duties. Under no circumstances are they to be apprised of the date, time, or location of the attack."

"Sir, perhaps we should find a substitute for this woman?"

"There isn't time. The shipment will be arriving soon and any delay only increases the chance of failure. Look Mazandarani, I could easily be wrong. The training school reports her to be a disciplined and eager student who got high marks on her training courses. But at my age, I have learned to go with my gut. Remember that fool of an actor who was the American President, Reagan . . . he said one smart thing: 'Trust but verify.' I think that applies to our Vashti."

As they were leaving for the Beirut airport to board the Air France flight to Paris, Hannah and Niaz received last-minute information that when they arrived at LAX they would be met by people carrying a sign that said "Cohen" on it. The ethnic implications of the name were completely lost on Niaz but Hannah got the point. When they arrived in Paris, they were supposed to assume their identities as Jews. They were given Lebanese passports to use for the trip to Paris, but were instructed to switch to Canadian passports when they boarded the plane there.

The two women got on the plane looking every bit like Western women. They wore fashionable tight jeans and skimpy tank tops which showed their cleavage. Niaz was shocked at the attention they received. Although there were numerous secular Lebanese women who dressed in Western clothes, it was a new experience for Niaz. She wore her long brown hair pinned high on her head as Hannah had taught her. Hannah, of course, was a Westerner, but she was in fact a modest dresser. Her fashion style was "Israeli hippie" and, at home, she wore her thick curly hair in braids or tied at the back. She favored loose-fitting, comfortable clothes. So, in reality, it was also something of a first for her to be dressed in a sexually provocative manner. She found the whole thing stupid and embarrassing, but resigned herself that it was just another uniform she needed to wear. If her mother saw her, she'd make a "tut, tut" noise and tell her not to dress so provocatively. Her only regret was that she couldn't wear more comfortable shoes or at least ones that she could move quickly in. The strappy sandals she was wearing were killing her feet even if they were attracting the stares of Arab and European men.

Hannah had come to the conclusion that Niaz was a bad girl stuck in a good girl's body and so it was not surprising that she was thoroughly enjoying every evil moment of her sinfulness. As they got settled into their seats, Hannah amused herself visualizing Niaz getting off the plane in Los Angeles, grabbing the unlimited-balance American Express cards they had been issued, hopping in a cab and heading straight to Rodeo Drive in Beverly Hills—never to be heard from again. Hannah must have laughed out loud because Niaz actually elbowed her and asked what was so funny.

They sat next to a middle-aged French-Lebanese businessman who flirted with them for virtually the entire flight. Because he was like most men, Hannah was able to keep the conversation going by asking the man, whose name was Pierre something—or—other, questions about himself. She got long-winded answers from Pierre; he evidently did not suffer from a modest ego. He kept looking at the women's breasts and making not so subtle hints about showing them a good time in Paris.

They had a three-hour layover in De Gaulle airport before their plane for Los Angeles was scheduled to depart. As instructed, Hannah put on the Star of David necklace and Niaz the Hamsa. They decided to kill time window-shopping at the various stores in the airport and headed straight for Hermes, Louis Vuitton, Chanel, and Gucci. There were many Europeans and Arabs in the airport and Hannah noticed that their jewelry was attracting attention and not all of it was positive. Niaz noticed too and she was puzzled. "Why are those Arab women staring at us?" she asked.

"Because they think we're Jews."

"Really?"

"Yes, Niaz, really."

As they entered the Hermes store, they saw a family of Hasidic Jews looking at scarves. The thickly bearded father wore a dark black suit and black hat, the mother had on a long dress with sleeves and a wig, and the two young sons wore long sidelocks—*payeses*—under their yarmulkes.

"Who are they?" whispered Niaz. Hannah steered Niaz back into the walkway so she could provide an explanation.

"Those are very religious European Jews called *Hassid*. They wear modest clothing. The women wear wigs after they marry so that men who are not their husbands cannot see their real hair."

"Oh, yes, those are like the Jews in the cartoons in the newspapers that always steal from people." Niaz looked disgusted, as if this harmless family were repulsive aliens. Ironically, they resembled the traditional Muslim families throughout the Middle East whose modest dress set them apart from their more modern coreligionists. But all Niaz could see was "the other."

Hannah hoped her sense of revulsion was not evident on her face. She felt protective toward the family; so many people hated them just because of their religion. Why did the old hatreds still persist? Could people ever move beyond their primitive tribal impulses?

Hannah felt exhausted. The weariness and tension of the trip was getting to her. When they finally boarded the plane an hour later, now pretending to be Canadians, she fell asleep almost immediately.

Chapter 69

Hannah woke up about two hours into the flight feeling groggy but rested. She slept through the first meal and was hungry. She got up to stretch her legs. As she walked down the aisle, it looked to her that the passengers were probably half Americans and half other mostly French tourists heading for their Southern California vacations. She went to the rear of the plane, where a few passengers were gathered and got into a conversation with two young American women who were returning home from a post-graduation European adventure. This had been the first time either of them had been abroad; their naiveté combined with their infectious enthusiasm seemed definitively American. The conversation was good practice for Hannah; she was able to talk about her cover story and use her slightly rusty English.

When she got back to her seat, Niaz was talking to a tall, lanky American college student who was leaning over her seat. It was obvious some serious flirting was going on. Hannah was starting to wonder whether the Islamic Republic of Iran had chosen an agent to send to the decadent West that was turning out to be a little too attractive to the opposite sex. When she sat down, she felt vaguely embarrassed, as if she was interrupting something that was not her business. Niaz introduced the young man, who was a graduate student from UCLA. Eventually, after trying hard to get Niaz' phone number, he gave up and went back to his seat.

"Well," said Hannah, "you seemed a little sweet on him."

To Hannah's surprise, Niaz turned to her and winked.

When they landed, they were directed to a large holding area for passengers deplaning from international flights. Illuminated signs warned travelers that Transportation Security Administration regulations strictly prohibited taking photographs in the customs-controlled area of the airport.

Once Hannah and Niaz retrieved their luggage from the big conveyor belt, they were directed along with the other foreign visitors to a series of segregated lines for passport control. Hannah found herself feeling nervous. Of course, if she was caught and arrested, the Israelis would secure her release. She realized that she had lived undercover for so long that she had become psychologically connected to her own false persona.

Hannah was first through passport control. She presented her Canadian passport to a cool, if not unfriendly, Immigration officer. The officer, a thirty-something Asian woman, looked briefly at Hannah and matched her face to the photograph in her passport. She then slid her passport through a digital reader. For a few seconds, she stared at her computer monitor. When the response arrived, the officer quickly stamped Hannah's passport and handed it back to her. "Welcome to the United States," she said, smiling.

Hannah pushed their luggage cart through the line and waited for Niaz, who came through the line a few minutes later, a triumphant smile on her pretty face.

They exited through a series of guarded doors into the public passenger arrival area and immediately ran into a crowd of limousine drivers, tour guides, and relatives waiting behind a barrier. Many of them held up signs with names on them. They were looking for a man and a woman holding up a sign that said, "Cohen." At first they didn't see them, probably because they unconsciously expected to be met by Middle Easterners. Then at the end of the line, they saw a blonde woman wearing sunglasses holding a small sign with the name Cohen written in black marker.

When they walked up to her, the woman said, in European-accented English, "Your aunt will be so glad to see you."

Hannah answered with the counter sign, "Grandmother sends her greetings."

The woman held out her hand and shook each of theirs.

"Sisters, we've been waiting for your arrival. Welcome." She turned to a taller, dark-complexioned man, who was standing behind her. "This is Mohammed and I am Ingrid." The man nodded at the women in greeting.

"Ladies," he said in heavily accented English, "let's gather up your luggage. You must be tired from your journey. Let's get you settled."

Chapter 70

Abid lay face down on the large, white hotel towel. Sepehr slowly rubbed sun lotion onto his back and shoulders. The sun, the warm sand, and the beach made them both feel languid and sensual. He turned his head up and whispered to Sepehr that he loved him and then lay back down and closed his eyes. Sepehr put more sun lotion on his hands and moved down Abid's back, massaging the lotion into his skin.

It was their third glorious day in Dubai and so far the trip far exceeded their expectations. There were several other gay couples at their hotel and most were very friendly. No one seemed to care about them or their sexual orientation and this allowed them to experience a sense of liberation and freedom that was unimaginable in Iran.

Abid heard someone say in English, "Hello, do you mind if we put our things down here?"

Sepehr's English wasn't great but he understood and said, "Yes, yes, OK."

Abid sat up and smiled at the two men. One had very dark skin and curly hair and looked African. The other man was smaller and older, but very handsome, and looked European or American.

It turned out they were Americans and had just arrived. The smaller one was named Jack and he seemed to do all the talking. The black man, who was originally from Ethiopia, was named Tesfaye. They made no effort to conceal that they too were a couple. When the hotel waiter came by to take their orders, Jack bought drinks for everybody. He spoke amazingly fast and the two Iranians had to keep asking him to speak more slowly.

Abid and Sepehr bought the next round of drinks and then there was a third. The two Iranians were pretty drunk. Tesfaye brought out a camera and they had the Filipino waiter take some pictures of them arm-in-arm, the turquoise blue of the Persian Gulf in the background. Jack regaled them with stories of his adventures in the Castro district of San Francisco, while Tesfaye laughed uproariously. All of Jack's tales, the wild parties, the gay parades, the clubs, were intoxicating to Abid and Sepehr.

When it started to get dark, they made plans to have dinner together. They met the two Americans at a restaurant overlooking the sea. At dinner, Abid told them how much he envied their freedom and told them about how gay couples in Iran had to carry on their relationships totally in secret because they faced arrest, public lashings, or even execution. Jack asked them why they didn't simply leave Iran and move to Europe or America. Abid responded that, because of his father's job, it wasn't that simple.

After dinner and still more drinks, they headed to the Atlantis disco. The crowd was young, hip, about half expat and half local, both straight and gay. Scantily clad blonde Russian girls were pole dancing on the stage and a DJ blasted out Western music. The dance floor was crowded. Abid, Sepehr, and the two American men joined in. The night went by in a whirr of sweaty, undulating bodies, alcohol, and laughter. At one point, another man asked Sepehr to dance and as Abid watched Sepehr disappear into the crowd, a German man, who must have been at least fifty and whose arms were covered by tattoos, asked him to dance. The man impulsively kissed Abid on the mouth at the end of the dance, just as Tesfaye snapped a photo.

The four men stumbled out of the club at 3:00 am exhausted, exhilarated, and thoroughly inebriated. Arm in arm, they weaved along the Corniche, talking loudly.

They did not notice the white delivery van pulling over besides them. There was a screech of tires, the doors flew open, and several men in dark clothes jumped out of the back of the van. They were at the side of the startled revelers in less than a second.

"You will come with us," one of them said in Farsi. Abid and Sepehr were in no condition to resist. Black hoods were thrown over their heads and they were hustled into the van.

"What is happening?" Abid pleaded. "Sepehr, are you all right?"

One of the men said in Farsi, "Shut up. If you talk, I'll stuff a rag into your mouth, you fucking pansy." He slapped Abid.

"Now listen closely," said another man in a deep voice. "You're going back to Iran to face a religious court. I swear by Allah, if you deviant pigs so much as squeak, we'll slit your throats and feed you to the fucking fish."

They drove for a while and stopped. "We're going to walk a few meters and then you'll be on an Iranian Navy craft. Do not talk."

When they opened the van door, Abid could hear the low rumble of idling marine engines. Hands pulled him roughly out of the van and stood him up. His legs felt rubbery and he wanted to retch. The heavy fabric of the hood made it difficult to breathe.

They walked for several meters, firmly in the grip of men on each side. Someone said to Abid, "Watch it," and pushed his head down. Abid could hear the big diesel engines revving up.

"Sit them down," a voice said.

The boat started to move slowly and then picked up speed. Someone lit a cigarette.

They passed the next few moments in silence. They must have cleared the harbor, thought Abid, because the engines went into high speed.

The door to the cabin opened. "Take off his hood."

The agent who pulled Abid's hood off was a little wiry man with a short crew cut, a cigarette in his mouth, and a pistol in a shoulder holster. Abid looked for Sepehr but he wasn't in the cabin. But Jack was there along with another man.

"All right, you little queer, you can relax now."

"Shlomi, can you please stop with the homophobia, already?" asked Jack in Hebrew. "It hurts my feelings."

The man named Shlomi grunted in annoyance.

To the shocked Abid, Jack said, laughing, in English, "Don't mind Shlomi, he's a Neanderthal when it comes to gay issues."

"What have you done with Sepehr?"

They laughed. Sepehr poked his head in the cabin and said, "I'm right here, Abid."

"What is going on, Sepehr?"

"I'm sorry," said Sepehr, matter-of-factly, "but you know what they say, Abid, 'business is business.' And we had a fun time, didn't we?"

Abid looked at Sepehr uncomprehendingly.

"What Sepehr is trying to tell you is that he works for us."

"Us? Sepehr, what does he mean."

Sepehr just shook his head sympathetically.

"Let's put it this way," Jack said. "You've won an all-expense paid cruise courtesy of the State of Israel."

"Israel?" stammered Abid.

"Hey, look on the bright side, Israel is a pretty tolerant place for gays. How many Queens do you think work for the Pasdaran? The Mossad is an equal-opportunity employer. They hired me."

"But we thought you were the Pasdaran and you were taking us back to Iran."

"Oh, that was just something Shlomi said to shut you up when he and the boys snatched you." Jack paused and took a deep drag on his cigarette, blowing the smoke out of the side of his mouth. "Incidentally, don't be confused here. I'm a nice guy, but we are going need you to cooperate with us. And if you don't, it won't be very pleasant for you."

"What are you going to do to me?" asked Abid, his voice now controlled, but the fear palpable.

"Well, for starters," interjected Shlomi, "what if we just drop your queer little ass in downtown Tehran with a photo of you kissing that German in the club pinned to your fucking chest?"

Jack rolled his eyes.

"Abid, as I'm sure you've noticed, Shlomi has a way with words."

The handsome young man that Abid knew by the name of Sepehr was a male prostitute whose real name was Mafooz. Dr. Boomla had rescued him from the streets of Shiraz a few years earlier and given him a job and an education. In return, Mafooz was occasionally called upon to perform certain services for Dr. Boomla's organization of a sexual nature. For Mafooz, who had experienced violence and abuse as a teenage prostitute, these duties were quite pleasant and usually consisted of a little romance and a lot of blackmail. He had grown quite fond of Abid and was sad that their relationship had come to an end. But business was business and it was time to return home.

The Israelis took Abid's passport and skillfully substituted a photograph of Mafooz. They also gave him Abid's wallet and a ring he owned and instructed him to give them to Dr. Boomla when he reached Shiraz. They brought him back to Dubai and from there he flew home to Iran in the guise of his former lover, Abid.

The Iranian border control agents detected nothing amiss and logged in the return of Abid Honari from his getaway vacation in the Emirates.

Chapter 71

Zahedan, Iran, August 10

Zahedan is strategically located where the borders of Iran, Pakistan, and Afghanistan meet. In the 1930s it was a sleepy village of a few hundred people when it was chosen to be the capital of the province of Sistan va Balochestan. Lying east of the Dasht-e-Lut desert, Zahedan is isolated from the rest of Iran and is more culturally and linguistically connected to Pakistan than it is to Iran. After the Soviet Union invaded Afghanistan in 1980, large numbers of refugees crowded into the city and its population swelled to nearly half a million. The vast majority of its residents are ethnic Sunni Baluchis, who feel little love for Iran's fundamentalist Shiite regime. Zahedan has the look and feel of a colonial outpost.

It was a clear day and to the south Mordechai could see the peak of Mt. Taftan rising three thousand feet from the surrounding plain. Although it hadn't erupted since 1993, volcanic steam still rose from its active vents. The view was breathtaking. But Mordechai was not interested in nature. Instead, he felt angry and impatient. The Americans were already forty minutes late. Mordechai's little delivery van was parked in an abandoned soccer field next to a big truck stop. He felt exposed at this location and kept looking around nervously. At the other end of the field there was a local market where farmers were selling their vegetables. Immediately behind the truck stop, some old Baluchi men were on their knees gambling. Mordechai counted twelve trucks parked next to the restaurant.

The semi that he was looking for was blue and white, the same colors as the Israeli flag. It was a coincidence that Mordechai found more unsettling than amusing. There was supposed to be a string of red balls hanging from the roof of the cab. He had also been given the license plate number.

Mordechai got out of the van to stretch his legs and get a better view of the area. There were no police or army around, which was good.

The sun was bright, but it was hazy and the light hurt Mordechai's eyes, so he put on a pair of sunglasses. If he looked like he was an out-of-place, slightly irritated Tehrani stuck in the middle of nowhere, it was because that pretty much described Mordechai's situation. He looked at his watch for about the fiftieth time that day.

A blue and white truck rolled into the field and came to a stop near the van. Mordechai looked up as if he was slightly interested in its arrival and confirmed that it was the right vehicle. A man and a woman got out of the passenger side door, each carrying a large suitcase. The driver stayed put. He had a big smile and waved at Mordechai, who nodded back. Idiot, he thought.

Mordechai looked at the two. The man didn't look American, but the woman was tall, tanned, and athletic, perfectly matching Mordechai's preconception of American women. She wore traditional clothes and the man wore an old black suit, a sweater, and black shoes. He had a cap on his head. To the average observer, they looked like farmers from the countryside who had hitched a ride into town with a truck driver. It was a common enough scene at the truck stop and did not arouse suspicion.

As they walked up, the young man said, "Hello, cousin" as he'd been instructed. Mordechai responded impatiently, "Hello, cousin. Now let's put your things in the back of the van and get going. You're late. Say your goodbyes and let's get out of here."

Mordechai opened the back of the van for them and got in. The couple loaded their suitcases in the back and shut the lift hatch. They waived at Aqil, who responded with a brief honk on his air horn and drove off.

Since there was no back seat in the van, Ivana and OJ squeezed into the front bench seat next to Mordechai.

OJ started to introduce himself and Ivana in Farsi. "Stop," Mordechai said, "I speak English." And as if to prove his command of the colloquial, he said, "Jesus Christ. What's the story with that guy blowing his horn? Maybe I should have had a sign out like those guys at the airport that said, 'Mr. and Mrs. CIA.' Anyway, my name is Mordechai and you must be Mr. and Mrs. CIA." He stuck out his hand and shook both Ivana's and OJ's.

"I am OJ and this is Ivana, but you can call her Irv," said OJ in Farsi.

"You are Iranian?" asked Mordechai in Farsi as he drove on to the highway heading toward Shiraz.

"Born here, left as a child and brought up in America. So that makes me . . . ."

Mordechai interrupted, switching back to English. "It makes you just like the rest of us, a little of this, a little of that. You are a Jew?"

"No, a Muslim."

"OK, you with the Slavic name . . . what are you?" Mordechai asked, a slight smile breaking out on his gaunt face.

"My family is part Serbian, part Bosnian. Half Christian, half Muslim. But not religious. And what are you, Mordechai?"

"An Iranian Jew. And like you, I work for my government doing things that need to get done."

Ivana turned to OJ. "'What Is to Be Done?' That was a book by Lenin we had around the house when I was a child. I remember the picture of a very serious Lenin on the front in which his eyes seemed to follow you no matter where you went."

"Oy," said Mordechai. "Communists. The CIA has finally started hiring Communists." He shook his head.

"Correction. Children of Communists," said Ivana.

Mordechai said, "Are you armed?"

Ivana lifted up the bottom of her skirt. She had a holster with a small automatic in it. "I've got this and we have a couple of MP-9s in the luggage."

"Ah," said Mordechai, "the improved Uzi. Irv, does your boyfriend know how to use it?"

"In a pinch," responded Ivana.

After that, they fell into silence. Ivana fell asleep against OJ's shoulder.

———————————————

Dr. Boomla owned a large house on the outskirts of Shiraz. It was surrounded by a thousand hectares of land that he leased out to farmers. He was well known in Shiraz for his hospitality. Boomla entertained often at his home and had a reputation for putting on lovely parties. He especially liked to entertain visiting government dignitaries. As both an eligible widower and an elegant man, Dr. Boomla was often seen in the company of a certain type of wealthy older woman, typically—but not exclusively—those whose husbands had departed for Paradise. They found him a charming but elusive target for their affections. Still, he was not beyond having the occasional dalliance with an attractive widow or divorcee, from whom he often learned interesting tidbits of information.

The Boomla house was, therefore, a lively place, with many guests coming and going. Boomla's wealth allowed him to maintain a domestic staff of long-term employ and extreme loyalty. The house's isolation afforded him privacy from prying eyes without arousing suspicion.

The old delivery van carrying the two American CIA agents and their Israeli Mossad driver arrived after midnight. It had been a long trip and they were exhausted. The Boomla compound was surrounded by a tall stone wall and the gate was guarded by a young man who only looked sleepy. They were expected and he let them in. Ivana and OJ were shown to their rooms by an elderly couple who had worked for the Boomla family for nearly fifty years. The old man insisted on carrying their luggage, which made OJ and Ivana uncomfortable. As Americans, they were not used to servants and it seemed unnatural for an old and frail couple to be carrying things for the young and strong. Mordechai, who didn't care about such conventions, simply picked up his bag when the old man tried to grab it and said, in Farsi, "I'll carry my own things." The old man bowed graciously and said, "As you wish."

Dr. Boomla met them in the grand foyer of the house and treated them with a formal Old World graciousness that seemed out of place in the twenty-first century. It was as if they were members of the Persian aristocracy who were paying a social call. He shook Mordechai and OJ's hands, but when Ivana stuck out her hand, he took it gently and brought it to his lips. Ivana turned red and Mordechai just rolled his eyes as if to say, "Crazy Gentiles." Dr. Boomla personally showed them to their rooms upstairs, all the while telling them about the history of the house.

As he bid them good night, his tone changed and he said, "Rest well; tomorrow we get down to the very serious business at hand."

Chapter 72

SHIRAZ, IRAN, AUGUST 11

D r. Boomla, OJ, Ivana, and Mordechai met over breakfast served in a beautiful sunroom with a view of the fields of wheat and the mountains in the distance. Dr. Boomla and Mordechai, as it turned out, knew each other well. Although they were opposites in personality, Dr. Boomla being talkative and friendly while Mordechai was taciturn and cynical, they were clearly very fond of one another. Dr. Boomla explained in his clipped British English accent that he and Mordechai had been involved in "quite a number of capers" together.

Now that Dr. Honari had responded to the emails, Boomla felt that he was ready to be exposed, as the dentist gleefully put it, to the next "level of hell in our little drama." Assuming that he responded to the blackmail by agreeing to help the Americans gain entry to Bala Deh, after the mission was accomplished Honari and his family would have to disappear. Moreover, the disappearance of the Honari family would have to be accomplished in such a way as to convince the Iranians that Honari was not implicated in the sabotage operation. The whole thrust of the mission was to make it look like an accident.

Therefore, the only logical choice was to make it looked like Honari killed himself and his family in a moment of extremis precipitated by the nuclear accident. Mordechai responded that he was disappointed because he wanted to shoot Honari.

Ivana looked at OJ, who looked as puzzled as she was, and she said, "Dr. Boomla, I think I may be missing something. How are you going to make Honari and his family appear to have died while actually getting them out of the country?"

"Well," said OJ, "I suppose you could acquire some dead bodies, but that won't hold up for long under even routine police scrutiny and the death of Dr. Honari in the wake of a nuclear incident will prompt a very high level investigation. If all goes well, Bala Deh will be an international incident and everyone in the Iranian security system will want Honari."

Boomla laughed in his gentle way. "We need Honari's body and yet the real Honari will, with any luck, be safely ensconced on some US Air Force base in the Indian Ocean. It is a conundrum, to be sure. Don't you agree, Mr. Nasim?"

"Do I agree? OK, yes, it's a big problem. But I bet you're about to give us the solution," responded Mordechai.

"You are correct, Mr. Nasim. The solution lies in the practice of dentistry. You see, we really don't need the entirety of Dr. Honari's body, simply enough of it that a positive identification can be made. When a body is burned beyond all recognition, as I propose should be our goal with respect to the cadavers of Dr. Honari and his family, the only way to identify the body is by looking at dental records. As is the case in many countries, dentists in Iran must register the names of their patients with the police so that identification can be made in just these kinds of situations. It would be a simple matter for the Honari family to choose me as their dentist and have their records transferred. In fact, it is likely that having recently moved to Shiraz, the members of Dr. Honari's family may not have even seen a dentist here and their records are still in Tehran. We would then be left with the task of obtaining a cadaver of the approximate age and gender of the deceased, take x-rays of the skull, and substitute those dental records for the real ones."

"Wouldn't you be taking a tremendous risk, Dr. Boomla?" asked Ivana.

"I think not. If I may boast a bit, I am a well-known dentist in this area. My patients are from the ranks of the wealthy and influential of Shiraz and I do not believe that suspicion would easily fall on me. I am, for example, the dentist for the head of the Revolutionary Guards in this province. I would simply be confirming what the police already strongly suspected to be true."

"OK, Dr. Boomla, so we substitute bodies. I take it that you know somebody who can burn the house down."

"I believe we have those connections to the appropriate person."

"All right. Now how about getting these people out of the country without arousing suspicion?"

"I believe, Madame, that is your department."

Chapter 73

On a small side street two blocks away from the Russian Embassy on Rehov Hayarkon, there is a small falafel restaurant. Boris Antonoff, the third assistant to the commercial attaché, sat waiting for the little woman to arrive. Boris was trying to quit smoking and was fidgeting with the ashtray, wishing he had a cigarette. He sipped from his cup of coffee, which was getting cold. The woman was late and he was becoming more irritated by the minute. Boris stared out the window onto the street. It was already hot, which made Boris even more taciturn than usual. However, he'd take a Tel Aviv summer over a Moscow summer any day. Anyway, he had no reason to complain; at least he had a job. A lot of the old KGB comrades had been laid off after the end of the Soviet regime and even though Putin was in power, not everybody had gotten their old jobs back. Moreover, a posting in Israel was good. There was some real spying to do and the food was good.

Finally, he saw Elena Markova crossing the street from the bus stop. She was a little round woman who rocked from side to side as she walked. Markova wore a kerchief over her dyed-red hair, an old house coat, and thick black shoes; another member of the age-old army of long -suffering Russian women. Elena was a Jew, although her late husband was not. They immigrated to Israel in the late 1980s. They had a son, but he did not come with them. He had become a heroin addict while serving in Afghanistan and when he returned to Russia he tried to kick his addiction but never succeeded. In 1997, he was arrested for possession of heroin. Elena went to the Russian embassy to inquire about posting bail and hiring a lawyer for her son. When the Embassy's intelligence officer found out that she worked as a janitor for the Israeli Foreign Office, they offered her a way out for her son and a little extra income. Elena started to work for the Russians. Her son was let free but was found not long after frozen to death outside an entrance of the Moscow underground, just another Afghanistan war veteran dead of a drug overdose. But Elena needed the money and continued to work for the Russians; it was easy enough for her to pilfer papers and pass them along.

When Elena opened the door, she looked around and spotting Boris. She shuffled over to his table.

"Hello, Elena Sergeyevich, do you want something to eat?" Boris and Elena always used the patronymic; it made them feel more at home.

"No, thank you, Boris Petrovich. I don't want to waste too much time. I have to get back to work. I have something for you."

"Yes? That's good. And I have something for you, too."

They traded envelopes. Elena's contained an intelligence report and several photographs that she had intercepted on the way to the shredder. Boris' contained cash.

"Thank you, Elena Sergeyevich."

"Goodbye, Boris Petrovich."

The little woman got up and shuffled out the door. She walked two blocks and got on the bus. An old man wearing a fisherman's cap and an ancient cardigan was sitting at a seat in the back. Elena sat next to him.

"Did you give him the envelope?" the man said in Hebrew.

Elena turned and answered him in Russian. "Did I give him the envelope? Such a stupid question, Moshe. Do I look like someone who wouldn't do my job?"

He patted her gently on the knee. "That's my girl." He picked up her hand and held it between his own.

"You know, Moshe, we're getting to be very old spies," she said, gently, her almond-shaped eyes glistening.

Chapter 74

The Israelis realized that the Russians had taken the bait when they starting spotting Slavs hanging around Van and conducting surveillance activities in the Heshmand Valley. For the operation, the Israelis flew Lubin in from his current posting in Athens. He was the obvious choice because, earlier in his career, he had worked out of the Israeli embassy in Moscow and so the Russians would immediately identify him as a Mossad agent.

Both the Israelis and the Russians had the Iranian under surveillance. The trick for the Mossad team was to keep the mark under surveillance without tipping off the Russians. Going back to the NKVD days in the 1930s, the Russians had always been very good at assassinations and blackmail; they were less competent at the more subtle arts of the espionage business.

The Israelis thought the Russians were so clumsy and obvious they might scare off the Iranian. They were posing as a Russian tour group and were running around downtown Van snapping pictures like crazy. Fortunately, he seemed to accept them at face value and his suspicions were not aroused.

The operation went off without a problem. The Iranian got up from his table at the café and, as he was leaving, Lubin walked straight up to him, and said, in accented English, "Hello, you must be Zaid." The Iranian stopped, not sure if the man was mispronouncing his name or not.

"Who are you looking for?"

"I am supposed to meet a man named Zaid who is going to show me around Van."

"You must be mistaken. I am not that man," Zaid said tersely.

"Oh, I'm so sorry to have bothered you," Lubin said with a big smile. He patted the Iranian on the shoulder and turned around and walked off.

Chapter 75

Although Mohammed and Ingrid were cordial to Hannah and Niaz, they were all business and it was understood that they were to operate under strict military discipline. Mohammed was their commander, Ingrid was second in command, and the two younger women were expected to follow their orders without question. They were not to reveal their real names but to use the names on their passports. That way, their identities would be protected if they were they captured.

Mohammed and Ingrid moved the two younger women into the team's other apartment, which was about a mile from their apartment. Despite the fact that both Hannah and Niaz carried forged California drivers' licenses, Mohammed prohibited them from driving. He felt that they should limit their potential exposure to automobile accidents or run-ins with the police. Every day, he and Ingrid would come by their apartment building and pick up Hannah and Niaz and they would drive together to the warehouse.

Two days after they arrived, Mohammed briefed them on the general outline of the mission. Mohammed told them they were going to hijack a gasoline tanker truck and detonate it next to its target; he did not reveal that they would be attempting to detonate a giant dirty bomb. Hannah and Niaz would be responsible for building bombs that would boost the explosive power of the fuel. When Hannah began to ask questions, Mohammed cut her off with a wave of his hand, telling her firmly that, for security reasons, they would not be given further information.

On the orders of General Yazdi in Tehran, Mohammed told Hannah and Niaz that there was a second terrorist team that would participate in the attack so that if they were captured or killed the attack could proceed. This was also a lie.

Hannah had a choice. She could walk away from the mission now and go to the authorities or stay and gather more information. If she went to the police, they might capture Mohammed's team, but the other terrorist team would remain at large to complete the mission. Redundancy was a standard operating practice for military planers and she had no trouble believing that General Yazdi had put a second team in place. She decided to stay until she could learn specific target information—and possibly the whereabouts of the second team.

"When will we have the details of the attack? And what about weapons? Do we have guns?"

Mohammed stared at Hannah for a long second. "You ask too many questions, Vashti. You needn't worry. We have sufficient weapons. This mission has been planned out to the last detail and I will tell you everything you need to know in good time. And nothing more."

Chapter 76

It was a Thursday evening when Dr. Honari received the next anonymous email message. There was no text, only a photograph. It showed his son Abid kissing an older bald European man in a night club. The man was not wearing a shirt. Honari was disgusted. What had happened to his son? Why had he turned away from Allah and become a *hamjesbāz*? He was sickened and angry and heartbroken all at the same time. For this offense, traveling to a foreign country and carrying on with foreign men, he was certain they would hang Abid. He remembered clearly how in the early 1990s, Dr. Ali Mozafarian, the Sunni Muslim leader in Fars province, was executed in Shiraz after being convicted on charges of espionage, adultery, and sodomy. The government repeatedly showed Mozafarian's videotaped confession of homosexuality on television. The man looked dreadful and had obviously been tortured by the secret police.

Honari stared at the image. He felt thoroughly exhausted. He clicked on the "reply" icon and typed: "What do you want?"

He received a response back almost immediately. "We have your son and his friend."

Honari felt panic rising in his chest.

"You lie."

"Their plans have changed and they will not be returning home next Thursday on Air Arabia Flight 226 as planned."

"I will go to the police."

"And tell them what? Please think carefully Dr. Honari about the consequences of your actions. We will contact you soon. Do what you are asked and your son will not be harmed."

Honari sat staring at the blinking computer cursor. He wrote back, "Is my son hurt?"

There was no response.

The next morning, as Dr. Honari waited for his ride to arrive, a teenage boy rode down the street on a bicycle. He stopped by Honari.

"Good morning, *Āghā ye Mohandes.*" The boy used the formal title for "Mr. Engineer" that would be used when addressing a governmental official. Is he mocking me, thought Honari?

"Good morning," responded Honari warily.

"I have a message for you. Make an appointment to see the dentist named Boomla."

"Boomla?"

"Yes, and you must telephone him this week." The boy started to pedal away. He looked back at the stunned Dr. Honari and said, smiling broadly and waving, *"Khodā hāfez Doktor Honari"* —Goodbye, Doctor Honari.

On Saturday morning, Dr. Honari drove his wife and daughters downtown to do some shopping. While Mrs. Honari and her girls were in a dress shop, Dr. Honari used a pay phone to call Dr. Boomla's Surgery and make an appointment. He would see the dentist on Monday morning at 9:00 am. He called Colonel Abadi, the military commander Bala Deh, and told him that he was taking the day off because of illness. The Colonel gave his approval, detecting nothing abnormal in the request.

Dr. Honari decided that he needed to try as hard as he could to make things appear normal and not show his fear. At dinner that evening, Honari informed his wife and daughters that Abid had emailed him to get his permission for the boys to say a week longer in Dubai and that he had agreed to their request. His wife seemed happy with her husband's decision, taking it as an indication that the recent tension between father and son had abated.

After dinner, Honari went into his study. There was another email. It said: "Abid thanks you very much and hopes to see you soon. By the way, you really ought to have that birth mark on his left inner thigh looked at." The point was obvious and any lingering doubts that Honari still had regarding the fate of is son were now gone.

On Monday morning Dr. Honari awoke from another restless night with the overwhelming sense of dread that had become his constant companion. Dr. Boomla's dental surgery was located in an older building that housed numerous medical professionals. When Honari arrived, a pretty young woman behind a counter looked up and said cheerfully, "Good Morning, Dr. Honari. Please sit down. Dr. Boomla will be with you shortly." The personal greeting unnerved Honari and threw him even more off balance.

Honari sat down in the empty waiting room and tried to read a magazine. There was a fish tank there. He once read that Western doctors had discovered that the presence of a fish tank in a waiting room made patients feel more relaxed. Honari was staring at the fish when he heard a deep voice say, "Good morning, Dr. Honari."

Honari looked up and saw a distinguished-looking man who appeared to be in his late sixties, with thick silver hair and a beard. He was dressed in a well-tailored, dark-gray suit. Dr. Boomla smiled congenially at Honari and stuck out his hand. Honari shook it and then found himself amazed that he was treating this blackmailer so cordially.

"Please follow me, Dr. Honari."

Honari followed Dr. Boomla down the corridor past several dental examination rooms to a large spacious office. The walls were hung with Boomla's degrees and photographs of him as a young dentist posing with his father. Another wall was lined with a lifetime of books and professional journals on medicine, dentistry, and science.

Boomla's desk was a large antique from the late Ottoman period and was equipped with a brass bankers' lamp, a pile of patient medical records, and an old bakelite model of an upper and lower jaw. In addition to Dr. Boomla, two men and a woman were in the room. They were sitting in chairs in front of the desk, but when the door opened, they stood up and turned to greet Honari and Boomla. One of the men was probably thirty, short with a dark beard. He was wearing the uniform of a high-ranking Pasdaran officer. When Honari saw him, he felt the jerk of fear. But the young man must have read his mind because he stuck out his hand and said, "Don't be alarmed, Dr. Honari, I am not what I appear to be." Switching to English, he said, "You may call me Ishmael."

The other man was taller and thinner than Ishmael, but quite a bit older. He was wearing a short-sleeved shirt and the muscles on his arms were tense and sinewy. To Honari, he looked like a bird of prey. He said his name was Mousa.

The woman was taller than either of the two men and her thick brown hair was covered loosely in a *hijab*. She was introduced as Dina, an "associate" of Ishmael. Dina did not speak, but looked Honari straight in the eye and nodded. Dr. Honari was shocked. No young Iranian woman of decent upbringing would ever make eye contact with a man to whom she just had been introduced.

The dentist guided Honari to one of the chairs. The woman sat on a small settee in the corner.

Dr. Boomla went behind his desk and sat down in his old-fashioned leather desk chair.

"I suppose you want to know what this is all about, Dr. Honari," said Boomla.

"I know what it is all about. You've got my son; it's about blackmail. So get to the point. Tell me how much it will cost to get my son back and purchase your silence about his . . . situation." Honari's voice was quivering with anger and, just beneath that, fear.

The thin man named Mousa said to no one in particular, "At least he's direct."

"Please, Dr. Honari, permit me to explain before you jump to conclusions." Boomla sounded slightly hurt by the accusation. "The people that have your son do not want money from you. They do not wish to hurt you or your son. And I, Dr. Honari, am motivated by pure altruism mixed with just a tinge of patriotism."

Honari looked dumbfounded and remained silent.

The man named Ishmael interrupted. "Doctor, we very much need your help. If you cooperate with us, no harm will come to your son and his . . . lover. In fact, if you help us, we will help Abid and Sepehr leave Iran or whatever else you or they desire."

"And if I don't agree to help you?" asked Honari.

"Why dwell on unpleasantness, Dr. Honari?" asked Boomla. Gesturing toward the other two people in the room, he continued, "Suffice it to say that these people and their compatriots are very serious and they mean what they say."

"If it is not money, what do you want?" asked Honari.

"We want information about your work at Bala Deh, Dr. Honari," answered Ishmael.

Honari turned pale and began to rub his hands together. His voice rose to a hysterical pitch. "So that is your game. You are spies and traitors. I will not help you. I am leaving. I am going to the police."

Honari stood up and turned around. Ivana was blocking the door; the barrel of her Beretta pointing at Honari's chest. Mordechai put a hand on Honari's shoulder.

"You will do no such thing, Doctor," said Boomla calmly. "Please sit down. There is no point engaging in theatrics. My friends here will kill you before you take two steps."

Mordechai put gentle pressure on Honari's shoulders and he sat back down.

Boomla picked up his pipe and began to tap it in an ashtray. The others watched in silence. Boomla looked up. "Now let's level with one another, Dr. Honari. These people are representatives of the Western democracies. It should come as no surprise that their superiors are extremely interested in Iran's nuclear program and naturally they will go to extraordinary lengths to acquire information about it. Your son and his friend have engaged in sexual behavior which the spiritual leaders of our country consider evil and criminal. As you know, our mullahs will punish them severely. They will be lucky to get away with imprisonment and a public whipping. They could very well be executed as an example to others. That, after all, has been the pattern with those convicted of sodomy. Overwhelming shame will be brought upon your family and you will be terminated from your job. You will lose your wealth and status. But, Dr. Honari, such a fate can be avoided. All that you need do to ensure the safety of your son and your family is to cooperate with these people and when they have finished gathering their information, Abid and his friend will be returned, their secret safe. My friends will leave you and your family alone. In fact, for your trouble, you will be paid handsomely. And as I said earlier, if Abid and Sepehr would rather leave Iran permanently, we would be willing to arrange that as well. That offer also applies to you, your wife and daughters, if you are so inclined."

Dr. Honari slumped in his chair. "Have I any choice?" he asked.

"Not really. You can choose death or life. What will it be, my good doctor?"

"Who are they?" Honari asked Boomla.

OJ answered. "We are Americans, Dr. Honari, and the sooner you help us, the sooner we will finish our mission and you will never see us again."

He turned toward OJ and said bitterly, "Ishmael, or whatever your real name is, you have come here to destroy Iran and attack Islam. And now, to save my child, my firstborn, my only son, I have no choice but to help you and betray my country. It is true, you people are the Great Satan."

Mordechai rolled his eyes and muttered something in Hebrew, which no one in the room understood.

"Look, Dr. Honari," said OJ, "our country has no quarrel with the Iranian people. I was born here and only wish your—our—country a future of peace. We must avoid war at all costs and to do so we and our allies need to know about your nuclear capabilities and to stop your government's attempts to acquire nuclear weapons. All we want from you is a little information. Then we will leave you and your family alone."

"What you want from me will get me executed if it is discovered."

"That is true, Dr. Honari. Like I said earlier, if you help us, there is a chance that nothing will happen to you. If you refuse to help us, then something very bad will certainly happen to you and your family."

"I believe, Honari," Boomla said as if teaching a school lesson, "it was Homer, the bard of our ancient Greek enemies, who described his hero, the wandering Hercules, as being 'between Scylla and Charybdis.' Like Hercules, you are in a similar predicament."

"How do I know that Abid is still alive?"

"A fair question," said Boomla. "Would you like to speak with him?"

"Yes."

Boomla took a satellite telephone out of his desk drawer and punched in a long string of numbers. He put the phone to his ear and when someone answered, he said, in English, "put the boy on." He handed the phone to Honari.

"Abid. Is that you?" His voice was now a cry.

Evidently Abid was on the other end of the line, because Honari said, choking up, "Are you safe?"

Honari listened to his son for a few seconds and then said, "Hello. Hello. Abid, Hello." The tears welling up in his eyes, he looked up at Dr. Boomla and said in a voice choked with emotion, "He's gone."

Honari put the phone down on the desk and slumped in his chair, the weight of his life bearing down on him.

Boomla said quietly, "Dr. Honari, you must make your decision."

As they waited in silence for Honari to speak, Dr. Boomla calmly began to pack his pipe with tobacco. Ivana caught OJ's eye and she smiled and winked.

Finally, Honari made a strange puffing noise and sat up in his chair. "You leave me no other choice, I will do as you ask."

Dr. Boomla smiled warmly. "Excellent, Dr. Honari. Now shall we spend the rest of the hour talking about your work?" Boomla picked up the telephone on his desk. "Hami, please bring in some coffee and pastries for our guests."

"So, Dr. Honari, tell us about your typical work day."

Later, after Honari had left, Ivana turned to OJ and said, "'Call me Ishmael?' I can't believe that you said that."

OJ, looking very satisfied with himself, replied, "I didn't think I could get away with 'Jesus wept.'"

"Thank goodness," said Dr. Honari. "That would have sent the man right over the edge."

"What are you people talking about?" asked Mordechai impatiently.

"Landing the big fish," replied OJ. Honari and Ivana laughed. Mordechai looked annoyed. Suspecting that he was the butt of a joke that he didn't understand, Mordechai said, "Enough with the smart American talk. We need to go."

Chapter 77

GRIFFITH PARK, LOS ANGELES, CALIFORNIA, AUGUST 14

G riffith Park is one of the largest urban parks in the United States. Its seventeen square miles of mountainous terrain sit at one end of the Santa Monica Mountains. On the south slope, the park overlooks Hollywood and downtown Los Angeles; on its north side lies the San Fernando Valley.

Mohammed and Ingrid sat in the parking lot of the Observatory which stood on a plateau with a spectacular view of the city. "This is breathtaking," she said. "What a beautiful place."

"It's a shame to blow it up but in wars such things are necessary," Mohammed replied casually.

Since he had been informed by Tehran that this was to be their target, Mohammed had gotten on the Internet and learned everything he could about the Park.

"The story of this place is one of typical American decadence," said Mohammed. "In the 1890s, the land was given to the people of the city by a wealthy man named Colonel Griffith J. Griffith. It seems the Colonel tried to murder his wife."

Ingrid interrupted. "Mohammed, you sound like a professor."

"You forget, I almost became one. "

"After the Colonel returned to Los Angeles from a short time in prison, he attempted to rehabilitate himself by donating money to the City of Los Angeles to build an observatory at the park. At first, the city leaders refused, calling the donation 'blood money,' but they eventually relented after Griffith died. In the 1930s, they finished the Observatory. Now, Ingrid, one of the reasons that this target was selected is that in the fall, hot winds, like the desert *Khamsin* we have, blow through these mountains. They call them 'Santa Anas.' God willing, those winds will be blowing when we attack."

"Yes," Ingrid replied quietly.

"Here's something interesting. It is a fact that crime increases when the hot Santa Ana winds blow; they were blowing the night Colonel Griffith shot Mrs. Griffith."

They got out of the car looking like just another pair of tourists visiting one of the iconic places of Los Angeles and walked toward the Observatory. It was a windy day and the gusts made it difficult to walk against the wind. Ingrid was in a happy mood. She loved seeing new things and couldn't believe that she was in Hollywood. Ingrid realized that for her this was a land of dreams, formed in her imagination by countless movies and songs. It was also the cultural heart of all that she hated and that they were sent here to destroy.

They entered the observatory and stopped at the Foucault pendulum in the main rotunda. Twenty-four stone pegs stood equidistant from one another at the outside of a circle. A pendulum suspended from the ceiling swung perpetually. At the top of each hour the pendulum would knock down another peg. Mohammed and Ivana stood watching the pendulum swing slowly back and forth, getting imperceptibly closer to knocking down the next peg. Mohammed spontaneously kissed Ingrid on the cheek.

"It is going to happen," he said cheerfully.

They walked out on to the observation desk. While Ingrid enjoyed the view, Mohammed noticed that the closest gas station to the Observatory was located near the Los Feliz Boulevard entrance to Griffith Park.

Chapter 78

From the moment their second meeting with Dr. Honari began, it was evident that he had undergone a change in attitude. "Before you start your questions, I have made a decision," Honari said.

"And what would that happen to be, my good Doctor?" asked a clearly bemused Boomla.

"I want my family and myself to be taken out of Iran to a safe place."

"OK, we can make that happen," Responded OJ.

"There is more. I want asylum."

"OK."

"And I want $3 million dollars for me and a job on the faculty of a good university. I want you to buy me a house there. I want my children to be able to attend private school and the university for free."

OJ responded, "Doctor Honari, we will take your request to our superiors and have an answer for you at our next meeting. Now let's get down to business. When we last talked, you were describing the security procedures at the facility."

Dr. Honari called Colonel Abid and told him that he would have his third and final root canal the following day and would need to be absent from work. The Colonel was sympathetic, since he firmly believed that all dentists were butchers.

When Honari arrived at Dr. Boomla's office, he was greeted by a smiling OJ.

"I am pleased to inform you that my government has authorized the relocation of you and your family to the United States and payment to you of up to $2.5 million. You will be given a teaching position at the United States Defense University. You will be required to cooperate fully with our government and to tell us everything—and we mean everything—you know about Iran's nuclear program. This means the names of individuals who work in the nuclear program, the roles they play, your foreign contacts, how technology is acquired, everything. Is that agreeable?"

Honari paused. "It is."

Ivana stood up and walked over to the chair where Honari was seated in front of Dr. Boomla's desk. She thrust out her hand and Honari looked a little shocked.

OJ said in Farsi, "Shake her hand, Doctor. You need to get used to these things if you are coming to the decadent West."

Honari stood up and shook Ivana's hand. "We're in business," said Ivana.

"From God's mouth to your ears," added Mordechai.

"What does he mean by that?" asked Honari, who clearly disliked the Israeli.

"Nothing, nothing," said Mordechai, "It's a joke."

"OK, Doctor Honari, let's get started," said Ivana. "Can I explain what we need from you?

OJ began to translate.

"If I may interrupt," interjected Dr. Boomla, "there is an important preliminary matter we must resolve. I know this may sound odd, but please bear with me, Dr. Honari. Have you and your family seen a dentist since you moved to Shiraz?"

"What do you mean?" Honari looked puzzled.

"Doctor Honari, please answer the question," said OJ.

"No, I haven't and I don't think my family has seen one either."

"What was the name of your dentist in Tehran?"

"Dr. Ghalazy."

"I know him. Good man. And your wife and children?"

"We all saw Dr. Ghalazy."

"Very convenient. Well, then, we will contact Dr. Ghalazy and have him transfer your dental records and that of your family to my office."

"Will he do that?"

"Of course, it is routine."

"Why do you need them?"

"Because, Honari, when the moment comes for the Americans to make you and your family disappear, we will need to convince the police that a tragic accident has occurred—a terrible fire—which killed all of you. Although your bodies will be burnt beyond all recognition, they will be identifiable by their dental records. What I will do is change your dental records to be consistent with those of the skeletons that we will incinerate in your place."

"And . . . where will you get these skeletons?" asked an astonished Honari.

"My professorship at the medical college affords me ample access to an array of body parts."

"I see."

"Forgive my interruption, Ishmael," he said to OJ. "Please continue."

"Dr. Honari, we need to understand how the Bala Deh facility is laid out, the security system, the work processes. And we need to know how to get inside."

"That is no simple matter."

"We didn't think it was. If we had, we wouldn't have gone to all the trouble of getting acquainted with you."

"And what of my son? Is he healthy and safe?"

The taciturn Mordechai answered. "At the moment, Doctor, he and his boyfriend are enjoying a free Mediterranean cruise."

Chapter 79

Bill Victorine and Ray Einhorn sat in a small reception area outside the large conference room where the Joint Chiefs of Staff held their regular weekly meeting. Two Marine guards stood at attention on each side of the large double doors that led into the conference room. The carpet was a luxurious deep-blue pile. In front of the doors, the seal of the Joint Chiefs—four intersecting gold swords with a red, white, and blue shield over them—was woven into the carpet.

After they had waited for about forty-five minutes, an officer came out of the meeting to get them. He led Victorine and Einhorn inside and directed them to sit on two vacant chairs behind a lectern in the rear of the room. The conference room was dominated by a massive oak table. The members of the Joint Chiefs sat at the table with an entourage of high-ranking officers. The aides and specialists sat in the chairs lining the walls. There were evenly spaced windows around the room but they were closed off by dark wooden shutters and trimmed with thick, gold brocade drapes. Between each window was a framed painting depicting a famous military scene from each of the four branches of the military. The near-perfect symmetry of the room gave the impression of order and power.

Appearing more like a bank auditor than a warrior, the Chairman of the Joint Chiefs of Staff, General Gundry, looked up over his half-glasses at the two younger men on the opposite side of the table. "Mr. Victorine, Commander Einhorn, you're up. Let's get a status report on Operation Whirlwind." All eyes in the big conference room turned toward the two men. The lights were dimmed. On a large screen appeared a detailed aerial photograph of the Bala Deh facility, with various locations labeled. One of the men stood up and went to a small lectern near the screen onto which the image of Bala Deh was projected.

"Sir, I'm William Victorine, Deputy Director for Foreign Clandestine Operations for the CIA, and this is Commander Raymond Einhorn, Navy Special Warfare Command, CENTCOM, and coordinator of Operation Whirlwind, the planned attack on Bala Deh.

"Since the last time we reported, we have begun execution of the final phase of the mission. Our team is in place and fully operational. The three-man SEAL team is currently in a safe house near the Afghan border training for the incursion. They are being resupplied by air. Our contacts in the Baluchi separatist movement will transport them back to Bala Deh when the time is right. Two of our people, Agents Svilanovic and Hamsid, are now in Shiraz. They are coordinating with the Israelis, who run a well-entrenched indigenous network, code named 'Novocain,' which is providing major operational assistance. The target of the coercion operation, Dr. Majid Emami Honari, Scientific Director of Bala Deh, is now fully cooperating."

"Now where are we with the incursion planning and execution?" asked the Chairman.

Victorine took out a laser pointer. "This is the facility at Bala Deh that the Iranians call Concrete Works Number 31. Here is the front gate, guard towers, barracks, command center, gravel pit, and gravel-processing facility. As the canyon narrows, there are blast doors that cover a cave . . . here."

Victorine clicked something on a laptop computer at the lectern and a series of photographs came up of the cave. "This is the cave entrance. Inside is the centrifuge cascade. According to Dr. Honari, there are three thousand linked centrifuges running half a kilometer back into the mountain." Victorine clicked again. The image switched to a blueprint. "This is a schematic drawing of the inside of the cave based on information reported to us by Dr. Honari. As you can see, the cave complex is very large, with a number of side chambers off the main tunnel. It is equipped with modern radiation detection, fire suppression, motion detection, and video surveillance systems. It is powered by underground cable from the main power line that parallels the access road to the facility. There are auxiliary generators."

Victorine brought up another slide, an aerial photograph of the mountain in which the cave was located. "At the rear of the facility is a ventilation shaft that also serves as an emergency escape route. It reaches the surface on the top of the mountain . . . here. The area is lit up and there are surveillance cameras.

"Honari says that there are only two ways to gain entry undetected, either to rappel over the side of the canyon wall entering through the blast doors or to secure entry through the escape shaft into the rear of the facility. In either case, Dr. Honari strongly advises that we shut down the electricity or, at the very minimum, darken the area at the time of entry."

A high-ranking Air Force General spoke up. "General, if I may? My question is this: if we take out the electrical supply, presumably through the use of bunker-buster ordnance or sabotage, how are we going to convince the Iranians and, more importantly, world opinion that the subsequent explosion and release of radiation was an accident?"

"That is a good question, Sir," responded Victorine. "We don't think it is possible to cut the electricity. However, we do believe it may be possible to get the Iranians to turn off the exterior lights themselves."

"How so?" said the Air Force General, looking skeptical.

Einhorn got up from the table and went to the lectern. "If I may, Sir. According to the information provided by Dr. Honari, whenever there is a flyover, the Revolutionary Guard Commander at Bala Deh has standing orders to cut the external lights for the entire facility in order to render it invisible from the air. One hour after the aircraft passes, then the lights are turned on.

"And what is the proposed solution to this problem?"

"We think that overflights of the facility are the solution."

The Air Force General asked, "What kind of anti-air defenses are there at this facility?"

"The SEAL team counted six SAM missile batteries," replied Victorine.

"If we fly over Bala Deh with fighter aircraft or any aircraft, for that matter, the Iranians are going to scream bloody murder and try to shoot them down. Hell, they'll probably bring half the world press to Bala Deh just to show how outrageous we've acted."

"General, we agree that we can't endanger human pilots, but we do think that we can use unmanned aerial vehicles to much the same effect. Moreover, we believe the Iranians will not attempt to shoot down the UAVs because they are reluctant to bring attention to Bala Deh.

"Why?" asked one of the officers.

"Since it is an undisclosed nuclear facility, if an incident occurs and its existence becomes public knowledge, the IAEA will demand to inspect it, causing all kinds of headaches for the Iranians."

"So, Commander," asked the Army Chief of Staff, "you believe that they will turn off the lights and this will create enough darkness to allow our team to gain entrance undetected? It sounds like the timing is going to have to be perfect."

"Sir, we agree with that assessment."

Victorine brought up another slide, this time a map of Iran. "In addition to the overflights, just east of Shiraz, we are now in the final planning stages of a diversionary attack. The target is a small paramilitary police facility off the main east-west highway. The Novocain group is arranging for an Arab Sunni separatist group to attack the facility with RPG's and small arms. We have provided funding. We expect this will cause chaos for a day and dominate the attention of the Iranian security apparatus."

"So this matter is proceeding on track. My understanding is that you are briefing the White House this afternoon, correct?" asked the Chairman of the Joint Chiefs.

"That is correct, sir."

"Very good. If there are no other questions for these gentlemen, let's move on to our little problem in Venezuela."

Chapter 80

Mohammed's team spent a week observing the operation of Antonio's Chevron station on Los Feliz Boulevard: when it had its rush of business and when it was quiet, how many people worked there, and the pattern of fuel deliveries. The fuel truck delivery was made every Wednesday and Sunday evening just after the station closed at 11:00 pm by a tanker truck operated by Veneto Tank Lines. The driver would pull into the station, unlock three round metal plates sunk into the concrete, haul the hoses over to the plates, and then he would start the refueling process. When he was finished, he would fill out an invoice and leave it in a drop box. The whole process took about fifteen minutes.

One evening after a long and mind-numbing day of watching the gas station, Mohammed and the three women went out for some coffee at an all-night restaurant in Hollywood. Mohammed told them that the Chevron station met the criteria to be chosen as the location where the truck hijacking would occur.

What he did not tell them was that it was also very close to their real target.

Chapter 81

Tom Harter was walking his dog in the park when he noticed that the stick was pointed up. He had mail. He checked to see that no one was looking and went over to the drop. He picked up the message and shoved it in his pocket and continued his ambling walk.

When he got home, he took the key Sayeed had given him out of its hiding place and decoded the message. He was to contact a man named "Mohammed" at a telephone number of a business in Wilmington. He was told to tell Mohammed that he was interested in arranging to ship a container of shoes from Austria. Mohammed was then to inform him that he could arrange shipping through the Port of Constanta in Romania.

The next morning, he called the telephone number and a woman with a European accent answered, "Smith and Jones." As instructed in the letter, Tom asked for Mohammed and she said, sounding wary, that she would get him. When Mohammed got on the telephone, Tom gave the sign and Mohammed duly gave the countersign. Mohammed asked Tom when he was available to meet in person and

Tom said that he could arrange to take a day off of work later in the week. Mohammed said that the time had come to "plant an oak tree" and Tom's heart started to race. That phrase was what Sayeed had told him would be the signal that he was being activated to participate in a Jihad operation.

The moment had arrived which Tom Harter had dreamed of for so long. He was being made operational and would, at long last, become a warrior in the Jihad against the West.

Tom Harter was Abdul-Haq once again.

Chapter 82

Mohammed asked Tom Harter to come to the warehouse for their first meeting. Hannah and Niaz were posted outside at opposite ends of the street to make sure that Harter was not being followed. They had no reason to believe that he had been compromised, but they were taking no chances.

The street was wide and, even in the early afternoon, there was very little foot or automobile traffic. Almost all of the buildings were commercial. Down at the end of the block was a little taqueria and a gas station, but they were the only retail businesses nearby. Harter parked his Toyota pickup truck on the street in front of the warehouse. The front glass doors were blacked out and the door was locked. To the side was a buzzer and an intercom. A little sign said, "Press to Enter." Harter pressed the button.

"Yes?" It was a woman's voice.

As instructed, he said, "Acorn".

Ingrid responded, "Oak tree," and buzzed him in.

The lights were off in the entry way and so when the door closed behind Harter, he was temporarily blinded after the bright sunlight outside. He felt a hand on his shoulder and cold metal on his neck.

"Don't move, brother," a man said in heavily accented English. "Not a millimeter or I will have to kill you. Now, slowly put your hands behind your back."

Tom did as he was told. Another set of hands quickly put a plastic cinch tie around his wrists and tightened it. A cloth hood was placed over his head. Tom's heart pounded; was this a trap?

Tom heard someone open a door up ahead.

"Now walk forward."

Tom started to move. At one point, the man said, "Watch your head, brother," and gently pushed down on his head. "OK, now we are going to turn left." Tom did as he was told.

"Sit down." Tom sat.

"Now, brother, I am going to ask you some questions. If you get them wrong, I will kill you. Do you understand?"

"Yes."

"What is your name?"

"Thomas Harter."

"When were you born?"

"August 23, 1982."

"Where?"

"North Hollywood, California."

"What was the name of your primary school?"

"John B. Monlux Elementary School."

"Your middle school?"

"Robert Milliken Middle School"

"Your high school?"

"Ulysses S. Grant High School."

"What is your contact's name?"

"Sayeed. I don't know his last name."

"Where was your last meeting with Sayeed."

"Rick's Burger Hut in Pomona."

"What is your religion?

"Islam."

"Were you brought up as a Muslim?"

"No, as a Christian."

"What is the *Shahadah?*

"It is the words one says to convert to Islam."

"And who was the Imam of the Mosque where you converted?"

"Dr. Wazzam."

"Say the *Shahadah* in Arabic."

"*Ashhadu Alla Ilaha Illa Allah Wa Ashhadu Anna Muhammad Rasulu Allah,*" Tom said, remembering the words.

"And what is your Muslim name?"

"Abdul-Haq."

"Welcome to the fight, Abdul-Haq," the man said, as someone took off the hood. An older man, dark and very handsome, with burning eyes, was standing in front of him. He put the automatic in his belt and thrust out his hand to shake Abdul-Haq's. "I am Mohammed and this is Ingrid." From behind him stepped a very beautiful older blonde woman, who nodded at him.

The office they were in was almost bare. It contained a computer terminal, a telephone, and a few pens and pencils. There was nothing on the white walls except an old calendar from a Mexican-restaurant supplier.

"Abdul-Haq, there is ship now at sea named OPCL Pusan traveling from Karachi, Pakistan to the Port of Los Angeles. On it is the container we are interested in. The container is number OPCL2948572." Mohammed handed a piece of paper to Abdul-Haq. "That particular container is consigned to various Wal-Mart stores in Southern California. Will you be able to determine when the ship is arriving?"

"Of course. If it is a consignment that is going to any Southern California Wal-Mart store, it will come through my distribution center."

"Excellent. Now, will you be able to tell us what truck will be dispatched to pick up the container after it is unloaded?"

"Yes, when the truck is dispatched to pick up the load, we receive the information electronically and it attaches to the shipping record for that container."

"How about the route that the truck will travel? Do you know that, Abdul-Haq?" asked Mohammed.

"No, not specifically, but if you parked outside the terminal and waited you could look for the truck when it pulls out and follow it."

Mohammed turned to Ingrid. "Could you please ask our two comrades to join us? I think they need to meet our brother."

Ingrid left the room punching numbers on her cell phone to call Hannah and Niaz.

"Here is our operational problem. We need to locate and remove three boxes from that container. One alternative is to intercept the truck, neutralize the driver, and hijack the vehicle. This involves significant risk since we don't know the route the driver will take and will have to improvise a plan of attack. A better choice would be to change the delivery point to a location where the driver would detach the container without arousing suspicion. A variation of that choice would be to divert the load to a location where the driver could be subdued and the load taken forcibly. A last alternative would be to bribe the driver to divert the load. What is your opinion of these alternatives Abdul-Haq?"

Abdul-Haq was deeply flattered that such a seasoned warrior would ask for his opinion. "I can get into the master traffic control computer program and change the bill of lading to direct the shipment to another location. The important thing is not to draw attention to the shipment by changing the tariff. If the location is a shorter distance than the original delivery point, it is not likely to alter the tariff. If you wanted the truck sent here, for example, then it will not cause a change in tariff because the consignment would be going a much shorter distance."

"You could make it come here?"

"I think I can make that happen."

"If a driver was routed here, would it cause suspicion?"

"It depends. It's not that unusual for us to reroute a load because of different distribution needs, but usually to another Wal-Mart distribution center not to a little warehouse in Wilmington. However, if the shipment is sent here, the driver is probably going to make the same money on the load. Since his turn-around time will be faster, he'll be happy. Anyway, most of the drivers are immigrants and don't want to make waves."

"And what about your employer? How long will it take them to figure out that a container is missing?"

"Well, it depends on when the stores that are supposed to get the freight start missing inventory. I suppose anywhere from a few days to a few weeks."

"Well, Abdul-Haq, we plan to hold on to the freight for probably one or two days at the most. So I believe that you should go ahead and divert the freight to this location."

"I'll do it first thing tomorrow."

"Excellent. And one more thing. In a moment you will meet Vashti and Niaz. For security reasons, they know nothing about the truck shipment and will not be told until later in the operation. So you must keep our conversation confidential."

"Commander Mohammed, I have a great deal of experience keeping secrets and I will never let you down."

Ingrid returned with Niaz and Hannah. Mohammed introduced them to Abdul-Haq, who bowed and said, in well-practiced Arabic, "*Salaam Alechem,*" to which they replied, "*Alechem Salaam.*"

"We have some food at a table out in the warehouse. Let's go out there and break some bread to welcome Abdul-Haq to our team."

"I can't tell you how happy I am to join the Jihad."

Niaz blushed. Hannah could tell that she was taken by the big blond American man.

Over a meal of falafel, ful, pita, and salad, they discussed the plan in further detail. Mohammed did not reveal anything about the real goal of the mission, but did explain to Abdul-Haq that it would not be safe for him to remain in the area after the mission was completed; he would have to leave the country with them. Mohammed asked Abdul-Haq if he possessed a passport. Abdul-Haq said that he had gotten one some years before at the urging of Sayeed. Mohammed explained that Abdul-Haq's complicity in the mission would certainly be considered treason by the American government; if he was caught and tried, he would probably receive the death penalty. He seemed a little shocked at the realization that suddenly he was now facing a future that included permanent exile from the country of his birth and a life on the run.

When the women left them to clean up, Abdul-Haq said quietly to Mohammed, "I have something I must confide in you. I have a

Christian wife. Sayeed encouraged me to marry her as part of my cover. What shall I tell her?"

"I am sorry, my brother, but in a few weeks, she will be a widow no matter what happens. Where you are going, she cannot follow. You must leave her and never contact her again." Mohammed patted Abdul-Haq on the shoulder. "War is hard on the warrior. But remember, many of our brothers who have performed martyr missions had to say goodbye to their wives and mothers without ever letting them know what they were going to do. God willing, this is not a martyr mission, and we will all survive." Mohammed laughed. "Besides, brother, when we return home, there will be many women for you. Abdul-Haq, I sense that your soul faces Mecca. After this mission, you will be a hero to our people. The dark-eyed beauties of the Middle East await you."

"That is a pleasant thought."

"Now here is what I want you to do. Tomorrow, you will go and change the computer program. You will ask to take the next four days off from your work. Is that possible?

"Yes, that will be no problem."

"You will tell your wife that you are going on a business trip."

"OK."

"Then you will come here tomorrow night. Bring extra clothes. Tell your wife you are going to Seattle for a meeting. We will make a reservation for you and pay for the room. We will arrange for you to call her to tell her that you are well.

"The next morning, Abdul-Haq, we will drive—all of us—to Seattle, Washington. You will then drive the van back to California. The rest of us will enter Canada on US passports that we possess. Then we will get on a flight using Canadian passports and return to Los Angeles. It will look as though we never left Canada and are beginning a short vacation. Then when the mission is completed we will drive to San Francisco and take a flight out of the country."

Niaz sipped her tea as she cleaned up their kitchen. "What do you think of Abdul-Haq?" she asked pensively.

"He seems dedicated. I like him," answered Hannah.

"Yes, he does. A true believer in the cause of justice. A good man. Imagine a person that can endure being alone in a sea of unbelievers. And to marry a Christian woman whom he does not love to provide a cover story for his mission."

"Niaz," Hannah said, "we don't know that he doesn't love his wife."

"I can tell he doesn't."

Chapter 83

Colonel Abadi was very understanding of Dr. Honari's dental problems. The Colonel, with whom Honari had a cordial, if not intimate working relationship, asked him who his dentist was. Upon hearing that it was Dr. Boomla, he told him that he was lucky because Boomla was supposed to be the best dentist in Shiraz. Although the Colonel was not a patient of Boomla's, he knew a number of officers who went to see him. A few of the Pasdaran officers didn't like Boomla because he was Zoroastrian, but personally, he thought that was ridiculous.

The Colonel's positive response to Dr. Boomla's name made Honari feel more secure that his treachery would escape detection. He was on an emotional roller coaster. Every night he woke up in a cold sweat thinking about what he had done. At various times of the day and night he would suddenly feel his stomach roil. He had betrayed his country to the enemy of Islam, the United States. He wasn't sure, but he suspected the gaunt Iranian man they called Mousa was a Jew. If he was caught, being executed would be the least of his problems. He would be tortured and put on trial. God knows what they would do to his wife and children.

The American agent named Dina impressed Dr. Honari with her depth of knowledge about nuclear technology. He found her very interesting to talk with. She questioned him at length about Iran's nuclear program and how close Iran was to having sufficient stockpiles of highly enriched uranium to build a nuclear device. She was also interested in the design details of the centrifuges, how they were linked, and the fuel-loading and gasification processes. When Honari told her that it was a replica of the Pakistani model Zippe type gas centrifuge, she seemed pleased. "Just as we had assumed," she said.

The plan for the "evacuation," as Dr. Boomla euphemistically put it, of Honari and his family was simple. The American penetration of Concrete Works Number 31 was planned for the early hours of Monday, August 24. That day was chosen because the 23rd happened to be Dr. Honari's birthday. It had been a tradition in the Honari family to have a picnic to celebrate his birthday. This year, he would tell his family that he wanted to picnic at the Daryacheh-ye-Famur Lake near Kazerun.

The plan was for the family to drive out to the lake in the morning. There was a small picnic area shielded from the road by a windbreak of oak trees; it was almost always deserted. Boomla's people would take up all the other picnic tables, thus dissuading any unwanted visitors from the temptation to enter the area. Then they would put the family in a truck and drive them to a deserted location on the coast where a US Navy team would pick them up and take them to a waiting submarine. All of the telephone calls to Honari's house or cell phone would be automatically routed to a secure satellite phone aboard the ship. OJ and Ivana repeatedly reassured Dr. Honari that Abid would be waiting for them on the US submarine.

For a short time, Dr. Honari considered confiding in his wife, but rejected the idea. While they loved one another, they were not particularly intimate and Honari could easily imagine her panicking at the very idea of leaving the country under such frightening circumstances. She was neither a well-educated or nor a worldly woman and she certainly would not easily adapt to the thought of her husband committing treason or their family having to leave Iran forever.

Chapter 84

It was General Yazdi's turn to report. He sat at the opposite end of the large conference table from the President of Iran, who served as Chairman of the Supreme National Security Council. The Council was made up of the leaders of legislative and judicial branches of the government and Iran's defense establishment. The President was a small man and he sat on a chair that allowed him to raise the seat. Yazdi wondered if his feet were touching the ground. Although he was popularly elected, real power resided in the unelected Supreme Leader of the country, the Grand Ayatollah. Any decision made by the National Security Council could not take effect unless ratified by the Supreme Leader. The little President was largely a figurehead.

The President nodded in General Yazdi's direction, signaling him to start his report. Yazdi was in his finest dress uniform. "Esteemed Chairman and members of the Council. It is my extreme privilege to address you today and report on the progress of our mission, Operation *Khamsin*. Like the '*Khamsin*,' the hot winds that blow out of the desert wrecking everything in their path, this operation will destroy the arrogance of the Imperialists. We will show the world that the American government cannot protect its people from the holy wrath of the *Umma*."

The Pasdaran's Chief of Internal Security, General Zahedi, a bitter rival of Yazdi, scowled and said, "Get on with it, Yazdi."

General Yazdi shot Zahedi a sharp look, but controlled his anger and his voice did not betray the hatred he felt for the man. Zahedi never passed up an opportunity to try to point out his superior rank. Yazdi thought Zahedi was a fool, but a cunning fool and not to be underestimated.

"Operation *Khamsin* is fully operational. Our agents are in place in Los Angeles. As you will recall from my last report, part of the team was arrested in Mexico. Unfortunately, it became necessary to have the captured agents liquidated in order to insure that the mission was not compromised. We have sent a replacement team to Los Angeles. The combined team of four has obtained a building from which to conduct operations. They have made contact with a deep-cover agent who is employed in the distribution warehouse of the company which is receiving the shipment. The shipment left Karachi and is in the Eastern-Pacific; it will reach the Port of Los Angeles within twenty–four to thirty–six hours. The team, with the assistance of our deep-cover agent, will intercept the shipment and carry out the mission."

"And the date of the operation, has it been determined?" asked the President.

"Based on our current estimates about the arrival of the shipment from Pakistan, in four days," replied General Yazdi.

"Excellent work, General."

General Zahedi said, "If you had any literary imagination, General Yazdi, you would have planned this mission to coincide with the date of the September 11th Attack."

They all knew it was a joke and Yazdi laughed right along with them, but it was just another dig at him. I would really like to put a bullet in the head of that fat peasant bastard, thought Yazdi.

Chapter 85

Mohammed stood over Hannah and Niaz while they built their fourth bomb of the day. Hannah was desperately trying to think of a way to render the devices ineffective, but she never had the opportunity. To her horror, she was now helping to construct a bomb that would be used in a terrorist attack.

Trained to build simple but powerful bombs using readily available materials, Hannah and Niaz were able to purchase virtually all of the components for the bombs at a nearby hobby shop and hardware store. The explosive was made from altered model-rocket fuel. The primary component of the fuel, nitromethane, could be converted into a liquid explosive twenty times more powerful than TNT by simply boiling it for thirty seconds to evaporate a retardant and then adding ordinary household ammonia. For the detonator, they attached a small resistance igniter used for launching model rockets to a dry cell battery and an electric kitchen timer.

With Mohammed looking over their shoulder, Niaz carefully poured the liquid explosive into a large metal funnel they had plugged and proceeded to seal the large end with modeling clay mixed with epoxy to make impermeable to liquids. Finally they inserted the detonator through the clay. Then they attached large magnets to the sides of the funnel so that the bomb would adhere to anything made of steel. The pyramid shape of the funnel would create a forced charge that would direct the explosion out of the large end of the device.

When they were finished and removing their protective gear, Hannah casually asked Mohammed, "What is the final target?"

Mohammed replied, "For security reasons, I cannot reveal that to you until the operation has begun."

"We understand," said Niaz submissively.

Hannah nodded her head in agreement, but she wished that the facts were otherwise.

Chapter 86

Surrounded by their supplies and equipment, the SEALS waited on the front porch for their transportation to arrive. There wasn't the usual banter; each team member was lost in his own private thoughts. They all knew the risks and they all knew that there was a high probability that some or all of them would die.

The day before, at dusk, an unmarked black helicopter had come in over the mountains from the east to deliver their final supplies for the mission. Gonzales was glad that it was time to go back into action. He was bored. Murphy and Amalakai were getting antsy as well. But they were rested and in shape.

In addition to receiving ammunition and demolition charges, inside a camouflage bag there was a small stainless-steel tube only a foot in diameter and two feet long. The top could be unscrewed, but it was sealed with tape and it had a triangular yellow sticker on it that read, "Danger: Radiation," along with the universal symbol for a radioactive hazard.

They spotted the dust kicked up by the pickup truck from at least two kilometers away and Gonzales understood why the old man's ancestors built this place where they did. He imagined the soldiers of Alexander the Great's army marching up the same dusty road.

Ted said, "Hey, Skipper, here he comes."

"Yeah, I see him."

"I'm ready to get back into it," said Murphy. "This place is getting old."

"We needed the rest."

"That's because you're getting old."

"Fuck you too, junior."

They all laughed.

Aqil pulled his truck off the road and lit up a cigarette. He had started smoking again when the police arrested his younger cousin for smuggling. He was worried that the kid would implicate him in one the many crimes he had committed as part of the Baluchi independence movement. They did beat the boy, but, bless Allah, he stayed silent and they eventually let him go. Without tobacco, Aqil was irritable and edgy all the time. Finally, he announced to his family that he was going to smoke again. At first, his wife and daughters clucked at him angrily but they knew that trying to stop him was futile.

He saw the dust coming from the pass and knew that the American soldiers were near. He liked them, especially the Iranian one. The others were tough, like the soldiers in the American war movies he had watched. Sure, they were infidels, but then they probably thought he was an infidel too. Anyway, Aqil didn't put much stock in religion. The truth was he thought most preachers, regardless of religion, were just a bunch of thieves anyway. A man should be judged by whether he was loyal to his family, his clan, and his people. Everything else was irrelevant.

The pickup truck was a half–kilometer away bouncing on the stony path. Aqil took a last draw on his cigarette and tossed it on the ground. He walked to the back of the truck and opened the doors. There were sacks of bulgur wheat, lentils, and pasta that he had taken on in Zahedan bound for delivery to a wholesaler in Shiraz. He had created a narrow pathway, so that the Americans could once again load their equipment and supplies into the hidden space in the front of the trailer.

As the dirty Toyota pickup pulled up, Aqil waved. The boy who was driving waved back. The two American soldiers in the truck bed were wearing dust goggles. Aqil could see that OJ was missing and he was disappointed. He wondered what had happened to him. None of the rest of them spoke Farsi, so he would have to make do with his few words of English and a lot of sign language.

When the pickup came to a stop, Gonzales got out of the passenger side and came over to shake Aqil's hand. "No OJ?" asked Aqil. "No," responded Gonzales, pointing out toward the distance, "he went on ahead and will be in Shiraz." Aqil wasn't sure what he meant by that but the boy said in Baluchi, "The Persian Yankee Ojay, he went with the girl soldier last week."

"OK," said Aqil in English and then said to the boy in Baluchi, "What girl solider?"

"She came with the helicopter over the mountains from Afghanistan. She is tall and very beautiful and she is their General."

"A woman General?"

"Yes. My grandfather says they are crazy, the Americans. My grandmother, she said it was a good thing because women are smarter than men."

"Are you joking with me? She said that?"

"It's true. And you know what else?"

"No. What?"

"My grandmother said that the girl General likes Ojay, the Persian-American one."

"Really? He's shorter than her."

"It's no joke. And I think he likes her too. Do you think they will get married?"

"I don't know."

The three Americans just stood there watching the conversation. The only thing that Gonzales could glean from it was that it was about OJ. Gonzales interrupted, pointing at the back of the trailer. "Aqil, do we load the truck?"

"Yes, yes, you load," said Aqil, who understood.

"OK, boys let's get this shit loaded and get out of here. The taxpayers aren't paying for us to hang around and watch a couple of Iranians bullshit with each other."

Dr. Boomla's guards must have seen the truck coming because as Aqil pulled up to the entrance of the compound, the gates swung open. As soon as the rear of the vehicle cleared the gates, they were immediately closed. Aqil got out, stiff-legged and sore from the long drive, and greeted the guards warily.

"*Salaam* brothers. Can you help me get this thing unloaded?"
They walked to the back and opened the trailer doors. The three Americans were already moving forward with their things and started handing them down to the men below. It took two of them to handle the container marked with the radioactive symbols on it.

As they were unloading, Ivana and OJ came out of the house. OJ gave Aqil a big hug; the two men liked each other. OJ introduced Ivana, who was dressed in Iranian clothes, including a scarf covering her hair. The boy was right, she was beautiful. Tall and willowy, with a confidence around men that most Iranians could not imagine. She smiled warmly at OJ. The boy was right, these two were soft on one another.

They unloaded the truck in about fifteen minutes and brought everything to a storage garage at the side of the compound. Aqil hopped back in the truck. If he hurried, he could make his delivery to the warehouse on the edge of Shiraz before it closed for the day. Then he would come back and the real work would begin.

Chapter 87

WAL-MART DISTRIBUTION CENTER, ONTARIO, CALIFORNIA
AUGUST 20

It was a simple matter for Abdul-Haq to log on to a computer in the traffic department and find the bill of lading he was looking for. He performed a search using the container number Mohammed had given him and found all sorts of information about the container: its location on the OPCL Pusan, the ship's whereabouts in the Pacific Ocean, and the estimated time that the Pusan would arrive at the Port of Los Angeles. He smiled when he saw that it was a container full of cat litter manufactured in Pakistan. He went into the section of the program that allowed him to view ground transportation instructions for the container and entered a change order to switch the delivery from the Wal-Mart Distribution Center to the address of the Smith & Jones warehouse in Wilmington. He couldn't believe how easy it was. The load was scheduled to arrive in two days.

That afternoon, Abdul-Haq asked his supervisor if he could take four days of vacation. He was granted permission, but his supervisor asked him to give more notice next time. Abdul-Haq apologized and his supervisor seemed satisfied.

He telephoned the warehouse and Ingrid answered. "It's done," he said, "the shipment will arrive in forty-eight hours and then it will take a day to unload."

"Thank you, Sir. We appreciate your business," replied Ingrid.

They both laughed.

By the time Abdul-Haq got home that night, he had already begun to shed his existing persona and transition to his real identity as a warrior in a holy Jihad. He found it exhilarating to think that in a few days his life would assume its full meaning. He would be leaving his wife, his job, and the land of his birth forever and he would be a fugitive.

His wife greeted him warmly and he hugged her. He had mixed feelings about her. He was fond of her but he had married her because it provided him a convenient cover. He did not love her. Her unquestioning Christian faith was alien to him and the truth was, he found her boring. She had made no effort to understand him and would be repelled if she really knew him. Although it made him guilty to think this, leaving her was a minor sacrifice given the greatness of his cause. The reality was that he was sick of living a lie and he yearned to be free. He did not know exactly what the mission entailed, but it was going to happen imminently and he would play a major role in it.

He told her about the business trip to Seattle and she helped him pack. As Abdul-Haq drove away from his house, perhaps for the last time, he felt more excited than he had ever felt—mixed with a little guilt.

He pulled up in front of the warehouse and called Smith & Jones on his cell phone. Niaz answered, sounding suspicious, but when Abdul-Haq identified himself, her voice grew warmer and a little throatier. She told him to drive around the back and they would open up the rear rollup doors so he could park inside.

They were planning to start the drive early the next morning, so Mohammed ordered them all to sleep at the warehouse that night. He had laid out pads and sleeping bags.

Mohammed shook Abdul-Haq's hand and put his arm around the big American. "We are so happy you are here. My brother, I know that you have sacrificed much. Is there something we can do for you?"

"I would like to pray with you."

"I understand," said Mohammed.

For the first time in many years, Abdul-Haq was able to pray openly as a Muslim. He and Mohammed put down small prayer rugs and faced east. Abdul-Haq placed a small white skullcap on his head and knelt down to repeat the suras. He had not felt this sense of liberation and inner peace since living in the apartment with the foreign boys. The intensity of his emotions surprised him. He had returned home.

The three women prayed separately at the other end of the warehouse. Niaz was fascinated with the blond man across the way. It had never occurred to her that there were Western converts to Islam. Her image of blond European or American men was formed by popular culture in Iran. They were evil crusaders, colonial oppressors, or athletes. It was beyond her comprehension that a man who looked like Abdul-Haq could be an appropriate object of her affections.

Chapter 88

The carrier group was within seventy-five miles of the coast of Iran. The sun had just gone down over the horizon. The young Lieutenant in charge of the five unmanned MQ-9 Mariner aircraft that were lined up on the flight deck called up to the Executive Officer on the Bridge to request permission to launch. The XO gave his assent and the five camouflaged drones took off into the wind, gained altitude, and turned east toward Iran. They climbed quickly to 40,000 feet to avoid detection by Iranian radar. During the remainder of their flight to their targets and back, the aircraft would be controlled by signals relayed through a satellite. For the next three nights, the Mariners would be directed to fly over the nuclear facilities at Ishfahan, Karaj, Nantanz, Ardekan, and Bala Deh. Although the gas centrifuge facility at Bala Deh was the real target, the Iranians would think that the Americans were casting a wider net.

When the drones reached their targets, they were programmed to descend quickly to a very low altitude and to start taking photographs. Unseen in the night, their powerful turboprop engines would be audible, although the Iranian anti-aircraft batteries would have difficulty getting a fix on them. As soon as their flight pass was completed, they would climb rapidly again to 40,000 feet and head west for their return to the carrier.

At approximately 8:50 pm, the Mariner assigned to buzz Bala Deh started to make its pass. The soldiers on guard duty could hear an airplane coming toward them, but they could not see it. They called Colonel Abadi who, in accordance with standard procedure, immediately ordered the lights to be turned off. He did not order them turned back on for one hour after the plane departed. He called his regional commander in Shiraz, who duly reported the incursion to Tehran.

From a turnout along the main highway four kilometers away, one of Dr. Boomla's agents sat in an old car recording the elapsed time that the lights remained off at the Bala Deh complex.

The next morning, Iranian newspapers reported American spy planes violated Iranian airspace at Ishfahan, Karaj, Nantanz, and Ardekan. Bala Deh was not mentioned. The President of Iran, speaking at a rally attended by hard-line students, denounced the Americans as aggressors who were destroying the peace of the Middle East and who should leave the region immediately. Would the American government tolerate spy plane flights over its territory by the Iranian air force? Of course not, he yelled to thundering applause. If the Americans did not leave the region voluntarily, they would be forced to leave by the divine wrath of the Almighty.

The next night, the Mariners were launched again, this time flying over Bala Deh and the Uranium mines at Saghand. Colonel Abadi plunged his facility into darkness at the first sound of airplane engines.

At Dr. Boomla's compound, the team was pleased. The plan was for the Navy to skip the following night at Bala Deh, but hit some of the other nuclear targets.

The night after that, they would launch the mission.

Chapter 89

D r. Boomla led Ivana, Mordechai, and Gonzales to a large grain silo in the back of the property. When he unlocked the doors, the two Americans couldn't believe what they saw. Not only were Aqil's truck and trailer parked inside, but there were two Iranian armored personnel carriers parked there as well. The walls were lined with a virtual arsenal: rocket-propelled grenade launchers, boxes of ammunition, machine guns, assault rifles, communications equipment, and stacks of uniforms.

"Impressive," said Gonzales, "where did you get all this?"

Dr. Boomla laughed. "We stole a little, we bought a little, some of it we even received as gifts. The important thing is that there are sufficient supplies to carry out the diversionary attack."

Mordechai said, "Boomla, maybe after this is over, you should leave Iran. If your identity is compromised, the response will be savage."

"You old Jew, you worry too much. My wife is dead, my children and grandchildren live abroad, and I have cavities to fill. What would become of my patients? Anyway, I must stay long enough to confirm to the authorities that the bones in Dr. Honari's house belong to his family. And if I live that long, it will mean that I am probably safe."

Chapter 90

They got up well before dawn and said prayers. Mohammed wanted to get on the road before the morning rush hour. They had a quick breakfast and washed in the small bathroom.

By 4:30 am they were already in the San Fernando Valley heading north on Interstate 5. They planned to stop briefly every four hours to switch drivers. The next driver was supposed to sleep so that he or she would be refreshed for their turn. Abdul-Haq took the first shift. Niaz sat up in the front with him while Hannah lay down in the back to sleep. Her turn to drive was next. The night before, she had slept fitfully on the floor of the warehouse and was exhausted. As she dozed off, Abdul-Haq was telling a rapt Niaz all about the story of his conversion to Islam, the purity of his beliefs, and the sacrifice that he had made to the cause of Jihad. When she awoke two hours later, it was silent in the van, but when Hannah stuck her head over the front seat, Niaz was asleep with her head resting on Abdul-Haq's lap. He was absentmindedly stroking her hair. Mohammed and Ingrid were also dozing on the rear bench seat.

"Hey," said Hannah, "it must be my turn soon." Abdul-Haq looked embarrassed and pulled his hand away.

"In another hour," Abdul-Haq replied.

"She likes you, Abdul-Haq," Hannah said. "But you have a wife."

"Not any more. That part of my life is over."

"Don't you love her?" asked Hannah.

"Not really. It was, as we say in America, a 'marriage of convenience.' But that doesn't mean that I don't feel some guilt over what I've done. It was necessary, that's all."

"I understand and I can see that you care for Niaz. You know, she is a sensitive, caring woman and not experienced with men."

"I would never take advantage of her. I am not that kind of person, praise Allah."

They spent the first night just across the Oregon border in a cheap motel about ten miles south of Ashland. It was near midnight and they were dead tired. The old man at the front desk asked them if they were there "for the Shakespeare." The four foreigners were nonplussed but Abdul-Haq, who once dated a girl whose family had gone to the Oregon Shakespeare Festival, said, "No, no, not this time. We're on our way up north."

"Oh, that's too bad," replied the desk clerk, handing them their room keys. Mohammed and Ingrid took one room and Hannah, Niaz, and Abdul-Haq would share the other room.

The room had two queen-sized beds. Rather than getting a rollaway, they decided that the two women would share one bed and Abdul-Haq would have the other. When Abdul-Haq went into the bathroom to take a shower, Niaz put her hand up to her mouth and started to giggle. "You really like him, don't you?" asked Hannah.

"Yes. When you were asleep, he took my hand and kissed it. It was . . . I don't know, very . . . what is the word in English?"

"Moving . . . romantic? What are you trying to say, Niaz?"

"All those things."

They were interrupted by the ringing of Abdul-Haq's cellular phone. Hannah ran over to the desk, thinking it was Mohammed or Ingrid calling from the next room, but it said "Home" on the screen. It must be Abdul-Haq's Christian wife.

When he got out of the shower, Hannah told Abdul-Haq that he had a telephone call, but that she didn't answer it because it was not from Mohammed or Ingrid.

Abdul-Haq went over to the desk and picked up the phone. He looked at it and said under his breath, "Shit." Turning to the two women, he said, looking embarrassed, "Excuse me, I have to make a private phone call," and left the room.

Hannah told Niaz that she wasn't ready for bed and wanted to take a walk and get something to eat. She would be back in an hour.

Niaz looked at Hannah, smiled, and thanked her.

As she walked out of the room, Hannah saw that Abdul-Haq was standing near the elevators talking quietly on his cell phone. She hesitated when he saw her and he motioned her over. From a few feet away, she heard him say, "Good night."

"Vashti, that was my wife," he said.

"I bet that was difficult."

"You don't know the half of it."

"I'm going to take a walk for an hour. This is your chance to be alone with Niaz," she said quietly, putting her hand gently on his arm. "We all might be dead in a few days. Be sweet with her."

"Thank you. You are very kind."

Hannah pushed the down button on the elevator and Abdul-Haq walked back toward the room.

When Abdul-Haq opened the door to the room, Niaz was sitting on the bed crying softly.

"What's wrong, Niaz?" he asked. "May I sit down next to you?"

Niaz nodded her head in assent and the tall blond man sat down and put his arm around her.

She looked up at him and smiled, embarrassed by her show of emotion.

"Abdul-Haq, I am not experienced with men. But you make me feel different. I know that you care for me."

"That's true," he said, wiping a tear from her eye. "I care very much for you. For the first time in my life, I think I am really in love with a woman."

"It is so fast . . . I don't know."

"Everything is speeded up for us because of our mission," he said.

"And you are a married man. It would be a sin."

"Niaz, the Koran tells us that a man may have more than one wife. But in my case, I have divorced my wife in the eyes of Allah. I am no longer married and I want you to be my wife."

"Yes . . .," she whispered. He kissed her gently on her lips, then her eyes, and then kissed her on the mouth. She lay down on the bed, pulling his head down to her's. He kissed her harder on the mouth and on the neck and shoulders and breasts. She shook slightly and a low murmur came out of her throat.

"Wait," he said, and got up and turned off the lights. It was a full moon and they could see each other's bodies in the dim light coming through the window. Abdul-Haq returned to the bed and silently began to take off his clothes. Niaz stood up and did the same.

Stepping forward to embrace him, she whispered in Farsi, "I love you, husband."

"I don't understand," he said.

She giggled slightly. "I forgot. You don't speak Farsi. I said, 'I love you.'"

They kissed again and he guided her to the bed. They began to move to the rhythms of their passion.

After they finished, exhausted and satisfied, they both must have fallen asleep, because they were awakened by the hotel telephone ringing. Abdul-Haq woke up and wandered to the phone. It was Hannah, who told Abdul-Haq that she had gotten her own room and she would see them at breakfast. "Thank you, sister," he said.

Niaz rolled over and said, groggily, "Was that Vashti? Is she all right?"

"Yes, Niaz, she called to say that she has gotten a separate room so we can be alone tonight."

"She is such a good person."

to a stop about fifty feet offshore from Pier 73 and parallel to it. On the dock, two teams of linemen waited fore and aft to tie up the ship. The tugs pushed the Pusan to the pier.

On board the Pusan, two crew members tossed a ball of thin rope tied to the eye of the ship's big two-inch tie lines down to the linemen below. They caught the ball of rope and began to haul the big rope hand-over-hand until they got a hold of the eye and attached it to a cleat on the dock. Then the ship's crew members turned on the huge electric wenches which drew the tie line taut and pulled the Pusan firmly against the dock. More ropes were then thrown down from the center of the ship and tied to the dock.

Just after 8:00 am, three groups of longshore crane gangs went up into the ship and began to scramble over the deck, removing the long metal tie rods that secured the containers to the deck. They also unlocked the interlocking cones between each container so that the boxes could be pulled apart. At their signal that all the preparatory work was done, two gantry cranes swung around and began pulling the containers off the ship.

At 7:30 am, as a cool summer breeze blew inland, container number OPCL2948572, whose manifest showed that it was filled with prepackaged cat litter, was removed from the Pusan and placed gently on the dock. It would be approximately another twenty-two hours of round-the-clock work before the longshoremen would have the ship completely unloaded.

Just after 1:00 pm, the agent for Wal-Mart sent an email to B & G Trucking in San Pedro directing it to pick up container number OPCL2948572 at the Avco terminal gate on Saturday, August 21 between 8:00 and 10:00 am.

PART III: THE FINAL DAYS

Chapter 91

The OPCL Pusan was now only three hours from the Port of Los Angeles. As required by the United States government, some thirty-three hours earlier the Captain of the OPCL Pusan had called the US Coast Guard to request permission to enter the Port. He also called the OPCL shipping agent in Los Angeles, who arranged for a bar pilot to board the vessel and guide the ship to its berth at the Avco Terminal on Pier 73. As the ship passed a buoy known as "Federal Buoy," a small Coast Guard patrol craft appeared on the starboard side of the ship to escort it into the port. The escorting of ships coming into port was initiated after the 9/11 attacks to defend against suicide ship attacks similar to the deadly Al-Qaeda attack on the USS Cole in Yemen in 2000.

As the sun started to rise over southern California, the ship slowed to a crawl and the bar pilot was brought aboard. The Captain stayed on deck, but the bar pilot took over steering the Pusan. As they approached Terminal Island, two tugs moved in close to the starboard side of the Pusan. The pilot expertly put the ship's big diesel engine into reverse and then took them out of gear, causing the vessel to com

Chapter 92

While Abdul-Haq stayed behind to drive the van back to LA, the other four team members drove to Canada in a rental car they picked up on the US side of the border. They crossed into Canada just after midnight. It had been a tense few moments when the Canadian immigration officer took their counterfeit American passports away to check them. However, when he retuned, he waived them through.

The night before, they had checked into a Marriot Hotel by the Vancouver airport. Mohammed got two rooms. No one said a word about getting a third room. When he discovered that Hannah had gotten her own room the previous night, he was furious. They had compromised security and violated his direct orders. If he had a choice in the matter, he yelled at them, he would have shot all three of them right on the spot. When they went upstairs, Mohammed informed them that he and Abdul-Haq would sleep in one room and the three women would sleep in the other room.

Their flight back to Los Angeles took two hours and they slept on the plane. Immigration was a breeze. They now appeared to be Canadians who had just arrived in the country for the first time.

As they rode back to Wilmington in the blue SuperShuttle van, in a whisper, Niaz asked Mohammed how far Abdul-Haq was from Los Angeles.

"You worry too much," replied Mohammed tersely.

They were silent the rest of the way.

Chapter 93

The first man to arrive at Dr. Boomla's house was a young, bearded tribesman on a motorbike. The guards brought him into the house where he was given food and tea. Then an old Ford F-150 pickup truck—it must have been forty years old—arrived carrying four boys with turbans over their heads who looked to be in their mid-twenties. They joined the first tribesman. By 7:00 pm there were twelve of them. Except for the youngest one, all had served in the Iranian army. Their leader, a grizzled and weathered man in his late forties or early fifties named Azarbod, was a combat veteran of Iran's bloody war against Saddam Hussein in the 1980's. The remaining seven members showed up during the afternoon, on foot, by automobile and motorcycle, and in one case, on a farm tractor.

The plan of attack was very simple. Just after dark on Sunday, the telephone lines would be cut by two of Boomla's operatives, who happened to work for the State Telephone and Postal Communications Company. They would also activate portable radio frequency-jamming equipment that had been supplied to Dr. Boomla by the Americans. This would make it impossible for the officers inside the compound to use cell phones, radios, or intercoms to communicate. When the raid started, they would effectively be cut off from the outside world.

Chapter 94

Adriano Mayorga had been pulling cans for B & G Drayage for two years. He was an angry man. The harder and longer he worked, the less money he seemed to make. He was paid by the load. These days, he got maybe $50 a load. When he had started as a port driver a decade earlier, he was getting three or four turns a day. Because of the increase in freight traffic, he was now getting two turns a day. So he started working six days a week and longer hours. Some days, he worked sixteen hours a day. The price of fuel was going up and the *jefe* kept raising the deductions for insurance. His wife was complaining that he never saw his children.

Adriano started working when he was nine years old to help his family scrape together enough to eat, but when he left Nicaragua as a teenager he believed that if he worked hard in America, he would get ahead. It seemed as though the so-called "American Dream" was a very elusive thing. He hated the way they made him work as an "independent contractor." As far as he could tell, it was just a scheme for the boss to rob the workers of money. He was no business man; he was a worker and he wanted to be treated with a little dignity. Another driver introduced him to Pat Johnston, the Teamster organizer. The older workers knew Johnston when he was a Catholic priest and they said you could trust him. One day, Pat brought an American Professor to a union meeting. The Professor was trying to find the *terroristas* and stop them from coming into the country. He asked the drivers to call Pat if they thought something about a load that did not feel right.

It was a light day at the Avco terminal and Adriano had to wait only thirty minutes before he got to the gate. As he moved up in the queue, he noticed from the shipping papers that the load was supposed to be delivered to Wal-Mart, but the destination was not the big warehouse in Ontario, but an address nearby in Wilmington. He had driven many Wal-Mart loads and they all went to the same place. Oh, well, he thought, things change. He presented his papers to the gate operator, who directed him to the terminal staging area in the sprawling yard where he was supposed to pick up his chassis and can.

After hooking on, Adriano returned to the gate. As he passed through the big radiation scanners, the alarm went off. This had happened to him once before. A Customs Agent came over and asked to see his shipping papers. "This is a Wal-Mart load, right?"

"Yes," replied Adriano.

"Oh, and I see you are carrying animal litter." The agent called someone on his two-way radio and told the person on the other end that he had a weak positive. He described the load and asked whether the container should be inspected.

He got his answer. "Driver, it's a false positive. This stuff is naturally radioactive. You can take the load through."

"Thank you, sir," said Adriano, relieved that he wasn't going to waste half the day while they opened up the container to inspect it.

It took Adriano only ten minutes to drive to the address of the warehouse in Wilmington. It was a small tilt-up concrete building with a one-bay loading dock in the back. He thought it was strange that a load for a company like Wal-Mart would go to such a small warehouse. But, he thought, it is none of my business. He took the truck around to the rear of the building and backed up to the loading dock. The big rollup doors opened up and out walked two men. One was tall and blond with the beginning of a scraggly beard. The other was smaller, older, and darker. Adriano got out of the cab and went around to get the papers signed and the trailer detached. He was in a hurry and wanted to get out of there.

The big blond man smiled at Adriano and took the clipboard to sign for the load. Adriano thought he looked familiar.

"Hey, man, don't you work at the Wal-Mart place in Ontario?" Adriano's accent was thick and Mohammed couldn't understand what he was saying.

But Abdul-Haq did. The blond man looked up with a passing look of surprise in his eyes.

"No, you must be confusing me with somebody else," replied Abdul-Haq.

"Probably."

As Adriano drove back in the direction of the Port to pick up his next load, he kept thinking that the whole thing was wrong. It bothered him all day and on the way back home from his final delivery that evening, he decided to call Pat Johnston. He picked up the cell phone and punched in his number.

The Teamster organizer answered on the second ring. He remembered meeting Adriano.

"Hey, you said to call if something was funny with a load. Well this morning, I delivered a Wal-Mart load to a little warehouse in Wilmington."

"That is odd, Adriano. What was in the load?"

"It was . . . I don't know how to say it in English or Spanish . . . you know the things that the *gatos* they take a shit in. *Comprende*?"

"Kitty litter?" asked Patrick.

"*Sí*, that is it. And you know what else is strange, Patrick?"

"What?"

"The guy there. I've seen him before. At the Wal-Mart warehouse in Ontario. He's a security guy there."

"That's weird. Maybe he got a new job. I will pass it on."

When they hung up, Patrick called Lee Sandahl and told him about Adriano's load. Lee had never heard of a Wal-Mart load going to a warehouse in Wilmington. It was definitely strange, a theft maybe.

But why steal kitty litter? Anyway, he called Jake and told him.

When Jake heard that it was a load of kitty litter and it was consigned for delivery to a small warehouse in Wilmington, he got very excited. Lee gave him the address and the container number.

"It's definitely weird," said Lee. "As far as I know all of Wal-Mart's freight goes to their distribution center in Ontario."

"I'm going to drive over there in the morning and see what's going on."

"Don't you think you ought to call the FBI or somebody like that?" asked Lee.

"Listen, I've already blown my credibility and I've gotten canned. I think they might lock me up if I make another false report."

"Yeah, I hear you," replied Sandahl.

All five of them worked throughout the morning to unload the truck. Mohammed instructed them to look for three boxes that weighed more than the others. By mid-morning they found them. Mohammed and Abdul-Haq carefully put the three boxes on a moving cart and wheeled it into the warehouse.

Mohammed ordered the other four members of the team to leave the building. They went out into the parking lot. Mohammed retrieved the radiation suit and lead-lined storage container he and Ingrid had purchased from a medical supply house in downtown Los Angeles and kept hidden from Hannah and Niaz. Until this moment, for security reasons, he did not wish to reveal to them that their ultimate mission was to launch a dirty-bomb attack.

Mohammed donned the bulky white suit and carefully cut open the packaging tape on the three boxes. Inside of each box were a dozen packages of cat litter, four of which contained the lead-shielded packages of highly enriched spent nuclear fuel. He retrieved the cat litter packages containing the spent fuel and put them in the lead-lined box. When all four were placed in the lead box, he sealed the lid and proceeded to drag the heavy box over by the rear doors of the van.

A few minutes later, Mohammed opened the front door and asked the rest of his team to come in. He was no longer wearing the white protective suit. Mohammed led Abdul-Haq to the van. The rear doors were opened and on the ground was a steel box the size of a large suitcase with handles on four sides.

"OK," Mohammed explained, "we need to lift it into the truck. It is heavy—one-hundred kilos or more—and so it will take four of us to get it in there. Vashti, you take the front handle. Niaz, you take the back handle and Abdul-Haq and I will take the two handles on the sides."

The four of them got into position and Mohammed said, "I will count to three and say 'lift' and we will lift the box and take it to the van. 1 . . . 2 . . . 3 Lift!"

For some reason, Hannah expected it to be harder to lift but it wasn't as heavy as she thought. They carefully walked the steel box over to the van and rested the corner on the end of the cargo bed. Then Mohammed let go and went around to help push the box into the van. "Now push," Mohammed ordered and they pushed the box into position. They secured it with ropes to the cleats on the interior walls of the van and covered it with several blankets. Mohammed placed the neatly folded protective suit on top of the blankets.

Mohammed locked the rear doors of the van and, turning to Abdul-Haq, Niaz, and Mohammed, said, "There is something that I can now reveal to you." He paused, breaking into one of his rare smiles. "The day we have all been waiting for has arrived. We will launch our attack in the next twenty-four hours. Now that our attack is imminent, I can reveal to you that the shipment we received was enriched nuclear material and we will detonate the tanker truck with the nuclear material inside. The explosion will release radioactive fallout into the atmosphere. Our attack, God willing, will permanently destroy the arrogance of Americans forever and, perhaps, bring down their evil regime. Are there questions?"

"Where will the attack take place?" asked Abdul-Haq.

"That I cannot reveal. But you will know soon enough."

"Any other questions?"

There was silence.

"One last thing. Unless otherwise ordered by me, between now and the time we launch the attack we are to remain together at all times. Is that understood?"

They shook their heads in assent.

Hannah now knew that she had waited too long to act.

Chapter 95

Dr. Honari often worked on Saturdays because it was quiet on the weekends and he could catch up with his reports, evaluations, and correspondence. He also conducted personal inspections of the uranium fuel-processing equipment and the centrifuge cascade. Although the three thousand linked centrifuges operated continuously day and night, the process of transforming milled uranium ore—yellowcake—into uranium hexafluoride gas took place only during the week. On the weekends, the plant ran with a skeleton crew. It was also the time that the maintenance engineers made repairs and replaced worn-out parts.

The uranium conversion process took place in a large side chamber off the main tunnel that housed the centrifuge array. The system looked like a strange brewery with huge pressure vessels, pipes, and valves everywhere. There were storage tanks for ammonia, hydrogen, and fluorine gasses as well as nitric acid, all of which were central to the uranium gasification process.

The process for turning yellowcake into uranium hexafluoride gas is complex. The yellowcake is dissolved in nitric acid, yielding a solution which is then treated with ammonia to produce a compound called ammonium diuranate. Then in a three stage process, hydrogen gas is introduced, followed by hydrofluoric acid and fluorine to produce the final product.

For Dr. Honari, this was to be the last day that he would ever spend at Bala Deh. With feelings of fear, defeat, and resignation all mixed up with one another, he methodically went about helping to sabotage the very factory that he had so enthusiastically helped to build. As Dr. Honari knew quite well, nuclear fuel itself is neither volatile nor explosive, but some of the gasses that are used to make uranium hexafluoride gas most certainly were. Hydrogen is highly flammable and nitric acid is actually so volatile that it is hypergolic— self-igniting—when combined with certain organic chemicals like turpentine or gasoline. While the rest of the maintenance team was busy in another part of the facility, Honari began his own inspection of the uranium gasification equipment. With a piece of red plastic tape, which was the usual way in which equipment was designated for inspection, Honari marked the outlet valve on the nitric acid tank. Although there were security cameras, Honari's actions were part of his normal activities and unlikely to arouse the suspicion of the security team.

It was more than a quarter of a mile to the rear of the facility and Dr. Honari walked slowly along the centrifuge cascade. The noise produced by three thousand centrifuges operating in a cave sounded like a billion angry hornets. Everyone who worked inside the facility was required to wear ear protection and hard hats and it was almost impossible to be heard above the constant din of cylinders turning at thousands of revolutions per minute.

At the back of the plant was an air shaft that doubled as an emergency escape tunnel. It was perhaps five feet in circumference and covered by a large steel grate. It also had a thick hinged airtight hatch that could be sealed in the event of an emergency. Normally, however, it was kept open to ventilate air to the outside.

As Dr. Honari stood in front of it he could feel the air rushing past him into the shaft and up to the plateau above. To the right of the door was a yellow handle that was labeled, "Pull Down in Emergency" in

Farsi, which opened the inner grate. There was a security camera high on the cave wall pointed at the ventilation shaft. His heart thumping, Dr. Honari walked up to the handle and stood over it, effectively blocking the camera's view of the handle. Honari took out some tape and tied it around the handle. While doing so, he quickly pulled the handle down, unlocking the grate, and then turning the handle so that it was not quite in the locked position. Unless someone in the security center happened to be watching very carefully, it would look as though Dr. Honari had simply put tape on the handle to trigger an inspection.

On his way back to the front of the cave complex, Honari placed more pieces of red tape on the gas-intake pipes on some of the centrifuges and on the inverters that powered the electric motors of the centrifuge array. He then returned to his office in the control room near the blast doors. As he entered his office, he passed the security center, which adjoined his office. Two guards were supposed to monitor various television monitors that showed views from each security camera. But he noticed that the guards hastily put away magazines as he walked by. He and his American "friends" were depending on their lack of vigilance to insure that he was not discovered. Sometime the next day, the security center would, in all probability, be a burning hulk.

At 5:00 pm, Dr. Honari left Concrete Works Number 31 and was driven home by his two military escorts.

Honari had never taken a risk before in his life and now he was risking everything to save his family. But the enormity of his actions were weighing down upon him. Hundreds, perhaps thousands of innocent Iranians could die because of his complicity in the American attack. Would Allah forgive a man who would kill other people's children to save his own?

Chapter 96

Gonzales went over OJ and Ted's orders one final time. He did not know when he would see Ted again and both of them knew that tomorrow at this time one or perhaps both of them could be dead. At such moments, soldiers sometimes make jokes and sometimes get serious or sentimental. Amalakai and Gonzales merely shook hands, nodded at each other, and smiled. Then OJ and Ted got in the back of the trailer of Aqil's truck.

Ivana stood about ten feet away and waived at the two men and the two men waived back. OJ yelled out, "*Hasta la vista*, Irvita!" Gonzales shut the trailer doors and the truck rumbled off to the west.

There was a heaviness in Ivana's heart. She was worried about OJ. He was no soldier, just a sweet guy with a keen intelligence and a somewhat offbeat sense of humor. She felt protective of him and nervous about the mission. As Gonzales walked away to get ready for tonight, he said to Ivana, as if he could read her mind, "Don't worry, Irv, your goofy little CIA friend will be all right."

"I hope so," she replied.

The Iranians sat cross-legged and leaned back against the corrugated metal walls of Aqil's trailer, which was empty except for some food, first aid kits, water bottles, and blankets. They didn't talk and some of them were sleeping. OJ surveyed the operatives in Dr. Boomla's network: a teenager with a mop of curly brown hair, a man in a turban who looked eighty, but was probably twenty years younger, two swarthy twin brothers who never seemed to say anything, a tall Turkoman who was Dr. Boomla's gardener, and an elfin little Azeri woman, who had piercing blue eyes, carried a small automatic in an ankle holster under her long skirts, and smoked a pipe. Where did Dr. Boomla collect all these people, who seemed fiercely loyal to him and utterly detached from any part of Iranian society?

It only took them forty-five minutes to get to the picnic area on the shore of Daryacheh-ye-Famur Lake. They left early because they wanted to occupy all four of the picnic tables so that they would have the area to themselves when the Honari family showed up. Aqil parked his truck across the road and waited. He was supposed to call them when Honari pulled off the main highway onto the access road that led to the picnic ground. The picnic area was ideal for their mission because it was behind a small hill and not visible from the road.

They waited and watched. At 10:45 am a family drove up and parked. Aqil called OJ and told him it was not the Honaris and to get rid of them. When they entered the picnic area, the young husband and wife looked frustrated at the unexpected crowd and their two young children began to whine. Abdullah, the Turkoman, told them that there was another picnic area a little further down the road and they thanked him and left.

An hour later, Aqil saw Honari's Mercedes pull off onto the access road. Aqil called OJ on the two-way radio and said, "Look alive. Your friends have arrived. I will pull in behind them."

Dr. Honari parked the car and climbed out of the Mercedes. They stretched their legs and Mrs. Honari and the two girls grabbed the food and drinks out of the trunk of the car. They walked through a break in the trees to the picnic area. To the Honaris' surprise, all the picnic tables were occupied except one. It was an odd assortment. Country people, thought Mrs. Honari.

Mrs. Honari said to her husband, "Is this suitable?"

"Oh yes, let's sit down."

Mrs. Honari was just finishing cleaning the picnic table with when two soldiers approached them.

"Good morning," said OJ in upper-class Farsi.

"Good morning," replied Dr. Honari warily.

"I really hate to bother you, but we must ask you to come with us."

Ted had unholstered his service revolver and had it pointed at the family. From across the way, the old man had pulled a shotgun out from under a blanket and pointed it at the Honaris while the Azeri woman had the nasty little snout of her automatic aimed at them as well.

The two teenaged daughters screamed. Dr. Honari said, "Shut up, do you want to get us killed?"

"Yes, please girls," said OJ evenly, "please stop screaming. It won't do any good. In any case, we need to get going."

Mrs. Honari said, "Is this a robbery?"

"No, no. We have no interest in your possessions or harming you in any way. Let's just say you are about to embark on a surprise vacation. So now," continued OJ, "I must ask you to stand up and come with us."

"Do as they say," said Dr. Honari.

The Honaris stood up. Each was handcuffed and blindfolded. They were escorted to Aqil's truck, which was waiting in the parking lot. Thoughtfully, Aqil had placed a stepstool in the rear of his truck and helped the Honaris get into the trailer and get seated along the front wall on blankets. As Dr. Honari was led into the trailer, OJ asked him for his car keys, wallet, and watch. The women's purses were locked in the trunk of the Mercedes.

When they were all seated, the two young sisters began to sob quietly. OJ felt sorry for them and undid the handcuffs of their mother so that she could comfort them.

"Who are you?" she asked OJ.

"Friends," he answered.

"Unless, of course, we try to escape."

"Suffice it to say, in situations like this, friends don't let friends escape. It could really be harmful to your health. My advice to you is to keep your wits about you and don't do anything heroic."

"Your Farsi is good, but you are not Iranian, are you?" asked the older daughter.

"Thank you for the compliment," replied OJ, without answering the question.

OJ walked to the rear of the trailer and hopped out, tossing Dr. Honari's keys to Abdullah. Ted came over and shook hands with OJ. "See you stateside, OJ," he said and walked back to the trailer.

OJ told Aqil to head to the rendezvous point on the coast. "Thank you for everything you have done for us. I will not see you again after today."

"Perhaps when I am Minister of Transportation in the Republic of Baluchistan, you can come visit me in my palace with your wife and all the little Hamsids."

Dr. Honari closed his eyes and leaned against his wife's shoulder. He was spent. At least the torment of having to make decisions was over; there were simply no more decisions left to make. His life and that of his family were now under the total control of others and never again would be their own.

Chapter 97

J ake noticed that the Volvo was running a little rough; he would have to remember to take it in for servicing. On the way over to the warehouse in Wilmington, he stopped at a place called "Bagels Galore" on Western Avenue. He bought a thermos full of coffee, three bagels, and some lox schmear. He also bought the Sunday LA *Times*. Thus fortified, Jake was ready to start the first—and probably last—stakeout of his abbreviated career in the national security bureaucracy of the US Government.

The Smith & Jones warehouse was located on North Neptune Street about five blocks from the Port. With most of the terminals shut down on Sundays, there wasn't much traffic. Jake drove slowly by the warehouse. It looked closed. He continued down to Harry Bridges Boulevard, turned left and came back up Lagoon Avenue and parked about half a block behind Smith & Jones. Behind the warehouse, enclosed by a chain-link fence and padlocked gate, there was a dumpster and an intermodal container backed up to a small loading dock. Oddly, there were quite a few unopened cardboard boxes stacked haphazardly around on the loading dock. Stranger yet, the doors of the container were wide open.

Jake sat in the Volvo, waiting and watching. There was no activity and within an hour he was bored out of his mind. He called his mother just to pass the time. Then he ate two of the bagels and drank all of the coffee. Finally, he read the paper cover to cover.

Jake opened the glove compartment and gingerly took out the paper bag that held the little 9 mm Ruger automatic that one of the Longshoremen had given him. He looked inside. He took the gun out of the bag and carefully unwrapped the cloth holding it. He stared at it for a few seconds and then picked it up, studying it from various angles. He held in his hand and practiced changing the clip. Just having it in the car made him nervous. He wrapped it up again, put it back in the bag, and returned it to the glove compartment, making a mental note to remember to get it out of there before it was time to give the car back to his father. God, he thought, he'll have a heart attack if he finds it.

The night before, when he met Lee and some of the guys for a drink, they told him they thought he needed a gun to protect himself. A wiry little crane mechanic named Luis took him out to the parking lot and retrieved a paper bag from the trunk of his car. When Jake looked inside, it contained a gun and an extra clip. Looking around to see that no one was watching, Luis showed Jake how to click off the safety and how to change the clip. Jake really didn't want the gun but it was, in its own way, such a thoughtful gesture that he couldn't say no. He thanked Luis and stuffed the gun in the glove compartment of the car.

Jake started thinking that he ought to use the time to do a little research about Smith & Jones. He turned on his laptop and searched the Internet for information on the business. The company had no website and a search found no Smith & Jones doing business in Southern California. He went to the website of the City of Los Angeles and found that a Smith & Jones had received a business license only a month before. The business license had been taken out by a person named Danielle Smith. He found the property listed on the search engine of the Los Angeles County Recorder's Office. It was owned by a man named Samuel Oh, who had purchased the property on December 16, 1987.

Jake started to make a "to do" list. Tomorrow, first thing, he would contact Mr. Oh and try to find out something about Danielle Smith. Also, he would speak to the people at the Wal-Mart Distribution Center; that is, if they would talk to him. With their record of getting sued, investigated, and generally beaten up in the press, the last thing Wal-Mart was likely to do was talk to an exiled academic about weaknesses in its transportation security system.

Jake called Lee Sandahl and explained what he had discovered so far, which wasn't much.

"Jake, I've got to tell you, there's just no way that I can see how Wal-Mart would piece off one container and send it to some tiny independent warehouse in Wilmington. It makes no sense."

"I agree with you, Lee. Also, don't you think it's strange that they unloaded the container and left a whole lot of the merchandise sitting around with the container doors wide open?"

"Well that's certainly a recipe for getting your merchandise stolen. I'm amazed it's still there," said Lee, incredulously.

"Can you check out this company—Smith & Jones—and see what other loads have gone to them?"

"Yeah, I can do that. At least for the past 120 days; records for earlier transactions are already archived."

"Would you? I mean, this is a pretty odd situation, don't you think?"

"Yeah, I can go into the office. I've got nothing better to do on my day off, right? And besides, what are friends for?"

"To abuse. Anyway, misery loves company."

"Apparently. OK, I'll call you back when I have something to tell you."

Jake finished the coffee, which was now cold and thick, and ate his last bagel. It must be dreadful to be a cop, he thought. When he had to urinate so badly that he could stand it no longer, he started the car and drove to a gas station a few blocks a way. While he was standing at the urinal in the filthy restroom, his cell phone rang. It was Lee.

"Jake, there's nothing on Smith & Jones. As far as I can tell, this Wal-Mart consignment is the only intermodal load they've received. That doesn't mean that they didn't receive nonmaritime freight consignments."

"Well, that doesn't clear up any mysteries. Then again, maybe they are terrorists and received the only load they care about."

Jake drove back to his spot behind the warehouse and resumed his stakeout. This was turning out to be the longest and most boring Sunday of his life. At the gas station, he had stocked up on necessities for the second half of his stakeout: a six-pack of Coca-Cola, two bags of pretzels, various flavors of corn nuts, and an assortment of candy. He even bought a doughnut for the symbolic value. No wonder cops got fat.

As the day wore on, it got hotter and hotter. By late afternoon, the sea breezes had died and there was a hot wind blowing west. The Santa Anas were back.

Some time in the early evening, Jake started to feel sleepy again and decided he needed to stretch his legs. He figured that there was nobody in the place anyway, so it probably wouldn't hurt if he took a walk around the block and got a closer look at the warehouse. He got out of the car and half way across the street he felt for his cell phone. He had left it in the car.

It felt good to be out of the car but Jake felt conspicuous strolling down the empty street as if it was the most natural thing in the world. He put the newspaper in the crook of his arm, but it just made him feel more foolish. When he got close to the locked gate of the chain-link fence, he slowed to stare into the yard. The boxes strewn around the loading dock were labeled "Pet Clean All-in-One Disposable Cat Litter." Most of them were unopened and some were dented and on their sides as if they were tossed randomly around. Was someone looking for a particular box? If so, Jake thought, that would be further evidence that there was something not quite right about this operation.

Jake was staring into the yard when the door to the loading dock opened and a woman stepped out carrying a trash bag. She was in her mid-thirties with dark skin and thick curly hair covered by a scarf. Probably Latino, he thought. She had an odd expression on her face, a mixture of attraction and repulsion. He couldn't just walk away; it would look suspicious. Jake figured the best thing to do was to bluff it out.

"Beautiful evening, isn't it?" he asked, as if it was the most natural thing in the world to be watching a woman carry out the garbage.

The woman didn't smile back. She whispered to him, "Wait, Mister, I need to talk to you." Her tone was urgent and demanding. She had an accent, but he couldn't place it. It didn't sound Hispanic

The woman walked toward him.

She whispered, glancing back over her shoulder, "Listen to me. Call the police. These people are terrorists inside and they have radioactive material and explosives. Now go."

A blond man appeared on the stairs and yelled, "Move out of the way, Vashti." He looked at Jake and slowly raised a shotgun.

Before Jake could react, he felt cold metal on his neck. A foreign-accented voice from behind him said quietly, "Do not move. Do exactly as I say or I will kill you. Do you understand?"

The blond man pointed the shotgun at Hannah, who had her hands up. "You traitorous bitch; I should shoot you now."

Mohammed pushed Jake forward toward the fence. A bleached blonde woman was unlocking the gate.

Mohammed stood in front of Hannah and Jake. Both had their hands and legs tightly bound with rope. They were barefoot. Jake's nose was bleeding from both nostrils and his eyes were puffy from the beating Mohammed had just administered. He breathed heavily through his mouth, tasting his blood. Hannah's chin was swollen and blue. Her lip was split. Abdul-Haq and Ingrid were behind Mohammed, their faces consumed by an expression of hatred mixed with disgust. Niaz stood to the side in a state of shocked disbelief.

Mohammed knelt down and brought his face close to Hannah's. He stared into her eyes. She met his stare with a passive look. Even now she was measuring her odds and trying to gain some advantage. "Did you think, Vashti, we did not see this man; that we were not watching him? You are not just a traitor, but stupid." Mohammed slapped her as hard as he could across the face. Hannah's head flew to the side. She cried out.

"Who is this man?"

"I told you; I don't know," she said, choking on her blood and coughing. "He was just standing there when you sent me out. That's the truth."

"They were right about you. They said to watch you. You are a traitor."

"I'm sorry," she whimpered. "I couldn't bear the thought of so many innocent people dying. I know you must kill me." She put her head down in an effort to look resigned to her fate.

Mohammed pulled his revolver from his holster, cocked the hammer and put it into Hannah's mouth. She closed her eyes.

"You betrayed us, your brothers and sisters. Killing you now would be too kind. You must suffer for your betrayal."

Mohammed stood up and put the gun back in his holster.

He turned and kicked Jake in the head. There was an ugly thump as his shoe landed on Jake's temple, opening up a nasty gash on the side of his head. Jake's eyes momentarily rolled up in his head.

Mohammed held Jake's DOE identification card up, looked at it briefly, and threw it at him.

"Abdul-Haq, what do we do with this pig of an American spy?"

"It would be an honor to kill him," replied Abdul-Haq.

Mohammed was silent for a moment. "Let's pack up to leave. I will think about what to do with these two while we get ready."

When they walked away, Hannah looked over at the man. She whispered, "Can you hear me?"

"Yes," he croaked.

"I'm so sorry that I got you into this."

"It's OK . . . they saw me anyway . . . you did the right thing."

They were silent for a while.

Jake said, "They'll kill us, won't they?"

"Yes."

"I hope it's quick."

"Me too."

"Why did you betray them."

"I'm not one of them. . . . Don't talk . . . I need to think."

"You are an overachiever," Jake croaked. He managed a crooked smile, his teeth stained with blood.

"A what? I don't understand."

"Forget it. You can think for the both of us. I'm tired."

Chapter 98

The drive to the coast was long and dull. They pulled over once on a side road to let everyone stretch their legs and relieve themselves. The Honari family seemed subdued and less scared than at first. The little Azeri woman who worked for Dr. Boomla escorted the mother and the two daughters into a stand of trees. No one tried to escape; there was no screaming. Boomla's people squatted by the truck and smoked cigarettes in silence. The dark-skinned American soldier politely refused their offer of cigarettes. Aqil thought one of the most baffling things about the Americans was that none of them smoked.

Aqil's truck reached the coast just as the light was just beginning to fade. He parked the truck on the side of the coast road and they waited for darkness to come. When an army patrol came by, he feigned sleep and told the officer in charge, a grumpy sergeant, that he was resting before he started the long trip back to his home in Zahedan. The Sergeant felt sorry for him and told him he could stay for two hours longer and then he really needed to move along. Aqil thanked the Sergeant for his help.

Aqil sat in the cab of his truck watching the sun disappear on the horizon, smoking one "57" cigarette after another. His cell phone rang. It was Ted, the American, calling from the trailer. He told Aqil to be ready; the American sailors would be coming soon. Aqil finished his cigarette and threw the butt out the window. He got out of the truck, stretched his legs, and walked around the truck, pretending to inspect it. When he saw the black-rubber boats coming, he banged on the side of the trailer, signaling to Ted that it was time to hustle their hostages down to the beach.

The USS Connecticut lay low in the water, its matte-black conning tower the only thing visible above the lapping waves. It was the second time in three months that the ship had surfaced off the Iranian coast. In the spreading darkness, several officers came up to the bridge to survey the coastline through advanced night-vision equipment. They signaled to the Captain below that all was clear and preparations were made to launch the inflatables that would carry the shore party to the beach. Within ten minutes, two boats were launched off the side of the Connecticut and were making their way to the shore.

From the beach, in the last bit of fading daylight, Ted could just make out the bobbing silhouettes of the inflatables as they bounced on the surf. Ted was starting to feel good. It was almost over—at least for him. He had changed out of his Iranian military uniform into his black Navy-issue jumpsuit. They could no longer shoot him as a spy, he thought, although they would probably shoot him for some other reason if he was caught. The submachine gun he carried was slung over his shoulder and he was holding Dr. Honari by the arm. The other prisoners were each held by one of Dr. Boomla's agents. Somebody whispered in Farsi, "Keep Silent."

When the two inflatables were 100 meters from shore, they cut their engines, but the speed of the boats swept them on to the beach, helped along by the choppy surf. Four sailors armed with the short-barreled version of the M-16 favored by US Special Forces units jumped out of the inflatables and ran the twenty feet toward the little knot of people on the beach. The women whimpered at the sight of the Americans, who were dressed completely in black, with black watch caps pulled over their heads, and their faces smeared with black paint. The whites of their eyes stood out, making them look like 21st century Banshees.

As the sailors approached, Ted held up his hand and said in a voice that sounded loud in the tense silence, "You want these four," and waived his hand over the Honari family. "One," he said, tapping on Dr. Honari's head and pushing him forward. The first sailor grabbed Honari by the shoulder and arm and started moving him down the beach to the boats. Ted touched the head of Mrs. Honari. "Two," and a second sailor said, "Come with me Ma'am,, and gently but firmly pulled Mrs. Honari forward. The pattern set, Yasmin Honari stepped forward toward the next sailor who, it turned out, was female. "Let's go, Miss," she said, directing her toward the second inflatable. Her older sister, Laila, also stepped forward and was led quickly to the boat by the last of the naval crew members.

Ted saluted Abid and said, "Thanks, man, for everything."

"OK, Yankee Doodle, goodbye," responded Abid, exhausting his limited English, and vigorously shaking Ted's hand. Then, unslinging his assault rifle, Ted said, "Abid . . . here," and handed it to the driver. "You'll need this more than me." Abid nodded solemnly. Ted turned and ran down toward the inflatables, which were already turned around and starting to move into the surf. He ran into the water and the sailors hoisted him into one of the boats. On the warrant officer's signal, the engines revved up and the inflatables started moving quickly into the warm water of the Persian Gulf.

Chapter 99

The police barracks was off the main highway about ten kilometers east of Shiraz. It normally housed about twenty officers of the Basij paramilitary police force, who patrolled the mountainous region of Fars province. It also held a communications center. It was no coincidence that Dr. Boomla's men chose to assault a Basij installation. The mission of the Basij, which was personally established by Ayatollah Khomeini in 1979, was to hunt down and destroy any resistance to the reactionary government of the Islamic Republic. Later, the Basij became infamous during the Iran-Iraq war for recruiting children to act as human mine detectors, eventually sending 150,000 of them to their deaths. More recently, the Basij patrolled Iran's major cities, beating and arresting women who violated the regime's strict Islamic dress code and students who dared criticize the government. The Basij had no shortage of enemies among the Iranian people.

The first person to die was a young Basij recruit who stood guard at the gate. From atop the dark green armored personnel carrier, Azarbod cut the man down with a few rounds from the heavy machine gun mounted there. The vehicle rammed through the red-and-white-striped barrier. Inside the barracks, the officers, who were eating dinner, heard the loud thumping of the machine gun outside. They froze. Then came the sound of the APC crashing through the barrier. Somebody yelled "gunshots" and they all got up simultaneously, running for their weapons, which were in a gun rack on the front wall. A few of the braver officers pulled out their side arms and ran for the front door and the metal shuttered windows; another ran to the communications room. When he got there, the officer on duty said all the lines were dead. He looked scared and confused.

From the back of the APC, the raiding party jumped out and deployed in a ragged skirmish line, while a few of the men headed for some of the outlying buildings. The raiders fired through the windows and at the front door. The heavy machine gun was punching holes in the cinderblock walls of the building. Two of the men had RPGs. They got on their knees and fired point blank at the windows and front door of the main building, just as the first Basij officers came through the door. They reloaded and fired once more. The sound of the explosions was deafening and almost all of the police officers were either killed instantly or seriously wounded. There were three large smoking holes in the front wall of the barracks. Azarbod fired a stream of bullets into the now-burning building. The members of the raiding party who ran to the other building tossed grenades through the windows, but there was nobody in these other offices and storage rooms. One of them was a small armory, which exploded as the ammunition inside cooked off.

Azarbod stopped firing his machine gun and blew a whistle and the raiding party ran back to the APC and jumped in. The vehicle turned around and rumbled out of the front gate, leaving the police barracks a burning hulk behind them. The pickup truck that had been guarding the access road pulled up behind them and they hurried west, back toward Shiraz.

Less than five minutes had elapsed since the APC entered the Basij base.

The communications officer was one of the few people in the compound who was still alive. Although in shock and with a head wound inflicted by falling masonry, he managed to get out a back door, gingerly stepping over the smoking and blackened corpse of his commanding officer. Once outside, he fell to his knees, sobbing. He turned on his cell phone and called his parent's house. This time the connection worked, since the jamming equipment was now several kilometers away in the APC. When his mother answered, he began to cry incoherently.

One of the raiders called Dr. Boomla to report that the mission was completed. The two vehicles then turned onto a country road and parked in an old barn behind a deserted farmhouse. There were two other vehicles there, old cars. They transferred to the two cars and headed off in the direction of the distant hill villages where they came from.

At Dr. Boomla's house, Mordechai signaled Tel Aviv that the diversionary mission was successfully completed. Moments later, in Beirut, a communiqué was delivered to the Al-Manar Television network stating that a group called the "Ahvaz Liberation Front" was responsible for the attack and denouncing the apostasy of the heathen Shiites that had embraced a false Islam. Al-Manar began broadcasting stories of an attack by a group of Arab separatists "linked to Al-Qaeda." From an autonomous region of Waziristan in western Pakistan, a spokesman for Al-Qaeda denied the involvement of his group in the attack, but praised it nonetheless. Caught off guard, the IRNA, the official Islam Republic News Agency, at first denied that an attack had occurred.

The first people on the scene of the attack were firefighters called by passing motorists who saw smoke rising from the police barracks. The firefighters were revolted and angered by what was clearly a terrorist attack. They found the communications officer dazed and semi-conscious. Seventeen bodies were discovered.

The Basij commander of Fars Province was notified of the attack while attending a reception for the Mayor of Shiraz. He quietly left the party and arrived a half-hour later. By that time, the President of Iran had ordered a nationwide search for the suspects, who, given the claims made in the communiqué to Al Jazeera, were presumed to be Sunni militants from the western region of Iran. Forty-five minutes after denying that an attack had taken place, IRNA released a press statement announcing that an attack had indeed occurred and blamed it on terrorists financed by the United States and Israel.

In his study, Dr. Boomla looked up from the television and said to Mordechai, "They certainly got that right, didn't they?"

"This ought to draw every spare policeman and soldier away from Bala Deh and to the east and north of the city."

As if to confirm their speculation, Mordechai and Dr. Boomla heard the wailing of sirens moving from west to east in the city below.

Chapter 100

Jake must have lost consciousness. When he woke, he looked at the woman they called Vashti next to him. She was still, her head bent forward. He could see from the gentle rise and fall of her chest that at least she was still alive. From his vantage point, Jake saw across the warehouse floor that the roll-up gates were open and that the white delivery van was pulling out into the loading dock area.

Mohammed and Niaz walked back in from the outside and came over to them. Vashti must have awakened because he heard her say, "Shit" quietly.

They stopped directly in front of them.

"Vashti, because you were her closest comrade, I am going to give Niaz the privilege of shooting you and the American." He pulled his gun out of his holster, clicked off the safety, and handed it to Niaz. "Shoot them in the stomach. They will die more slowly and in great pain."

Mohammed turned and walked back toward the exit.

"Niaz, don't do this. Please," Hannah pleaded.

"You betrayed us, Vashti. If the Americans come they will kill us. You wanted me dead, so why should I spare you? What you have done is an offense against God and all of Islam. We are at war and you are a traitor." Her voice was angry and yet there were tears in her eyes.

"Niaz, listen to me, we cannot harm your mission. You will go on and even if we live, you can still accomplish what we were sent here to do. I'm not a traitor, Niaz; I'm a coward. I couldn't do it. I failed, I know that. After what I've done, no matter when I die I will still suffer the eternal torments of hell. Please don't kill us; I beg of you."

Hannah too was crying now.

Her eyes streaming with tears, Niaz raised the gun in front of her. It shook. "Vashti," she said, "I will not betray our cause. I have cared for you; part of me always will always care for you, but I am a loyal soldier." She pointed the gun at Hannah's stomach. "Close your eyes, Vashti," she said and pulled the trigger.

Out in the loading area, Mohammed, Ingrid, and Abdul-Haq heard two shots. A few seconds later, Niaz came through the door of the warehouse. When she got in the van, she said, "It is done," and handed the gun back to Mohammed.

Chapter 101

"What just happened?" Jake asked, his ears still ringing from the sound of the gunshots.

"She couldn't do it, I guess," said Hannah.

"Thank God, Vashti."

"Enough with the Vashti. My name is Hannah. Hannah Parras, OK? I work for Israel, you understand? What is your name?"

"Jake."

"OK, Jake, we don't have time for a lot of small talk. Listen to me: These terrorists have radioactive material. I didn't realize that until today. Before that, all I knew was that they planned to blow up a gasoline tanker truck. But I did not know the time of the attack or the target. We still don't know the target. What I do know is where they plan to steal the tanker truck from. There may be more than one terrorist group out there. "We have to get out of here, alert the police, and stop them. I don't know how much time we have. So come here and use your hands to try and untie me. Quickly."

With great difficulty, as Jake was in tremendous pain, he crawled over behind Hannah. It took him a while, but he finally untied her. She then freed him.

They helped each other up and limped arm-in-arm toward the rollup doors at the back of the warehouse.

"God, I'm in total agony," he said.

"You have pain? I have pain. So what? You have a car outside, no?"

"Yes."

"Did they take away the keys?"

Jake felt in his pocket. His keys were there. "No, I have them."

"That was stupid on their part. He should have just shot us in the head in the first place. Too much drama, these Arabs."

It was dark outside and the street was poorly lit. The air was hot and the wind strong. It felt soothing on their wounds. "The Santa Anas . . . Fire weather," Jake said.

"What?" asked Hannah.

"The wind; it's hot. We call it fire weather."

"'Dirty bomb weather' is more like it."

They stumbled over to the car and got inside.

Jake started the engine. "What now?"

"You got a phone?"

"Yeah, it's somewhere in here." Jake turned on the interior lights, which barely illuminated the inside of the car. They scrounged around and Hannah found Jake's cell phone under her seat.

"Here," she said, handing the phone to him. Start driving; call the police."

Jake pulled slowly into the street, turning east on Neptune.

"Where am I going, Hannah?"

"Oh yes," she tried to smile, which must have hurt her face because she winced in pain. "It's a petrol station on Los Feliz Boulevard."

The name came out sounding like "fellis" and Jake didn't recognize it.

"Fellis, I don't know a Fellis Street."

"It's spelled 'F-E-L-I-Zed'—Do you understand now?"

"Los Feliz! I got it."

Jake punched the accelerator and headed toward the onramp to the Harbor Freeway. The freeway was virtually empty and so Jake flew toward downtown LA at about eighty miles per hour.

"Hannah, before I call 911, can you tell me where on Los Feliz is this gas station? That's a big street."

"Near the big park with the Hollywood sign."

"That's Griffith Park.

"Do you know the name of the station?"

She struggled to remember and then it came to her. "Yes," she said, "it's the one with the three stripes like a sergeant has."

"Chevron?"

"Yes that's it."

He dialed 911.

The operator answered. "911 Operator," she said.

"There's going to be a truck hijacking of a gasoline fuel truck by terrorists at a Chevron station somewhere on Los Feliz near Griffith Park."

"Slow down, Sir. Tell me your name."

"Dr. Jonathan Elliot." Jake figured using the "Doctor" title couldn't hurt.

"Where are you now, Dr. Elliot?" the 911 dispatcher asked evenly.

"I'm on the Harbor Freeway headed there.

"Headed where, sir?"

"To the gas station. To stop the hijackers!" Jake yelled.

"Please stay calm, Dr. Elliot. We strongly advise civilians not to go to potential crime scenes."

"Are you sending somebody?"

"Dr. Elliot, what is your home address?"

"What?"

"Your home address, sir. We need your home address and the telephone number you are calling from."

"OK." Jake gave her his parent's address and his cell phone number.

"Ma'am, I think you don't understand the gravity of this situation. These people are planning to hijack a truck and blow it up with radioactive material inside."

"I understand, Sir, what you are saying. Please stay calm and don't raise your voice. I am here to help you. Now, what is the cross street of the gas station on Los Feliz?"

"I don't know. All I know is that it's near Griffith Park. You need to send somebody over there."

"Have you witnessed any criminal activity at that location?"

"I'm not there. I'm telling you what is going to happen if nobody stops it."

"I understand, Sir. We will get someone over there as soon as possible."

"Look, I'm not a nut. You need to call Homeland Security and the FBI. I'm not kidding. If people die because you're not taking me seriously, not only will it will be your fault but there will be a tape recording of your failure to take me seriously playing on the nightly news for the next ten years."

"Calm down sir, I am taking you seriously."

"OK, OK, just get them there," Jake yelled, hanging up

"Are the police coming?" asked Hannah.

"Honestly, Hannah, I don't know."

"Call the FBI."

Jake called 411 and the operator connected him up to the number for the FBI's Los Angeles Field Office.

He got a recording: "This is the Los Angeles Field Office of the Federal Bureau of Investigation. Our office is now closed. Please call back during normal business hours, which are Monday through Friday, 8:00 am to 5:00 pm. If this is an emergency, please hang up and dial 911. If this is a nonemergency and you wish to leave a message in our general mailbox, please dial 1. Thank you for calling."

"Jesus Christ. They're not home," said Jake. "But I've got another idea." Jake had the cell number for Agent Connoughton. Maybe he could stir something up. But he didn't answer and Jake just left a message saying that there was going to be an imminent dirty-bomb terrorist attack using a hijacked gasoline tanker truck to boost the explosion. If he got the message, he should get anybody he could to a Chevron station on Los Feliz near Griffith Park.

"Jake, do you have any kind of weapon?"

"Yes I do. There's a gun in the glove compartment."

Hannah pulled out the paper bag and unwrapped the gun from the cloth. She removed the clip and checked that it was loaded. She put the other clip in her pants pocket.

"You look like you know what you're doing, Hannah."

She didn't answer. She sighted down the gun and pulled the trigger. "Not bad," she murmured. "It's not a Desert Eagle, but it will have to do." She reloaded the clip and put it in her belt.

Just past Civic Center, they merged onto the Golden State Freeway and then quickly exited at Los Feliz. It had taken them twenty minutes to get downtown; some kind of record. They were actually quite close now to Griffith Park.

"There, up ahead," Hannah pointed. "That's the gasoline station. I remember now, Antonio's Chevron."

The station was closed, the illuminated sign dark. There was one bank of fluorescent lights illuminating the pump area. They could clearly see that a large silver gasoline tanker truck was parked in the station.

"Slow down, Jake."

"OK, I'm slowing." Jake felt a bolt of pain shoot through his head.

When they were two blocks from the station, they saw the white van suddenly make a U-turn from the other side of the street and pull up behind the tanker truck. Mohammed and Ingrid jumped out of the van. Both were carrying assault rifles and walked quickly to the driver's side window of the truck.

"Jake, pull over and stop. We are too late to save the driver. We must not do anything stupid."

"OK," he responded, and pulled the Volvo over about a block away from the gas station.

The driver never saw the terrorists. Simultaneously Mohammed and Ingrid raised their weapons and fired at the driver's head. The window glass shattered. Jake and Hannah watched in horror as the driver's head was blown apart by the hail of bullets. They could see him fall over to his right. Mohammed opened the door of the truck and got on the running board. He unbuckled the driver's seatbelt and pulled the bloody corpse onto the concrete driveway. Mohammed got in the truck and closed the door. He started the engine and signaled for Ingrid to go back to the van.

Mohammed put the truck in gear and drove out of the station.

With the van following, the fuel truck headed slowly east on Los Feliz. Jake could see that Abdul-Haq was driving the van and that he was wearing a green headband with red writing on it.

"Follow them," said Hannah.

Jake pulled onto the street. In his haste and out of lifelong habit, he made a stupid mistake and turned on his headlights. Hannah, distracted and in pain, did not notice. They were now two hundred yards behind the white van.

The tanker truck and the van turned left into the southern entrance of Griffith Park.

"Follow them," Hannah said.

They had gone about a half-mile up the twisty access road when Abdul-Haq saw the Volvo in the side mirror.

"Shit," he said, "there's somebody behind us."

"The police?" asked Ingrid.

"I don't know. I don't think so."

"Ingrid, shoot at the guy," yelled Abdul-Haq, trying to see the car in the side mirrors.

Ingrid opened the passenger-side window and stuck her head out. The hot dry wind blew in the window. Because of the curves in the road, she could not get a very clear shot.

She fired.

Jake did not hear the gunshot, but felt it. His right arm was burning and his shirtsleeve was quickly getting soaked with blood. He felt a wave of dizziness and nausea. "Oh shit," he said. He put on the brakes and stopped the car. He felt the wound with his left hand. There was blood and shattered glass everywhere.

The fuel truck and the van rumbled on up the road. Jake turned off his headlights. "What an idiot I am," he said.

"Oh yes, I see, the lights; that was stupid. Let me look at your arm." Hannah tore his shirt open and examined the wound. "You'll live. It's not deep."

"Can you drive?" she asked.

"I think so," answered Jake, holding back the urge to vomit.

"OK then. Don't go until you see the last of the brake lights of the van. Do you see those lights at the top of the hill? What's up there?"

"There's an observatory up there."

"So they will blow up the tanker there and with this wind the radiation will go everywhere."

"Jesus, these people really do have a flair for the dramatic," Jake said, laughing at the absurdity of his situation and wincing in pain.

"Didn't I tell you?"

The red brake lights of the van disappeared around a curve.

"OK, now go," She said, gesturing with the gun in her hand.

He started the engine and this time drove up the hill with his lights off.

"I don't see them," Ingrid said to Abdul-Haq.

"You must have him hit him or shot out the engine."

"I hope so."

They were making the last turn before entering the parking lot of the Observatory. It was lit up beautifully. Mohammed was parking the gasoline tanker truck. He got out of the cab and ran over to the van. He had his gun in a black military-style web holster.

Abdul-Haq got out of the van and came around and opened the back doors. He smiled at Niaz and took her hand to help her as she jumped out.

At this higher elevation, the Santa Anas were blowing hard and the air temperature was very hot.

"Niaz and Abdul-Haq," Mohammed ordered, "take the four bombs and attach them to the tank at the places where I instructed you."

Mohammed gave Abdul-Haq the backpack with the bombs. He and Niaz ran to the tanker. As instructed, they placed the bombs on the front and rear of the tank directly on top of the welded seams. The magnets grabbed onto the stainless steel. Just to be safe, they used duct tape to secure each of the four devices.

When Niaz and Abdul-Haq finished attaching the bombs and started back toward the van, they saw that Mohammed had changed into the white radiation suit. Mohammed ordered Abdul-Haq to help him carry the metal chest to the tanker truck. It was heavy and they walked slowly.

When they got near the tanker, Mohammed said to Abdul-Haq, his voice muffled by the clear face mask, "Now go back. Hurry."

Ingrid, Abdul-Haq, and Niaz watched with rapt attention as Mohammed bent down and opened up the chest. He withdrew the first box of cat litter and carried it gingerly toward the tanker. He rested it on a metal shelf where the fuel hoses were attached at the bottom of the tank. Then holding it in one hand, he climbed the ladder that went up the side of the tank to access the top hatch. Mohammed undid the large valve at the top and dropped the cat-litter container into the tank.

Mohammed climbed slowly down the ladder and walked over to the stainless-steel chest. He picked up another package of the highly radioactive cat litter and put it on the metal shelf.

Jake drove his car slowly up the access road toward the Observatory. He was feeling faint, his arm was throbbing uncontrollably, and he was in excruciating pain. They got out of the car well below the line of vision from the parking lot above and hiked up the road to the edge of the plateau. They were concealed by the bushes around the perimeter of the parking area. The van and, further away, the tanker truck were clearly visible in the reflected light of the brightly lit Observatory.

They saw Mohammed ambling toward the tank with one of the packages.

"Oh God, Jake, he's putting the radioactive material in the tank . . . and look, those are the bombs we made . . ."

Unconsciously, Jake looked at his watch. "When are the police getting here?"

"I'm afraid not soon enough."

Jake was starting to feel faint. His stomach was roiling and he felt very dizzy. He felt like he was going to throw up again. He put his hand over his mouth to control the sound and tried to stop it. But it didn't work and he threw up anyway. He slid down the hill a few feet and put his head between his legs. It helped.

Hannah grabbed Jake's chin and spoke slowly looking into his eyes. "Listen carefully to me now. The police are not coming. We have to stop this now. You are going to get in the car and drive up that hill. As soon as we get over to the top, you will stop the car, and I will get out. Then you must use the car to hit Mohammed. I will deal with the rest of them. Do you understand me, Jake?"

He nodded.

The Volvo came bounding up the drive and stopped with a squeal of the brakes. Hannah, who was crouched in the back seat behind Jake, opened the door and rolled onto the ground. She slammed the door shut, yelling "Go" to Jake. Jake floored the accelerator and headed straight for Mohammed, who was starting to climb the ladder again. Mohammed turned around and saw the car coming. He could do nothing but stare. He dropped the package of cat litter and reached instinctively for his gun, but it was zipped up inside the suit.

It took a half a second for Ingrid and Abdul-Haq to realize what was happening and another second for them to reach for their guns. Jake was already pressing down on his brakes. He didn't want to blow up the tanker himself. Mohammed continued to claw at his side in a frantic effort to get his gun.

Ingrid screamed, "Mohammed!" and emptied her weapon at Jake's car.

Abdul-Haq forgot that his gun was strapped in and was struggling to pull it out.

The terrorists, their attention drawn to Jake's Volvo, didn't see Hannah lying on the ground in firing position. For Hannah, a lifetime of training and the loathing and fear she felt came together in that moment. She carefully aimed at Ingrid, who was screaming and firing at the car. Hannah pulled the trigger twice, Mossad-style. The first shot missed but the second hit Ingrid under her raised left arm, entering her chest cavity and nicking her aorta. She spun around, dropped the gun, staggered and then dropped to the ground, already unconscious. In forty-five seconds she would be dead.

Ingrid did not live to see Jake's car pin Mohammed to the tanker, or more accurately, to the shelf that stuck out from the tanker's side. Jake was not trying to kill Mohammed and managed to succeed in that act of restraint. But the impact severed Mohammed's spine at the T-12 vertebrae. If Mohammed lived, he would be a paraplegic for the rest of his life. Still, he kept struggling to get his gun. He clawed at his suit and tried to tear at it, but he was pinned and no longer in command of his senses.

Hannah was walking toward Abdul-Haq and Niaz, crouching, her weapon held with both hands to steady her aim. She did not want to kill them. Abdul-Haq finally got the Beretta out of his holster and brought it up to firing position with both hands.

"Stop now, Abdul-Haq," yelled Hannah, taking aim. She took deep breaths to steady herself and said, trying to keep her voice controlled, "Stop. Put the gun down. You don't have to die. It's all over. Just stop." Hannah saw total hatred in the man's eyes. He lifted up the gun to fire at her. Niaz yelled "Noooo" and dove in front of Abdul-Haq to protect him. Hannah pulled the trigger, intending to kill the American, but hit Niaz squarely in the chest. Niaz fell to her knees. Abdul-Haq tried to pull the trigger. Nothing happened. He had forgotten to release the safety.

Hannah said slowly, "I said, Drop the gun."

At that moment Abdul-Haq's expression changed. All the fight seemed to go out of him. He dropped the gun and knelt down to hold up the wounded girl.

Niaz looked at Hannah, confused, in pain, her hand over the wound bleeding through her clothes. When she spoke, it was barely above a whisper, "Why?" she asked. "You are my friend. I saved you." Her eyes were wet with tears.

"*Israeli injast*", replied Hannah, as she had been trained to say by the Mossad. The tears began to flow from Hannah too. "I'm so sorry, Niaz," said Hannah, but the girl was already dead.

Jake opened the car door. He could see the man he had pinned with his father's Volvo screaming with rage and pain behind the mask.

"Fuck you, you asshole terrorist. Just shut the fuck up!" He knew that wasn't the right thing to say and that he wasn't in his right mind. When he turned around, he saw that Hannah was holding a gun on the big blond guy. The two women terrorists were crumpled on the ground.

Jake could hear sirens now and the sound of a helicopter. He slowly walked over to where Hannah was. She was crying softly and pointing a gun at Abdul-Haq. The blond man was on his knees, cradling the girl named Niaz in his arms. He laid her down on the ground and kissed her gently on the forehead.

"We're alive," Jake said, amazed at all that had happened in the last few minutes.

"That's true."

At that moment the police helicopter put a spotlight on them. From a loudspeaker a voice said, "This is the LAPD. Put down your weapons and lay on the ground. Put down your weapons."

Hannah pressed the release on the grip and the clip fell out of the handle. She then threw the gun down. Police cars with sirens blaring were coming up the drive. She and Jake got on the ground and spread their arms out as the first officers, guns drawn, ran toward them. Hannah looked over at Niaz. Abdul-Haq was crying softly, Niaz's head cradled in his arms, his headband with the Arabic writing on it half-off. Several officers ran to Abdul-Haq and Niaz. Jake saw other officers by the tank truck grabbing at a limp Mohammed and trying to free him.

The officers held them down, cuffed them, and pulled them to a standing position. Jake howled in pain as the officer touched his right arm. "Hey, go easy. I've been wounded. I need help."

One of the officers said into his radio, "We have wounded here. We need at least two ambulances."

Hannah said, "There are live bombs strapped to that truck . . .."

"And," Jake added, "what I believe to be enriched nuclear fuel in the tank. You need to call the NRAD clean-up team. That stuff is highly radioactive."

"Who are you people?" asked one of the officers.

"We're the good guys," said Jake. "You're the cavalry and you're late. Can we go now? A guy could get killed around here."

Chapter 102

The young assistant producer ran to the group of her fellow Al Jazeera reporters who were gathered around the television monitor watching the first fragmentary news reports coming from Los Angeles. According to the Los Angeles Police Department, some sort of "attempted terrorist attack" had been stopped. It involved an attempt to explode a gasoline tanker truck. The US Secretary of Homeland Security had issued a press release stating that the matter was under investigation and it was premature to comment.

"Look," she said, "we've gotten an email claiming responsibility for the attack in America."

Her producer turned around and grabbed the piece of paper.

"Read it, Sammi," one of group said.

"OK, here's what it says:

> We can strike the Americans whenever and wherever we choose, Almighty Allah be willing. Today, we launched an attack in Los Angeles. It did not fully succeed. But it will not be the last attack. This is but one battle in a Holy Jihad which we will inevitably win. We will not stop until the last pagan leaves our lands and Al Aqsa is liberated.

"It is signed Ayman al-Zawiri, Al-Qaeda."

"We need to go on the air with this right away. Let's get moving."

Chapter 103

SUNDAY, AUGUST 24, 12:05 AM
BALA DEH NUCLEAR COMPLEX, IRAN

This time they approached the nuclear complex from the northwest, rather than from the wooded forest on the other side of the valley. The mountains here were more barren and afforded them little cover. So they resorted to the only cover they had: deception. They wore their Al Qods division uniforms; even Irv, who, with her clean-shaven face, looked like a teenage recruit.

A few kilometers north of the access road to Bala Deh, the jeep turned off the main road onto a narrow dirt road that ran toward the mountains. The grass was low and brown from the summer sun and made the land look flatter than it was. At times, they had to go slow because of deep ruts in the road caused by spring flooding.

At the base of the mountain, their way was blocked by a chain-link fence that was topped by razor wire. Signs warned that it was a military facility and that trespassers would be arrested and prosecuted. Murphy jumped out of the jeep, cut the lock on the gate with bolt cutters, and pushed it open. Gonzales drove through the gate and they continued up a switchback dirt road that led to the crest of the hill. It was a moonless night and pitch black except for the narrow beam of light cast by their slitted headlights. They did not speak, concentrating on the task ahead. The Americans had gone over the mission again and again at the safe house in the south, timing their actions down to the last second. They tried to think of every contingency. They studied detailed aerial photographs until they knew every inch of the terrain. Still, each felt the weight of fear. Gonzales looked at his watch. It was 12:27 am and in three minutes, the drone launched from the USS Truman was supposed to make its first pass over Concrete Works Number 31. If all went as planned, Commander Abadi would order the facility plunged into darkness and they could get on with their work protected by the night. Gonzales saw light rising from the edge of the plateau. They must be getting close.

They were now on a gentle slope leading down to the edge of the plateau. Off to the right, perhaps half a kilometer away, they saw the dark silhouette of a guard tower. There was a light inside, but they couldn't see much else. Then up ahead, just over a little dip, they spotted what they were looking for. It was a large metal grate that looked like a big drain built into the mountaintop.

Gonzales turned the jeep around and faced it in the direction from which they had come. If they were successful, when they came out of the hole in approximately thirty-five minutes they would need to get the hell off that mountain.

Murphy hopped out of the jeep and ran over to the steel post that held a security camera pointed at the vent. Using the barrel of his assault weapon, he placed a black cloth over the camera.

The four of them went over to inspect the vent. A strong current of cool air was blowing out of it. Somewhere along the ridge, thought Ivana, there must be intake vents as well. The vent was hinged and covered by steel louvers. There was probably a release handle inside but it was obvious that they would have to use explosives to gain entry.

Ivana set to work attaching an explosive charge to the two big hinges. She molded C-4 plastique around each hinge and the locked latch on the other side of louvered grate. She placed a radio-controlled detonator in each charge.

"Take cover," she whispered, and they all retreated behind the jeep.

They donned their night-vision equipment and waited. No one said a word. Ivana could hear the breathing of the others. Her heart was pounding and her neck was sweaty. The world was a sickly yellow-green color through the night vision goggles.

At 12:33 am they heard the noise of airplane engines. It was the drone, two minutes late. It began making its pass, low and from the west. The engines were very loud, which was the desired effect. In fact, they had been modified to be much noisier than usual for tonight's mission.

The lights at Bala Deh went dark.

They could not see the plane but could hear that it was heading toward them. When the engine sound seemed to be reaching its crescendo, Ivana yelled, "Fire in the hole!" and flipped the switch. There was a loud, sharp detonation. OJ had his hands over his ears, but still felt the shock wave hit his body and when he took his hands away, his ears rang.

They were now racing against time. They ran over to the smoking vent. The grate covering the vent had been blown completely off and was lying on the ground a few feet from the scorched concrete tube. Gonzales took out an infrared flashlight and they looked inside. There was a metal ladder which ran straight down into the darkness.

They removed their night-vision equipment. From their packs, each of them took out a white lab coat, identical to those worn by the staff of Bala Deh, and put it on over their military uniforms. Then they donned white hard hats, each of which was equipped with a small LED flashlight. Finally they attached earpieces and microphones that would allow them to communicate with one another when they got inside. They tested the communication system to make sure that they could all hear one another. Led by Gonzales, they climbed down into the vent and began their descent. The vent was wide, probably seven feet in diameter, and so there was plenty of room to move. OJ, who was mildly claustrophobic, felt relieved since he had been worried for days that he would panic and make a fool of himself. In his fitful and anxious night of sleep the day before, OJ had dreamed he was

Just as Murphy and Ivana pulled Gonzales and OJ over the side of the ventilation shaft, the first of the charges that Murphy had placed on the gas pipes transporting enriched uranium hexafluoride gas began to detonate. There was a hissing sound as the gas escaped into the atmosphere of the cave propelled by the air pressure of the spinning centrifuges. Every fifteen seconds another detonation occurred. Within one minute, the radiation level inside the cave had reached toxic levels.

From above, the detonations sounded like popcorn popping. They now had only a few minutes to get out off the mountain. After they got OJ and Gonzales untangled, the three of them carried OJ to the jeep. They sat OJ in the back with Ivana, while Murphy sat shotgun in the front with Gonzales. Gonzales hopped out and cut the rope off the winch and threw it back down the shaft.

In the gas-processing chamber at the front of the cave, the first micro-charge exploded, causing a small leak in the pipes leading in and out of the tank of nitric acid. A steady stream of nitric acid fell on the ground. Some of it made contact with the napalm that had been deposited on the floor by OJ. The jellied gasoline began to smoke and then with a sound like the poof of an old-time photographer's chemical flash, it combusted. The flames spread and became more intense.

The last charge, which was located on the front of the hydrogen tank, detonated and gas leaked into the room. It took a few seconds for the hydrogen gas to reach the requisite degree of atmospheric saturation, but then a violent explosion occurred. The hydrogen tank exploded as did the two other hydrogen tanks in the chamber. Unlike other volatile gasses, Hydrogen burns clear and the flames cannot be seen by the human eye. It also burns at an extremely high temperature. The flaming ball of hydrogen gas expanded quickly, destroying everything before it. First it engulfed the gasification area, then spread into the main chamber of the cave, sucking oxygen in from the outside and spreading flames all the way to the rear of the cave, then the flames—now concentrated—rebounded toward the front of the cave. It was now a powerful radioactive fireball seeking to escape from the confines of the cave at Bala Deh. Thousands of centrifuges

were blown apart, releasing radioactive uranium hexafluoride gas that mixed in with the flaming toxic fireball that got stronger as the milliseconds passed. The fluorine gas that was stored in the facility exploded and mixed with the unburnt hydrogen gas to form hydrogen fluoride, a deadly and explosive acid that can kill a human being in very small doses.

The blast doors were in the process of closing. When the fireball hit, the intense heat fused the huge hinges so that the doors could not be closed. With enormous force, the explosion pushed through the opening, vaporizing the two guards, Colonel Abadi, and Dr. Shakeil. One of the interesting characteristics of hydrogen is that its atomic weight is so small that its molecules rise quickly skyward in the atmosphere. And so, apart from the four people that were in the path of the flames, the explosion did not immediately kill anyone else, though the shock wave accompanying it severely injured a number of soldiers and plant workers.

Toxic smoke and radioactive gas were rising rapidly into the atmosphere above Bala Deh and within seconds there was a huge black cloud that reached almost 10,000 feet into the air. The prevailing winds were starting to carry it east toward Shiraz.

––––––––––––––––––––––

Gonzales decided to use the full beam of the headlights, even if it did make their jeep visible in the blackness of the night. With lights, they were able to drive much faster and put more distance between themselves and the cave complex.

When the explosion came, it felt like the mountain was shaking underneath them. Gonzales almost swerved off the gravel road. Ivana and OJ turned around to look. A tongue of light rose out of the valley and shot high into the atmosphere. Simultaneously, smoke and flames leapt up out of the vent. OJ grabbed Ivana's hand. "Thank God," he croaked.

"Why?" she asked.

"Because He made the wind blow east tonight . . . away from us and that radioactive nightmare we just created back there."

When they reached the bottom of the hill, Gonzales put his foot to

the floor and drove the jeep as fast as he could toward the main road. Very soon, it would be full of roadblocks and security forces. They took off their white coats to reveal their Al Qods Division uniforms. Hopefully, OJ's Farsi and their uniforms would get them through the next hours. The only problem was that OJ had once again lapsed into unconsciousness.

By flashlight, Ivana started a saline drip in OJ's arm to keep him hydrated. What he needed, though, was a blood transfusion. She felt his pulse. It was weaker but still regular.

Chapter 104

The ambulance took Jake to the trauma center at County-USC Medical Center. His vitals were good, but his blood pressure was low. The paramedics started him on a glucose drip to help elevate his blood volume. They bandaged up his wounds. "How'd ya do this?" the paramedic asked.

"Somebody shot me."

"Hey, we're experts at treating gunshots, aren't we, Phil," he said to the driver.

"That's reassuring," Jake said.

"You're not a gang banger, are you?" he asked.

"Do I look like a gang banger?"

"Yeah, kinda." He yelled up to the driver, "Hey, Phil this guy look like a gang banger to you?" Phil did not respond.

The cop that was crammed in the back with them said, "No, he's more like an international terrorist."

"Hey, can you give me something for the pain?" Jake asked.

"No, that will have to wait, buddy."

When they arrived, the trauma doctors shot Jake's arm full of

xylacaine so they could open up his wound, clean it, and pack it. They also put him on a morphine drip to help him with the pain. Within a few seconds the pain began to ebb. He had done a fair amount of bleeding and so they gave him several units of blood. When the orderly wheeled him out of the operating room, he was already asleep. He was taken up to the lock-up ward where they kept prisoners.

Chapter 105

AUGUST 24, 2:05 AM, THE SKY ABOVE IRAN

B ritish, French, and US satellites detected the explosion at Bala Deh. Ionizing radiation sensors on those satellites measured the presence of various radioactive compounds in the atmosphere. Within minutes, all three countries reported their findings to the International Atomic Energy Agency in Vienna. The Director-General of the IAEA was asleep in a hotel in New Delhi, but the matter was deemed to be of sufficient gravity that he was immediately awakened and briefed by his staff.

The Director-General telephoned the delegate to the IAEA from Iran to demand an explanation regarding the explosion. The Iranian delegate could not be immediately located.

Shortly thereafter, the Secretariat of the IAEA released a press statement:

> The IAEA has determined that at approximately 10:45 pm, local time (GMT + 3:30), there was a significant radiation release from a previously unknown facility sixty kilometers southwest of Shiraz, Iran, near the town of Bala Deh in Fars Province. The Director-General, Mohammed el-Kabalai, attempted without success to contact Mr.

Roozbeh Javanifard, Iran's representative to the IAEA, to demand an explanation.

The Director General said, "This is a very serious incident. We do not yet have a complete understanding of the consequences of the apparent radiation release and we are continuing to investigate and monitor the situation. Iran must comply with the requirements of the Nuclear Nonproliferation Treaty and come into compliance with the demands of the International Community."

The major news outlets in North America, where it was still daytime, and in Europe, where it was evening, began to report the story and it soon became major breaking news.

The Reuters headline was, "Explosion at Secret Iranian Nuclear Facility, Radioactive Cloud Drifts Toward Population Center." AP and UPI followed soon thereafter.

Across the Iranian diaspora, millions of telephone calls and emails started pouring into Iran as anxious family members attempted to check on their relatives.

Chapter 106

The exhilaration Hannah felt at the Observatory had quickly been replaced by relief and then exhaustion. The FBI agents kept asking her questions; she kept telling them the same answer. She was Mossad; she came here without the knowledge of her government as part of a mission to infiltrate an Iranian-sponsored terrorist operation. No, she was not a rogue agent; no, she just didn't have the opportunity to warn them; no, Israel was not running active operations in the United States. No, no, no. They showed her a photograph. Did she know a Jonathan Elliot? Yes, sort of, she met him the day before outside of the warehouse in Wilmington. Was he working with Israel? No, not that she knew of. What did she know about him? He worked for the government and he had *chutzpah*.

Later they brought someone over from the Israeli consulate in Los Angeles. He looked harried and nervous, a bureaucrat who would rather have been in bed. He confirmed that Hannah Parras was a Mossad agent, but denied that she was operating in the United States as part of an official Israeli operation. He told her not to say anything else, but the advice was unnecessary, as they stopped the interrogation.

At 7:00 am, the FBI released her into the custody of the Counsel General of Israel with the promise that she would remain in the United States and cooperate fully in the investigation and prosecution of the two surviving terrorists, Thomas Harter, who was also known by the name "Abdul-Haq," and the as yet unidentified suspect known only as Mohammed.

As they walked out of the steps into the bright sun of a southern California morning, there were dozens of reporters and cameras waiting for Hannah. The Counsel General put his arm around her and said, "Don't speak to them, Hannah."

She looked up and smiled. Then she waved.

Chapter 107

Since he was a little child, Ali loved to burn things and he had gone to jail many times for starting fires. Ali knew everything about fires: different kinds, how to make fires that were hard to put out, how to make fires that looked accidental. Ali was a professional. Ten years earlier, when he was in jail for starting a fire in an empty house, another prisoner told him that, when he was released, he could arrange to get Ali a job starting fires. Ali readily agreed. The thought that someone would pay him to do what he loved more than anything was, for Ali, a dream come true. When his sentence was completed, almost the first thing he did was contact the man on the piece of paper his jail mate had given him. The man promptly hired him.

Ali carried a big backpack and a ten-liter can full of gasoline. His instructions were to turn on the gas lines and then make sure that there was a huge explosion. It must look like a murder-suicide. Inside his backpack were five separate plastic bags full of bones and he had been carefully instructed to lay them about in a specific way. The house was totally dark, except for a light at the front entrance. His boss had given him a set of keys and instructed him to enter the house through a gate in the rear of the property. He walked through the neat garden past a small fountain that was gently gurgling water.

The back door was open and he went in. Using a small flashlight, he found the kitchen. It was laid out just as he had been told and he found the stove and oven. He made his way upstairs to the bedrooms. Ali unpacked the heavy backpack full of bones and arranged them in each of the bedrooms as he had been instructed, with the jaw parts on the pillow and the other bones arranged further down toward the foot of the bed. In the girls' room he found two beds and put bones in each. He also tossed their purses on the desk. In the son's room, he put a set of bones on the bed as well. He tossed Abid's wallet on the floor and put a man's ring in the bed. Finally, he entered the master bedroom and laid out another set of bones and some jewelry on the bed. Then he took a small automatic out of the backpack and went from room to room and shot it into each of the beds. He fired through a pillow to muffle the report. Finally, he opened the gasoline can and soaked the bed sheets with gasoline.

Satisfied, Ali went downstairs with the last set of bones and found Dr. Honari's study. There was a dull light in the room coming from the computer screen by the desk. He placed the last skull on the desk and shot it in the head. Then he placed the gun beside the skull. He also placed a bathrobe and the remaining bones on the desk chair as instructed. Ali doused the room with the remaining gasoline and left the metal petrol can. He loved the smell of gasoline and inhaled the fumes deeply. Now came the fun part.

Ali returned to the kitchen and turned the burners on in the oven and the stove, but only after he had blown out their pilot lights. It began to smell like natural gas almost immediately. All of the various gas odors brought back the old feelings of excitement in Ali. However, as much as he wanted to linger, there was now not much time to do so. Ali went into the dining room and took out a book of matches. He walked over to the thick drapes covering the windows and lit a single match, and held it to the dry material. The cloth ignited instantly. The drapes, the carpets, and the heavily lacquered wooden furniture in the living and dining rooms would burn like mad, Ali thought. When he was ready to die, Ali thought, he would love to die in a blazing explosion of flame and heat.

Ali left the way he came in, almost forgetting to leave the mother's purse. He put it on a table by the rear door as he was going out. He ran to the rear of the property and out the gate. He looked in the alleyway, but all was silent and he walked quietly down the deserted alley. He wished he could stay and witness the results of his work, but he knew that he could not. He did not want to return to jail and the surest way to get caught was to stay around to watch. He walked quickly away from the house, crossing the main street that entered the neighborhood. On the other side of the street was a car parked in the shadows. Ali could see the glowing red tip of the driver's cigarette. He had told his cousin that there was no smoking, but Gorazm did what he liked.

Ali got in the car and they drove down the hill toward the center of the city of Shiraz. As instructed, from under the seat, Ali grabbed the cell phone and called the number they had asked him to memorize. After one ring, a man said, "Yes," in Farsi.

"All done," replied Ali and hit the red button to terminate the call. As instructed, he took off the back of the cell phone and removed the battery. He took out his prized Zippo lighter and proceeded to melt the SIM card and circuit board with the flame. Then he broke the telephone into parts and flung them out the window into the bushes on the side of the road.

On the way down the hill, Ali and Gorazm passed three police cars speeding toward the neighborhood in the opposite direction.

They could hear the explosion but they did not see it. Sirens started up immediately, probably from the police cars that had been heading up the hill. Ali turned to Gorazm and said, "I think they will be happy with our work tonight."

"I hope so," replied Gorazm, turning the car into a street which took them in the direction of the crowded slums on the south side of the city. They heard the distinct wailing of the fire trucks going up the hill to the house. A few moments later, a huge explosion could be heard off in the west. Then they heard even more sirens. Lights began to go on in the houses that lined the dark streets as people woke up to the strange cacophony.

Gorazm stopped the car in front of the apartment he and Ali shared. While the people of Shiraz might be awaking to the noise of explosions and fire, the two cousins were exhausted. Their work was done and it was time for bed.

The telephone that Ali had disposed of was actually a satellite phone and so the call he made was not traceable within the Iranian telecommunications system. The person who answered the phone was sitting at a desk in front of a computer terminal in Tel Aviv. When he got the call, he pushed a key on his computer that caused Dr. Honari's computer to send an email to the head of the Iranian nuclear program, the esteemed Dr. Reza Khosravi:

Sir:

I have learned a few minutes ago about the explosion at Bala Deh. I do not know how this accident occurred, but I must take full responsibility for it. I cannot bear the thought of my family facing the shame and humiliation of my trial and punishment. And so I must do the honorable thing. May Allah, the powerful and the merciful, protect our souls. We will enter heaven cleansed by fire.

Long live the Islamic Republic of Iran!

Your Faithful Servant,
Dr. Majid Emami Honari

Chapter 108

When the explosion came, it blew out every window of the Honari household. Blue flames shot through the windows and reached out like the tongue from some primordial god of fire. The walls of the neighboring homes were scorched and a cypress tree in the Honaris' front yard caught fire and began to burn. Adding to the intensity of the blaze, the gasoline soaked beds and carpets burned. The plastic and vinyl throughout the home melted and then burned. Shocked neighbors came outside and stood in their bathrobes and underwear staring in disbelief.

The police cars were just pulling into the street when the explosion occurred. The officers were confused, but one managed to call the fire department and within seconds sirens could be heard coming up the hill. When the fire trucks arrived, they hooked up to a fire hydrant, but there was no water pressure. So they tried put out the fire with the available water in their trucks. They gave up trying to contain the fire at the Honari house and concentrated on preventing the fire from spreading to the neighbor's houses. By dawn, the fire had burned itself out. There was nothing left of the house but a smoking, blackened shell. When the police and fire inspectors went inside, they found almost nothing that had not burned completely. In the bedrooms upstairs and in a small room downstairs, they found some charred bones, which they carefully collected to give to the medical examiner at the city morgue. In the immediate aftermath of the fire, however, all available police and fire units were preoccupied with the catastrophic explosion at Bala Deh and the terrorist attack, the day before, at the police barracks east of the city.

Chapter 109

They had seen several military convoys moving east toward Shiraz while they were driving west. Gonzales refused to relinquish the steering wheel to one of the others. OJ woke up and seemed somewhat revived. Ivana put more morphine in the saline drip to control OJ's pain. She held his head on her shoulder. He fell back asleep. The next thing he knew, Ivana was shaking him awake. "Get up, OJ. There's a roadblock up ahead. We need you to get us through this." OJ shook his head to try to bring himself to full alertness. When he sat up, he could see a line of vehicles stopped on the road.

"Fuck me," said Murphy.

"OJ, you're going to have to talk us out of this one. Can you do it?"

"I'll try my best," OJ responded weakly.

"Everybody else, get ready, we may have to shoot our way out of this."

"Ivana, pull out this goddamned IV. We can't let them see it."

"Why?"

"Because they'll take me to the hospital and then we're all dead."

As they approached the line of cars and trucks, OJ could hear the sound of safeties being clicked off and grenades being placed where they could be reached.

"You all have your papers, right?" asked OJ. When no one responded, OJ said, "OK, give them to me." The others handed over their papers to OJ. He then put on his officer's cap. The rest of them put on helmets.

When they got up to the roadblock, there were several soldiers milling around with assault rifles. They thoroughly inspected the pickup truck in front of them and ordered the farmers who were sitting in the bed of the truck to get out. They lined them up with their hands over their heads and frisked them. The farmers were apparently clean because they let them go.

When it was their turn, a Pasdaran Lieutenant walked up to the vehicle, saluted, and asked them for their identification. OJ handed their forged identity papers to the officer. When he shined his flashlight on OJ, he realized that he was dealing with a high-ranking officer of the Al Qods Force. "Excuse me, Sir, I didn't realize . . ." and his voice trailed off.

OJ said, "I understand; it's late. Now inspect the papers, please, so that we can be on our way."

"Yes, Sir," said the officer, who left and walked over to an APC.

When he returned a few minutes later, he looked embarrassed. "Sir, I don't know how to explain this, but your names aren't in our system. I'm sure it's a mistake. My orders are to detain you until a further inquiry can be made."

"That's unacceptable. We need to get to Bandar-e-Gonaveh by dawn."

"Yes, Sir, I understand. But . . . ."

OJ interrupted him. "You, son, are lucky I'm a tolerant man. Give me the papers back."

The Lieutenant hesitated.

"Now!" OJ yelled.

"Yes, Sir," and the officer handed them back to OJ.

"Lieutenant," OJ said angrily, "you will not regret following my directions." He paused and said "We're leaving. I take full responsibility." OJ saluted the young officer. The Lieutenant saluted back. OJ tapped Gonzales on the helmet and said, "Now, go!" The message was unmistakable and Gonzales put his foot on the gas pedal and they took off in a whirl of dust.

They were silent for the first few kilometers, while they waited to see if they were being followed. When it was evident that they were not, Gonzales turned around and said, "I didn't understand a word of it, but whatever you said, it worked. Good job."

"Yeah, well done, OJ," said Murphy.

Ivana smiled at him and squeezed his hand, but he had already slipped into unconsciousness.

Gonzales told Murphy to start signaling the submarine about ten kilometers from the beach and to inform them that they had one casualty needing emergency medical care. It was getting close to 5:00 am when they parked the jeep on the coast road. The night was getting lighter and it would be dawn soon. They started to pick up the unconscious OJ. Ivana felt his pulse. He had none.

"Oh, OJ. My God, his heart's stopped. His pulse was weak but regular just a few kilometers back."

"Shit," replied Gonzales. "Murphy, Ivana, let's lay him on the sand and try to resuscitate him. I'm going down to the beach to signal them. They know OJ's wounded; they'll bring a doctor."

Frantically, Murphy and Ivana tried to bring OJ back. Ivana pushed OJ's head back, cleared his airways, and started mouth-to-mouth resuscitation while Murphy performed chest compressions to restart his heart. OJ did not respond. They tried it again. After the fifth cycle, Murphy stopped.

"Ivana, stop. It's over. He's gone."

Ivana lifted up her head. A strange guttural noise came out of her throat, half-keening, half-groaning. She pounded her fists on the sand.

Seconds later, Gonzales returned with three sailors and an officer. The three sailors went over to the jeep to attach a demolition charge to it. The officer was a doctor and he had a black backpack with him that contained an automatic external defibrillator.

"How long has he been without a pulse?" the doctor asked.

"At least two minutes," answered Ivana.

The doctor quickly knelt down in the sand and put the paddles on OJ's chest. "Stand back," he said.

OJ's chest arched as the electrical charge entered his body, but there was no response. He tried it again and once more OJ's heart remained still.

The doctor looked up. "This man's gone. I'm sorry, there's nothing more to be done."

"All right," said Gonzales, "let's get this soldier down to the beach. No one gets left behind."

Moments later, as they made their way through the surf toward the submarine off shore, there was a flash and an explosion as the charges on the jeep exploded.

Chapter 110

There were rumors flying all around the city. The foreign news sources reported the explosion at Bala Deh and were raising questions about potential radiation exposure in the surrounding areas in Fars Province. The Government refused to comment. People, particularly the more affluent, started leaving Shiraz and by mid-morning there was a long line of cars heading east out of the city toward Ishfahan and Tehran. The trains and intercity busses were also packed.

At noon, students from the University of Shiraz began to congregate on campus, passing out flyers asking why there needed to be a nuclear Iran. The long banned Communist Tudeh Party of Iran distributed leaflets calling for the overthrow of the "religious dictatorship from the dark ages."

The students decided to march on City Hall to confront the Mayor. There they clashed with local members of the Basij, who had been called out to protect government offices. Some local police officers tried to protect the students from the Guards.

By 2:00 pm, spontaneous demonstrations had erupted at

Tehran University and at universities in Tabriz and Abadan. At the demonstration in Tehran, some women students threw off their head coverings and were beaten by the religious police.

At 2:25 pm, the President of Iran issued a press release, stating that there had been an act of sabotage at a concrete plant near Shiraz which had been carried out by American and Zionist spies. He denied that there had been a release of radiation and characterized Western reports of a radiation accident as "pure propaganda."

From his headquarters in Vienna, the Director-General of the IAEA held a news conference to answer questions about the incident at Bala Deh. He called upon the President of Iran and its Supreme Religious Leader to "be honest with the world and, more importantly, honest with the Iranian people" about what had happened there. Atmospheric tests had conclusively proved that there was an explosion at Bala Deh and that a substantial amount of radioactive material had been released into the atmosphere. He demanded immediate access to the site under the express terms of the Nuclear Non-Proliferation Treaty, of which Iran was a signatory nation, so that the international community could assess the situation. He pledged the complete support of the international community to help the Iranian people with humanitarian and medical assistance in the present crisis.

Chapter III

Jake was finally moved to a private room in a civilian ward of the hospital. He still had a police guard sitting outside, but it was now for his protection, as much from the press as from avenging terrorists. He was no longer a suspect.

Jake's mother and father were sitting by his bed, talking and joking with him. He had been quickly identified by the press as a hero, along with the Israeli woman, Hannah Parras, for stopping the dirty-bomb attack at Griffith Park. The White House was quick to take credit for Jake's actions, implying that the Administration was somehow responsible for stopping the attack. However, the Mayor of Los Angeles, an up and coming young Latino Democrat with national political ambitions of his own, wondered out loud why the Administration would have let a plot of this magnitude get so far before stopping it. The senior Senator from Kentucky, a leading Republican critic of the President on national security issues, commented, "That dog don't hunt." A chorus of politicians, journalists, and self-appointed national security experts said, with the kind of perfect clarity that is available only in hindsight, that there was a dire need for enhanced programs to protect our ports of entry.

There was a knock at Jake's door and in walked Hannah Parras, her curly hair loosely piled on her head, all smiles. She looked a little battered and her face was swollen.

"Good morning, Dr. Elliot."

"Good morning, Ms. Parras."

"Mom, Dad, let me introduce Hannah Parras. We met yesterday, or was it the day before? I'm losing track."

Hannah shook his mother's and father's hand. "You're quite famous, young lady," said Jake's father.

"And so is your son. If it wasn't for him, we'd probably both be dead." Hannah absentmindedly put her hand on his left shoulder.

"Your family must be very proud of you, Hannah," said Mr. Elliot.

"Yes, I suppose they are. I spoke with my mother who told me to stop acting like I was some kind of movie star."

"And what are your plans? Do you go back to work?" asked Mrs. Elliot.

"Jeese, Mom," Jake interrupted, "give the poor woman a chance to catch her breath."

"It's OK, Jake, your mother is just curious."

"Mrs. Elliot . . . ," Hannah started to explain.

Jake's mother gently placed her hand on Hannah's arm. "Please call me Joan."

"OK, Joan," said Hannah, "the answer to your question is that I am finished with government service. It's time for me to go home for good. As they say in America, I've 'done my time' for the Jewish state. Besides, my cover is blown now. I'm no use to them any more."

"That's kind of how I feel. Actually, I felt that way before all this happened," said Jake.

Mrs. Elliot turned to her husband and elbowed him. "Isn't she just adorable, Lou?"

"Mom," Jake said, "please, you're embarrassing me."

"I'm so sorry, Hannah," said Mrs. Elliot, "did I embarrass you?"

"No, no. Not at all. I have a Jewish mother too."

Jake's father tapped his mother on the shoulder. "Joan, let's let these two visit for a while. We'll go get a cup of coffee and come back later."

"OK," Jake said. Both of Jake's parents kissed him on the forehead.

When they left, there was a moment's silence. Then they both started to speak at once, throwing off the cadence of their conversation. They laughed and Jake said, "Let's start over."

"Have you ever been to Israel, Jake?" Hannah asked.

"No. I've always wanted to go but never got around to it."

"It's a beautiful country. We have our troubles. Anyway, you should come. I will show you around."

Jake looked at her. She had rosy cheeks and all that thick hair. Her eyes were dark too and there was something else in them, an expression that was a combination of intelligence mixed with weariness. She was an "old soul" as his mother would say.

"You know, Hannah, I was fired from my job. They will probably want me to come back now, but I won't do it. I start teaching again next year. So I may just take you up on the offer. But can you guarantee me one thing?"

"Sure. What's that?"

"You won't shoot anybody."

Chapter 112

USS Connecticut, Persian Gulf, August 25

It was twenty-four hours since the radiation release at Bala Deh. Finally, the Iranian Government admitted that there was a nuclear facility there and that radiation had entered the atmosphere. The President of Iran was defiant and continued to blame the Americans and the Israelis for sabotaging the facility. While he now admitted that facility was kept a secret from the IAEA, he said that the government had only acted out of a desire to prevent the sort of attack which had now occurred. The Director of the Iranian Nuclear Regulatory Agency assured the Iranian people that the release had been minor, that alarmist news stories coming from the West were inaccurate, and that the story was being exploited for propaganda purposes.

Ivana and Gonzales sat quietly in the officer's mess sharing a cup of tea. Gonzales asked Ivana if she thought what they had done was right. "If it brings about a change in the regime and they abandon their plans to develop nuclear weapons, then yes, I'd say it was worth it."

"Are they telling the truth about the lethality of the release?"

"I don't know. Disbursed at it was, it is certain that there will be an increase in cancer rates and birth defects in the region near Bala Deh. Nothing like Chernobyl."

They sat quietly for a while. Then Gonzales looked at Ivana.

"I liked OJ. He was a good guy, as brave a man as ever I've met."

Ivana stared into her cup of coffee and after a few seconds of silence, said, "Yes, and no one but us will ever know what he did or how he died. Not his family, not his friends. It will be as though he never existed."

EPILOGUE

Chapter 113

Pasdaran Headquarters, Tehran, Iran, August 30

The Russian, whose name was Ivanich, sat impatiently in the outer office of his counterpart, Colonel Zandipour, waiting to be called in. Ivanich was an agent of the *Sluzhba Vneshney Razvedki*, Russia's post-Soviet foreign intelligence service, known by the acronym SVR. It was 9:30 in the morning and Ivanich lit a cigarette, his tenth for the day. He had the distinct feeling that the Colonel was just sitting at his desk making Ivanich wait for no other purpose than to demonstrate his importance. There was once a time, during the old Soviet days, when the Iranians treated the Russians with respect and, better yet, fear. Now the Russians were just another trading partner who sold them military goods at high prices. As a bonus, the Russians also passed along selective intelligence information to the Iranians. Ivanich was on such a mission.

The rude little bastard of a military clerk who sat at the desk in front of Zandipour's door didn't even bother to ask Ivanich if he wanted a cup of coffee or tea. And Ivanich certainly needed a cup of coffee. He was tired and hung over from having spent the previous evening with some visiting SVR comrades drinking vodka and reminiscing about their old KGB days. Ivanich's head throbbed and his eyes ached. All happy things were followed by sadness, the old villagers of his childhood used to say.

The phone on the clerk's desk rang. He picked it up, got some instructions, and hung up.

"Mr. Ivanich, you may go inside now." The clerk got up from his desk and opened the door to Zandipour's office.

Zandipour was a healthy and fit-looking man in his mid-forties. Another reason to hate him, thought the Russian, who was fat, drank and smoked too much, and was in a state of general physical decline.

The two men shook hands in a desultory sort of way.

"To what do I owe this pleasure, Ivanich?" The Iranian's smile was not particularly friendly.

The Russian sat down. "Well, Zandipour, my government has a little gift of information for your government."

Ivanich opened his attaché case and removed a large manila envelope from which he took out several large color photographs and some documents. He put one of the photographs on the desk facing the Colonel.

"I believe you know this man as Commander Zaid. He is one of your operatives in Eastern Turkey." Ivanich enjoyed the look of surprise in the Iranian's eyes, which he attempted to suppress.

"Perhaps," responded Zandipour with an indifferent shake of his head.

The Russian placed another photograph next to the first one. It showed Commander Zaid talking to another man on the street.

"The other man is a Mossad agent known to us by the name of Zev Lubin. They are talking to one another in a street in Van, Turkey. We took both photographs last month. It is apparent that they know one another."

The Iranian studied the photographs.

"Is there more?"

"One more thing. We received this document from a source that we have in Israel." The Russian handed the Iranian a copy of a document in Hebrew.

"I don't read Hebrew, Ivanich."

"I don't either, but our people tell me that it refers to the Mossad's operations in eastern Turkey. Apparently, they have an agent whose code name is 'Prince' who operates out of a safe house in the Heshmand valley. We sent some people to the Heshmand valley and it didn't take long to discover a farmhouse with significant activity. Yours, perhaps?"

The Iranian didn't respond.

"And guess who we saw at the farmhouse? Our friend Zaid. Is it possible that Zaid and the Israeli agent code-named 'Prince' are one in the same?" Ivanich was enjoying the humiliation this was causing the Iranian.

"I really couldn't say, Ivanich."

"Colonel, you wouldn't mind asking your man out there to bring me a cup of coffee, would you?"

Since the failure of the mission in Los Angeles and the revelation of Hannah Parras' role in stopping the attack, Commander Zaid knew that he would be sacrificed. He recruited the woman named "Vashti Palmeni", he was in charge of performing the investigation into her background, and he recommended her to General Yazdi. Within a day after the failure of the mission, he and his agents went to Van to seek out the family of Vashti Palmeni. The electronics store was boarded up and all the members of the Palmeni family had disappeared. General Yazdi demanded a full report. It was only a matter time, Zaid knew, before they would come for him.

Zaid woke up from his dream feeling the hot fetid breath of the other man on his face. He opened his eyes, but couldn't tell who it was that was trying to hurt him. Someone was pinning down his arms. There was a knee pushing down on his chest. He tried to struggle, but it was no use. They lifted his head up and slipped something underneath. Then he felt the wire around his neck, twisting into his skin, cutting off his breath. He tried again to fight back. He was growing weak; he couldn't breathe. The pain was all-consuming. He heard the grunting of the man using the garrote; he was working hard to kill Zaid.

Zaid heard somebody say, "Shit," and then he entered the blackness.

Chapter 114

Aqil was asleep next to his wife when the secret police simultaneously broke through the front and back doors of his house. He woke up immediately and grabbed the assault rifle that was next to his bed. His wife was awakened by the noise as well and he told her to get under the bed. Aqil went to the door of the bedroom and in the filtered moonlight coming through the window saw the shadowy silhouettes of the soldiers coming through the front room. He leveled the gun and fired. The flash illuminated the scene for a split second. There was a thumping sound and a grunt as the bullets hit home. One of the black-clad soldiers had a light on the end of his assault rifle and flashed it in Aqil's eyes and fired. The first bullet ripped through Aqil's esophagus, the second his shoulder; the rest missed. Aqil tried to fire his gun again, but for some reason he couldn't pull the trigger. He dropped the gun and grabbed his throat, trying clumsily to put it back together. One of the soldiers walked up to him, pointed a pistol at his head, and pulled the trigger.

Chapter 115

Hannah walked through the museum galleries not really paying much attention to the art. She was trying to divert her attention from the stress of the constant interviews with the investigators and prosecutors. She refused to tell them about the events that preceded her arrival in the United States. She did not wish to give away her country's secrets, even to its closet ally. They wanted to know more, to understand how she had infiltrated the terrorist group. She told them, politely, to ask the Prime Minister of Israel.

"Shalom, Hannala," said a voice near her left ear. Hannah knew that voice. She didn't turn around.

"Shalom, Avi, welcome to Los Angeles."

"It's time for you to come home, Hannala. We need you."

"I'm finished, Avi," she said, staring at the large Jackson Pollack canvas in front of her.

"You like this paint-spattered art?" Avi said. He took a step forward and stood next to her. He put his arm around her.

"It's very restful." She smiled and looked at him. Her eyes were moist.

"OK, so you're finished. That's good. Now what? Plant avocados at Kibbutz Etzion? Teach nursery school?"

"I don't know, Avi."

"You know, Hannala," picking up her hand, "far be it from me to be a *yenta*, but I just left that Professor Jake. Nice boy, unmarried. The mother's Jewish, did you know that?"

"It was hard to miss," She responded dryly.

"Are you doing anything for lunch, Hannah?"

"No, it just so happens that I'm free today."

As they walked out of the museum, Gerstner turned to Hannah and said, "Do you want some unsolicited advice?"

"Do I have any choice?"

"Of course not."

"So what's the advice, Avi?"

"Go back and see him. You never know."

Chapter 116

The *taweez* sat in Commander Abu Khalid's desk drawer for almost four months. It was a forgotten loose end. Not quite forgotten.

Two Israeli F-16s began their mission at an Air Force base in the Galilee at 2:00 am. They flew out to the Mediterranean Sea, turned sharply north and then, a few moments later, east, entering Lebanese air space over Sidon. They headed straight for the Bekaa Valley at an altitude of 5,000 feet. Their mission was to drop their ordnance on the target, make a rapid turn to the south to avoid crossing into Syrian airspace, and to return to base. Each fighter carried a pair of one-thousand-pound laser-guided precision bombs. The computers in their fire-control systems were programmed to drop the ordnance right on top of the pulsing *taweez* sitting in Abu Khalid's desk drawer.

Abu Khalid died in his sleep, which was a fate that he had often joked would never be his. His mistress, a young Lebanese woman, died with him, as did over thirty other people that night. Some were innocent, some were guilty, all were young.

The next morning, a tearful and enraged representative of

Hezbollah announced that the Israelis had bombed an orphanage, killing many children. He vowed revenge. A spokesman for the IDF insisted that they had struck a terrorist training camp. In the United Nations, the Ambassador of Oman, who was serving temporarily on the Security Council, introduced a resolution condemning Israel's "cowardly and vicious attack on innocent civilians."

The United States vetoed the resolution.

Chapter 117

THE TEHRAN ZOO, TEHRAN, IRAN, SEPTEMBER 16

General Yazdi held the hand of his grandson, a little curly haired boy of five, his daughter's youngest child. The General did not see the boy very often but when he did, he doted on him. He told him adventure stories and read him fables. The boy, in turn, adored his grandfather. General Yazdi bought the boy a bag of peanuts and they tossed them into the cage to feed the elephants. The little boy laughed and laughed.

Tomorrow morning, the General's visit with his daughter and son-in-law would be over and he would return to work. He needed to finalize a plan to transfer 500 cases of Chinese made RPGs to the Sudanese government for use by the Janjaweed militia in Darfur. Due to the current wave of civil unrest as a result of the incident at Bala Deh, the operational issues were turning out to be more complicated than expected.

And then there was General Yazdi's most vexing problem: how to counter the persistant criticism that he was to blame for the failure of the mission in the United States and even more damaging, the apparent penetration of the Pasdaran by the Jews. So far, he had successfully deflected the criticism by quickly exposing the Zionist spy ring operated by Commander Zaid and having him and his agents eliminated. That he knew that Zaid was innocent was a fact that gave Yazdi little pause. Although, at least so far, General Yazdi's loyalty had not been questioned, his reputation had suffered enormously and there were persistent rumors that he would soon be asked to retire.

General Yazdi's gaze shifted to the exhibit in front of him. It was the Chimpanzee exhibit and the General knelt down next to the little boy. "Look," he said, putting his arm around the child's shoulders and pointing.

"What is it, *pedar bozorg*?"

"Look, over there. Do you see the mother chimp with her baby? She is very gentle with it."

"I see it!" the boy said excitedly.